Second Chance

Second Chance

JEANETTE SKALSKI

For more information, address: jeanetteskalski@outlook.com

First Edition: June 2023

Book interior design by Alison Cnockaert
Cover design by Robin Locke Monda

Library of Congress Control Number: 2023907597

ISBN 979-8-9877701-1-5 (paperback)
ISBN 979-8-9877701-2-2 (hardcover)
ISBN 979-8-9877701-0-8 (ebook)

This book is dedicated to the most selfless and loving person I know...my mom.

1

Alex

THE CLOCK ON my phone blared loudly. I peeked one eye open: it was 6:55 a.m.

"Yeah, yeah," I said to the inanimate object. My phone's alarm clock and I had a love/hate relationship. It loved to annoy me until I'd eventually roll out of bed. I hated that such a feature was necessary. I didn't despise mornings. Waking up, in general, had never been an issue. *The early bird gets the worm*, so to speak.

"Alex, I think you need to get up." Stacey rubbed her hand along my abs and pushed me back and forth to jostle me awake. Or was her name Sammie? I had doubts.

I was considered a millennial by whoever created the arbitrary generational categories. Millennials got a bad rap. We were labeled as lazy, entitled, and selfish. I understood the stereotypes would remain unless we, the millennials, did our part to change opinions. And so I put full effort into everything I did. I never wanted to be viewed as a "typical lazy millennial." My positions within my father's and my companies were not challenging. For the most part, as long as I showed up, checked in, and kept the peace in each place, my job was complete for the day.

That was only the explanation for one of my jobs. I also trained clients at my health club, FLEX GYM—Clients who would be waiting on me soon if I didn't leave my bed.

"Yeah, babe, I'm up," I reassured Sammie. Or maybe it was Summer?

The alarm blared again. With a deep sigh, I heaved myself off the mattress to get dressed. Sauntering downstairs, I decided to skip my morning cup of coffee to head to the gym early. The woman—who remained nameless—followed me down to the kitchen.

"Hey, so I have early clients today. I have to run. But maybe I'll see you later?" I kissed her on the cheek and went to find my keys.

Her eyes glared at me. "I'm your first client today, Alex. And my session isn't for a couple of hours."

"Oh. In that case, I'll see you soon. You know your way out?"

Her arms were crossed. She nodded slowly.

I slipped on my sneakers, grabbed my phone and keys, and headed to the back door. "Okay. See you in a bit."

It was a beautiful, crisp spring day in the town of Crystal Lake, a northwest suburb of Chicago. The parking lot of the gym was packed, a good sign that my first task of the morning would progress quickly.

Most days I came to FLEX for the workout, whether it was for me or my clients. A lot of days I had business to take care of. Sometimes I went there just to be social. As a trainer and owner, I knew most people who walked through the door. They knew me too. The men would stop me to ask questions about their workouts. The college kids would watch my form and try to mimic it (anything to get out of paying for training sessions). Lots of ladies would bashfully look down and grin as they walked by me. I'd give them a genuine smile and nod.

The atmosphere as I walked through the parking lot was no different. The regular flow of clients came and went out the front doors. People rushed in wearing workout gear and rushed out wearing suits, skirts, and scrubs. Watching everyone hustle around made me grateful for my career. I was my own boss. I made my schedule. It was beautiful.

I walked in the back entrance and confirmed it was just another day around FLEX. Customers sweated out their anxieties while wearing earbuds blaring their favorite music. Babies played in the nursery while moms or dads enjoyed their hour-long break. I did my rounds through the club, making sure customers and employees alike were happy and excited to be there.

I took my usual stance at the counter, near the check-in desk, to greet and wave to the clientele as they went about the club. I also stood there daily to read the newspaper and discuss current events with Stan and Patti before my first client came in. Well, Stan and I discussed those topics. Patti nodded and smiled at the appropriate times.

Stan was one of my closest buddies. He doubled as an assistant and personal driver when needed. He wore many hats, and he wore them well. He'd been working at FLEX for about ten years. Having Stan around always made my job easier and more enjoyable. He didn't ask for much but gave a lot in return. He was in his late fifties, had two ex-wives under his belt, and two twenty-something-year-old daughters who had taken their mom's side of any conflict. Stan had sworn off the female species. I met both his exes and his daughters. I couldn't say I blamed him.

Patti worked at the check-in counter full-time and went to college in the evenings. She'd been studying exercise science since I met her about five years ago. Somehow she hadn't finished yet. She was twenty-seven years old, of average height, and had sandy blonde hair with hazel eyes. Her body was made for exercise ads. She paid for it to be that way. When I looked at her, I often thought of a song lyric I heard once: "The bodies look great, but they're fake." She wasn't the brightest crayon in the box, but her ass made up for it. She and I had hooked up a few times in the past. We were great in bed together, but I'd never wanted to take it any further. While that was always enough for me, it wasn't for her. She wanted an exclusive relationship I could not give her.

After a while of regulating the herd and shooting the shit with Stan, it was time to complete a quick workout. It was stair climber day. That was another love/hate relationship I had. It loved to torture me and to trip me occasionally. I hated the time spent on it but loved the results. As much as weight training was my go-to favorite, and as much as the masses nay-sayed cardio-based workouts, I forced myself to wrestle with the stair machine at least once a week.

I was finishing up the sports section of the newspaper, ready to head to the machines, when I saw a woman out of the corner of my eye. In the ten years since I owned the gym, I'd never seen her. Her blonde hair was loosely braided down the center of her back. The end of her blonde braid touched the space below her exposed shoulder blades. I watched her hesitantly approach a treadmill, and when she turned to face me, I couldn't help but stare. She looked past me, searching for something...or someone. Her face flattened, and she turned back to the treadmill. She seemed to be deciding whether she wanted to put the effort into stepping onto it.

I rubbed the back of my neck and took a few deep breaths before I looked in her direction again. She was the most spectacular sight I had ever seen. And yet she looked disheveled. She was pale with dark circles and bags under her eyes. She was thin, much too thin, with clothes that didn't seem to fit. But even with those imperfections, I still couldn't remember ever seeing anyone so beautiful.

"Hey, Alex, did you see the game last night?" Stan suddenly knocked me out of my staring fest.

Distracted, I couldn't form a proper sentence. "Uhh...yeah, no. Um, it was a good one."

"You all right?" Stan raised one eyebrow in concern.

I turned around to answer him in the shortest amount of time possible. "Yeah, you know. Just had a late night." Turning from him quickly, as if it was an involuntary choice, I fixed my eyes back to find the girl. The treadmill was now unoccupied. She'd somehow disappeared during my short interaction with Stan. But she couldn't have gotten far. "Stan, did you see that girl who was just on treadmill five?"

"Nah, I didn't see—" Before he even finished his sentence, I'd left his side. I had an unshakable urge to go after her, to find her. She'd looked unwell at the machine, unkempt. I needed to know her name, find out who she was, and see if she was okay. I searched every area of the club. It felt like hours, but it must have been fifteen minutes of searching. I even made Patti do a sweep of the women's locker room, which was unsuccessful. It was like the girl had vanished out of thin air.

Frustrated, I decided to take a breather and head up to my favorite forbidden spot—the roof. Through the years, it had become my place to get away and think. Nobody ever looked for me there. If I *casually* left my phone in my office, I would be gifted with a few minutes of silence before I continued putting out fires throughout the day.

It was mid-March, so the brisk Illinois air would wake me from this dream. I opened the door to the rooftop and walked to my favorite spot. I was in a deep discussion with myself about what had gotten into me when I noticed I wasn't alone.

I blinked a few times dramatically to make sure I wasn't seeing things. The blonde beauty was sitting on an old, low, rusty pipe. She had no coat on and was visibly shaking from the chilly temperature. She looked like she was in her own dream, so I approached slowly. When I was about three feet away, I attempted to speak in the kindest voice I could muster.

"Hi. My name is Alex." I waited to see if she would look up and acknowledge my words. Nope. Maybe a question would get her to react. "What's your name?"

She didn't budge or move. She was almost in a fetal position with her knees up by her chest and her arms wrapped around her legs. She was distraught.

"I'm not going to hurt you, but I'd like to put my jacket around you."

No answer.

Very slowly, I shrugged out of my Under Amour jacket to place around her shoulders. She still didn't say anything. I remained at her level to examine her better. She wouldn't look at me. Her skin was paler than it had been in the gym. "I'm not sure why you're up here, but your lips are turning a beautiful shade of blue."

She tilted her head up and stared past me with vacant, despairing eyes. Even with all that sadness, I couldn't help but notice—again—how lovely she was. It knocked the wind out of me and made my head spin. Her hair was a natural blonde shade—not like the others who dyed their hair. She was born a blonde; it was almost platinum from root to tip. The sun illuminated it to make it appear as if each strand was on fire. Examining her up close, she was thinner than she had looked from afar. Her cheeks were sunken in and her collarbones were protruding. Her almond-shaped, deep blue eyes were the color of the ocean on a cloudy day. They had a gray shade to them too, which made me wonder if they always had that tint or if it reflected her mood. She had the kind of eyes one could see right through. A few strands of her hair fell from her braid and whipped around her face. I tucked them behind her ear in an attempt to wake her from the trance she appeared to be in.

It didn't work.

I stood and paced back and forth, trying to decide what to do. I couldn't just leave her alone. My mind was empty of solutions. I bent back down to her level and tried one more time. "Are you hurt?" I asked while trying to reach her eyes.

My attempts to communicate with her were futile. She continued to stare blankly with her ocean-gray eyes. When a deep shiver shook her more noticeably, I decided to take action so she wouldn't suffer from hypothermia. "I'm going to lift you. Is that all right with you?"

No answer.

I slowly walked to her side and put one arm under her knees and one arm around her ribs to lift her. She was as light as a feather. She made no attempt to resist and quickly passed out into the heat of my body.

Something was terribly wrong with her. I didn't know her name, who she was, where she was from, or if someone was looking for her. But I needed to take care of her, at least for the moment. I spontaneously decided to take her back to my house and let her rest until she came around. I hoped that didn't count as kidnapping.

With her still passed out and cradled in my arms, I swiftly went down the stairs to the main level. Stan was there and stared at me, one eyebrow lifted. "Treadmill five?" he asked suspiciously.

"Yep. Please cancel all my clients today." I knew my behavior would pique his interest. I didn't cancel clients lightly.

"But Sierra is already here," he informed awkwardly.

Sierra! I knew it started with an S. "Tell her something came up. She'll understand." I walked out without seeing Stan's reaction to my hasty decisions. He would, no doubt, question me about it later.

I brought the girl to my Jeep and gently buckled her into the passenger seat. She came to but didn't seem to be concerned with a stranger putting her in his vehicle. Once I knew her name and story, I'd have a talk with her about keeping oneself safe in public.

We drove in silence back to my place. I couldn't tell if she was awake or still in a dream. Her head lay back on the headrest and her eyes would open briefly and then close again. Her gaze never fixed on any certain thing. I pondered detouring to a hospital but thought better of it.

It did not go unnoticed that my worry for her was acutely exorbitant for knowing nothing about her.

After carrying her into my house, I decided to let her sleep first before going to extreme measures, like a hospital. After about six hours of her sleeping in my guest bed, I felt on edge for a couple of reasons. First, I was concerned the police would show up any minute, accusing me of abducting her. Also, someone had to be worried about her. I looked for a wallet in her jacket, but the only thing I found was her phone. I immediately typed in 'ICE' (In Case of Emergency) and it came up with "ICE/Graham." I called the number. Disconnected. Hmm, why would she have an emergency contact that was disconnected? I found her favorites list and saw Reese Delvani's name. I rolled my eyes...*of course* Miss Reese would somehow be involved with her. I hesitantly clicked on her name.

"*What in the hell did you do to her?*" Reese, who seemed to be a mutual friend, barged into my house almost an hour later. While I'd never had a problem with her, she seemed to be irritated by everything about me. She turned to face me with her hands on her hips. Reese always reacted in extreme ways. Keeping my cool was imperative around her.

"Reese, how lovely to see you," I stated sarcastically.

"Tell me, Alex. What did you *do* to her?" she shouted again.

My hands went up to my chest in surrender. "Whoa, whoa. I didn't do *anything* to her. I found her shivering, near death on the rooftop of FLEX. She was incoherent and distraught. I brought her back here, put her under the covers, and hoped she'd sleep it off. That was seven hours ago. She's still asleep."

"Well, did you check for a pulse?" Reese pulled a hair tie off her wrist and twirled her long, straight, dark hair into a messy bun. She looked like she was ready to brawl.

I rubbed my forehead conspicuously to cover my eye-rolling. Reese was exhausting. With a sigh, I assured her, "Yes. She's breathing."

Reese calmed herself. She walked over to the sleeping beauty and gently brushed the back of her tan hand along her friend's pale cheek. She hovered there a minute with a look of sorrow. I didn't know Reese was capable of such an emotion. Usually, I only saw anger and annoyance when I was in her presence. Reese met my eyes and walked back to me. "Let's chat somewhere private for a moment." We went into the hallway and closed the door. "Do you know who she is?" she asked.

"No. I've never seen her before today."

"Don't you watch the news? Or read the newspaper? I'm always seeing you read that damn paper at the club like it's the most important part of your day. And you've never seen her before?" She was flabbergasted.

"The newspaper *is* the most important part of my day, most days. And no, I haven't. I skip sections, you know." I folded my arms and tried to maintain some patience that I didn't feel. "Who is she?" I asked curtly. Reese was taking too long to spit it out.

She rubbed her face and already looked tired of being in my presence. She and I, like my damn alarm clock and the stair machine, also had a love/hate relationship. Well, I had a love/hate with her. Her opinion would be more in the hate/hate category.

She took a deep breath through her nose and let it out. "I'll give you the short version. I feel bad talking about her like this when she's in the next room. Her name is Jane. She's my best friend." I gave her an incredulous look. *Best friend?* I met Reese in high school. We'd known each other for well over a decade. She cut my hair. We had mutual friends. She frequented my gym. Yet I had never seen Jane, nor had Reese ever talked about her best friend. I paused my train of thought to let Reese continue before she became angry again.

Too late.

She stopped when she saw my disbelieving face. "Why are you giving me that look? Yes, my best friend. You don't know everything about me, Alex." She crossed her arms defensively. "Anyway, she's my best friend and she works for me." I couldn't help but raise my eyebrows at that new information. She scoffed at my reaction. "Oh my God, what now?"

"She works at your salon? How have I never run into her?"

"Because she works afternoons, Alex. Well, she used to. You always come in the morning after the gym. Why is this important? Stop interrupting!" She eyed me to see if I approved of the newest info. I remained silent and let her continue. "*Anyway*...she had a perfect family: a husband, a daughter, and two beautiful boys." She stopped for a moment to gain composure. I could tell it was hard for her to talk about. She quieted to almost a whisper. "They all passed away in a car accident a month ago." Her eyes closed in pain. "A month ago today, actually."

The blood drained from my face. "Holy shit."

"Yeah. She's been through more than anyone could imagine. I have taken her under my wing this week and tried to get her out of the house. I told her I'd meet her at the gym this morning, but when I arrived, she wasn't there. I figured she wasn't having a good day and stayed home." She paused and looked worried, as if she didn't know how to help her broken friend. "I thought FLEX would be a safe, easy place to be, especially if I was there. It may have been too soon." Reese let out a sigh and leaned against the wall. "She hasn't been able to be alone. Her parents live overseas, so she moved in with her in-laws and has taken a leave of absence from work. She has not been back to her house since the accident." In a rare Reese moment, she looked vulnerable. Tears welled in her eyes. I almost went to hug her but thought otherwise. Reese and I didn't hug.

She paused, wiped her eyes, and became serious again. "And you," she poked my chest with her pointer finger, "need to stay away from her. Got it? She isn't another trophy to hang on your wall."

I suppressed the laugh that wanted to emerge from my throat. "I don't hang girl trophies on my wall," I stated sarcastically.

She pushed her finger into my chest even harder. The look in her eyes was menacing. "You know what I mean. Leave her alone. You have a long history of breaking women's hearts."

I pulled her hand away from my chest and placed it down at her side. "Wow, I didn't realize you thought so highly of me." It was so easy to rile Reese up, even during a serious conversation.

Reese kept intense eye contact with me. She was trying hard to get her point across. "Jane is not going to be another notch on your belt. Just leave her alone. She has been through enough."

"I can't promise—"

Before I could say anything else, I was pinned against the wall. "Look. I'm *not* fucking around." Her big hazel eyes glared at me as if they could fling fire. Her messy bun flew around the top of her head with the same intensity as her words. To be honest, she looked fierce. She had the body of a cross-fitter. Or gymnast. Or one of those competitive cheerleaders with six-pack abs. For as little as she was, nobody could deny Reese's strength, inside or out. If she wasn't so irritating, I might have thought she looked hot. "Jane has been through more pain than you and I will ever see. Leave her alone." She let me go, went into my spare bedroom, woke Jane, and carefully dragged her out of my house. Jane didn't even look at me as she left, still out of it from her mini-coma.

"You heard me!" Reese exclaimed as she passed me and headed toward the door. "Stay away."

"It's always a pleasure chatting with you, Reese." I shut the door behind them.

2

Alex

FOR THE NEXT few months, I watched every move Jane made at the gym. I used that time to also collect information about her on the Internet. She had no social media accounts, but there were a lot of local articles and links to news clips about the crash.

After a couple of days of research, I gained enough courage to read one of the articles. Her husband, Graham, and their kids were part of a thirty-three-vehicle pile-up on I-90 in Schaumburg, a suburb about twenty miles southeast of Crystal Lake. There had been ice on the roads and fog low in the air—the perfect storm for a multiple-car accident situation. Vehicles, including a semi-truck in front of the Coras' van, halted abruptly to a stop, which created a domino-crashing effect. Graham had no time to react and plowed into the semi-truck in front of him. The vehicle behind him, also a semi-truck, crashed into the back of the van. The photos were difficult to look at. There was hardly a vehicle to be seen in between the two semi-trucks. Graham and the children were pronounced dead on scene, along with seven other people in different vehicles.

The article went on to detail the survivors of the incident and the loved ones left behind. They highlighted Jane's story because it was the most tragic. She and Graham were high school sweethearts who had married a few months after high school graduation. Graham was an accountant. Their three kids were young when they passed away.

Every time I learned something new about her, it drew me in more. How could someone endure so much pain and find the strength to keep on living? I had the urge to comfort her, to protect her. But I needed to *actually* say hi to her first.

She became a regular at FLEX during the week, always arriving around 7:00 a.m. and staying an hour. Seemingly overnight, my alarm clock and I became best friends. It reminded me every day of why I needed to wake early. A frail and sad girl, who so easily had captured my attention, was worth it. I had never felt so strongly about pursuing a woman in my life. And I'd had a lot of women. It felt as if she was the sun and I was the Earth. I revolved around her.

I sighed. It used to be the other way around in my relationships. I shook my head at myself. I didn't know what had come over me, but I didn't mind the change either.

Every morning, I looked forward to heading to the club so I could be somewhat near her. She never smiled. She never made eye contact with anyone unless Reese was there. Her favorite class appeared to be yoga. I decided I needed to become more limber and hung out in the back of the class. Watching her. Always watching her. It was like my eyes, as well as the rest of my body, were pulled by a magnetic charge right to her. I couldn't stay away.

That being said, I did my best to not send her stalker vibes. I meant her no harm, obviously.

"Hey Alex, what are you doing this weekend?" asked Patti, a "trophy," according to Reese.

"Nothing," was all I could muster up. I had no patience for small talk the past few months...or for women who wanted in my pants. Before I'd laid eyes on Jane, all I'd wanted was to satiate my desires—partying, sex, alcohol, wealth. Now all I wanted was for Jane to notice me.

"Aw, come on," Patti whined. "Let's go have some fun at Las Cazuelitas like we used to. We could drink margaritas and eat chips and guac!" The idea had her excited. We always had fun at a Mexican restaurant. "Oh! And tequila shots! Maybe Stan will come too. He needs to get out of the house and out of this gym." She could be very long-winded. "And what about Tanner? Where has he been? I haven't seen him in forever. Let's see if he can go. It's been so boring around here lately."

"I'm sorry, but I'm busy. And Tanner has been out of the country. He'll be back tomorrow, though. Maybe he'll go with you. Shoot him a text."

I had more important things to tend to. It was the day I was going to talk to Jane. I needed to say hello. It had been almost three months since I'd brought her to my house. She has never spoken a word to me. Not one word. I would fix that very soon.

If Jane wasn't doing yoga, her usual routine would be to run on the treadmill for a half hour before doing some weight machines. It was 7:30 a.m. on the dot. She had just finished the treadmill, so I headed up to the rooftop to get some fresh air before approaching her. I had thirty minutes to figure out what I was going to say.

We were nearing summer, which meant it was relatively warm in the Midwest. I didn't want to miss my opportunity but needed to clear my head and shake off my nerves. I figured a quick fifteen-minute breather couldn't hurt. The idea of sparking a conversation with Jane had my mind completely empty of ideas. I knew I should start by saying, "Hi," but after that, my brain was blank. Once again, I was shocked at how much one girl, whom I hadn't even had a real conversation with yet, could affect me.

I opened the door to the roof and headed to my spot. I immediately stopped dead in my tracks. Miraculously, as if it were a sign from someone above, there she was, back on that old pipe. Now, I wasn't very religious. I simply didn't know what I believed anymore. But the fact that Jane Cora was back on the roof on the *exact* day I decided to talk to her *had* to be some sort of kismet. I quietly thanked whoever was responsible for my good luck before slowly approaching her.

Sitting with her knees up to her body, rocking with her head in her lap, she hummed to herself. The feeling of déjà vu was eerie. "Hi, Jane." She didn't look up. "I'm Alex. I'm not sure if you remember me, but I helped you a few months ago. You were sitting right in that same spot and were so cold." She kept her eyes down and her arms wrapped around her thin legs. I continued with my nervous explanation, "I took you back to my house and let you rest."

I bent to her level and searched for some eye contact. "Reese picked you up. Do you remember?"

She nodded without looking in my direction.

"And now here you are again. It's a weird coincidence because I decided to come up here to gain some courage to speak to you."

Her eyes shot up at me—those sad, gray-blue eyes. She looked confused. "Why would you need courage?"

And there it was: she finally spoke to me. It took me by such surprise that I nearly fell backward. Who *am* I, and where did the old Alex go?

It took me a few seconds to realize she'd asked me a question. I sighed because the answer was ludicrous. The words came out before I could convince myself otherwise. "Well, I think I'm in love with you."

That would normally provoke some sort of response out of a girl. Especially coming from me. But she said nothing. She didn't even react. Maybe she didn't hear me.

I hope she didn't hear me.

"Today is his birthday," she said solemnly.

"Whose birthday?" I asked, already feeling choked up, knowing she was talking about one of her boys.

"Marric's. He would have been four years old today."

My heart dropped down to my stomach. I didn't know what to say. I didn't think anything would have been appropriate, so I stood there like an idiot, unable to help in any way—until an idea came to me a few seconds later.

"Come on." Before I could change my mind, I grabbed her hand. She looked weak, so I helped her to her feet. Keeping her hand tight in mine, I pulled her back into the gym slower than I wanted to go. Her frailness had me worried. She definitely had lost a few pounds since the first time I'd noticed her in March.

"What are we doing?" she asked cautiously. It was the first thing she didn't say in a monotone voice. She seemed genuinely curious and clutched my hand tight. I tried to keep that from distracting me. Her skin was so soft...

"You'll see when we get there." I pulled her through the entire gym while nosy onlookers gawked at us. They hadn't seen me show interest in anyone in months and were eyeing the lucky beauty. Little did they know I was the lucky one. I had her hand and never planned to let it go.

Dude, get a grip, I told myself. Not since I was in the fourth grade had I been excited to hold a girl's hand. I was regressing, but I refused to care or think about it too much. I felt lighter than I had in months and allowed myself to enjoy the soft skin of her hand in mine.

I guided her out into the parking lot to my Jeep. Regretfully, I had to let go of her hand to unlock the door. She turned to me, looking skeptical. "Don't worry," I said, giving her the most genuine look I could.

"Reese warned me about you." Her eyes narrowed.

My pulse raced, and my eyes narrowed to match hers. "She did, did she?"

"Yes, when she picked me up from your house that day, she said I should stay away from you."

I ran my hands through my hair, trying to figure out the right words to say to convince her to come with me. "Look, we can talk about what Reese said about me later. And I'll speak to her too. But I'd like to do this for you and your son. I promise I'm trying to help."

She stared at me for a moment, probably contemplating what to do—run away or trust me. Finally, after what felt like an hour, she entered the Jeep and allowed me to close the door. Once I was in the driver's seat, we headed to the first stop. Sweet Treats was just around the corner. They specialized in gourmet cupcakes.

"So, which one would Marric have liked?" I asked once we were in the bakery.

She eyed me both curiously and apprehensively. She looked at the glass case with all the beautiful desserts. She gave it lots of time and thought and finally pointed to the devil's food cupcake with chocolate frosting and chocolate sprinkles. The teenage girl at the counter, who must have recognized Jane because she had tears in her eyes, boxed it up for us before we headed off to the next stop.

"Where is Marric buried?" I asked Jane.

We headed to the cemetery. It was very close; I knew that wasn't a coincidence. I let Jane put the cupcake on Marric's headstone. I said a prayer with her and told her I would give her some space to let her celebrate her boy's birthday. I walked around the cemetery grounds for probably an hour, just thinking. There was a wave of change brewing inside me. I was thirty-two years old. I had never been in love before. Was what I was feeling love at first sight: unconditional, overwhelming emotion, and a strong, intense bond to someone? I'd only said a few words to Jane, and vice versa, but I knew if I were never to see her again, it would bring me physical pain.

I'd had many relationships in the past. Looking back, they all seemed more for convenience than anything else. As I continued to walk, I thought about my more serious relationships. I'd "played the field" my whole high school career, in more ways than one. Football and having fun were my main priorities. Having a girlfriend seemed like a lot of work—and a lot of wasted opportunities. There had been an abundance of hot girls in high school.

My first "real" girlfriend, Jodi, was in college. We'd met at school and started dating almost right away. It lasted a few years. She was from Iowa and planned on moving back there. She tried to convince me to plan on moving there with her, but I had no interest in living in the land of corn. My undergraduate degree was in business administration and entrepreneurship. I knew I wanted to stay around a bigger city, such as Chicago, to get my MBA and start my career. Because our end goals were so different, we knew it would never work out and mutually agreed to end the relationship before it became too serious. We mainly kept in touch on social media, but that was it. I never missed her once it was over. We moved on. It felt natural.

The "no strings attached" concept appealed to me after having a girlfriend for a couple of years. The last two years of my undergrad were the best times of my life. I started my MBA the year I turned twenty-one. I was young, carefree, and enjoyed what the single life had to offer. I hadn't planned on dating anyone again for a long time.

But then I met Cameron while taking my master's degree night classes. She was four years older than I was, incredibly smart, and challenged me in ways that nobody else could—in and out of the bedroom. She was gorgeous, experienced, and charming. I thought I was in love with her. We dated for a few years until she ended it abruptly by saying I wasn't giving her what she needed. Apparently, she wasn't into me as much as I was into her. That breakup affected me for a while, but could I say I was heartbroken over it? No, more like

I had a wounded ego. That was when I realized maybe I had never been in love with her in the first place. In my mind, there were plenty of fish in the sea. I had been ready to catch any that landed in my net.

Since Cameron, I had been a bachelor. Looking back at the last eight years of my life, I started to realize that maybe I had been out of control in the lady department. Suddenly, I felt guilty about it. I couldn't help but think it was Jane who was making me reevaluate some past choices. Sleeping around no longer appealed to me. That chapter of my life was closed. My life belonged to one girl now, a girl I hardly knew but was irrevocably obsessed with.

Maybe obsessed wasn't the correct description. It sounded too disconcerting. But I couldn't deny that she consumed every bit of me.

Right about the time I decided I was crazy and should be admitted somewhere for a psych evaluation, I was back at her family's headstones. It turned out to be an unseasonably warm day. We had already been sweaty from working out. When I left her, she'd had an Under Armour workout shirt on and capris leggings with her sneakers. When I arrived back to her, the shirt was gone, leaving her thin, pale body in a tight tank top. Her shoes were kicked off. She was lying next to Marric's headstone, humming again. Even with all the pain she must have been feeling, I had never seen anything more exquisite in my entire life. I didn't want to interrupt her, so I turned back around to wander some more.

"I'm ready to go," she said suddenly when she saw I was near. She seemed sure of herself for the first time since I'd known her. And she also seemed... content.

I smiled at her. "Okay then." I'd planned to take her back to her car at the gym but remembered I'd never seen her drive herself there. She was always dropped off or rode with Reese. The ride was quiet as we headed to her in-laws' home. She was deep in thought, and I didn't want to interrupt.

"How did you know?" she asked quietly.

"Know what, Jane?" I asked in the shyest voice I had ever heard myself speak.

"How did you know that bringing Marric a cupcake and allowing me to celebrate him would help me?"

Did I want to go there with her already? *Not yet.* "I know how much little guys like cake. My sister is a strict mom. My niece and nephew don't get many sweets, but when they do, they're in heaven."

Shit. I cringed at my words. *Pun not intended.*

She didn't seem to notice my tasteless mistake. "Thank you, Alex," she murmured, taking a long pause afterward. "You made this day brighter than expected. I'm not sure how I can repay you."

Without even thinking, I met her gaze and blurted out, "Marry me."

Her almond-shaped eyes went wide with concern.

I rubbed my eyes with my free hand and shook my head. *Idiot.* "I'm sorry. I didn't mean to say that out loud." I'd waited so long to hold a conversation with her, and I was ruining it with all my confessions.

We drove the rest of the way in silence. After the most awkward and uncomfortable car ride, we finally approached her in-laws' house. "How did you know where I lived?" Worry laced her tone.

I parked, sighed, and turned toward her, hoping she would see nothing but concern in my demeanor. "I've been watching you at FLEX for months. Not in a creepy way. Well, I hope you don't think it's creepy. But I know your entire weekly schedule at the gym." The worry dropped from her face and was replaced with confusion. "The first time I saw you, you were standing at a treadmill, and my entire world stopped. It hasn't been the same since." I paused for a moment to allow her the chance to run up to the house screaming. Since she didn't, I kept going. "After Reese told me what happened with your family, I knew it was too early to approach you again. So I found other ways to be near you...like hanging out with you in yoga, which I have to thank you for. My back hasn't felt this good in years." The corners of her mouth lifted in a semi-smile. "I also followed you home once." Her eyes went wide again. "I know that sounds like a stalker, but I intended on putting flowers outside your doorstep one morning. I just hadn't mustered up the courage to do it yet. So that's why I know where you live..."

Maybe my speech was too intense, but I had a hard time keeping things in. I wanted her to know where my head was at, even if she couldn't return the same feelings.

She paused before she spoke, her eyebrows furrowed. "Wow, okay. Well, thank you so much for helping me today. I will forever be grateful." And like that, she opened the car door and left. She walked up the hill to her in-laws' house. Waiting for her at the front door was an older-looking man. His lips pulled down into a frown; he appeared angry and weathered. It didn't help that his handlebar mustache followed the same pattern as his pout. When she made it up the hill to him, he put his arm around her shoulder gently and spoke to her. They were too far away for me to hear the conversation, but I could assume what it was about. He didn't look friendly. In fact, he looked ridiculously protective. He gave me a nasty glare, which confirmed my assumptions. I killed him with kindness by waving at both of them with my best smile plastered on my face. You catch more flies with honey...

He didn't return the wave. Instead, they turned away and headed into the house. The door closed without another look in my direction from either party.

3

Jane

"WHO WAS THAT, dear?" *Dear* was a pet name Robert started calling me after I moved in. It was meant with sincere fondness and nothing else. He was my father figure and my rock. He also acted as my driver, chef, safe space, and counselor. I owed a lot to my father-in-law.

"His name is Alex. He works out at the health club, I guess. He told me he was in love with me." That was as much detail as I could muster up at the moment. I needed a hot shower. And a nap.

"Have you ever seen him before today?" Robert looked skeptical, as if I had been keeping a secret.

"No..." I had to correct myself as soon as I answered. "Well, yes, actually. He said he's at the club every day, but I've never noticed him."

My mother-in-law, Deb, moseyed into the room to listen to my explanation. Deb was the sun on a cloudy day. She was one of the main reasons I woke up every morning. Her presence in a room made everything—and everyone—lighter and better. Even after losing her son and grandchildren, her supreme faith in God kept her natural positive disposition in place. Yes, she struggled hard with the "whys" after the accident. She wasn't immune to the pain. She had her intense moments of sorrow and anguish. However, her faith was bringing her back to life more quickly than Robert's or mine was.

She also happened to be the nosiest woman east of the Mississippi.

With a sigh, I filled them in with all the details I knew. "He said he has been watching me for months...since I started going there. On the one-month anniversary of the accident, I was in rough shape. Alex found me passed out and took me back to his house."

Robert turned red in the face.

"Before you get your shotgun, he didn't touch me, I promise. He called Reese, and she came to get me. Fast-forward to today, I was on the gym rooftop getting some air. Alex came up, saw I was upset, found out it was Marric's birthday, and took me to a cupcake shop." I stopped for a moment, again realizing how much my day had turned because of him. Robert appeared to want more information, so I continued, "Alex bought a cupcake, and we took it to Marric. We said some prayers together, and then he let me lay with Marric for a while. When I was ready to go, he dropped me off here."

Deb stayed quiet but had her hand over her heart like she was touched by my experience with Alex. The color came back to Robert's face. But in case he was still upset, I went over and gave him a bear hug. "Please don't be mad. Alex saved the day for me. Taking that cupcake to Marric was exactly what I needed."

Robert continued to hug me but seemed absorbed in thought. "What is Alex's last name?"

I peered up at him, trying to see why it mattered. He looked at me and then glanced Deb's way, who was already in on the secret. "I'm not sure. Why?"

"Could it be Lombardi?" Deb asked with a hopeful tone.

"I'm not sure," I repeated.

Deb had a little twinkle in her eye. She was a sucker for the news and all things celebrity gossip. "Janey, I'm pretty sure that's Alexander Lombardi. He is the owner of FLEX GYM. He also owns a few other local businesses, as well as some bigger companies. Well, part owner. He runs them with his father. He is," she added air quotes for emphasis, " 'Chicagoland's Most Eligible Bachelor.' At least that's what they say on the news now and then," Deb mused. Robert rolled his eyes and shook his head. She kept going with more excitement in her voice. "Anyway, they were trying to get him on *The Bachelor* a couple of years ago, but he refused. He comes into Jewel often." Deb had worked part-time at the local grocery store as a cashier since the dawn of time. She knew just about every patron by name. "He's a very nice man. And so handsome!" She waved her hand in her face as if to get some air.

"I don't like him," Robert muttered.

I pulled away from him, feeling the slightest bit defensive. "You haven't even met him." I scoffed.

He grunted at me and started what Deb and I call his *anger mumbling.* "Well, I don't like him. Stay away from him. He's declared love for you already?" His face turned a unique shade of red again.

"And he proposed..." I admitted.

Robert's eyes tried to bulge out of their sockets. "He doesn't even know you...who you are or what you've been through. How does he know he wants to *marry* you?" He would pop a vein soon if I didn't calm him.

"Pretty sure he was kidding," I mumbled with an eye roll. "Nobody *actually* proposes after meeting someone forty-five seconds prior." I hoped teasing him about it would lighten his mood.

It didn't.

"Stay away from him, Jane. He's no good."

It didn't escape me that Robert was the second person to give me that exact warning. He was in his full-blown parental mode. I had known him for almost half my life. He was one of my biggest supporters, but he was stern, stubborn, and fiercely protective.

I had no energy to argue. "Okay." I headed to my room to shower. Going to the gym and celebrating Marric was the most activity I'd had in months. I was spent. I lay on my bed...well, Graham's bed from his childhood, and the room spun. It was the first time I'd felt any happy feelings since the accident. I'd been living half numb, half wounded since February 13th, the day that ruined my entire life. Everything I'd lived for had been taken from me in an instant. My husband, the love of my life, Graham, was driving the kids to a birthday party. I had to work that Saturday, so I stayed behind. I often wondered why I couldn't have been with them. Survivor's guilt was debilitating at times.

We had been married for twelve years. Since Graham was a good Catholic boy who'd had ethics—and our teenage hormones had been raging—we chose to wed the autumn after high school. We were young and madly in love. People told us it wouldn't last. I never thought they'd be right. We had our first baby four years after our wedding vows. Barely past drinking age, we welcomed our blonde-haired, blue-eyed baby girl, Clare. Four years later, our feisty daughter gained a brother, Marric, who was the spitting image of his sister. Graham and I thought we were done. We were in our mid-twenties, had our careers, and had two kids. He was an accountant and I was a hairstylist. We were happy with our little life. One girl, one boy. Perfect. Little did we know that God had other plans, and we welcomed our pleasant surprise baby, Arlo, a couple of years after Marric's birth. Arlo had the same features as his siblings: blue eyes, blond hair, and pale skin. It turned out the Swedish genes were strong in my blood.

At the time of the tragedy, our little angels' ages were seven, three, and one. Arlo was still my little nursling when it happened. That thought, one of the most painful parts of it all, both physically and emotionally, had me detour from the shower and brought me to my knees on the side of the bed. Prayer. I constantly tried reasoning with God.

Lord, please help make the pain go away. I feel like I'm dying from the inside out. I need your help, today and always.

Just then, my mind involuntarily went to my morning. Alex. The man who had come into my life so suddenly. Maybe, just maybe, I could gain a new friend—someone who wasn't afraid of my past. As soon as the thought crossed my mind, I dismissed it. I was a hollow shell of a person. Who would want to invest in me? But then again, he'd said he loved me. While I never planned on getting married again or being in a relationship for that matter, the thought of having a new friend was so appealing.

I had a lot to think about.

THE FOLLOWING WEEKS turned into months, and I became a person on autopilot. I tried to keep myself as busy as possible to keep the darkness and pain at bay. I wasn't ready to go back to any of my pre-accident routines, which included working with Reese at the salon, teaching fitness classes on the side, and having my weekly Tuesday night cocktails with coworkers and fellow instructors. Those activities felt too close to what was a customary and happy life. I needed more time before I could consider even trying to have a normal, productive routine.

So I continued to exercise every morning at Alex's gym. It wasn't the same as teaching my own classes, but it forced me to leave the house and was hopefully strengthening my very weak body. Sometimes I would do yoga. Sometimes I'd run my anxieties out on the treadmill. Other times I attempted to be good at Pilates. When I came home from the gym every day, Robert and Deb always made sure to have something planned for me. It reminded me of planning out my kids' days to keep them occupied. But the fact that my in-laws tried to keep me busy didn't upset me. I felt the opposite toward the gesture. I was grateful they cared enough about me to go the extra step. I needed them, and since they also were struggling with tremendous loss, I knew they needed me too.

Audrey, Graham's sister, lived about forty minutes away and was busy with her own family. She didn't need too much assistance from her parents. With Robert retired and Deb working limited shifts at Jewel, we all had a lot of spare time on our hands. When you're recovering from such an emotionally destructive event, having too much free time can make moments debilitating. So we continued to help each other daily. We would go to Sunday Mass. We worked in their garden together. I went to a weekly grief group and saw a personal therapist. I volunteered at a local animal shelter for a few hours a week. Playing with the cats and walking the dogs became another type of therapy. One of the few activities the Coras did, but I skipped, was tend to my home—the modest, three-bedroom, two-story house Graham and I purchased about a decade ago. I had not stepped into it since the morning of the accident. I couldn't bring myself to do it. Not yet. Luckily, Robert loved cutting grass and maintaining a home. Deb handled the logistics of having a vacant dwelling for months. They had not once asked me what I planned to do with it. They must have known I didn't have an answer. Once again, I owed them so much.

Aside from Reese, Robert and Deb became my best friends. They were two of the few people who weren't afraid to talk to me. The experience of losing my family made me realize people don't know how to process grief.

Pre-accident, I had a good group of friends. We went to coffee or had our weekly happy hours. They all came to my kids' birthdays. Post-accident, they were all pretty absent from my life. I couldn't say I blamed them. They didn't want to upset me with anything they said or did. But it was a very lonely way to live when hardly anyone was brave enough to talk to you.

The days started flying by even faster, something I was grateful for. Before I knew it, we inched closer to spring. The busier I was, the less pain I felt. The past several months of staying busy had done wonders for my psyche. Immediately after the accident, I had been put on some heavy medications to numb the pain to a tolerable level. I was ready to wean off some of the stronger pills and dip my pinky toe into a new productive life.

I couldn't say "happy" life. One step at a time.

I made a few decisions through the winter, as we were fast approaching the first anniversary of the tragedy:

One—I wasn't going to let the upcoming anniversary affect me negatively. Every waking moment for the last year, I thought about my husband and kids. The in-laws and I frequented their graves and had picnic lunches with them when the weather allowed. We talked to each other when we had bad days and shared little stories about one of our lost loves when the time felt right. I went to bed thinking about them and woke every morning to my babies' faces at the forefront of my brain. There was no shortage of grieving.

Therefore, I was steadfast in my pursuit that February 13th would be no different from any other day of mourning. I would not torture myself more than I usually do. I had to give that gift to myself.

Two—It was time to go back to work. I needed to contact Reese and see if my position was still available. Somewhere in the back of my mind, I remembered that she filled my open spot when I needed an extended leave.

I also needed to work on my endurance so I could eventually get back to teaching my fitness classes. Spin was my favorite by far, so that was what I planned to return to first. I taught a few different formats, including strength classes and some dance fitness too. I began to miss being an instructor.

Three—I didn't want to be alone anymore. I still wasn't willing to have any sort of romantic relationship, but a friendship would be nice. All my friends, besides Reese, kept their distance. Alex was the only person who was brave and willing to accept the challenge of befriending a broken girl. He hadn't approached me since Marric's birthday last spring. Maybe he realized the proposal was a bit much. He did, however, give me pleasant smiles and nods from across the gym. And he watched me. It seemed crazy that for three months before Marric's birthday, I'd never noticed being watched by Alex. Once he confessed to it, I felt like I had a big target on my back. The intense burn of his brown eyes followed me wherever I went. I would be lying if I said his awareness bothered me. He was intimidatingly sexy and confident. There were girls always trying to hang on him. But as far as I saw, he never took notice of them. Only me.

Mind-boggling.

As I was coming out of my yearlong fog, I collected information about Alex from Reese, much to her dissatisfaction. Reese had always frequented Alex's gym and knew him quite well. He'd even been her personal trainer at times. Selfishly, I wished I could have watched those sessions. Considering her distaste for him, Reese could *not* have been an easy client.

Reese confirmed what Deb had said about Alex being the desirable bachelor of Chicago and the surrounding suburbs. Not surprising. He was in his early thirties and never married. He owned many companies that made him wealthy. He was somewhat tall, dark, and handsome, which of course, made most single ladies desire him. Reese let me know he'd had his fair share of partners. That part made me uneasy. However, since I met him, I had never seen him openly flirt with a woman. Reese said the same thing; he hadn't been out on the town in months. He also hadn't come into the gym looking hungover, she told me. With all that being known, I wanted a new person to talk to, to spend time with. I *needed* a friend. One that wasn't afraid to be near me.

The day after the anniversary, I built up some courage to text Alex. I had obtained his phone number from Reese. I remembered how the conversation went with my protective best friend:

"Ew. Why him? Do you know the number of STDs he probably has?" Reese tended to be a little dramatic.

"I'm not trying to bang him, Reese. I just need a friend."

"What about me?"

I took her hand and kissed it. "You're a better friend to me than I deserve. But you're my only friend. I need to get out of the house and do something besides go to the gym, church, and walk dogs. You work a lot, and I'm lonely." She looked guilty, which then made me feel guilty. "And you have more to your life than your broken friend. You can't babysit me all the time. You need to go enjoy yourself too."

Reese shook her head in frustration. "But why him? There are literally seven billion people on this planet. You choose the one person who I know will hurt you in the end. What about your instructor friends? What happened to Luis? Hey, what about Dean? He could use a friend. Text one of them instead."

"Reese, they've all ghosted me. I know they mean well. They just don't know what to say or not say anymore. I will text them all eventually, I promise. Especially Dean. He'll be in town soon. We're planning on getting together, okay? Please don't worry about my intentions with Alex. It isn't romantic. I want to start fresh with someone who isn't afraid of my baggage."

It had taken a little more pleading, but she'd finally agreed to hand over the number. After a long, deep breath, I typed before I could change my mind:

> Hey Alex. It's Jane from the health club. I was wondering if you'd like to go out for coffee or something sometime.

He answered within a minute:

> Of course. You pick the day, time, and place, and I'll be there.

A few minutes later, as I was deciding where we should go, Reese texted me:

> You make him nervous. Look:

She sent me a screenshot of Alex's social media page stating: "After more than a half year of waiting, she finally did it. She asked me out on a date. My nerves are on overdrive. Wish me luck, everyone."

The responses were as follows:

> **REESE:** "I thought I told you to stay away from her. I guess I cannot intrude because *she* asked *you*, not the other way around. But listen, I'm watching you. If you hurt her, I will cut your tongue out and feed it to my hypothetical dog."
>
> **PATTI:** "Who's the lucky lady? I ask you out all the time."
>
> **KRISTEN:** "Where are you going? You didn't invite me."
>
> **JODI:** "You haven't been out to Des Moines in a while. Come visit me! *I'll* take you out on a date."
>
> **TANNER:** "Dude, get a grip."
>
> **COLETTE:** "I haven't seen you around Marley's as much. Come by tonight, and we can catch up when I'm off work."

My phone pinged with another text from Reese:

> Don't mind my response. I may be a little protective of you. So where are you headed on said date?

I tried not to be distracted by all the responses so I could reply to her:

> I don't know. I have to think about it. I don't want him to get the wrong impression.

Reese answered immediately:

> Girlfriend, I think you've given him the wrong impression by asking him out.

I hoped she was wrong.

I sent Alex a text back, letting him know the details. I settled on Conscious Cup, the local coffee shop in town, after church on Sunday. It was a place that couples, business associates, and/or friends went to. Hopefully, an informal coffee shop would keep any sort of romance out of the equation.

CHURCH WENT SLOWLY on Sunday as I was anticipating my *date-but-not-really-a-date* with Alex. I couldn't hide my anticipation that I was going to a food establishment with someone other than my in-laws. I reminded myself that being a little excited was okay. It didn't mean I loved my angels in heaven any less. That had been something we'd been working hard on in therapy.

As excited as I was, during the service I tried to remember why Mass was so important to me. In the past year, not one person had outright asked how it felt to lose my entire immediate family. It was not a question that would seem appropriate. But if someone *had* asked me, I would've told them it first felt like an out-of-body experience...

On that terrible Saturday in February, I was taking care of a client when two police officers showed up during the middle of my shift. There were a few of us working that day, so immediately the jokes started about who was going to jail and for what. When they entered the salon, the look of sadness on their faces made my heart drop into my stomach. Something was wrong. Reese approached them and spoke quietly for a moment before she walked them over to me. One of the only things I remembered was the worry on her face. I'd heard the brain shuts down during extreme moments of trauma. I could attest that to be true. I had very little memory of the time between the officers' visit and Reese picking me up from Alex's house a month later. The processes of identifying bodies, viewing photos of the scene, funeral arrangements, family coming into town, and moving into the in-laws' house were completely blank. I was thankful for the shutdown of my fragile brain.

During that first month, Deb and Robert, along with my parents and Reese, dragged me—quite literally—to every place I needed to be. Deb thought church would be a good first public setting, a place where people would always support and pray for me. It was times like those that made me feel very guilty.

The Coras lost so much too, but they always considered my comfort, protection, and safety.

So I went with them every Sunday and never stopped. Graham and I never went to church religiously. We had married there and had baptized our babies, but that was about as far as it went. It wasn't that we were against church; we just had our hands and hearts full in other ways. Church had been on the back burner.

Now Mass was the most significant activity in my life. It was where I felt closest to my kids and husband. I felt their presence every Sunday. I silently spoke to them for the entire hour. I asked for signs that they were okay in heaven. I sang the hymns and liked to think they were singing along with me. Their burial sites were a place of sadness, a place where I mourned. Church was a place of deep comfort. I had no plans to stop attending any time soon.

When Mass ended, I felt like I should ask permission to go on my *date-not-date*. "Hey guys, I'm going to pick up my car and go out with a friend for coffee. Is that okay?"

"What kind of friend?" Robert's face was turning the lightest shade of crimson.

Deb waved off Robert's fowl reaction. "Janey, you do not need to ask our permission. You're thirty years old."

The car ride home was completely silent, and I couldn't help but think Deb was going to get an earful as soon as I was out of the picture. She didn't seem concerned about it. She had a smirk on her face the entire ride home.

"Have fun, honey. Don't stay out too late," Deb said with a wink, knowing it was currently 10:45 a.m.

As they walked into the house, I heard Robert whisper to her, "Don't you want to know whom she's going out with?"

"Hush," Deb demanded gently. "She hasn't had a social experience in a year. Let her be. It's just coffee in the middle of the day."

I loved them so much that it brought tears to my eyes. Crying had become a daily event for me lately. I had been numb for months. Some tears had flowed, but I had mostly felt hollow. A week after the first anniversary, my cheeks were always wet with tears. I counted it as a step forward in my recovery process.

Going on my *date-not-date* proved to be more nerve-wracking than I had anticipated. I stayed in my church clothes: a silver-metallic, loose-fitted blouse tucked into a black pencil skirt. The heels were too dressy, so I ran inside quickly to put on sleek black boots. My hair was in its typical braid down my back. As nervous as I was, I still couldn't get myself to fuss with my hair or makeup. I wore the standard mascara, eyeliner, and blush. Every other type of makeup seemed like too much work.

Before I could talk myself out of going, I said one last goodbye to my roommates, started up my Subaru Outback, and headed to the coffee shop. My brain became overwhelmed on the drive there with different emotions bubbling up to the surface. Every time I blinked, I saw a flash of Graham's face. I couldn't ignore the adulterous feelings coming out of me. *This is not a romantic date*, I kept telling myself. *This is nothing. It means nothing.*

Other emotions began stirring within that thought. Somewhere hidden in my subconscious, a deep, quiet inner voice was waking up. She was trying hard to push through to say, *Even if it is romantic, you're doing nothing wrong.*

"Hrmph. Tell that to my family in heaven," I mumbled, suppressing that deep inner voice.

I met Alex right inside the door of Conscious Cup. He looked me over respectfully. "You look lovely. I thought you didn't drive." His stare was so intense I found it hard to return, so I looked away.

"Thanks," I responded shyly. "I started driving again. I felt bad asking others to take me places all the time. Did you order?"

"I thought the 'ladies first' approach would be appropriate. This is a date, after all, isn't it?" He smiled shyly.

His words made my cheeks heat up. For being nervous, as Reese informed me by text, he sure knew how to keep cool. My hands trembled, and I giggled quietly from my nerves. My inner voice clapped her hands in excited approval. I hadn't had *nervous-around-a-boy* types of feelings in over twelve years.

But it's just a friendship date, my stronger, louder, sensible surface voice reminded me. I needed to make that clear to Alex right then, while in line to order our coffees. "Yes, it is a date, I guess. But I'd just like to be friends." I looked anywhere but at him. For some reason, I felt guilty about putting Alex, who was a—stranger? Acquaintance? I didn't know what to call him at the moment, in the friend zone. "I hope that's okay with you."

"Anything is okay as long as you're involved." He kept his intense eyes on me, and I had a moment to get a good look at him. He truly was a sight to be seen. His skin was a creamy dark tan color that complemented his dark hair perfectly. It made me wonder if he was Italian or Greek, or if he had a little Latino in him. His last name was Lombardi. He had to be Italian. His complexion made my Scandinavian skin look colorless. His hair was the perfect amount of messy and styled. His face was flawless, with a strong jawline that was covered with the perfect amount of facial hair stubble. He'd definitely had a facial or two in his adult life, along with a healthy layer of Botox. His teeth were very white and perfectly straight. And he had the most desirable shallow dimples when he smiled. I could stare at him for quite a long time and not feel bored.

Alex must've taken my assessment of him for something else, because right there in the coffee line, while he was still staring back at me, he lifted his hand and gently cradled one side of my face.

And there it was. Reese was right: I was giving him the wrong impression. He had already declared his love for me last spring. My loud surface voice, who seemed to be my conscience, sternly reminded me that my sole intention was to just gain a friend.

Sighing quietly, I slowly pulled my face away from his hand. A friendship would never work. We ordered our coffees and found a table. I tried to stay vague for the rest of the date. I couldn't shake my anxiety. I worried if I looked too interested he would take it as flirting. So I kept answers short and planned to leave as soon as possible. Alex picked up on my mood change. About a half hour in to our *date-not-date*, he looked concerned.

"Did I say something to upset you?" Even his voice exuded sexiness.

I didn't know how honest I should be but decided to just lay it all on the line. While not being able to meet his eyes, I began, "No, not at all. It's just... Reese showed me your post after I asked you out. I guess I'm realizing we shouldn't do this...try to be friends. We're looking for two extremely different things." I looked at him and couldn't read his eyes. They seemed surprised. Or worried. Or both. "It's not fair of me to string you along just so I'm not lonely. I'm sorry I asked you on this date. I have to go." With that, I pushed myself from the table to leave. Alex's hand caught mine and held it in place. His intense chocolate eyes bore into me.

"Don't go." He looked a little bit desperate, but mostly caring. "Jane, I want to be your friend. I want to make you happy in any way you'll allow. I won't ever push you to do something you don't want to do. I've waited nearly an entire year to sit with you for a cup of coffee. Stay. Please." His eyes were so sincere that I lowered back into my seat.

We stayed at Conscious Cup for another hour, discussing light topics. He was sure to steer away from anything that may trigger me. He asked me questions about my job. We talked about the members at the gym. He discussed some of his most interesting clients.

"Tell me something I don't know about you," Alex said inquisitively.

I paused in contemplation, feeling stumped by his request. I tried to think of something interesting about myself besides the size and amounts of poo I picked up during my shelter dog walks, my thoughts on the homily at Mass, or what type of vegetables grew in my garden. His question made me realize I was currently very lame.

"Hmmm. I teach fitness classes on the side. Well, I used to, and I hope to start again soon."

Alex grinned and looked moderately shocked, those perfect dimples showing their adorableness. He leaned back into his chair and crossed his arms. "I had no idea I was sitting across from competition." His demeanor remained light. He was teasing me.

His reaction made me blush again. I rolled my eyes and grinned back.

Yessss, very good, my deep inner voice exclaimed. *Baby steps...*

My deep inner voice seemed to want me to get in trouble with my conscience.

I scoffed playfully at Alex's remark. "Hardly. I'm not an owner."

"No, but I'm sure you draw people in with your charm and talent." His stare became intense again.

I thought about that for a moment. My main format, spin class, always had a lot of customers. Looking back, it was hard to deny that more than half my class participants were always middle-aged men. *Huh*, I thought to myself. How could I have missed that for so many years?

I waved my hands at him, dismissing such an idea. "I teach at a local recreation center. Nothing as fancy as your gym. No competition here." I resisted the urge to wink. He laughed quietly as if he knew I was right in the end. The light banter felt so good and I didn't know why.

Because you've missed it. And you deserve it, deep inner voice informed.

I wondered if my opinionated internal voices were in my head to stay. I didn't remember hearing them so loudly before I reached out to Alex. It would have to be something I brought up to my therapist.

After we finished our coffees, as we were saying our goodbyes, Alex's demeanor changed from playful to nervous. He walked me to my car and opened my door. He couldn't know, but chivalry was very important to me. That earned him extra points.

He's just a friend, Jane, my surface voice reminded...again. She was getting on my nerves already.

"Thank you for inviting me today. Can I see you again soon?" he asked, the smile not meeting his eyes.

"I'll see you at the gym tomorrow, right?" I asked sincerely as I sat in the driver's seat.

"That's not what I mean." He bent down to meet my eyes. "I'd like to take you on another date."

My heart went into my stomach. I gulped awkwardly. Did I want another *date-not-date*? My inner voices were battling out that question. "Just a friendship date, right?"

He nodded slightly. "If you're up for it." His gaze made my body ache in ways it hadn't in years.

My conscience waved her finger at me in disapproval. I needed to keep our *date-not-dates* light before she had a stroke. "We can do coffee again next Sunday if you'd like." For some reason, daytime coffee dates seemed safe. Nothing too heavy would happen at a coffee shop.

He grinned. "Okay, I'll take it."

Once he walked away from my car, I opened the windows and took a few deep breaths of cold winter air. The tension was radiating off me in waves. I wondered if he felt it too.

On my way home, I took a detour to Reese's apartment to see if she was home. I knocked on her door, suddenly really hoping she would answer. I was desperate for some girl talk. She opened the door in a thin, short, silk pink robe with old-fashioned curlers in her hair. She was on the phone.

"Okay, yay! I can't wait to see you! Text me when you know more. Okay, sounds good. Love you. Bye!" She hit end and gave me a hug. "Hi, Janey! What a pleasant surprise!"

"I didn't know anybody used those anymore," I said, pointing to the curlers wrapped into her chestnut hair. "Going on a hot date or something?"

"Nah. I don't need an excuse to get pretty. You know that. Besides, there are no new boys in this town. I'm so done with all the ones here." She worked her way into the kitchen, where I pulled a stool to her breakfast bar. "Want some coffee or tea?"

"Hmmm, I don't know. I just had a big latte."

"Oh, come on, Jane. Live a little. Whatcha having?" she asked with a wink. I always thought Reese was very beautiful. She naturally exhibited all the traits I aspired to have. First and foremost, she was confident. We'd known each other since high school. When we met, she was a senior and I was a freshman. Every freshman was assigned a mentor. I was fortunate enough to get Reese, the girl all the other girls wanted. Even back then, I always noticed her self-assurance. She, of course, was the most popular girl in school. Not only was she well-liked because of her looks, but she was genuinely friendly to people, even to freshmen like me.

Before high school, I'd been naturally soft-spoken and reserved, but Reese pulled the extrovert out of me. She signed me up for her cheerleading squad and convinced me to join committees with her. Having that great freshman year set me up to have the best high school experience I could have hoped for. We kept in touch even after she graduated. She went to a local cosmetology school and stayed active in my life by being the cheerleading coach during the rest of my high school years. After I graduated, she convinced me to attend the same school she did. It didn't take much for me to agree. Graham worked full-time with his dad while taking online classes for his Bachelor's in Accounting. Since I was engaged already, I needed to stay close to home.

By the time I graduated from cosmetology school, Reese had rented out a small space to do hair. She had two chairs: one for her and one waiting for me.

Once I had my license, she put out ads to establish new clients. Before we knew it, she had a full clientele base for both of us, and we were ready for a bigger salon.

We eventually moved to a more desirable location in town with room for more chairs. Throughout the years, she added a couple more stylists and a nail technician. I had worked with her full-time until the day of the accident, which brought me back to why I was there. Reese stared at me, and I realized I'd never answered her about my beverage choice. "I'll take chamomile, thanks." She made our beverages while I sorted out everything I wanted to talk to her about.

"Who was that on the phone?" I asked curiously.

"It was Brooks. He'll be on leave soon. Within the next few months!" Brooks was Reese's baby brother. He'd left for the military right out of high school. He was three years younger than she was. They had a playful relationship that I envied. I had always wanted a brother or sister. "Want to know a secret?" she asked deviously.

I looked at her in surprise. "Um. Sure?"

"Brooks always had a huge crush on you. Borderline obsessed."

"Oh my gosh, no he didn't." I rolled my eyes at her.

"Yes, he most certainly did. He made me swear to secrecy. I can't believe I never told you."

"Aww, he's such a baby." I wrinkled my nose. "Wouldn't that be like robbing the cradle?"

"Janey, he was in your grade. He's your age." She laughed at my cluelessness. "All I'm saying is he'll be in town this summer, and I know he's going to want to see you."

"I'll definitely make an effort to see awkward, pimple-faced Brooksy." I hadn't seen him much since he left for boot camp many years ago.

"Oh, he's not pimple-faced anymore. Or awkward. The dude is ripped. He's a different guy than you remember." With a sly smile, she added, "I would totally do him if we weren't related."

I gasped loudly. "Reese Marie Delvani! *Gross!*"

She cackled. "I still got it!"

I rolled my eyes at her playfully. She loved getting a rise out of me. It worked every time.

She brought my tea and her coffee over and sat next to me. "So what brings you over? How was your date with douchebag?" she asked dryly and took a sip from her mug.

"Well, two things brought me over. First, why do you hate him so much?"

"Ugh, I don't hate him, Jane. I've known Alex longer than I've known you. He's fine...tolerable. I just don't want him anywhere near you."

"How'd you meet?" I couldn't help my curiosity.

"I don't even remember how we met. A party, maybe? He didn't go to Central High School. He went to Cary-Grove High School. I was a couple of grades ahead of him. We had some mutual friends. We always saw each other at parties or football games, and he'd hit on me, of course. But I never gave in to him."

"I'm surprised by that," I said, trying to picture a younger Reese saying no to Alex.

"Why do you say that?" she asked defensively.

"Oh, come on. Everybody knows you love up on hot guys. Alex is...well, he's sort of gorgeous."

"Yeah, he is." She raised and lowered her eyebrows. "Have you seen him with his shirt off? Dang."

I giggled. "See what I mean?"

"Yeah, I never felt anything like that toward him. He's more like my annoying brother or something."

I looped the conversation around to stay on topic. "Back to my original question...why are you so upset that he's interested in me?"

She sipped her coffee and took a deep breath. "I've told you a lot of this already. I can't speak for the last year because I've seen a change in him since he met you, but *previously* to him meeting you, he took advantage of women. Girls are always ready and willing to be with him. Of course they are, right? He's handsome, single, wealthy, and very charming. He knows he's all those things and has used them to his advantage. These girls, some of them my friends, would fall in love with him, and he'd drop them for the next girl who walked in the door. He's one of *those* guys, Jane. And quite frankly, you've been through enough already in your life. You don't need to mess around with a guy like him. If you started having feelings for him and he hurts you, I couldn't forgive him. He'd be dead meat." She finished her speech by pounding her fist into her other hand, looking angry. Her theatrical side was shining through.

"Hey, calm down." It was hard to suppress the giggle that was brewing from the image of little Reese attacking Alex. "I just had coffee with him. He hasn't proposed marriage or anything." As soon as I said it, I remembered I was wrong. "Oh, wait. Yes, he has..." My cheeks turned bright pink.

"*What?*" She nearly dropped her mug.

"Jeez Louise, Reese, relax! He was kidding." She was so hot-tempered about him. I would have to be careful about the information I divulged to her. "I'll take it slow with him, okay? I'm not looking for anything but a friendship."

"Janey, I trust your judgment. Just be extra careful with him. Please. I don't think he's going to let you keep it at 'friend' status. But I'll leave it at that. For now." She paused and took a sip of her coffee. "What else did you want to talk to me about?"

"Well, I was wondering if there was a place for me at the salon."

She answered without hesitation. "Of course."

"Don't you have Shawna helping you? I don't want to take her job." Shawna worked out of her home usually but was enjoying taking a break from her toddler twins a few hours a day.

"She knew it was temporary. And ironically, the other day she asked me when you were coming back. She was offered a spot at a different salon. It's a part-time position closer to her home."

"So I wouldn't be taking her job away?" I asked in relief.

"No. You helped me build my salon. The job is yours," she stated firmly.

"You've helped me too, you know." Words really couldn't describe how thankful I was for Reese.

"I know, honey." We smiled gratefully at each other as we clinked mugs.

4

Alex

I MET JANE the following Sunday and tried my best to keep the conversation light. Everything about her exuded fragility. It took my reserve to keep my discussions and expressions happy and playful. No tough topics. Nothing too personal. She seemed much more comfortable that way.

We developed a pattern for the following several weeks. We saw each other during the week at FLEX with not much more than a wave, smile, or short conversation. On Sundays, we went out for coffee. I knew from experience there would come a time when she would want to discuss her lost family. I didn't know when that would be, but I would wait patiently for the cues.

At times I would see the pain surface on her face. It happened so randomly that I never knew when to expect it. As much as I wanted to brush the back of my fingers across her cheek or grab her hands while we were chatting, I thought better of it. It was harder than it should have been to keep my hands off her. The magnetic pull was powerful, but I would wait. If the last year taught me anything, it was patience.

After about two months or so from our first daytime date, we were headed to our cars after coffee when something came over me. I turned to face Jane and grabbed her hands so she had to face me. She didn't pull away, which seemed like a good sign. Her hands were warm despite the chilly April air. It was only the second time we'd held hands, and I couldn't help but feel the racing in my chest. There was so much I wanted to say, but I knew I had to choose wisely.

"Jane, I've loved meeting you here every Sunday." I gently squeezed her hands for emphasis.

Her perfect blonde hair whipped around in the wind. She looked down with a bashful grin and squeezed my hands back. "Me too, Alex."

My heart swelled at her reaction. "If you're up for it, I'd like to take you out on a date this Friday evening."

She released her hands from mine and narrowed her eyes at me in skeptical concern. "Evening?"

"Do you have something against nighttime?" I asked in a teasing tone. "You don't turn into a werewolf, do you?" I winked at her with a smile.

She grinned for a moment before becoming serious again. She wrapped herself in a hug, looking anything but comfortable with the conversation. She appeared torn, as if she had an angel and a devil on each of her shoulders and she was trying to decide who should win. "Uh, no. Evening is fine. Do you have a place in mind?"

"Oh, *I* get to pick this time?" I asked with a timid grin. "Hmm. Let me think about it and get back to you."

I walked Jane to her car to say goodbye, as I always did. Every week I had an empty, aching feeling when I closed her door, knowing I had to wait another week to spend time with her. I also ached for a physical connection. Every cell in my body needed it, and that need grew by the minute.

JANE HAD SOME obvious reservations about an evening date. I assumed she thought I'd want to take it to the next level. If I were being honest, I *did* want to take it to the next level. I would even be content with the next *half* level, but my needs and desires were not a priority. I was never a worrier before Jane. Now I was anxious all the time. Mainly, I worried I would push her away. Every action, every word, every movement were all calculated. *Baby steps and patience*, I reminded myself.

I called my pal, Reese, to get some much-needed info. I sighed and dialed her number. Reese picked up right away. "What's going on? Everything okay with Jane?"

"Yes, of course. Why are you so paranoid?" It didn't take long for her to irritate me.

"Oh, you know...my best friend lost her *entire* family a little more than a year ago and now she has decided to hang out with the one guy I disapprove of...the one person I know who could hurt her again. Sorry, not sorry about my overreacting."

"I don't even know what to say to that." Part of me approved of her protectiveness. Part of me was offended by her prejudices against me. I wondered what it would take to earn her trust.

She huffed out a sigh. "What do you want, Alex?"

Patience. Kill her with kindness, I told myself. In my calmest voice, I told her I needed a favor.

"Oh my God. *You* need a favor. Let me bend over backward for you..."

"Just let me finish, dammit!" Yeah, patience ran out quickly. *Reese.* So unbelievably infuriating. "I need to know what Jane's favorite restaurant is."

Shockingly, she filled me in on what I needed to know and ended the conversation with another sigh before she spoke once more. "Don't hurt her, Alex," was all she said before she hung up on me.

I don't intend to, Reese.

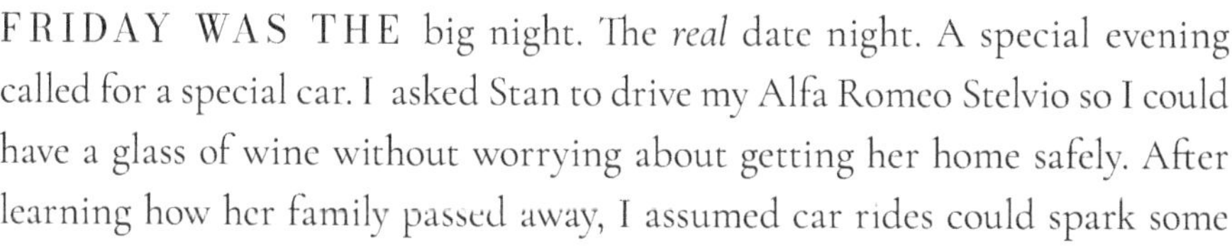

FRIDAY WAS THE big night. The *real* date night. A special evening called for a special car. I asked Stan to drive my Alfa Romeo Stelvio so I could have a glass of wine without worrying about getting her home safely. After learning how her family passed away, I assumed car rides could spark some anxiety.

Stan and I arrived at her in-laws' house promptly at 6:30 p.m. I rang the doorbell and found an angry, seventy-something-year-old man in front of me as the door opened. "Hello, sir, Mr. Cora?" I reached out to shake his hand. He stared at it and moved out of the way to let me in. Okay then. No shaking hands. Message received.

A heavyset woman in an apron welcomed me. Her blonde hair was different from Jane's. It looked artificial. She paid to be a blonde. She was all smiles, drying her hands with a dish towel as she walked to the door. "Hi, Alex! What a pleasure to meet you! I'm Deb, Jane's mother-in-law. She's finishing up getting ready." She directed me to the living room with a glass of water and the crabby man. I felt like I was in a scene in some tween movie. Mr. Cora sat next to me, cleaning his 12-gauge shotgun. I refused to let that intimidate me.

After a very long uncomfortable silence, he finally spoke. "Back in 'Nam, we used to have to kill or be killed. I'm no virgin to death. I've killed before. Don't forget that."

Luckily, before I was able to respond to his welcome speech, my blonde beauty walked into the room. Time stood still for a moment as I took in every bit of her. She looked more beautiful than any of the times before. She had on a gray and white striped dress that flowed to just below her knees. There was a belt at the smallest part of her waist, which reminded me of how thin she was. It was good we were going out for dinner. Maybe a hearty meal would add a couple of much-needed pounds to her frame. Her silky blonde hair was pulled to the right of her head into a low bun. And if my vision was correct, she had more makeup on than I had seen her wear.

Jane Cora was breathtaking.

Deb woke me up from my involuntary ogling. "Telling old stories again, Robert?" she asked sarcastically.

Robert stared at her with zero guilt in his eyes.

"Alex, were you formally introduced?" Jane asked my direction.

"Introduced enough, I'd say." I stood and brought my attention to her in-laws. "Mr. Cora, Mrs. Cora, thank you for letting me steal your daughter-in-law for the evening."

"Enjoy! Have a drink for me!" Deb said as she walked back into the kitchen.

"Mr. Cora, I assure you I'll bring her back better than when she left."

"Mmhmm." Robert was a man of few words, it seemed.

"Robert, please be nice," Jane ordered with a smirk as she bent down to kiss him on the forehead. "I won't be gone long. Enjoy your evening alone, you two."

We walked outside and down the little hill to where my car was parked. "Well, he seems lovely," I said flatly.

She turned to me and eyed me defensively. "He's worried about me. Can you blame him?"

"No, I can't blame him at all." That was the truth.

Jane looked surprised when we stopped at the Stelvio. "No Wrangler today?" I was flattered she knew what I drove most days. Sometimes she seemed very unobservant to the world around her.

"A night like tonight called for an upgrade." To her surprise, I opened the back door for her. She furrowed her brow in confusion and then noticed Stan in the driver's seat. After another uneasy look on her face, she entered the back seat. I ran around to the other side to get in next to her. Stelvios weren't the roomiest of SUVs, which meant we would be close to each other.

That may have not been by accident.

Once we were on our way, she looked more nervous than I had ever seen. She was fidgeting and breathing heavily. As to keep myself from respectfully admiring her up and down again, I made small talk to ease whatever concerns she had. "So Robert was in Vietnam?"

"Yes. He speaks of it a lot. It really affected him." Her voice was soaked with tension.

"My father was in Vietnam as well. He earned the Purple Heart by tending to the wounded after being shot in the butt—Forrest Gump style." Considering my father was more than fine, I hoped my little joke would make her laugh. She looked genuinely surprised but didn't say anything. She was still full of visible nerves.

I couldn't stand her being anxious anymore. I had to help somehow. Slowly and cautiously, I moved over to her side of the seat, where she was looking out the window, and grazed her left cheek with the back of my fingers. "Jane, have I told you how beautiful you look tonight?" She shook her head but continued to look out the window. I saw the subtle ways her body reacted to my touch. Her breathing quickened and her face warmed. "Jane, look at me, please."

Ever so slowly, with a few hesitant sighs, she turned her head toward me, but wouldn't meet my gaze. Her eyes were filled with tears. I faced her completely and let her cheek fall into my hand. "I'm not going to hurt you. Is that what you're worried about?"

She shook her head and wiped the fallen tears. My hand fell from her face and rested gently on her leg. She still wouldn't look at my face.

"Anxiety is radiating off of you." Her sadness was killing me slowly.

She was deep in thought once again. Tears fell to her cheeks and off her chin. "I'm not afraid you're going to hurt me." I didn't say anything. I didn't know what to say. She continued, "This last week, in between dates, you've been at the top of my mind. While I welcome a distraction for my brain, I'm... scared."

"Of what?" I wanted to keep her talking. It was deeper than she had ever gone with me.

"Of so many things, Alex. I'm scared I'm going to forget what my kids felt like in my arms. I'm scared I'm going to fall out of love with Graham. I'm scared of loving another and having them ripped away from me. I'm scared of myself. There are too many things..." She turned toward the window again as the tears continued to flow.

It took all my willpower not to fully embrace every part of her right there in the back of the car, with Stan listening to every word. Her worries were my worries. There was no difference between us anymore. I needed to find a way to help her. But I knew if I overstepped, she would shut down. So I approached cautiously. My right hand was still brushing against the fabric over her thin thigh. I took my fingers and brought them up to trace her ear. Then I trailed the back of my hand down to her neck and slid back and forth over her skin as delicately as I could. She leaned into my touch.

"I cannot imagine all the fears and worries you have. Please know that I'm honored just to live in the moment with you. I'm not going anywhere." I took her hands in mine and kissed them tenderly. "We'll go at your pace. I've waited a year. I will keep waiting." We were silent for a minute while I continued to lay gentle kisses up and down her hand, from her wrist to her knuckles.

She interrupted the enjoyment I was having at the taste of her skin. "Why me?"

"I'm sorry?" I asked, my lips still on her wrist.

"Why me, Alex? Reese said you can have any woman you want. Women who are far less broken." She asked the question as if there was no right answer. Or if I should say in return, "*You know what? You're right. You're not worth it.*"

She needed the truth, and I didn't know how to express it without scaring her. I had already stupidly confessed my love and proposed to her on the first day we'd ever held a conversation. I needed to choose my words carefully. Reluctantly, I put our entwined hands down to look at her and hoped to answer her question as honestly as I could.

"Why *not* you, Jane? Are you unworthy of friendship, or love, or whatever this will turn into?" It was a rhetorical question, and she knew it. "Since the moment I laid eyes on you, I knew I needed you in my life. Nothing has changed except I care more for you every day." Okay, so being careful with my words was more challenging than I thought. She didn't say anything in response, but it did seem to placate her.

We rode the rest of the way to the restaurant in silence. I didn't let go of her hands the entire way. When we arrived, I opened the door for her with the best smile I could put on after the intense car ride. "Madame, restaurant végétarien pour toi," I said with a grin. I was determined to get the anxiety out of her face. While I was so grateful she'd opened up to me, I still had to tread lightly.

"You brought me to a vegetarian restaurant?" She sounded impressed. "But...how did you know?" She looked at me questioningly. "Reese?"

I nodded happily and grabbed her hand to officially start our first date.

When we sat down to dinner, I told Jane that the evening was about getting to know her more. Our coffee dates were always surface conversations. I was dying to know the ins and outs of Jane Cora—*pun intended.* She looked a little uncomfortable at the idea of talking about herself, but I had been so careful about the topics I'd brought up over the last few months. It was time to dive a little deeper.

My priority was to learn about her family outside of her husband and kids. She told me she was an only child. Her parents currently lived in Sweden to take care of some elderly family members. Both her parents were born in Sweden. Jane was born in Chicagoland. Her dad had been transferred to Illinois for work before she was born. Prior to her parents moving back to Sweden, they had lived in the McHenry County area Jane's whole life. She had no blood relatives in the States. I began to understand how truly lonely she was and how special her in-laws were. Graham had a sister who lived in Schaumburg with her husband and four kids. They, along with Deb and Robert, were Jane's only local family. As I learned all about her, she tried to ask me the same questions. She was genuinely interested in my responses, but I kept them vague. Talking about me would be a waste of precious time.

"So, the name 'Jane.' It's not Swedish, is it?" I asked.

"No, it's not. My mom wanted me to have a normal American life. Against my father's wishes, which were to have a more traditional Swedish name, my mom insisted on choosing an easy name to say and remember. She told me she worried about me being looked at as different or weird because my parents weren't from here. She picked my name because she heard the saying 'plain Jane' and figured it would be a good name to help me fit in."

I put my hand over hers and squeezed gently. "Your name is lovely. And it suits you. However, you are anything but plain."

Jane blushed and looked at our hands. "Thanks. My mom didn't mean anything negative by it. She was trying to help." She had a sentimental look in her eyes. I could tell she missed her parents.

As the end of the evening fast approached, I started silently panicking with the unreasonable thought that our first date would be my last chance with her. Everything had gone fine—more than fine, in my opinion—at dinner, but I still couldn't shake an uneasy feeling. We entered the Stelvio and it became my turn to get anxious. It was 9:30 p.m., and the lights from oncoming traffic shone on her face. She was so beautiful. Every single part of her was perfection. Why had I ever wasted my time with anyone else? I knew why I had never married. I was waiting for the woman sitting next to me.

She noticed me staring, smiled a shy smile, and turned her head to look out her window. The feelings I'd been having for an entire year were too intense to ignore anymore. Without thinking it through, I moved toward her a bit and gently kissed the nape of her neck, right below her left ear. An immediate electric charge ran through my body. I knew she felt it too when I heard the quietest intake of air escape her lips. The noise must've startled and embarrassed her because she closed her mouth and shrugged her left shoulder to push me away.

"Jane," I whispered breathlessly against her ear. "Did you feel that?"

She nodded ever so slightly.

"Did it upset you?"

She shook her head without meeting my eyes. Her hands were fidgeting restlessly in her lap.

I reached down to calm her anxious hands. "Please, Jane. Please let me..."

She paused for a moment, then relaxed her left shoulder to allow me entrance. As gently as before, I kissed the same area of soft tissue on her neck. Her mouth parted, and she once again let in the smallest of audible breaths. Her scent was overwhelming. It almost knocked me out. She smelled of lilacs and strawberries. I could be suspended in time with her scent all around me, and I would call my life complete.

"You are intoxicating. I could breathe you in all day." As I did with her hands in the Stelvio before dinner, I placed gentle kisses up and down her neck, never letting my mouth leave her skin. I could feel the heat of her cheeks blushing. I wanted so badly to kiss those cheeks. Those lips. Her shoulders...

Suddenly, the car stopped and woke me from my worshiping. I had lost track of time. I was still high on her aroma. I could hardly speak but was able to whisper a request. "Come home with me. I'll bring you back first thing in the morning. You can stay in the guest suite if that would make you more comfortable." I kissed her neck again. "I just want you near me."

It took her what seemed like hours to respond. She hadn't spoken the whole way home. "I can't. I'm sorry." She looked at the house. "They're waiting for me." She was feeling the high from my touch too. It was emitting off her.

With the promise of taking it slow in my head, I sighed reverently and nodded. I didn't want the dream of a night to end. I left the warmth of her presence to be a gentleman until the end and exited the car to open her door. I laid my hand on the small of her back on the way up the hill. I tried to decide how I would end our date...a kiss on the lips? A hug? A high-five? Nothing seemed right. I knew what *I* wanted, but it wasn't about me...

"Madame, I had a wonderful evening. Thank you for honoring me with your presence." She blushed in the moonlight, and I nearly fell over with lust. It wasn't fair how much she affected me.

"Thank you, Alex." She paused. "For everything."

"My pleasure." I kissed the back of her hand and let her walk into her home. I knew going on a true date had been way out of her comfort zone. I hoped she sensed my appreciation.

As much as I had wanted to touch her lips to mine, I'd refrained. I was on a slow-moving train with her and could never increase speed too quickly.

Patience.

Baby steps.

I could still wait. Even with the lust waking up in me.

The evening couldn't have ended better.

Jane

AFTER ALEX ENDED our night with a gentle kiss on my hand, I shut the door behind me and rested my body against it. I needed a moment. The feeling of him was all over me, especially in a few specific areas. I placed a hand on my neck where his soft lips took full advantage of my weak moments on the ride home. The skin was still warm where he'd kissed. I closed my eyes and let myself relive and evaluate the evening. Blush flushed my cheeks. My thoughts drifted to each place he tenderly touched through the evening.

It made me ponder...

Touch. Such a simple act that could imply so many things. We were meant to give and receive physical touch. Every single human showed emotion that way, often subconsciously. Whether it be a friendly touch, an empathetic or sympathetic touch, a silly "slap someone gently because they said something funny" touch, *a sexual touch,* or so many more, we needed physical human connections. Alex has awakened me to the realization that I missed it. Hardly anyone touched me anymore. Aside from Deb, Robert, and Reese, everyone seemed afraid to hug me, fearing that I would spontaneously break into pieces.

But Alex did plenty of touching on our date. He wasn't afraid. More than that, he took every opportunity he had to lay his gentle and willing fingers on me. It wasn't just the obvious experiences in the car. At dinner, he couldn't help but brush my fingertips with the backs of his when in conversation. If I mentioned something even remotely amusing, he used the opportunity to gently grab my hand or my shoulder as he reacted to whatever I had said. If I had a hair in my face, he grazed his fingers along the strands and put it back into place.

I took a deep breath and let myself feel the sensations in all the areas he laid his hands on me. A teeny tiny inner part of me, deeper than my deep inner voice, made me feel guilty that I'd made him wait so long to touch me. That tiny inner part of me also made me feel *so* guilty I'd hardly reached out to touch him. Had he noticed? Of course he had. Nothing seemed to get by Alex. I wondered how it made him feel. Surface voice told me to let that shit go. That I had enough crap to deal with and feeling guilty for Alex Lombardi was not on the list. Deep inner voice was pushing herself to the top of my brain, past surface voice, to remind me of one point I had been trying not to think about...he asked me to go home with him.

He asked me to go home with him.

I refused to admit that I *indeed* wanted to spend the rest of the evening with Alex. Nor did I want to admit that an internal ache was building for him to keep touching me, in all the places he already had...and maybe some new places too.

I stopped my daydreaming abruptly. What kind of hussy was I becoming? My annoying inner voices weren't the only things waking up after over a year. Other parts were coming out of hibernation too. I didn't know how I felt about it.

Not a hussy, deep inner voice explained, *just a lonely, sad, broken woman who feels a little more put together around Alex.*

Surface voice scoffed.

I shook my head in an attempt to quiet the disagreement. All the internal dialogue made my heart race and head spin. I was too dizzy to make it upstairs, so I rested on the foyer floor for a moment. The cold tile felt good on my warm cheeks. What was happening to me? Was I falling for him already? How could I let myself do that? Last week I was still adamant I just needed a friend. Now I blushed and felt an unbearable amount of unfulfilled chemistry between us. I was so confused.

Once my breath and heart returned to normal rhythms, I crawled my way to my bedroom upstairs to sleep away any worries or guilt. As much as I tried to think of something else, anything else, the man who'd made all my nerve endings come alive was my last thought before I drifted off to sleep.

I dreamt that evening. Graham and the kids were at the zoo with me. We went to see the monkeys, Clare's favorite, then the giraffes, Marric's favorite. We followed the bigger two kids around, trying to keep up as they skipped to each exhibit. Graham was pushing little sleeping Arlo in a stroller, whistling the way he did when he was at his happiest. It was the most beautiful day in Brookfield. Based on the weather, I would guess it was mid-June. It was about seventy-five degrees and partly sunny. The white fluffy clouds were keeping the perfect amount of shade.

The dream went on and on. We treated the kids to cotton candy and milkshakes before the dolphin show. The older two kids picked out souvenirs in the gift shop. When Arlo awoke, I stopped at a bench near the zebras to nurse him. The other kids played around me, giggling and kissing the baby while he ate. Graham sat on a bench across from me and stared at his riches...the only riches he ever cared about. Family. Our eyes met, and he nodded at me once, as if he was trying to finish an unspoken conversation we'd had together.

I woke up in a sweat. My heart raced as I sat up to gasp for air and wipe wet hair away from my face. That was the first time they'd starred in my dreams. Was it a coincidence that I dreamt of them the first night I went to bed thinking of someone else? I had been waiting for a sign from one of them for over a year. Was the dream Graham's sign? Was he giving me the okay to love again? Maybe he was trying to remind me of who my true family was. I had absolutely no idea, and I was instantly overwhelmed with so many emotions. Familiar tears welled up again. My chest shook from the inside out. Anxiety was taking over; I knew the pattern. The dark clouds started surrounding me the same way they had the first couple of months after the accident.

Sometimes there was no fighting the darkness.

I curled up into a ball under my covers to get warm and to try to contain the quivering. Flashes of the dream were behind my eyelids. Each flash showed me a perfect image of one of my lost treasures.

Graham. Clare. Marric. Arlo.

The flashes abruptly changed to images of my night with Alex. One was of his brown eyes so concerned. One of his dimples. One of his gentle kisses...

It was all too much. I squeezed my eyes tighter to remove the images. I wasn't being fair to any of them. I was at a loss as to how I should be honoring and remembering my family. I didn't know what was considered appropriate behavior with Alex. My heart felt like it was being torn apart. And I was certain nobody could understand or help me with the raw, agonizing pain expanding deep in my chest.

The clouds surrounded me without any chance to escape. All the images were gone, and total black nothingness appeared. The darkness completely took over as I drifted off with an "I'm sorry" before falling asleep.

5

Alex

I NEVER HAD trouble falling asleep. However, hours after I dropped Jane off at her in-laws', my adrenaline still pumped hard through my veins. No amount of sheep counting would save me from replaying every moment of the night. At about 4:00 a.m., staring at the ceiling while trying to get her image out of my brain so it could rest, I thought back to the end of the evening. Maybe if I replayed the whole night through to the end, my brain would be satisfied...

Stan had remained dutifully quiet on the way home from Jane's, but I would have been naïve to think he was going to let me off without twenty questions as soon as the car was in park. I grabbed two beers from the garage fridge, tossed one in his direction, and let him start the interrogating. Stan seemed pensive. He kept staring at me with a smug expression.

"Well, get on with it, Stan," I teased. "What would you like to know?"

"I don't know, man. I don't even know where to start." He took a swig of his beer. "How long have we known each other? Ten years now?" I nodded. "Well, in the ten years I've known you, I've never seen you act that way with a woman."

All I could do was smile at him. I was still on a high from the date.

He continued, "Not even with Cameron."

"Two totally different relationships," I clarified with a pointed finger in his direction.

His eyebrows raised in surprise. "Oh, come on, man. You were head over heels for Cameron."

"I can't deny that." I chuckled quietly.

"And this is stronger?" he questioned.

"Much." I tried to get my point across with my tone.

He narrowed his eyes at me with a giant grin. "Are you in love with her?"

I took a long sip of my beer, gaining the courage to answer his question. There was no point in denying it. "I am."

Stan's eyes doubled in size. "So soon?"

"Yep." I ran my hands through my hair, knowing how crazy my admission sounded.

Stan shook his head in disbelief. "Are you dating?"

I sighed and shook my head. "Unfortunately, no."

His eyes narrowed again. "Why not?"

I closed my eyes and took in a deep breath. "It's complicated."

"Are you going to give me any more than two words at a time tonight?" He laughed.

I smirked. "Probably not."

He laughed again and took a big gulp of his beer.

Somewhere between me replaying Stan's questioning and him going on a tangent about how women weren't worth all the trouble, I finally fell asleep.

I WOKE UP to my doorbell ringing as if a toddler had gotten a hold of it. I looked at my security camera and found one asshole with a giant grin peering right at it. I quickly ran down to the door in only my boxer briefs to greet my long-lost bud.

"Tanner. What's up, man?" I went in for a handshake and hug. "Where the hell have you been?"

Tanner looked me up and down, as any good friend would when seeing their buddy in my state. He smirked. "Handing out hugs in your underwear. Some things will never change." He laughed at his joke. "Where the hell have *I* been? Where the hell have *you* been, bro?" He looked at me expectantly.

I didn't reply. I had no good excuse.

He continued, "I've been back in Chicago since last June. It's what...April? You've been MIA." He sounded mildly offended and suspicious. "I figured if you wouldn't answer my calls or texts, I'd come to make sure you were alive myself."

I sighed and ran my hand across the stubble of my beard. "Sorry, man," I apologized with a sheepish grin. "I've been distracted."

Tanner narrowed his eyes. "What's her name and where did you meet her?" he asked as he walked past me into my house. He knew me too well.

Tanner and I had a lot of history together. He'd moved to the area his sophomore year of high school, and we'd clicked instantly. He was a jock and liked the ladies, so of course we were fast friends. Our other buddies in high school would say Tanner and I had a "bromance" because we were always together. I wasn't offended by the teasing. He became my brother rather quickly.

We went to separate colleges but always stayed in touch. He would come to visit me in Chicago at UIC, and I would go visit him at U of I-Champaign/Urbana. Once Jodi was out of the picture, we were a force to be reckoned with at bars and clubs. We often joked that we had something for everyone. If the ladies preferred tanned skin, dark eyes, and dark hair, they'd eye me all night. If they liked the naturally highlighted blond with baby blues, they eyed Tanner. Neither of us went home alone.

After college, he'd moved to Chicago to start his business. He traveled all over Europe, tending to the wealthy while they were on their lavish holidays. I wished I knew what he actually did. I liked to poke fun at him, saying he was a glorified tour guide. He didn't deny it. His work life consisted of a repeat schedule of long extended jobs overseas and then having a break for a few months.

"I'm sorry, Tanner. I didn't realize you'd been home so long already. When do you go back to Europe?"

He made himself comfortable on the couch, then turned on my big screen above the fireplace. "Not for a few months." He settled in to find something good to watch, then faced me with expectation written all over his face. "Who is she?"

"Who's who?" I grinned.

"The one keeping you away from all the bars...and me. How long have you been dating?"

I shrugged. "I'm not dating anyone."

"Who's the girl you're after then?" He was too smart.

"I don't know what you mean," I teased.

"Dude! Enough!" he exclaimed with a smile.

Why was I feeling so protective of her? Of our relationship? If I could even call it that yet. Stan and Tanner were my two closest friends. They'd earned my trust over the years. Never had I felt the need to be evasive with their questioning about a woman. Knowing that, I still couldn't shake the resolve to stay vague.

I sighed a loud, flabbergasted breath and sat on a recliner adjacent to him. He wouldn't give up. "Her name is Jane. I met her at the gym."

"Nice, bro! How good is she?" His eyebrows were doing a vertical dance in excitement.

I felt my cheeks getting red, so I chucked a throw pillow at his face in an attempt to divert his attention. "It's not like that, *bro*," I said defensively but still smiling.

"Alexander Lombardi, are you blushing?"

I turned away from him. I could feel the astonishment on his face.

He gasped. "Holy shit. You're *blushing*."

"She's different from all the others," I mumbled.

He raised one eyebrow and flattened his lips together. It would have been obvious to anyone—especially my best friend—that I was madly in love.

"Spill it," he demanded.

And that was it. I had no hope to keep anything from him. I knew him well enough to know he wouldn't leave until he was satisfied with my play-by-play description of the last year. I left out the parts when we were in the backseat of the Stelvio. I had a nagging urge to keep some things just between Jane and me.

After an hour of giving him all the details he demanded, he turned his attention to the TV, which gave me a break from the interrogation. Between my nerves being on overdrive, not being able to sleep, Stan's questioning, and then Tanner's interrogation, I was exhausted. I dozed off right there on the recliner and fell into a fantasy dream of Jane Cora.

"WHAT IN THE *hell* did you do to her?"

"Well, hello, Reese," I said to my phone with the most sarcasm I could gather. I was once again having déjà vu from last March.

"I'm not joking, Alex. What did you do to Jane?" she demanded.

Her alarmed tone sent a worried shiver down my spine. "What are you talking about? I took her on a date Friday and haven't heard from her since. We had a great time. Today's Sunday, so she should be going to church soon, and then we'll meet for coffee. What do you mean what did I *do* to her? What's wrong with her?"

"She's in the hospital for exhaustion, dehydration, and anxiety. She was admitted last night." She paused for a moment to let herself calm down. "I thought you'd dumped her or something."

"Reese, that will never happen, so you can stop worrying about it. What else do you know? Where is she?" My words may have come out a little too forceful. I was panicked now.

"Don't bother yet. Visiting hours aren't for another hour." She sighed as if she didn't want to give out any extra information to me. "All I know is the Coras went into her room last night because she hadn't come out all day. They thought she needed a day in bed. But when the sun went down and they still hadn't seen her, they went to check. She wouldn't wake up." Her voice hitched; she was trying not to cry. "They were worried and called 911."

I could feel the color drain out of my face. "Is she stable?"

"As far as I know, yes." She paused again. "Alex, if you visit her, please don't upset her. I can tell you're serious about her, and you haven't done anything yet to allow me to punch you in the face, but she's really fragile…" Her voice trailed off. Reese's worry was breaking her defensive nature toward me.

"I know. Thank you for caring about her so much. She's really lucky to have you," I said sincerely. "Now if you'll excuse me, I need to go to her."

"Wait. One more thing." There was silence at the end of the line for a while.

I hadn't used up all my patience with her, so I waited until she was ready. If Reese was keeping me on the phone, she had something important to say. "Jane used to be so happy. In high school, she blossomed right in front of my eyes to become this gorgeous, confident, bubbly girl. She's a great storyteller and loves stupid jokes. She has the best giggle. It makes you want to laugh along with her, even if you don't know why she's giggling." I listened with bated breath. "I don't expect her to return to her old normal self. But I can feel that some parts of her natural disposition are trying to escape. But it's like she's holding back." Her voice turned somber. "My only guess as to why she'd hold herself back is because she feels guilty for moving on. I can't say I blame her." There was another moment of silence. Reese was contemplating hard. "I've been trying for months to help her heal back to something closer to normal, but my efforts aren't enough. If you can pull out any of the happy, silly side of her, I'll—"

"Trust me and my devotion to her?" I interrupted eagerly.

Her vulnerability left in an instant. "*Ha*! No. Don't go that far." I suppressed a snort and shook my head. I had all the confidence in the world I'd win Reese's trust. It would just take time, and yes, more patience. "If you can do that, Alex, I'll wave the white flag in surrender. I will stop trying to convince Jane to stay away from you. And I'll trust her judgment—"

"Thank you, Reese."

"I wasn't done." *Of course not*. "I'll trust her judgment. Until you fuck up, then I'll break your teeth."

I chuckled quietly, thankful for our conversation. "Thank you for filling me in. It was nice chatting with you."

"I wish I could say the same, Alex." Her words were harsh, but there wasn't truth behind them.

EXACTLY AN HOUR later, I headed to room 417 of Good Shepherd Hospital with a bouquet of flowers and a card. As I approached the closed door to Jane's room, Deb was arriving too. Robert was not with her which had me grateful. I had promised him I'd return Jane better than she'd left. I'm certain he remembered that promise.

Deb and I smiled at each other and went to push the door in to greet our girl. A nurse came over quickly to stop us. "One visitor at a time," she instructed sternly. "We don't want her to get upset or exhausted." I nodded and made the "ladies first" signal to Deb. She smiled at me again and pushed the door all the way open. I was about to walk away to find a bench when I noticed there was a mirror in the room, angled in the perfect position to let me get a view of Jane without her seeing me.

"Jane, there's someone here to visit you. Are you up for some company?" asked the nurse as Deb trailed behind her. Jane sat up in bed and pulled the breathing tube from her nose.

Deb went in for a hug. "Oh, honey. How are you feeling?"

"Better, I guess. I don't know what happened."

Deb explained that when she didn't get up by Saturday night, they finally checked on her. They found her incoherent and breathing shallowly. "We were so worried," Deb choked out. "You looked sick and frail, just like you did right after..." She hesitated to say more. Jane nodded like she understood the unspoken words. Deb flattened out an area of the bed and sat down. "I'm glad you're feeling better, Janey, but what do you think triggered this?"

With fresh tears streaming down Jane's face, she told Deb about a dream she'd had Friday night, and how she had a mess of confusion in her head. She confessed she thought she was starting to feel something for me. She was terrified she wouldn't love Graham anymore if she made room for someone else. She was worried she'd forget the laughter of her kids if she were to ever have another child in the future. She didn't know how to embrace a new future without forgetting her past.

"Oh, honey. Those are all valid worries." Deb lifted Jane's chin so she had to look into her eyes. "But you have an opportunity to find happiness again. If this boy brings you joy, you need to take a chance on him. This feels like the right path for you."

"Does Robert feel that way too?" Jane asked, wiping away some tears.

Deb huffed a laugh. "I'll work on him. Don't you worry about Robert." She left the bed to find some tissue before she sat back down. "Janey, I can tell you have a lot of complicated thoughts running through your head. I see it in your face. Nobody expects you to forget the trails you've walked before." Jane's tears really started rolling. *So much for not upsetting her,* I thought to myself. Deb continued, "And you will never forget your gorgeous, perfect family. They're in your heart forever. Having fondness for another man will not diminish your feelings for any of them, Graham included. You need to be happy, Jane. You *deserve* it. Nobody expects you to mourn your life away." Jane wept as they hugged and worked through her concerns. Deb handed her a tissue and kissed her on the cheek.

"It doesn't feel too soon to you?" Jane's voice was worried.

"It's been over a year. Sure, that isn't a substantial amount of time, but for the last fourteen months, you've been learning how to cope and start healing. It's a long process to heal. Besides, who sets the parameters on this sort of thing?" Deb blotted Jane's tears. "There's no need to rush it. But there's also no need to suppress any feelings you have building. You're doing nothing wrong by trying to heal and find happiness."

Jane nodded in thanks and kissed Deb on the cheek. "You're such a great mom to me."

"And you're such a great daughter." They looked at each other lovingly for a moment before Deb continued, "There's someone else here that would like to see you. Are you ready?"

"I don't know, Deb. Am I? I don't know anything anymore," she said softly.

"You have our blessing. No matter what happens, you'll always be our daughter. We love you."

They hugged once more, and Deb prepared to leave the room. When she passed by me in the hallway, she winked at me through her tears.

I was beginning to become fond of Deb Cora.

I took a couple of seconds to steady my breathing after hearing Jane's private admissions. It was hard for me to feel any sort of hope or relief when she was struggling so much. *Baby steps,* I reminded myself once again. Her confessions didn't speed up any timeline. In fact, they may have slowed it down. With a deep yogic inhale and exhale, I entered the room. As I approached her, I couldn't hide my look of distress. "Jane..." I breathed out her name as I sat down next to her.

"I'm okay, Alex. You don't need to worry about me."

She would learn eventually that my concerns for her well-being weren't going anywhere. I let out a big sigh. "I'm so sorry if something I said or did made you unwell. I let my desires get the best of me..."

She stopped me before I could apologize anymore. "Alex, you didn't put me in here. You did nothing wrong." She looked at me, and I swear I could see her remembering how my lips touched the nape of her neck. "Friday was the best time I've had in over a year." She paused, like she wanted to say more, but didn't know how to say it. She focused on her bedding, deep in thought. She lifted her hands to find mine and connect us together. It did not go unnoticed that it was the first time *she* reached for *me*. My heart raced. "I'm struggling a lot right now. I have butterflies in my stomach all the time when you're around." She stared at our hands. "In the back of my head, my family is glaring at me in judgment." Tears welled up in her eyes again. "I don't know how to manage all this yet, but I want you to know I have...feelings for you." She huffed a breath. "That is hard for me to admit. Or say out loud." I knew where her head was: she felt like she was cheating on her family. "I just don't know to what extent yet. Or if those feelings can grow." She looked at me. Her almond-shaped eyes were a different shade of blue when she cried. They were brighter, almost translucent, but gorgeous all the same. "I'm sorry I can't give you more."

I tipped her chin up so she would look at me. "Shhh..." I said in a soft, disagreeing tone. "You've given me all I need." I kept her eyes focused on me so she could see the genuineness in my features.

"I really don't know why you're bothering," she whispered.

Between eavesdropping on her chat with Deb and the current conversation, she had given me a good look into her brain. It was only fair to give her something in return.

"Jane, you're the only person my eyes see anymore. When we're together, everyone else is blurry. When we're apart, I see you in my daydreams. At night, you star in my real dreams." I paused to gauge her reaction. She didn't look concerned, so I continued, "You are so beautiful." She looked down and shook her head in disapproval. She didn't see herself the way others did. "Do you know how stunning you are?"

She rolled her eyes and snorted quietly. "Oh yeah, hospital attire and dirty hair are the latest fashion trends."

I brushed my thumb across her cheek, gently guiding her to meet my eyes again. Her platinum hair was messy on the top of her head. She had strands falling out of the hair tie at every angle. Her face was puffy from crying. Dark eye makeup from Friday night was smudged under her eyes. Her full lips were so dry. She looked like she needed a hot shower and a toothbrush. However, even with all that, she was a sight to behold.

"So beautiful," I repeated, and meant it. She took a deep breath and closed her eyes as gentle tears fell to her cheeks. She leaned into where my thumb was grazing her skin. I could not mentally handle any more crying. It was tearing me apart, so I changed the subject to something less intense. "Do you know when you'll get discharged?"

"This afternoon or tonight, after the doctor makes his rounds. He's putting me on some new medications to help with anxiety and depression. He also wants me to see my therapist more frequently."

Good. There was no reason she needed to suffer more than she already did. "Can I see you this week sometime?" I asked hopefully.

"I'm not sure. I'm back to work on Friday, so I have a lot to do to prepare. And I'm meeting with the recreation center manager at some point to discuss getting back on the schedule to teach spin class."

"Are you sure you're ready for all that?" Concern had to be written all over my face.

"I think I am. It will be a welcome distraction. I won't be on the schedule to teach right away, so I have time to plan for that. As far as the salon, I'm only going to work one day a week to start. I'm looking forward to it."

"Well, good then. I'm glad." An idea hit me. "*I'll* look forward to being your first client back at the salon." Her eyes became large in surprise. "*What?*" I said playfully. "That way if you're out of practice and mess it up, it's only *my* hair, and I won't sue you." I winked. She chuckled quietly, which made me do the same. "Can I take you out to dinner after your shift?"

She looked uneasy all of a sudden. "Actually, I'm meeting a family friend for dinner on Friday." It was more of a confession than a statement.

"Oh," was all I could muster. I was surprised I didn't coax her into telling me who it was, but I would have been fooling myself if I said I didn't care. In fact, I desperately needed to know. Was it a guy? An old boyfriend? That was unlikely, considering she had been married since she was eighteen. All of a sudden not knowing whom Jane's friends were made me anxious.

She's allowed to have friends, Alex, my subconscious reminded me.

Jane shook me out of my contemplating. "Thank you for coming to see me. I had a feeling you were placing the blame on yourself. I didn't text you because I wanted to tell you and show you in person that it wasn't your fault, and that I'm okay. Maybe I should have texted you. I'm sorry. I have a lot going on. I'm overwhelmed in many ways." She laughed under her breath. "I think I'm in need of a vacation."

Before I could stop the words, they were already leaving my mouth. "Then let's go."

She furrowed her brow.

"I mean it. I have the perfect place we could get away for a couple of days. I'll have you back by Thursday so you can start work Friday."

"Alex, I'm not sure I'm ready to—" Her face screamed uneasiness.

I gently laid my hand on her leg. "This would be strictly platonic. Think of it as a friend helping a friend."

Her eyebrow raised in doubt.

"I'll be on my best behavior." I gave her the Scouts' honor symbol. "Let's go, Jane. Let's get out of here." Now that the idea was in my head, it had to happen.

I could almost see the wheels turning in her mind. It was as if she had the devil and angel pulling her in two different directions again. After a minute or so, she shook her head and took a deep breath. "You promise I'll get home by Thursday?"

I nodded. "I promise."

"And you promise we can go just as friends?"

"Of course." There was no hesitation in my answer. It was an easier promise than it should've been, considering the deep needs brewing in my body. But the last thing I wanted to do was push her away. If she would go on a little trip with me, where she could decompress and where we could get to know each other better, I could continue to be the perfect gentleman.

I smiled a giant smile at her, hoping to win her trust with my genuine promises.

"Robert and Deb may not think it's a good idea."

I made the prayer sign with my hands and pushed my lower lip out in a pout. "I promise it will be good for you."

She paused and stared at me for 176 minutes. Well, it felt like that many. Finally, she spoke. "Okay. I'll go with you, Alex." I let out the breath I didn't know I was holding and beamed a huge smile. She grinned hesitantly back at me. "Are you going to tell me where we're going?"

Just then a nurse came in to inform me it was time for Jane to get some rest. Reluctantly, I pushed myself up from the bed.

"Nah. A surprise sounds like more fun. But here's a hint. We're not going to a beach. You'll need warm clothes. I'll text you what else you need to pack." I kissed her hand. "Take care, Jane. I'll see you tomorrow."

She rested her head back on her pillows and closed her eyes. "See you then."

"YOU OWN A private plane?" Jane asked as we were buckling our seat belts. She looked more uncomfortable than surprised.

The plane started taxiing toward the runway. "Not mine, personally. It's our company plane. I hardly ever use it. I generally fly the way everyone else does. But since we have time constraints, I felt it was appropriate. There aren't many direct flights to where we are going."

"And you're still not going to tell me where that is?"

"Nope." I took her hand and kissed her knuckles. "Unless you want the surprise ruined." She looked down at her hand in mine. I realized I didn't know what quite constituted crossing the line. "Is this okay?" I asked sincerely. She nodded at me, appearing a little shy. We were silent for a moment while I enjoyed the scent and taste of her skin.

The plane picked up speed and my anticipation rose along with it. We'd be in the air shortly. In the past twenty-four hours, every time I thought about being alone with Jane for a few days, my heart would skip a few beats. Even if I had to stay on my best behavior, I was more than excited for the opportunity with her.

Once we were in the air, Jane interrupted my daydreaming. "If I guess right, will you tell me?"

I was still holding her hand, so I kissed her knuckles again to hide my grin. That was an easy bargain. She'd never guess. "Sure."

"Are we going east or west?"

I couldn't hide my smile anymore. "Not telling, but feel free to look out the window and see if you can figure it out by the sun."

She rolled her eyes. "Well, we're not leaving the country because you didn't tell me to bring my passport."

"That's correct. We're staying within the continental U.S."

She cocked her head to the side and grinned. "No hints?" She was so damn beautiful. She was trying to weaken my resolve, and she'd win if she kept trying. She was someone I never wanted to say no to. I chuckled under my breath. I wondered if she knew yet just how much of a hold she had on me.

"I gave you a hint. No more. Unless you want to ruin the surprise," I repeated, trying to stay strong.

She stared at me for a moment and then closed her eyes. "Okay, you win. I'll wait." She put her head on the back of the headrest and sighed. She looked too tired to ask more questions. She had dark circles under her eyes. She must still be fatigued from the weekend. I kept her hand in mine and let her rest.

We landed a few hours later. Jane had slept the entire flight, which had me thankful. I didn't want her to arrive back to Chicago on Thursday feeling more exhausted than when we left.

The airplane door opened and I let Jane travel the stairs first.

"Mountains?" she inquired.

I nodded excitedly. "Any guesses yet?"

6

Jane

"HMM. NO GUESSES yet." I hadn't been to too many areas of the country. I knew there were mountains east and west of Illinois, but I didn't know their differences enough to make an educated guess. The landscape definitely looked like a place I had never been.

We descended the stairs and were greeted by an attractive, cowboy-looking man who drove a pickup truck. He was probably in his mid-thirties and just under six feet tall, about the same height as Alex. I could tell he was full of muscle under his flannel, jeans, cowboy boots, and Stetson. His dark beard matched his dark hair and eyes. He looked a little weathered, as if he had seen some hard winters.

"Spencer." Alex pulled the cowboy in for a hug. "It's been too long. How have you been?"

The cowboy hugged Alex back and gave him a hard pat on the shoulder. "Doing just fine. We've missed you around the ranch. How are you?"

"I'm great." Alex took my left hand and pulled me in close to him. "This is Jane Cora." I looked at him as he said my name. I may have imagined it, but it appeared he had color in his cheeks.

Spencer reached to shake my hand. "Miss Cora, it's a pleasure to meet you."

"It's nice to meet you too, Spencer. Please call me Jane."

"Okay. Jane." Spencer smiled and let go of my hand. "I have to say, it's nice to have you bring a guest, Alex. You're not much fun by yourself. No offense."

"Offense taken." Alex pretended to look hurt.

We packed into the pickup truck with Spencer and Alex in front and me in the back. Alex asked if I wanted him to sit in the back with me, but I insisted he sat in the front so the two of them could catch up. I didn't know much about Spencer yet, but the two of them seemed to be friends who hadn't seen each other in a while.

I stayed quiet while listening to their conversation. It sounded like Spencer was newly married. He and his wife tended to the ranch year-round. Alex teased Spencer that he was offended he wasn't invited to the wedding. Spencer rebutted that he did indeed invite Alex, but he was—he air quoted—"too busy" to come. Their banter made me smile. They were like brothers.

About twenty minutes into our drive, I still didn't know what city we were in, or state for that matter. I had paid such close attention to their conversation that I'd forgotten I could find some clues by looking outside. It only took a few minutes for me to solve the puzzle and see MONTANA written on a sign.

Montana. That excited and terrified me at the same time. I'd never been to Montana or anywhere near there. It would be fun to explore a new area. However, if Alex hoped I'd hike those mountains I'd seen in the background, he would be very disappointed.

"Jane, you're quiet back there," Spencer hollered over his shoulder.

"Hmm? I'm just listening and enjoying the view outside. It's really pretty here."

Spencer looked out his side window and sighed contentedly. "That it is."

"Have you lived in Montana a long time?"

He nodded. "My whole life. I love it here. I wouldn't move if you paid me."

I looked back out the window at the gorgeous landscape around us. "I can see why. The views are way nicer here than where we live in Illinois. Sometimes I wonder why I live in such a boring state." Both boys chuckled at my admission. "I'm looking forward to finding out where we're going. Alex has kept me in the dark." Alex turned to give me a mischievous grin. "How much longer until we're there?"

"Not long now." Spencer looked at Alex with a raised eyebrow. "Why didn't you tell her?"

Alex shrugged. "I thought it would be more fun to see her reaction without any info." He looked at me again. "This is one of my favorite places. I'm looking forward to sharing it with you."

"I look forward to finding out what it is." An involuntary, quiet giggle escaped my lips. We weren't even at our destination yet, but it felt good to be there. I would be foolish to think all my problems would stay in Illinois. Nevertheless, I'd promised myself I would attempt to enjoy the next few days. I could give myself that. Or at least I could try. Everything would certainly be waiting for me when I arrived back home.

Spencer pulled off the main road onto a side street a few minutes later. We traveled along for a while until he slowly turned into a large property. Above the long driveway was a tall wooden entrance post and sign. The sign read "TRIPLE-A-RANCH."

Okay, so all signs pointed to it being a ranch. I'd gathered that much. Spencer drove down the long and winding driveway. After what felt like a mile, an enormous log cabin came into view. It had to be the largest cabin I'd ever seen. He pulled around to the side of it and parked the truck.

"Welcome to TRIPLE-A-RANCH." Spencer beamed with pride. There was no question he loved it there.

Alex opened my door and took my hand. I looked around and tried to absorb everything in sight. The incredible mountains were in the background. There were stables right behind the large house with about twenty horses roaming and eating hay. Cows rummaged for grass out past the horse stables. A couple of barns were scattered perfectly around the property. A few small cabins were placed on each side of the main house's backyard area, about 200 feet to the right and left of the horse stables. There were cute little paths from each cabin to the stables and the main house. The place was charming but also rustic. I loved it immediately.

"Is this a resort?" I asked anyone who was listening.

Alex wrapped my arm through his and led me to the back of the home. "In a sense, I guess. It's a dude ranch. People come here to learn how to be cowboys and cowgirls. It's a fun experience, especially for those who have never been on a farm or ranch."

My eyes couldn't stop studying all the beauty surrounding me. "Do you own this property?"

"No. As of now, this property is under my parents' names. I'm free to stay here any time I wish, but they ask that I keep my visits to the slow months, or months like April when the ranch is completely closed."

"Why is it closed in April?" I needed to find out as much as I could. The ranch was a little slice of heaven I hadn't known existed until four minutes ago.

"April is in between seasons. It's not cold or snowy enough to do winter activities, and it's definitely not warm enough for summer activities. Being closed in April allows Spencer and the other ranch hands to do property maintenance and recoup before the summer season starts." Alex opened the door to the large home and ushered me to go first.

"We're not staying in one of those cute cabins?" I looked out toward the little wooden buildings.

"Those are one-bedroom buildings. Well, more like studios. They aren't as warm as the main house. There's heat, but there are no fireplaces." He paused to take in my reaction to his explanation. "We can stay in one if you'd like. But I thought you'd want your own room. Those are usually for couples who want more privacy than what the main house can provide." Alex looked shy as he said the last sentence. He was trying to do the right thing—what he thought I'd want. And he was right. The charm of the property was making me not think straight. I wasn't ready, nor willing, to share a studio cabin with anyone just yet.

Maybe soon though? Deep inner voice chimed in.

"Right. Of course," I replied, feeling a little embarrassed that I'd even mentioned it.

Spencer had our bags and entered the cabin behind us. "Do these go in the master suite?"

Alex turned to him. "Only the purple bags. Mine will go into one of the other suites upstairs." Spencer gave Alex a puzzled look but didn't question it.

"Alex, I don't need the master suite. You can have it."

He grinned at me. "Absolutely not. It's yours." He took my hand again. "Come on, I'll show you around."

He brought me to the master suite first. The room was big enough to be its own house. The cabin sat on the slightest of hills, so the bedroom had a private balcony overlooking the mountains. It also had an en suite bathroom with a large Jacuzzi tub and a large gas fireplace. I could stay in that room for the full three and a half days and feel satisfied with my getaway. My eyes hovered over the large king-sized bed, which was way too much bed for one person.

"Alex, this room is incredible. But I truly don't need all this space. Are you sure you don't want it?"

He squeezed my hand. "This is your time to relax and unwind a bit from the real world. You deserve this room." He kissed my cheek quickly, which made my heart leap. "Let's go see the rest of the house."

The log cabin ended up being even more impressive than I'd imagined. Including the first-floor master suite, it had seven bedrooms and six bathrooms. The lower level was an open floor plan but had designated areas for everything. There was a giant kitchen with the largest island in existence. Eight bar stools lined one side of it, ready for guests to mingle and have coffee or a meal. Three large leather couches were placed in the middle of the open room with a few recliners placed around them. The main focus of the room was the grand fireplace, which was built out of large stones and spanned up to the tall ceiling. The mantle held a large art piece that appeared to be a painting of the property. On the opposite wall to the fireplace was a large floor-to-ceiling bookcase filled with hundreds of books. A few feet away from the living area were two large rustic dining room tables. Each table seated eight people.

Every bit of the cabin fit the wild west ranch feel without being overkill or tacky. There were no dead animal heads or hides anywhere. The colors were light and airy. The decor complemented the beauty of the outdoors shining through the large windows and skylights. Everything flowed well together. It reminded me of a fancy bed and breakfast. I could picture a dozen happy, relaxed guests in the cabin, ready to go out and learn how to rope cattle or ride horses—or do whatever cowboys and cowgirls do.

As we toured the rest of the house, Alex filled me in on how the ranch operated. During peak months, there were always workers buzzing around. There would be at least one cook, a maid, and an activities director. The ranch hands helped with any and every task too. In April, all the inside employees were on their month-long paid vacation. According to Alex, they worked more than forty hours per week most of the year and deserved the month off. The ranch hands remained, but they got vacation time throughout the year since there were more of them to cover for each other.

"So, it will be just us in this huge house?" I asked nervously as he pulled me from room to room, showing and explaining all the amenities.

"Just us," Alex confirmed while keeping his eyes away from mine. Generally, Alex preferred direct eye contact when we spoke. But he looked as nervous as I felt. It made me wonder if he worried about keeping his promises for the next few days. He cleared his throat and continued, "Spencer and the other guys will be around. And Spencer's wife, Betsy, said she'll help with meals and anything else we need."

We made it to the end of the upstairs hallway where Alex opened the door to a substantial-sized billiard room. Another fireplace was on the back wall with a large TV hanging on the brick. Come to think of it, that was the only room I had seen with a TV so far. The room also had a little bar tucked away in the corner, as well as a couple of dart boards and couches. There was a thick, solid wood door that separated the room from the hallway. That door was thicker than the rest of the guest room doors. I imagined it could get a little rowdy in there, depending on the clientele. The heavy door probably blocked out some of the noise. I had to admit it looked like a fun place to finish the night after a long day in the fresh Montana air.

"So they live here? The ranch hands...and Betsy?" I asked.

"They all live on the property, yes, just not in this cabin. This place is strictly for guests. Spencer and Betsy live in a cabin a quarter mile into the property. The other guys live in what may look like a college dorm building, which is near Spencer and Betsy's home. They're all single, so they're satisfied with having a dorm room, so to speak, instead of private homes. None of them pay to live here. It's part of the perks."

My eyebrows rose in surprise "Wow. That's very generous of your parents."

"It is. But it's a give-and-take. The ranch hands don't make a huge income. They get free rent and free food when the cooks make large meals. They have access to vehicles whenever they need one. Those perks help offset their wages. Plus, free rent keeps them happy and wanting to work hard. They're the hardest working group of men you'll meet."

"I don't doubt it."

Alex brought me back downstairs once he showed me all the rooms. "What would you like to do? I can give you the outside tour. We can have some lunch. Are you hungry?"

My body felt heavy and fatigued. "I'm not hungry. To be honest, I'm a little tired from the traveling. Would you mind if I lay down for a bit? If there is enough sun left when I wake, you can show me the outside stuff then."

Alex brushed his knuckles along my cheek. "Of course. Come find me when you wake up."

Before I lay down, I changed into more comfortable pants, washed my face, and organized my toiletries. The master bathroom was an impressive space. I promised myself that I'd get into that Jacuzzi tub before I went home.

I fell asleep before my head hit the pillow. I must have slept hard because I was a little disoriented when I woke. I didn't know how long I had been out. I forgot for a moment where I was until I saw the mountains outside my window. I remained in bed for a minute, stretching and feeling thankful for being there. I wasn't sure what Alex had planned for the following few days, but I was looking forward to any of the experiences at the ranch. I needed to remember to thank him for inviting me to one of his happy places. I could easily see how the property would fit "happy place" criteria.

I left the room in search of Alex. A delicious aroma came from the kitchen, but no one was cooking. I traveled upstairs and went to his bedroom suite. I knocked a few times with no answer, so I traveled down the hall to the billiard room. The heavy door was cracked just enough to be able to hear, but not see, a conversation taking place.

"She seems like a nice girl. How'd you meet?" Spencer asked Alex. My eyes went wide. They were talking about me.

Alex cleared his throat and then spoke. "We met at FLEX."

"Are you two dating?" Spencer asked.

"No. We're not," Alex's tone sounded disappointed. "I'm hopeful she'll be mine someday soon. I have to go slow."

"Separate rooms? That's not like the Alex I know." Spencer let out a low chuckle.

Alex sighed. "It's complicated right now."

"You seem different. Something has changed. For the better." There was silence for a moment before Spencer continued, "Do you love her?" His tone was incredulous.

Alex must have either nodded or shook his head because I heard no verbal response. My heart raced at his silent reply. I couldn't tell which answer would concern me more.

"Alexander Lombardi, Chicago's Most Eligible Bachelor...actually ready to settle down?" Spencer sounded more than surprised.

Again, I heard no words from Alex. I imagined he grinned and took a sip of his drink.

"I didn't think you had it in you." Spencer still had surprise in his tone.

Alex grunted in agreement. "I didn't think I had it in me either. It turns out you just have to find the right one." There was silence again for a minute or so. It sounded like Spencer was trying to process the new information about his promiscuous friend.

"And you're sure she's the one?"

Alex didn't hesitate. "Hundred percent."

"How long have you been talking?"

"We met a year ago, but have been talking for a couple of months."

"Wow. And you're already head over heels for her?"

"When you know, you know." I could hear the smile in Alex's tone. My heart raced a little faster.

"She has a sad presence to her..."

"Spencer!" a female with a southern accent chastised. "That's not nice."

"What? I didn't mean it in a negative way. I can just sense some despair."

"Yes. Spencer's not wrong." Alex must have turned to the girl, whom I assumed was Betsy. "She has a sad history. She was married to her high school sweetheart and had three little kids. The four of them were in a car accident fourteen months ago and all died on impact. Jane was at work the day of the accident."

"Oh...my...word," the female emphasized each word very slowly. "Oh, that poor girl. How do you even keep living after that? Alex, you better not hurt her."

My heart dropped into my stomach. I hadn't overheard a conversation like that before. Yes, I was living the nightmare, and it wasn't a secret. It had been on every local news channel and some national networks. Hundreds, if not thousands, of strangers knew my story. But to hear it out loud felt...I didn't have the right word. Bad. Really bad. How *did* someone keep on living after the worst tragedy imaginable? I didn't have the answer.

I attempted to push the door open a half inch more so I could see the sweet woman who was worried about me before we'd even met. The hinges creaked loud enough to blow my cover. Instantly embarrassed for eavesdropping, I swiftly turned and headed down the hall.

About five seconds later, I heard the big door creak all the way open. "Hey," Alex said softly. "You're up." I turned to face him and tried to hide the tears about to fall. His face turned to concern as he walked toward me. "What's going on?" His hands ran up and down my shoulders. "What's the matter?"

Spencer and his wife peeked their heads out the door of the billiard room. "Hi there! I'm Betsy. It's so nice to meet you, Jane." Spencer was right next to her, beaming with happiness he probably didn't feel. They were trying to be welcoming, especially after hearing my story.

There was so much emotion in my throat that I couldn't speak. So instead I nodded and waved my hand in hello.

Alex turned to his friends. "Excuse us, guys. We'll be right back." He grabbed my hand and walked me into his suite.

As soon as the door closed, he rested one hand on my hip, and gently pulled my chin up so he could see my eyes. "Are you okay? Did you have a bad dream?" His voice was so soothing.

I let the tears fall now that we were alone. "No. No bad dream. I'm sorry for the terrible first impression I'm giving Betsy—"

"There's nothing to apologize for. She's going to love you." He pressed himself to me, wrapped his arms around to the small of my back, and kissed my cheeks where the tears were flowing. His warm presence instantly started to calm my anxieties. "Tell me why you're so upset."

"It's hard to explain. I heard you sharing what happened to my family and it made me emotional. Betsy asked how someone keeps living after what I've been through. She's right. How *does* someone live through this, Alex? I don't know how to live again." The sobs were in full force now.

Alex pulled me in tighter and let me cry on his chest. He kissed my forehead and hair over and over but didn't say anything. His hands lovingly ran up and down my back. It felt really good to be comforted. The pain was still there, but it was easier to manage with his arms around me. I wrapped my arms around his low back and pulled tighter, trying to squeeze all the sadness out of my pores.

We stood there in a tight embrace until my sobs calmed. Once I was quiet, Alex gently pushed me away just enough to reach my eyes. "You live through this with the help of those who care about you. You go to therapy. You cry. You take time alone when you need to, and you reach out to friends and family when you need their support. And you give yourself grace to heal slowly."

New tears formed in my eyes, and I pulled myself into him once more. I counted the calming beats of his heart to distract myself. When I lifted away from his chest, I felt much better. I kissed each of the tear marks on his shirt. "Thank you. Sorry about your shirt."

He looked down and smiled. His dimples making an appearance made me smile in return. "You can cry on my shirt any time you need. I'll always be here for you."

I let go of the embrace and shook my head. "I don't know what I did to deserve your devotion."

He shook his head back at me. "You've got that backward. I don't know what I did to have the pleasure of being devoted to you."

I closed my eyes and shook my head again. There was no sense in arguing. "I have a question. Is Spencer psychic or something? How did he sense sadness in me?"

"Spencer can read people and animals easily. He's worked with ranch animals his entire life. Animals, as we know, are nonverbal. But I swear he can read their minds, especially horses. It's just a talent he has. He didn't mean anything by it."

"I'm not offended. I was just curious." I took his hand in mine and kissed *his* knuckles for a change. I hoped he took it as a symbol of thanks for being so good to me. His eyes brightened at my touch. "I'm ready to go meet Betsy and eat some dinner. Whatever is cooking down in the kitchen smells amazing."

7

Jane

"SO HOW DID you two meet?" I asked Spencer and Betsy after we'd sat down for dinner. They gazed at each other with the sweetest expressions on their faces. Betsy had long, wavy, strawberry-blonde hair pulled up in a ponytail. She had a cute, curvy figure and seemed a few inches shorter than I was. Her dark brown eyes and freckles on her nose made her face unique and pretty at the same time. "At a rodeo in Texas. Spence was in the bull riding competition with my brothers. He was, by far, the cutest one there."

Spencer chuckled and interrupted, "I prefer rugged. Handsome. Or manly."

Betsy pushed his shoulder playfully. "All those things too, babe." She turned to me and rolled her eyes. "Boys."

I chuckled under my breath. They really were all the same.

"After the rodeo, I went up to Spence to congratulate him for beating my brothers. And the rest is history." Her southern drawl was adorable. I could listen to her speak all day.

"So you're from Texas?" I asked.

She smiled proudly. "Yes, ma'am."

"Do you miss it?"

"I do. But it's beautiful here. Spencer was worth the move. And I love this ranch. It's a really special place." She glanced at Alex with appreciation.

I took a bite of the lasagna at the same time Spencer mumbled something about rabbit food.

"Hush," Betsy scolded. "It won't kill you to skip meat at one meal."

Alex must have asked Betsy to make a vegetarian dinner. I was instantly embarrassed. "Betsy, thank you for accommodating my food preferences, but you don't need to. I'm good at picking around any meat or eating sides. It's no big deal." I looked at Spencer. "Sorry."

"Nah, it's okay. She's right. One meal won't kill me. But two might." We all laughed at his joke. Spencer and Betsy were easy to be around. They had a good, happy vibe surrounding them. And their love was really sweet. I was looking forward to spending time with them over the next few days. I looked over at Alex and smiled at him. I was so glad I hadn't turned down the opportunity.

After dinner, we all helped clean up the kitchen, and then Alex suggested a bonfire. It was pretty cold outside, but he assured me there were patio heaters to help keep the heat.

Spencer and Alex went out to start the fire and heaters while Betsy ran back home to get her warm gear. I went into the master suite and unpacked all my finest winter attire. I laid everything out on the bed: long underwear, wool socks, boots, winter coat, hat, scarf, and mittens. I stared at it for a few seconds. That was a lot of stuff to put on my body when we could just sit inside and enjoy the sight of a gorgeous fireplace while it kept us warm.

Nevertheless, I was going to be open to any suggestion Alex made over the next three days. I trusted his judgment on what was going to give me the best experience. I could already feel the time was about to fly by too fast and I was going to miss the ranch when we left.

I pulled off my sweatpants and shirt to don the first layer: the long underwear. Just as I was bending over to pull the pants up, Alex pushed the door open into the room. He started speaking before the door was completely open. "Hey Jane, it's pretty cold outside, you may want to put on long..." His entrance startled me, which made my legs pivot uncontrollably to the point of losing my footing on the slippery hardwood floor. The pants were too low on my legs to allow me to catch my balance. I hit the edge of the mattress with my ribs and slid down to the floor, basically naked aside from my bra and underwear—and of course, the long underwear tangled around my ankles.

I sat there, laughing out of embarrassment at how ridiculous that probably just looked.

"Jane!" Alex rushed over and attempted to pull me up.

I resisted his assistance. "Hang on a second." My laughter turned to an uncontrollable cackle. There was no way I was going to be able to stand up yet. I was laughing so hard that happy tears formed.

The laughter was contagious. Alex started chuckling too. He brushed my overheated cheek with the back of his fingers. "I can't tell you how happy it makes me to hear you laugh."

His touch calmed my hysterics. I leaned into his fingers, the way I do when I try to show him that what he was doing felt right. "I guess I'm all different sorts of emotions today. Thank you for putting up with me."

"No thank you necessary." He kissed my forehead. "I didn't knock before I entered. I'm sorry. I will from now on." Alex kept his eyes on mine. I could see it written all over his face that he was trying his best to *not* take in my almost naked body. I figured I'd better help him out; he was concentrating pretty hard. I pulled my long underwear to my hips and then reached for his hands to pull me up. He found the long underwear shirt on the bed and grabbed it. "Maybe I should help with this layer," he teased.

"Hey, long underwear is hard," I playfully whined back at him.

"That it is," he replied while trying to suppress a chuckle. He bunched the shirt up and pulled it over my head. Then, as if I was a toddler getting dressed, he grabbed one of my hands and slowly pushed it into the right armhole. He repeated the movements with the second arm and then pulled the shirt down to my hips, being sure to graze my skin with his fingers. His simple touch had my body reacting more than I cared to admit. He held his hands at my hips for a moment before he leaned down and lightly kissed my exposed collarbone. The skin there heated up instantly.

With a quiet sigh, he turned around to walk out of the room. "I'll see you at the fire. There is a large wool blanket on the couch. I want it to stay warm for you for as long as possible, so grab it on your way out."

"Okay, thanks for dressing me," I chuckled again, obviously having a case of the giggles. I couldn't remember the last time I'd laughed uncontrollably. It felt so foreign.

We sat outside at the fire for a couple of hours. Alex had been right, I wasn't cold with the fire, heaters, and blanket. Spencer and Betsy were really good storytellers, which also distracted me from the temperature. They'd each had eventful childhoods. They'd both grown up on ranches and had similar stories about the animals they'd raised. Both of their fathers were strong, stubborn men, and both their moms were soft and sweet. Their descriptions and stories of how their parents engaged with each other reminded me of Robert and Deb. Opposites really do attract.

My giggles continued out at the fire when one of them would share a funny story. Alex laughed alongside me, but he didn't add to the conversations. Instead, he glanced at me every couple of minutes to see my reactions. He seemed more focused on watching me enjoy the night than anything else. We sat next to each other on a padded bench, sharing the large blanket and our body heat. Alex had his hand on my leg and would rub up and down, or squeeze it gently on occasion. I put my hand on top of his and squeezed back. "Thank you for bringing me here." I laid my head on his shoulder.

Alex kissed my hair. "Thank you for trusting me enough to take me up on my invitation."

"Hey, Alex, you need to take her out away from the house and show her the stars," Spencer suggested.

We all looked up at the same time. We could see so many stars already from where we sat.

I looked back at Spencer, who was excited for me to see a Montana starry night. "They don't call it Big Sky Country for nothing," he announced with a beaming smile.

I glanced at Alex to see if he was up for it. "Do you want to go?"

Alex's eyes brightened in the light of the bonfire. "I want to if you do."

How could I say no to that face? "Let's do it."

He wrapped the blanket around me so I was in a cocoon of warmth and then picked me up. I squealed out of surprise. I didn't expect to be carried all the way out there. Alex walked around to an all-terrain golf cart-looking vehicle that I'd seen Spencer and Betsy use earlier and placed me in the passenger seat. It was really cold when we got going out into the field, but I had a feeling it would be worth it. The only skin exposed was my face and I could handle that if it meant a beautiful view.

Alex didn't drive very far before we were in pitch blackness. He parked the vehicle and walked around to help me out since I had limited walking capabilities wrapped up the way I was. I'm sure he didn't want to see me fall on my ass for a second time in one night. The mental picture of me falling over wrapped in a large blanket made me giggle once again.

We walked over to where a giant log was on its side. "This is where I come when I want the best view." Alex unwrapped me from the warm blanket before he wrapped it around himself and sat down with his back against the log. I could hardly see him in the dark, but I could sense he was inviting me to sit in front of him. Keeping with the "I'm going to trust his judgment with these experiences" mindset, I sat down and let him wrap the blanket, and his arms, around me. I felt his warmth right away and couldn't help but lean my back into his body. A low hum escaped his lungs when I rested my head on the front of his shoulder. I suppressed the urge to hum back at him in contentment. I fit into his embrace perfectly.

"Look up," he ordered.

I did as I was told and let out an audible gasp at the most impressive night sky. It was so overwhelmingly magnificent I couldn't take it all in at once. I had to look at the stars in sections to truly see and appreciate all the beauty.

Alex kissed me on my temple and kept his lips there while he spoke. "What do you think?"

I didn't know how to describe my thoughts. It felt like thousands of stars shone down at us from different dimensions. I found plenty of the common constellations that our dull Midwest skies displayed, but there were so many more I had never seen. I understood why Spencer would never leave Montana. It was spectacular, both day and night.

I could've laid there all evening and not been bored of the view—or Alex's protective arms around me. I couldn't remember the last time I felt so comfortable. The best part, for now at least, was I knew he wouldn't try to take our relationship to the next level. He had promised it was a friendship vacation, and I trusted he would stay true to his word. While I wasn't quite sure friends would get cozy in a blanket staring at a very romantic night sky together, I knew Alex wouldn't take it any further than that. Even though Reese was often in the back of my head, reminding me of what kind of guy Alex used to be, he'd never given me any signs of his past indiscretions.

"Are you awake?" Alex whispered in my ear. I must have been in deep thought longer than I realized.

I shifted in his arms. "I am. I'm trying to figure out how to accurately describe how beautiful the sky is. Or how happy it's making me to be here. I'm a bit speechless, I guess."

"That's how I feel about you."

"Hmm?" I didn't know what he meant.

"I have a hard time accurately putting into words just how beautiful you are. Or how you make me feel when we're together." His confession made my heart skip a few beats. "Like this, right now. Life has never been better for me than it is at this moment." He wrapped the blanket tighter around my body and then unwrapped my scarf. "I still promise to behave. You have my word." It was almost as if he had heard the conversation in my head a moment ago. "But I'm going to breathe you in and enjoy this—if it's okay with you."

I nodded hesitantly. I wasn't quite sure what he had planned, but I trusted his word.

Alex ran his lips and nose up and down the nape of my neck. His face was so cold that the heat from my skin plus the sensation of his icy touch had goosebumps prickling my entire body. I quelled the moan that tried to surface. His caress had every physical part of me standing at attention, ready and eager for something more. I sunk into his chest a little deeper while he kept exploring my neck. His arms stayed protectively wrapped around mine and at some point, he grabbed my hands in his. I couldn't tell where he ended and I began. We were one—closer, both physically and emotionally—than we had ever been before. We sat in complete silent contentment for about ten minutes. As much as I wanted to keep viewing the night show above me, my eyes subconsciously closed. The sensation of Alex's greedy lips on my warm skin continued to overwhelm all my senses. It felt so good to be desired.

That was *really* hard to admit.

One moment, everything was as perfect as it could be. The stars were incredible and I was warm in the arms of a man I trusted. The next moment, the feeling of him intertwined with me became unendurable. Sweat started dripping from under all my layers for more than one reason. My body wanted so much more than what he was giving me, and it would win the battle soon. My brain shouted at me for allowing the cuddle fest to go on for far too long.

"Alex, I think we should go back." I didn't want to leave. But I knew if I didn't get up soon, my heart and mind would regret my actions.

Alex abruptly paused his kisses and let out a quiet sigh with his lips still on me. "Okay," he whispered as he unwound us and helped me to my feet.

I turned to face him. Our eyes had adjusted to the dark night, so I tried to meet his eyes. "I'm sorry."

He shook his head. "No need to be sorry. As I said before, this is the happiest moment of my life."

"Sitting on a freezing hard ground with a broken girl who can't let go of her past enough to fully enjoy the present with a wonderful man who adores her." I chuckled under my breath. "You sure are easy to please."

He pulled me in and kissed my forehead. "More like... being entangled with the most amazing and beautiful woman I've ever met while staring at the perfect Montana night sky. Feeling her heartbeat next to mine while taking in the scent and taste of her skin. Being able to show her, and share with her, one of the places in the world that makes me the happiest. Feeling fully present in the moment and totally understanding and accepting she might not feel the same way yet. Seeing her laugh more in one night than all the times I've seen her laugh put together." He leaned in and kissed my neck to drive his point home. "I'd call that a pretty perfect night."

His words stunned me in the best way. "Okay. You win." He was right. It was pretty perfect.

When we made it back to the cabin, the fire had died down and there was no sign of Spencer or Betsy. "We had their vehicle. They didn't have to walk home, did they?"

"No," Alex assured me. "We have more of these Gators in the barn."

Okay, good. I would've felt really bad if they had walked a quarter mile in the dark.

"Are you tired?" Alex asked once we were inside and had removed our winter attire.

"I am, even though I napped twice today. It's all the fresh air, I guess. You?"

"A little bit. But I'll stay up with you if that's what you want."

My nerves were still firing from our little snuggle session. I needed to calm down and be away from him if I was going to be able to sleep. "Considering what you have planned for tomorrow will most likely take a lot of energy, I think I probably should go to bed."

"We can do as much or as little as you want while we're here."

I shrugged my shoulders. "I'd like to see what this property has to offer. It's not every day I'm on a dude ranch."

"Okay then. You need your rest." Alex walked with me to the threshold of my bedroom door and kissed my cheek softly. "Goodnight, Jane."

We quietly stared at each other for the briefest of moments before I entered the room. "Goodnight, Alex." I shut the door behind me and rested my forehead and hands against it. I closed my eyes and took a few deep, steadying breaths. A few tears escaped my lids. I wished I could talk to my therapist. I felt so conflicted and needed some advice. I couldn't deny the small part of me that had hoped he would have taken it to the next level out in the field. The larger part of me obviously needed me to stay on the straight and narrow for my mental health. The conflict was exhausting. I didn't know how much longer my body was going to let my heart and brain win the battles.

8

Alex

WHILE RESTING MY forehead on Jane's door, I closed my eyes and tried to calm the intense burn firing through every cell of my body. Keeping my promise to her was becoming much more challenging than I previously thought. Seeing her in her lacy bra and panties...*fuck*. It took every ounce of self-control not to take her right there. When we were alone out in the field, all I could picture was making love to her under the Montana starry night. The desire became so strong I was thankful she spoke up and said it was time to go. She most definitely felt the sexual tension increasing. And it wasn't just me bringing the tension; she had it pulsing all over her body too.

Unfortunately, that didn't change anything. I still needed to have patience.

I walked away from her door and headed to the shower. If I was going to be with her for another couple of days, I needed to take care of myself. Probably every day. More than once per day.

The tension broke slightly after I finished in the shower. I lay in bed awake for too long, hoping and praying there would be a knock on the door that never came. I wasn't sure why I tortured myself with hope. She'd made it clear she wasn't ready. I finally fell asleep after imagining both of us old and gray and still waiting for our first kiss.

"GOOD MORNING, SLEEPYHEAD," Jane called up to me as I slowly walked down the stairs while putting a T-shirt on.

I couldn't tell her that I didn't sleep well because her aroma had my body too aroused to sleep, so I just moaned a hum at her. I looked for a clock but couldn't find one from the stairs. "What time is it?"

"It's after ten o'clock, you lazy bum. You missed all the morning chores. How convenient," Betsy teased.

"Hey now," I said mildly defensively. My voice sounded lower than normal. I still wasn't quite awake. "I never promised to be Spencer's bitch while I was here." Both girls giggled. "Where is he anyway?" I made my way to Jane, who was sipping coffee at the breakfast bar. When I kissed her cheek, her perfect morning scent hit all my nerves at once. My body immediately became excited again, totally wiping away all my efforts to keep myself calm. "Good morning, beautiful. Sorry I kept you waiting."

Jane blushed; I was affecting her more and more. "No worries. Betsy and I were just chatting about what we should do today."

Betsy moved about the kitchen, cleaning up after whatever breakfast the three of them had had while I slept. She stopped her cleaning to give me an update. "Spencer is getting a few horses ready to ride. We thought we could start by showing Jane the property. Here, eat first, and then we'll go."

"Sounds good to me. Jane, are you up for some horseback riding?"

She nodded and appeared nervous. "I've never ridden a horse. But sure, I'm up for it."

We all went to get dressed for the day after I had some breakfast and coffee. I put on my favorite jeans and flannel. Spencer had brought in some cowboy boots and hats for Jane to borrow. The ranch had multiples of every size, in case the guests forgot theirs or didn't own any.

Jane's door was shut when I went back downstairs. I finished getting dressed in my boots and Stetson before I went outside to find Spencer and my favorite horse. "Hey, where is Juliette?" I asked Spencer when he came out of a barn carrying a saddle.

He used his chin to direct my eyes the right way. "She's in that barn. She hasn't been feeling well lately. We won't be riding her today."

Juliette had been on the ranch for as long as I could remember. "What's wrong with her?"

"Alex, she's thirty years old. She's a senior citizen. Go and say hi, but don't take her out. She's looking better than she was a few days ago. I don't want to overwork her."

I found her eating some hay in her stall. "Hey, girl," I called to her. She immediately came over and pushed her muzzle toward me. She and I had always had a good relationship. Even though I only came to the ranch once or twice a year, I practically grew up there in the summers as a kid. She remembered me every time I visited.

"Hey, there you are," Jane called to me. My back was to her and when I turned around, she looked startled. She instantly softened her features when she saw I noticed. I'd totally just caught her checking me out.

"Like what you see?" I asked as I peered back at her with a sexy grin. I shook my butt right and left a couple of times. I knew I looked good in a pair of Wranglers and a Stetson, and I didn't feel bad using it to my advantage.

Jane cleared her throat and coughed a couple of times, trying to recover. Her hair was braided down her back like it was so often. She had on a white and blue flannel shirt that complemented her eyes. Her shirt was tucked into her perfectly tight jeans, which were tucked into riding boots. And she had a Stetson in her hands. She looked way sexier in riding gear than I ever could. "Um... Spencer said we're ready."

I nodded her over with my head. "Come meet Juliette first."

Jane walked to us hesitantly. Juliette started sniffing Jane's hair and face right away. Jane giggled at the touch and backed away.

"She's friendly. I think she likes you already." I grabbed Jane's hand and rubbed it up and down Juliette's muzzle. I watched them interact with a smile beaming on my face. Horses were so therapeutic. I hoped Jane could feel Juliette's calm aura.

"Is she yours?"

"No. But she and I have always had a good friendship. She's been here forever."

Jane looked at me with inquisitive eyes. "I wouldn't peg you for a horse guy."

I smiled and laughed once under my breath. "There's a lot you don't know about me yet."

She narrowed her eyes. "You're right."

"Yo!" Spencer shouted from outside somewhere. "We have lost half a day because your lazy ass slept in! Let's go!"

Both of us laughed and stopped petting Juliette. I kissed the side of her muzzle. "Bye, girl. See you later."

"So I'm not the only girl you steal kisses from, I see," Jane teased as we walked toward the stables.

"Are you jealous of a horse, m'lady?" I gently bumped my hip into hers.

"Do I need to be?" she teased again.

I stopped her and slowly leaned in to place a single kiss on her cheek. I kept my lips close to her ear. "You're the only one I want to steal kisses from. I'm hoping that one day, they won't be stolen. But instead, you'll invite me in." Jane grinned and shivered at my words.

Yep, she was definitely affected by me more and more.

"All right, all right," Spencer shouted over to us. "Enough of that. Come over here and meet your horse."

We walked over to where a large black horse was being saddled by Betsy. "Jane, you'll be riding with Alex today," she informed. "Say hi to Zeke."

I rubbed the side of his back and made my way to the front of him. He seemed anxious as Betsy buckled him into a saddle. "Hey, it's okay," I said in a soothing voice. "It'll feel good to get out of the stable, I promise."

Spencer walked over to us and rubbed Zeke's muzzle. "Okay, Alex. I want you to ride Zeke for a few minutes so he can get acclimated to you."

I nodded and lifted myself onto Zeke to guide him out of the stable and away from the others. I glanced back at Jane, who looked impressed with my skills already.

Once Zeke and I roamed away from the stables, I tried to get to know him. He felt anxious to have someone riding him. "Are you sure he's the right horse, Spencer?" Nobody heard me; I was too far away. I squeezed my legs to instruct Zeke to start trotting. I needed to make sure he was safe before my girl joined me. We trotted around for a minute before Zeke galloped without my instruction to do so. One moment I pulled on the reins to slow him down, the next I flew off him and landed hard on my hip and ribs.

"*ALEX!*" I faintly heard Jane scream from the stables. The wind was knocked out of my lungs, so I rolled around on the grass until I could catch my breath.

Spencer had already been on his horse, so he was over to me the quickest. "Alex! What the hell happened?"

I moaned a few times before I sat up on the hip that didn't hurt. "The bastard bucked me off."

Spencer dismounted his horse and chuckled. "Clearly." He grabbed my hand and helped me stand. "You okay?"

"Yeah. What made you think he was the right choice?"

He slapped my back. "That's what you get for skipping morning chores." I glared at him with a "you have *got* to be kidding me" look. He laughed and continued, "Nah, I'm just joking. I chose him because he's the biggest and could carry you both for the whole ride. I'm sorry, Alex. He's been really good with the ranch hands. He hasn't bucked anyone off in weeks."

"Weeks," I grumbled.

"Alex!" Jane ran toward me. "Oh my gosh! Are you okay?"

I brushed the grass and dirt off my jeans and picked up my hat. I limped toward her. My hip was on fire. "I'm okay. It won't be the last time I'll be bucked off a horse."

"You make horseback riding sound so appealing." She giggled as she brushed off some dirt and grass I'd missed. "Do you want to go back to the cabin and get some ice?"

"No, I'm okay. Let's go find a horse that won't buck us off."

"You really should rest," she scolded, one eyebrow raised.

I took her hand to walk back to the stables. "We'll rest later, I promise."

JANE AND I mounted Stardust, a mare I had ridden a hundred times and knew would behave. Spencer had another horse trailing us since Stardust wouldn't be able to carry us both for too long. Jane rode behind me, with her arms and hands tight against my stomach. Her delicious aroma was once again distracting and exciting my entire body. It reminded me of how entwined we had been the previous night, which made it hard to concentrate on controlling a horse.

We rode for a couple of hours, exploring the land. My parents owned over 3,000 acres. There was a stream that flowed through part of the property where the guests often fished. In the winter, snow machine and ski trails would be marked. I stayed quiet and listened as Spencer and Betsy gave Jane a great tour of the land. Spencer knew the property better than anyone else. It made me want to call my dad and remind him what an asset Spencer was to TRIPLE-A-RANCH.

We made our way back to the cabin at lunchtime and all ate sandwiches together. Spencer and Betsy had some errands to run in the afternoon, so Jane and I were on our own, which was what I'd hoped would happen. I told her to get her bathing suit on and put her clothes over it. She was hesitant but didn't ask any questions. We packed towels, snacks, and water in a backpack and headed out to our destination in one of the property's pickup trucks.

It took about twenty minutes to drive to the trailhead of our destination.

"You're taking me on a hike?" Jane asked with her eyes wide.

I chuckled at her expression. She was more than capable of hiking, but she looked terrified. "Not exactly. We have a mile hike. It's easy, don't worry."

We walked in silence, hand in hand, down the winding path. She seemed deep in thought and I didn't want to interrupt her.

Luckily, it didn't take very long to reach the end of the path. My injured hip muscles could not have handled much more walking. I'd forgotten to take ibuprofen before we left, so my entire right side throbbed in pain.

I walked to a steamy pond and smiled at Jane. "Okay, let's get in."

She raised an eyebrow. "In there?"

I nodded. "It's a hot spring. Have you been in one?"

She shook her head.

I raised my eyebrows up and down. "You're in for a treat." I took off my shoes and layers while she stared at the water.

She looked hesitant. "But it's so cold out here."

"It's not cold in there." I took off the rest of my clothes except my trunks and stepped into the hot spring. I made sure I kept my right side away from her. I didn't know if I was bruising yet from the fall, and I didn't want to ruin the moment with her being concerned about me. Hot springs were very therapeutic. She needed the experience without any sort of worries overshadowing it.

The temperature difference between the air and water was significant. I didn't waste any time getting right down into the hot water. I let out a satisfied sigh when the warmth overtook the cold. "This feels so good. Please come in," I encouraged. She must have trusted me because she took off her shoes and socks and started on her top layer. Once my body had acclimated to the heat, I found a place to sit and watch Jane undress. I knew it was probably wrong to do so, but I couldn't take my eyes off her as she stripped each article off her gorgeous body. She, on the other hand, kept her eyes far away from mine.

Once she was down to her bikini, she wasted no time stepping into the water. "Ohhh. This is so warm." Her whole face lit up in a huge smile.

I smiled back at her. "Told ya. This is a well-known hot spring. Usually, there are a lot of people here. We got lucky today."

She rested her head back and closed her eyes. "This place gets more and more incredible every second. I never want to go home."

"Let's stay longer then. Reese will understand if you cancel your day, right? We can stay until next week."

She shook her head. "She'd understand if I needed to wait another week. But I wouldn't do that to her. I have a full day booked. I have to go home."

"But *do* you?" I grinned at her.

She raised her eyebrow. "You promised."

"I know. It's just that you seem very relaxed. I don't want the effects to wash away when you get home."

"I don't think they will. I think Montana will leave a positive lasting effect on me. I'm hoping I'll be back here again sooner than later." She blushed. I guessed it was more from her admission than the heat of the water. She meant she wanted more time with me. More time for us.

I smiled at her. "I'm hopeful for that too."

Jane closed her eyes and rested back against the ledge again. She looked at peace. Montana was good for everyone, but it looked exceptionally good on her. She was so fucking beautiful. I stayed quiet and let my mind wander to unclean scenarios while I watched her enjoy the warmth of the water.

"Howdy!"

We turned our heads at the same time and saw two hikers, probably in their late sixties or early seventies, heading toward us. "Oh boy. We have company." I chuckled.

"I guess that's our cue to leave?" Jane asked.

"We don't have to go if you don't want to. People who hike to this hot spring know that they most likely won't be alone."

She watched them get closer. "No, it's okay. We can go. My fingers are turning into prunes anyway."

"Okay then." I stepped out of the water, wrapped a towel around my waist, and opened up a towel for her. She quickly popped out of the water and let me wrap it around her.

"It'ss ssoo coollldd outt herrre." Jane's teeth chattered right away. I wrapped the towel around her tighter and rubbed up and down her body, trying to create some heat.

"Don't leave on our account! We hope we didn't interrupt your honeymoon!" the male hiker exclaimed with a laugh as they got closer. He had a southern drawl that I couldn't place.

"No worries. You didn't interrupt anything," I shouted back at him while I continued to warm up my girl. "It's all yours."

"Are y'all *actually* on your honeymoon?" the man asked with a huge smile, as if he thought he was a master at reading strangers and situations.

The female hiker smacked him lightly on the chest. "Martin! That's none of your business."

He looked down at her, confused. "What? I'm just being friendly."

She rolled her eyes.

"No, sir. No honeymoon," I informed him.

"Well, when's the wedding? Y'all look like the cutest of lovebirds."

"Martin! Stop!" The woman looked embarrassed. She directed her attention to us. "Hi, I'm Linda. This is Martin. I'm so sorry. He doesn't get out much," she joked.

Jane waved at them and then answered Martin's question. "Umm... we're not engaged."

"What?" He looked genuinely surprised and also disappointed. "Son, you better snatch her up before someone else does."

Linda rubbed her forehead in disapproval. She looked as if she wanted to crawl in a hole and never come out. "Okay, we're going to let these two get dressed and be on their way. I'm so sorry for my husband. He means well."

I laughed. She was funny. She probably had to be, being married to him. "It's all good. Enjoy your dip. It felt great."

There was an awkward silence sitting in the air as Jane and I got dressed while they undressed down to their bathing suits.

"It was nice to meet you both," Jane hollered to them as we were leaving.

"Likewise! Oh and hey! When y'all get married, I want an invitation to the wedding! Martin Miller in Mountain Brook, Alabama! Look me up! Easy name to remember!"

"Martin! Enough!" Linda splashed hot water at him. "Don't listen to him, y'all! He's just a hopeless romantic!"

Jane giggled under her breath and shook her head. She didn't seem uncomfortable with the notion of a wedding at all. She just looked...happy. Happy in the moment. Maybe happy with the idea of marriage too? Doubtful. But one thing I was sure about was some of the deep sadness that Spencer had felt was melting away. I wouldn't get my hopes up that it was a permanent change. I knew she had a long way to go to heal. But the way she looked at me with the most intense ocean-gray eyes as we walked back to the truck had me more excited for the future than ever before. We'd taken some very large baby steps in Montana.

Okay, maybe this *was the best moment of my life.*

9

Alex

THE MORNING OF our last full day in Montana called for several hours of rain. It wasn't going to be the fun, "dance in the rain" type of weather. It was cold, windy rain. Rain that made you want to snuggle up in a blanket by a fire and watch movies, which is what I had planned. There were purposefully a limited amount of TVs in the cabin. My parents didn't believe guests should be watching TV when they paid for the Montana experience. However, they knew how much Americans were addicted to screens, so they reluctantly installed them in a few suites, as well as the billiard room.

Even though my hip and ribs were killing me from my fall off the horse the day before, I woke early to join Spencer for the morning chores so he wouldn't give me crap about it again. No way would I tell him how much pain I was in. He'd never let me live it down. Cowboys held themselves to different standards. There was too much work to be done to complain or wimp out.

We fed the horses in the barn when Spencer let me know all the ranch hands were going to move the cattle in the afternoon. He thought it would be something fun for Jane to participate in. Moving livestock was part of the "ranch experience" guests paid for. All the ranch hands would be on hand and did almost all the work, but it made the guests feel like they were an active part of a very wild west task.

I raised my eyebrow. "You're not going to give her a horse that will buck her off, right?"

"Nah. We save those for you." He chuckled. I gave him a serious look. "I'm kidding, man. I didn't know Zeke wasn't ready yet. I wouldn't have given him to you if I didn't trust him. I'm sorry."

"Mmhm," I hummed.

"Jane can ride Stardust. She's the best horse we've got." He went over to Juliette's stall and rubbed her muzzle. "This one's feeling better. She'd probably love to herd some cattle." He put his face by her nose and kissed her. "Isn't that right, girl? You wanna get out of this barn?" She sniffed him and nuzzled into his cheek. "Yeah. I think you're ready to move around a bit." He looked back over at me. "You can ride your girl today."

"Ha!" A laugh burst out of my lungs. "Pun intended?"

Spencer winked dramatically and put on his best cheesy smile. "You tell me."

I sighed. "I wish."

"It'll happen. She'll be yours...eventually," he stated confidently.

I shook my head. "You sure about that?"

He smiled, again with confidence. "Very."

I so wanted to believe he was right.

When we were done with all the chores, we were soaked to the core by freezing rain. Jane was still asleep, so I enjoyed a hot shower and once again took care of the deep ache in my body that I knew would build if I cuddled alone with my beauty for hours on a couch. In all the years I'd been with ladies, my hand didn't need to be put to use very often. Now we were best friends. I tried not to overthink it too much. It was a temporary solution.

Before Jane woke, I had everything ready in the billiard room for a morning of movies. I had told Betsy to stay warm in her home, so I prepared breakfast for the two of us once I heard noise from the master suite.

Jane opened the door and immediately looked out the windows into the dense gray weather. Her shoulders slumped as she walked toward me.

"Good morning, how'd you sleep?" I poured her a cup of coffee and kissed below her ear before handing her the mug.

Jane took an audible breath at my touch. I was beyond thankful she let me steal so many kisses. I wasn't sure I'd be able to resist touching her in other ways if my lips weren't allowed the occasional connection to her body. She hadn't looked uncomfortable when I'd touched her so intimately. In fact, her body language told me she enjoyed my stolen kisses. So, I took her cues and ran with them. Those little acts of affection seemed integral to my survival.

"I slept great. You?" she asked.

"Just fine," I lied. I'd had another sleepless night of both daydreaming and actually dreaming Jane would join me in bed. As much as I'd tried to push the unrealistic hope out of my head, it was there to stay. "Breakfast is almost done. Then we'll head up into the billiard room."

"Oh? In the mood to play pool?" She grinned and sipped her coffee.

"Nah. But since it's pretty crappy out this morning, I thought we could watch movies and relax, if that's okay with you. We have something fun planned this afternoon. We just need the rain to calm down."

"Sounds good to me."

The morning went pretty quickly for doing absolutely nothing. We watched a couple of movies and vegged out. We shared a couch and blanket, but I kept my hands to myself. As much as I wanted to hold her hand, graze her thigh or kiss her neck, I refrained from all of it. It was one thing to have an intense moment of lust when I knew the moment would be over in a flash. I could snap out of it before I did something to make her uncomfortable. But I didn't think I had the willpower to sit next to her on the couch for hours, teasing myself, and not push her limits. Nevertheless, it was a great morning. We didn't say much to each other, but I was okay with it. We were comfortable not saying anything at all. That, once again, felt like a big step in the right direction.

The rain finally stopped after we made ourselves some lunch. Jane looked out the window and saw the sun poking through. She instantly perked up. "What do we have planned this afternoon?"

"Well, Spencer needs us to help move cattle."

"Me too?" she asked, sounding surprised.

I grinned. "Yep. You too."

She looked nervous. "I don't know how to move cattle. I've never even ridden a horse by myself."

I grinned again. "You're at the perfect place to learn."

A few minutes later, Spencer hollered into the cabin that we needed to get ready. Jane and I dressed in our same riding clothes as the day before and headed for the stables. My injured side was hurting more and more. I must have overdone it with chores that morning. I could tell my gait was off from the pain shooting up into my hip and ribs. It didn't take many steps for Jane to notice.

"Are you limping?" she asked, concerned.

"What? Um. Maybe a little."

She grabbed my arm to stop me. "From what?"

"I sort of got bucked off a horse yesterday." I chuckled under my breath.

"Oh yeah! Of course you did. You hadn't mentioned anything so I thought you felt okay. Are you bruised?"

"I don't know, but it feels like it." I limped a few more steps.

"Where does it hurt?" She was morphing into mom mode with a worried look on her face. I hadn't seen that side of her yet. It was adorable.

I pointed to my entire right side.

She grabbed hold of my belt buckle and examined my side. "Let me see if there's a bruise."

I raised my eyebrows. "Right now?"

"Yes! Let me see so I can decide if you need to see a doctor."

I chuckled. "I don't need a doctor. I just need some ibuprofen. Besides, Spencer will roast me if he knows I'm complaining."

"You're not complaining. I'm asking about it, so you're informing me. He's in the barn anyway. Let me see." She untucked my shirt and pulled it up. I pushed my jeans down the best I could while keeping them buckled.

Her hands flew over her mouth. "Oh. My. *Gosh*."

"That bad?" I asked jokingly. I looked down and saw the entire right side of my trunk riddled with dark purple welts. Definitely that bad.

"I should've insisted on you icing it yesterday! And we went on that walk too? How did I not see this at the hot spring?"

Because I purposely hid it from you so you wouldn't worry.

I did my best to dismiss her concern. "It's no big deal. I'll be fine. It looks worse than it is."

"You have got to be in so much pain. Maybe we should just go back in so you can rest." As gently as possible, she grazed the bruised skin with the back of her fingers. Her caring, light touch sent an electric shock up my spine and straight into my heart.

"No." My voice broke as I spoke. "I'm totally excited to see you..." I closed my eyes and inhaled deeply, "...on a horse." I couldn't concentrate on speaking. The light sensation of her fingers on my sore and overly sensitive body felt like heaven. Her hand was on such an intimate part of me. Goosebumps took over the entirety of my skin.

She dropped her hand and narrowed her eyes. "Okay, fine. But you have to promise you'll take it easy the rest of the day."

I smiled and tried to recover from the intensity of the moment. "Will do," I promised. I took the same hand that had brushed my bruises so gently and kissed each of her knuckles. "Thank you for caring," I whispered.

She blushed in an instant. "Of course."

Spencer gave Jane a riding lesson while I saddled Juliette. Once we were all ready, Spencer put us to work right away. Herding livestock was not hard once you knew what to do. There was a reason there were jokes and stigmas about herds. They actually did tend to follow each other blindly. So as long as you could get the cattle started and keep them together, our work would be done pretty easily and efficiently.

Jane kept Stardust in the back of the group. It was obvious she was trying to stay out of the way. Betsy hung back with her, gently advising her on what to do and when to do it. I was at risk of getting shit from Spencer for slacking, so I stayed in the thick of the cattle. I kept an occasional eye on Jane, though. Every time I snuck a glance her way, she seemed cautiously happy, listening to all of Betsy's tips and advice.

We arrived at the stream, which was encroached with a lot of low-lying trees and brush right where we needed to pass through. That was the most challenging part of getting the cattle to the new pasture. The stream was not deep, so we would wade through it easily, but the trees were overgrown to a point where there would have to be some bending down to avoid getting hit by branches. As we approached closer, I heard Spencer tell a ranch hand they needed to do some maintenance trimming before their next guests arrived.

I turned back to find Jane before I made my way through the brush. She was about a hundred feet away and doing fine. I made a mental note to thank Betsy for being so good to her.

A few heavy branches smacked Juliette and me while we passed the dense opening, but it was manageable. We waded through the water as easily as expected and helped the ranch hands guide the livestock to the new grassy range. Everything was going great until I heard a horse neigh loudly behind me, followed by a few brief screams.

"*Spencer*!" Betsy shouted from the brush. Both Spencer and I turned around instantly at the panic in her tone and forced our horses into a gallop back through the water. A couple of the guys came with to guide the herd away from where Betsy shouted. When I got through the brush, I found Betsy on the ground, hunched over Jane, who was curled up in a ball on the left side of her body with her hands over her head. My heart fell into my stomach. I practically leaped off Juliette to kneel by Jane's side.

"Jane!" I exclaimed. "Are you hurt?" She didn't answer. I pulled her hands from her face to see tears in her closed eyes.

Spencer came up beside me and kneeled. "Jane, what hurts?"

She moaned when she tried to move off her side.

"It's okay, baby. Just tell us if you're okay," I said softly.

She opened her eyes, blinked away her tears, and searched around. "Is Stardust okay?"

I looked over at the horse who was a few feet away. She had a superficial puncture wound just behind her flank.

"Yeah, she's okay. What about you? What hurts?" I repeated Spencer's question.

She moaned again. "My whole left side. And my head."

Spencer shouted over to a ranch hand nearby. "Wade, go get a Gator!"

"No." Jane tried to sit but winced and lay back down. "I'm fine. I can walk."

I put my hand lightly on her forehead and brushed back the loose hair. "Just relax for a second."

I looked at Betsy, trying not to look accusatory. "What the hell happened?"

She shrugged. Her eyes were filled with concern. "I'm not sure exactly. We were headed into the brush, dodging the branches. Then, a few of the cattle in front of us stopped abruptly, which made Stardust back up. When she took a few steps backward, she slipped in some mud and a low branch must have bit her. But I didn't see her buck or anything."

"Do you remember what happened after that?" I asked Jane.

She shook her head. "Not exactly. The whole thing made me panic." She closed her eyes and looked mortified.

"It's okay. We've all been there. You're not a real cowgirl until you've fallen off a horse," Betsy ensured her.

"Is that true?" Jane looked around at all of us.

"It is now," I said with a grin. I scooped her up in my arms when Wade was in sight with the Gator.

She protested. "Alex, I can walk."

I ignored her protests and directed my attention to Wade. "I've got it from here, thanks."

I looked over at Spencer. "I can come back and retrieve the horses if you'd like."

"Nah, don't worry about it. We have it under control. Go get her some ice."

"ALEX, I'M FINE. I don't need any more ice." Jane hadn't stopped protesting since I laid her down on the couch. I had been ignoring her arguments over the last two hours and icing the side of her body and her head at intervals. "You wouldn't let me get you ice the other day," she grumbled.

"True. But I've fallen off a horse before. You haven't."

"Moot point," she contested.

"Okay, how about I have more meat on me than you do? You probably bruised your bones." She mumbled under her breath but didn't argue anymore.

"How's the patient doing?" Betsy inquired as she entered the cabin with a few bags of groceries.

Jane sat up and pushed the bag of ice off her body. "Betsy, thank you for the concern, but I'm totally fine. Just a little sore."

"Honey, I've been thrown off a horse many times. I know how it feels, and it *never* feels fine." She winked at Jane and held up the bags. "But we're going to make it right. I went to WinCo and bought some stuff that will certainly have you both feeling better."

I raised my eyebrow at her. I actually *was* totally fine.

"Don't look at me that way, Alexander. You fell off a horse too and have done nothing to help the bruising. Plus, you're pale with worry. Don't think I don't see it."

I wasn't going to argue with a strong Texan woman when she was right anyway, so I just shrugged at her with a grin.

"That's what I thought." She nodded once, happy that she won the argument. "This is your last night, so we may as well splurge." She unloaded a few cartons of ice cream, whipped cream, and a jar of microwavable fudge. "Dessert for dinner? Nothing says 'feel better' like hot fudge sundaes!" The look on her face was that of a kid who ransacked a candy store. Her excitement made me chuckle under my breath. Betsy was a really sweet woman. Spencer was lucky to have her, and I felt lucky she'd made Jane feel so welcome over the past couple of days. If we lived closer, I could see Betsy and Jane becoming close girlfriends.

Betsy then pulled out a large bag of Epsom salts and looked at Jane. "But first, you're going to soak in the tub to soothe your sore muscles."

"That sounds pretty amazing. Alex has been trying to give me hypothermia with all the icing." Jane giggled and glanced over at me. I attempted my best "I'm offended" face which made her giggle again.

Betsy rolled her eyes playfully. "Okay, let's go then," she ordered.

I could hear the running of the water in the master suite as I put all the sundae ingredients away. I tried my best to keep my thoughts clean, but I couldn't help the jealousy that brewed because Betsy was helping Jane into the tub and I wasn't. My mind went to a really dirty scene pretty quickly, and I had to shake my head a few times to remove the images. Right when I was about to go outside to clear my head by spending time with Juliette, Betsy called me casually into the master bathroom. Jane was in the water already. Her eyes were closed and she was resting her head on the edge. The jets were creating bubbles that covered her body, but it appeared she was in her bikini.

"Jane and I were talking, and we both agree you need to get your swim trunks on and join her." Betsy turned to Jane, whose cheeks were turning pink. "Isn't that right, Jane?"

Jane nodded but kept her eyes closed.

"The Epsom salts will do you some good too," Betsy advised.

I grinned at Jane's beautiful, contented face. "You don't have to tell me twice," I stated before swiftly going to find my trunks.

A couple of minutes later, I slowly lowered down into the hot water. It immediately felt great on my sore body. Jane scooted over to her right to give me space, even though there was plenty of room in the tub. Betsy left and shut the door behind her. I wasn't sure what she thought would happen, but she gave us privacy anyway. It wasn't necessary. I had made it almost three full days without pushing Jane's limits. I wouldn't start now. I had given her my word and planned on keeping it until the end. Even though it was torture to do so.

I sat back and enjoyed the therapeutic effects of the Epsom salts and jets. "Two soaks together in two days? How did I get so lucky?"

Jane didn't answer my question, but instead smiled and looked at the water pulsing around her. "I think we're going to have matching bruises."

"Hopefully you won't bruise as much since we've been icing so frequently."

She nodded but kept her eyes on the water.

"May I see?" I asked.

She nodded slowly and then shifted onto her knees to turn her left side to me. There were faint shadows of red splotches all over her ribs, hip, and upper leg. I gingerly ran my fingertips down her skin. "I'm so sorry."

She lowered back into the water. "It's not your fault."

"I should've stayed back with you." *What had I been thinking?* I shook my head in frustration.

She looked me straight in the eyes. "No. You shouldn't have. It's all good. Thank you for taking care of me."

"I like taking care of you," I admitted.

She grinned. "I can tell." She waved her hands back and forth on the surface of the water. Something had her deep in thought. Her eyebrows furrowed before she spoke. "I like that you want to take care of me, Alex. It makes me feel...I don't know how to describe it. A little less alone, maybe?"

My heart started beating faster. I lived for these little glimpses into her mind.

"My in-laws take care of me too. But I feel they have an innate obligation to keep me well." Her ocean-gray eyes stared right at mine. "You take care of me by choice."

I nodded slowly in agreement. There was nothing I wanted more than to take care of her for the rest of our lives.

She crossed her legs and tipped toward me. Her hands found one of mine and she pulled my palm to the side of her face. "Thank you."

I stared into her eyes while trying to hold back the emotion that surfaced out of nowhere. "My pleasure, Jane."

She shook her head in disbelief. "Don't you miss your old life? Where you weren't always so concerned about one sad, despondent girl all the time?"

I grinned at her. That was an easy question to answer. "I don't miss that life at all."

She shook her head again and huffed a laugh like something funny came to mind.

I eyed her speculatively. "What?"

"When I first walked into this huge bathroom, I told myself I wouldn't leave without soaking in this tub. I didn't expect it to be under these circumstances." She chuckled quietly again. "We both fell off a horse in two days' time. We're kind of hot messes."

I shrugged. "Even the most seasoned ranchers fall off horses," I stated reassuringly. "They've had much worse happen to them. You have to be tough out here."

"Spencer is pretty tough, isn't he?"

I nodded. "He sure is."

She stared at the popping bubbles around us. "You're pretty tough too."

"Well, thank you, m'lady." I pretended to tip my Stetson down when she glanced at me. "I could say the same about you."

"I'm not tough," she disagreed.

"You're the toughest." I meant it as she was mentally stronger than she realized, but there was an unintentional accurate double meaning behind my words. She was, by far, the toughest woman I'd courted. I'd never had to work so hard at something in my life.

She shook her head and closed her eyes. We soaked in silence until the water started getting chilly. I exited the tub first so I could retrieve a towel for her. She shivered as she stood and stepped into my waiting arms.

"Maybe we should rinse off in the hot shower?" I asked.

Jane immediately stiffened in my arms.

Shit. She took that the wrong way. I looked down at her and tenderly pulled her chin up so she met my eyes. "I didn't mean…"

She wiggled out of my embrace. "No, it's okay. I'm feeling warmer anyway." She went into the bedroom and grabbed her sweats. "Let's go have some ice cream."

We did indeed have dessert for dinner. As Betsy said, "Because why not?" Jane insisted she felt good and didn't want to lounge on the couch anymore, so we all traveled up to the billiard room to play a few rounds of pool and darts. Spencer and Betsy called it a night an hour later. They weren't late-night people. Their work at the ranch didn't allow for middle-of-the-night shenanigans.

When they left, Jane and I put on another movie and settled in on the couch, as we had earlier in the day. At some point, she fell asleep with her head resting in my lap. I gently played with her hair while I finished the movie. I had a hard time concentrating on what I was watching. All I kept thinking about was a life in which Jane would fall asleep in my lap every night if she wanted. A life where I would carry her to bed, tuck her in, and kiss her cheek goodnight. Or better yet, a life in which I would carry her to bed and make love to her all night.

I'm not sure how long I sat there in my daydream of far-off hopes. Once I snapped out of it, I lifted Jane and carried her downstairs. She woke up during the transfer but didn't say anything. I laid her down in bed and kissed her forehead.

"G'night, Alex," she mumbled. "Thank you for being so good to me."

I bent down close to her face and nuzzled my nose with hers. "Goodnight, Jane."

I made it to my bed and was once again too wound up to sleep. A couple of hours into laying in the darkness, it hit me we were leaving the following afternoon and Jane had yet to see a TRIPLE-A-RANCH sunrise over the mountains. That couldn't stand. She was about to have an early wake-up call in the morning.

"JANE." I GENTLY nudged her shoulder at 6:20 a.m. She didn't budge, so I leaned down and kissed her cheek as lightly as I could. I didn't want to startle her, so I whispered, "Wake up, my beautiful girl."

She stirred for a few seconds before she blinked her eyes open. "Mmm," she moaned in protest with a stretch. "It's not time to leave yet, is it?" Her voice was horse and sexier than ever.

"No." I kept my voice quiet. "Not yet. I have something I want you to see before we go."

She opened her eyes fully. "Right now?"

"Yes, right now." I grinned. She was wearing the same sweats she'd put on after the bath the day prior. "Don't bother getting dressed. You'll just need your coat and boots." I gave her space to use the bathroom while I poured hot coffee into an insulated carafe. She met me in the kitchen with a confused and sleepy look on her face. I opened the front door and guided her out to the Gator. "Don't worry. This will be worth it, I promise."

I drove back to the same place we stargazed the other night. Earlier that morning, I had placed a waterproof blanket next to the tree stump and had a few other blankets ready in case she was cold. She saw the setup and grinned at me. "When you said you came here for the best view, I thought you strictly meant the stars."

"Nope." I glanced at her with a big smile. "This is *the* spot for sunrises too." We settled onto the blanket and I draped another one around her shoulders. I poured us each a thermos of coffee and looked out toward the mountains. "It should be soon."

Jane stared at the same place in the distance that held my gaze. "Why do you ever go home? This place is heaven on Earth."

I nodded in agreement. "The offer still stands. We can stay a few more days if you'd like."

She sighed and stared out at the horizon. "I really have to get home."

I looked at her with a shy grin. "I had to try."

She looked down at her coffee and ran her finger along the rim of the thermos. "Can we...maybe sit the way we did the other night? If it doesn't hurt your ribs?"

My eyebrows raised at her request. "You mean over there?" I pointed to the edge of the stump. She nodded but kept her eyes down. It was as if she knew what she wanted, but was embarrassed to admit it. "Of course. It won't hurt me." *And even if it did, I would endure the pain to enjoy enfolding my body around yours.* "Will it hurt you?"

She shook her head, so I pulled the blanket from her shoulders and wrapped it over mine. I sat with my back on the edge of the stump and let her sit down in front of me before I swaddled the fabric around us. It felt as amazing as it had the other night. The warmth, comfort, and tension came back in an instant. I nestled my face into the back of her neck and breathed her in. I wished I had the courage to ask her what she was thinking. Aside from her being momentarily upset the first day when I shared her story with Spencer and Betsy, she had been in a carefree mood all week. I didn't want to do or say anything to ruin that. We were going home soon and I was sure that at least some of her worried, sad, and anxious feelings would surface once we hit ground in Illinois. As much as I would love for Montana to have healed her completely, that wasn't realistic.

We watched the first sign of the sun peak over the mountains and it did not disappoint. Every color of the rainbow was in front of us, shining up to heaven and back down to Earth. Jane didn't say anything. She looked to be taking it all in, as if she was snapping pictures of it for her memory bank later. Her expression made me reach for my phone to take a picture of us. She leaned into me as I took the snapshot. The sun shone brightly on her face, making her skin even more gloriously ivory than usual. I stared at the photo after I took it. Our first picture together. Our only picture. I instantly regretted not taking more photos over the past few days.

Cuddling with her again, watching her be amazed at the view, felt just as priceless as it had the other night. Jane had taught me a lot of lessons in the last year. One lesson was to be loving and affectionate with my partner without the act of sex. It didn't have to be all or nothing, which was what I was accustomed to. Sure, I'd have loved nothing more than to turn her around and have her ride me into the sunrise. But snuggling up together under a warm blanket was special and intimate too. And if I was being honest with myself, there was a part of me that wouldn't want our journey to be any other way. If and when Jane ever shared her entire self with me, it would be that much better. That much more of a gift.

I could wait.

10

Alex

REESE APPEARED TO be handling Jane's client appointments because I'd received a text from her after we landed yesterday that said "10:00 a.m. tomorrow." I wondered if she was that blunt and rude to all of Jane's clients.

Probably not.

At 10:00 a.m. sharp, I arrived at R & J's salon. While walking to the entrance, I realized something… for all the years I had stared at that sign before I entered, it never dawned on me to ask who "J" was. Jane was literally under my nose the whole time and I didn't know it. I shook my head in disbelief and opened the door.

There weren't many customers yet, but those who *were* there ended their conversations abruptly to stare in my direction. That was a sure way to feel self-conscious quickly. My blonde beauty was at a station in fashionable casual business attire, a look I hadn't seen on her yet. She wore black leggings with a silver loose blouse. A black apron covered her clothes. Her braid ran down her back, the signature look of hers that I loved. She seemed relaxed and very at ease while she continued her quiet conversation with Reese and a client. Apparently, they were the only ones who weren't fazed by my entrance. Jane made eye contact with me and waved me over.

"Hi, Jane. You look well. Very relaxed after a little getaway," I said with a genuinely happy smile.

"Well, Mr. Lombardi, I could say the same about you." She draped a smock over me. "How would you like it cut?" She looked comfortable in the role of hairstylist. For it being her first day back in over a year, she didn't seem nervous in the slightest.

She nodded along as I described what I wanted. Before she went to gather all her supplies, I gently grabbed her arm. "Do you ever shampoo men's hair first?" I caught her off guard, but she recovered with a grin.

"Sure, if you'd like. It'll cost you extra though." She winked, led me to the sink, and started the warm water. I'd never had my hair washed at a salon because Reese usually did the bare minimum. She would always ask me why I didn't go to the barber down the street. I'd tell her I liked the way she cut my hair, but in reality, I liked to annoy her by staying at her salon. It was so easy to push her buttons, which brought some entertainment to my days.

Maybe I liked going to R & J's because I knew subconsciously my entire world worked there...

The week I'd endured in Montana had given me plenty of time to daydream about how my first haircut with her would go. There weren't many scenarios that were appropriate in the company of others, so I had to take what I could get: a scalp massage. I selfishly wanted to feel her hands on me, instead of just a comb and clippers. My head was angled back, ready in the bowl, so she took the sprayer and wetted my hair. Using her hands, she made sure the water reached everywhere. Once she was satisfied, she pumped some shampoo into her palm and started rubbing it all over my head. It smelled like lemon and coconut. She used her nails to massage my scalp and embed the shampoo into my follicles and skin. Her body was so close to me; the scent of her skin, mixed with the shampoo, was intoxicating. I was lost in the beautiful abyss that was Jane Cora. It brought me back to Montana and cuddling in the blanket. No scent was better than hers. It was at that moment I was so thankful I'd decided on heavy jeans. Anything thinner would have posed an embarrassing problem. If she noticed, she didn't give any indication.

Once the heavenly scalp massage was over, she cut my hair quietly. She only spoke if she had a question about my requests. I wasn't sure if she just had nothing to say, or if she knew there were listening ears around us. Either way, she looked content, which was all that mattered. I was more than happy to soak up her presence in silence as she methodically moved inches away from me, grazing me with her body every so often. You would have thought I wouldn't be as affected by her proximity after being with her for four days.

You would have thought wrong.

After she finished, we went to the front desk so I could pay. The curiosity about her plans after work ate at me. I had to see if I could get any details before I left. "Are you still busy with a family friend tonight?" I asked casually.

"Yeah, I am. Sorry, Alex." She ran my card and handed it back to me.

"No, no. It's fine. I was just making sure. Where are you guys headed?" I currently had no idea how *not* to sound nosy. She eyed me cautiously and I could read her mind. "I'm not going to show up." I put on my best innocent smile. "I'm just curious."

"I'm not sure yet." She walked me to the front door. It would be easy for me to stand and chat with her all day, but she had a schedule to keep. "I wanted to ask you about Sunday, though."

"What about Sunday?" *Please don't cancel on me.*

"Well, it's supposed to be unusually warm all weekend. I was wondering if you wanted to have a picnic or something."

Alone time in a field with my beauty? Sign me up. "I'd love to. I'll pick you up after church?"

"Sounds great. Looking forward to it." She smiled.

I grabbed her hand and kissed it. "Me too, Jane."

I NEEDED A distraction. I hadn't been out in months so while Jane was with her "old friend," I went to have a couple of beers at the local pub I owned. (I used the term "own" loosely because I was a silent partner.) It was a place I frequented alone when I wanted to get away from work or women. Sitting alone at the bar would seem no different to the eyeing patrons, unless you paid attention to how I really appeared—lonely, horny, and worried. As long as nobody tried to hold a conversation with me, I could pull off the casual "drink alone on a Friday night" look. I texted Tanner, but he was unavailable to meet me for drinks. That irritated me more than it should have, considering I'd ditched the dude for ten months. I'd received a few texts from some of my past flings, asking me what I was doing over the weekend. But just as I had since the day I'd met Jane, I ignored their texts. I wasn't trying to be rude, but I felt no conversation was better than an awkward one.

So no Tanner and no ladies meant I was left to belly up to the bar alone.

Marley's was the hottest pub in the area. It also happened to be one of the only non-chain restaurants to serve dinner *and* have live music in McHenry County. It was always packed on the weekends. Locals and those traveling through came to the Irish bar that served green beer year-round. It was a warm night, a treat for the end of April. *Warm*, meaning 60 degrees. The band would play on the terrace, which would bring in a bigger crowd. Illinoisans never wasted nice nights in April. I was sure to have some good people-watching ahead of me. Sipping my beer, I started to daydream about Jane again. I tried and failed *not* to think about what she was doing, whom she was with, where they were going...

With my elbows on the bar, I ran both my hands through my hair and scratched my scalp. The feeling of it reminded me of the head massage she'd given me earlier, which made parts of me twitch that should once again not twitch in a public setting. I needed to get it together. Maybe finding a new hobby was in order. All my fantasizing and reverie could not be healthy.

Moments later, as if my daydream crashed into reality, Jane Cora walked in the front door of Marley's. She stood next to a tall man with wavy, sandy blond hair. I had to do the classic "blink and rub my eyes" to make sure I wasn't going crazy. Nope. She was actually there.

What are the fucking odds? Is this kismet again? It was hard to dispute all the coincidences over the past year.

The hostess directed them to the back of the restaurant. As they passed me, neither of them looked in my direction, which allowed me to evaluate the situation. She looked amazing, as always, in a very short *(too short when I was not involved if you asked me)* dark blue, open-back, cotton dress. There was a darker blue panel of lace that ran from the tip of her neck to her lower back. Most of her back was exposed, which meant there wasn't a bra involved. The tall dude was touching just above the small of her back as they walked by. I nearly fell off the barstool. I glared at his hand that rested on parts of her bare skin—skin I hadn't touched yet. It took every ounce of self-control to stay where I was and *not* break every finger that brushed against an intimate part of her. That would not go over well, and I needed to score all the points I could get. Every damn point counted if there was competition I hadn't known about. Now it was imperative I learned everything about her "family friend," so I kept cool and watched them. He pulled the chair out for her and sat in the next spot over instead of across the table. They were a distance away from me, with many tables full of people between us, but I could see their faces. I doubted she'd see me since she didn't know I was there. I felt the adrenaline pumping through my vessels. My muscles were gearing up for a fight. It must have been some primal, involuntary instinct kicking in.

My sensible side tried to relax my firing nerves. *Stay seated, Alex. She doesn't belong to you.*

I shook my head in frustration. She could go out with him, but not me? I watched them the entire time as they ordered their drinks and meals and then ate dinner. She looked so relaxed. I reminded myself she had a friendship with him. He was a familiar face. They drank red wine as they laughed and finished their plates. My stomach felt sick.

I had been staring at them for at least an hour and couldn't watch anymore. I directed my attention to the TVs in front of me while I finished my third beer. I kept my eyes straight for the most part but couldn't help glancing their way every couple of minutes. I could tell they were wrapping up and getting ready to leave. It was my cue to exit. I didn't want her to see me at the bar, alone, in a depressing state. I took another glance in their direction before I headed out. Jane was crying and holding Tall Guy's hands. He looked distraught too. Their demeanors were a change from the lighthearted, happy vibe they'd had all evening. My curiosity kept me from leaving and I stole another minute of staring. I assumed they were discussing the tragedy with Jane's family. That would explain the sudden sadness. I nodded to myself and stood up from the bar stool, ready to head out.

But because I was a glutton for punishment, I looked their way one last time. As I was turning my head toward them, Tall Guy leaned over and kissed her, right on the fucking lips! My heart dropped into my stomach. *I* hadn't even kissed her! She pulled away from him as fast as she could and pushed him away. She smiled awkwardly through her residual tears, but by the look of her, she was trying to get a point across. Without even hesitating, he went in for another kiss.

My feet moved in their direction before I could stop myself. When I made it to their table, I pulled Tall Guy out of his chair and pushed him away from her.

"What the fuck?" Tall Guy exclaimed.

"*Alex*!" Jane gasped and stood abruptly. Her eyes were as wide as they could get. "*What are you doing here?*" She was angry, an emotion I hadn't seen yet. She looked hotter than ever. I pushed the raging fantasy aside to direct my attention to Tall Guy.

"In case you need the reminder, chivalry isn't dead. And it includes only kissing a girl when she fully agrees to it." Tall Guy seemed too stunned to respond. "Better work on reading body language, bro," I said harshly. Then I directed my attention toward Jane and softened my voice. "I promise I wasn't stalking you. I was sitting at the bar having a beer and you came in. Total coincidence."

"Jane, who is this guy?" asked defensive Tall Guy.

Jane looked so angry and so embarrassed. "Dean, this is Alex." She swept her hand in my direction. "Alex, Dean." She glared at us both and in a serious tone, she asked, "Can we sit down now and stop creating a scene?"

I was still fuming. The primal testosterone raged through my veins. "I'll create a scene all day in this place!" Jane's eyes went wide again. I had never spoken to her in such a way.

Dean and I had some more not-so-friendly words with each other about how to be a gentleman. When I turned around to take Jane out of there, she was gone. I did a double-take of the entire dining area to make sure she wasn't around. No, she was gone, so I headed out to my Wrangler and took off in the direction of the Coras' home. I found her walking alongside the road. I slowed down so the Jeep was traveling at the same pace. After rolling down the passenger side window, I hollered to her in the most pleasant tone I could muster, "Jane, I'm sorry. Will you get in the car?"

No response. She kept going without even looking at me. She was in sandals and her dress was way too short to be walking alone at night. Her in-laws' house was miles away. "Jane, I don't know what came over me. Please forgive me. Get in the car." I wondered if I sounded as desperate as I felt.

No response again. She was furious. I could almost see fumes coming out of her ears. Finally, she spoke while keeping her face forward. "Don't you think I have enough to worry about? I don't need to be concerned about you being jealous of my friendships." I wanted to explain more to her, but just then a pickup truck pulled up on the shoulder behind her.

"Jane, sweetie. Get in the truck please." Dean's head was out the window as he inched toward her with his truck.

"Sweetie?" I shouted to Dean. "Last time I asked her, she was nobody's sweetie."

He ignored me. "Jane, it's getting colder out. I have your jacket right here. Please get in and I'll take you home."

"Jane, I can take you home. Please come with me. I won't accost you like sweetie Dean over there." I didn't know where the attitude was coming from. I wasn't the jealous type, or at least I never had been before her. She gave me a dirty look and stopped dead in her tracks. Dean and I stopped abruptly too, in the hopes she would get in our respective vehicles.

She took one last look and me and bitterly said, "I'm sorry," before she entered Dean's truck. They sped away and I lost it. I didn't know a Wrangler's steering wheel could handle so much beating. After a few deep breaths, and a couple of bloody knuckles, I headed home. I knew nothing would be resolved until we both calmed down.

First thing in the morning I'd go to her house to apologize with some flowers. It was Saturday, so I assumed both Robert and Deb would be home. It would be harder to have a conversation under the peering eyes of her in-laws, but she was worth it.

I did not sleep at all. Different scenarios played in my head all night...Jane forgiving me with a passionate embrace...Jane holding a grudge until I bent down on my knees and begged for forgiveness...Jane choosing Tall Guy over me...Jane never speaking to me again...

The hours dragged through the night. By 7:00 a.m., I couldn't stand it anymore. I left my bed, went for a seven-mile run, drank some coffee, showered, and checked my work email twice. Thankfully, all those tasks took the couple of hours I needed to pass until it was an appropriate time to head out.

I rang the Coras' doorbell, anxious about the prospect of resolving the previous night's quarrel. To my surprise, Dean answered—with his shirt off, no less. He was completely loaded with tattoos. The tops of his shoulders, his chest, the upper third of his arms, and his six-pack abs were covered in elaborate art.

"Can I help you?" Dean asked brusquely. I decided it would *not* be a good idea to take out sweetie Dean right there, although it made for a nice scene in my head.

From the kitchen, I heard a beautiful, sleepy voice. "Dean, knock it off. Let him in." With cocky chagrin all over his face, he moved over to let me into the foyer. I knew ignoring him would be the best choice. I went into the kitchen where my blonde beauty sat at the breakfast bar with a cup of coffee. Her hair was in a messy bun on the top of her head. It looked like "after-sex" hair, but since I didn't want to ruin the mood so soon, I kept that thought to myself. She had on a spaghetti strap tank top and loose thin cotton pants. It didn't look like there were any undergarments involved.

Relax, I kept reminding myself. I needed to keep calm, in more ways than one.

"Jane, can we speak privately for a moment?" I requested, unable to hide the urgency in my voice.

"Sure." She hopped off the bar stool and I tried *not* to focus on how her body reacted to moving without the support and layer of underwear.

How did this guy get to spend the evening with her? The thoughts piled up in my head, making it ache.

When we were alone outside in the backyard, I let out a large, surrendering exhale. The negative tension between us was insufferable. "Jane, I'm so sorry. It isn't like me to behave in such a way." She crossed her arms defensively, but let me continue. "I'm protective of you. I can't help it." The chilly morning weather made her body react; it took a lot of willpower to stay focused on her face.

"Alex." She exhaled out my name with annoyance written all over her face.

"That was so inappropriate last night. I still can't wrap my mind around it." I nodded in agreement. "I still hardly know you..." I went to interrupt, but she raised her hand at me. "Yes, we've been meeting for a couple of months and we went on a little getaway together. But we don't ever talk about anything personal! I know you try not to trigger me with certain topics, so I understand why our conversations are the way they are. But you said it yourself in Montana...there's a lot I don't know about you. I don't even really know what you do for work. Or your middle name. Or when your birthday is. Taking me to Montana does *not* entitle you to crash an evening out with a friend."

She was right on all accounts...except for one. "He kissed you. Seems like it's more than a friendship." She crossed her arms and looked away from me. I had her there. Friends did not kiss on the lips.

I sighed and walked toward her. I didn't want to go on fighting. "Salvatore," I said quietly.

She looked at me with confusion.

"Salvatore is my middle name."

She rubbed her forehead and shook her head at the same time.

"I know I overstepped last night and I'm truly sorry," I replied sincerely. "I can't say it won't happen again, because I don't want to lie to you. But I promise to try to behave better around your friends."

She attempted to suppress a smile. My apology seemed to calm her down. "Nothing happened between Dean and me. He slept in the guest bedroom. We talked, had some more wine, and went to bed. That's it." My body visibly relaxed a little as she continued, "Maybe you'll be less upset about our dinner date if I tell you about him..."

Jane filled me in on Dean's story. He had been married for six years to a grade school teacher. His wife started feeling sick last fall. After many tests, they learned that she'd had asbestos poisoning, which turned into cancer. She'd passed away a couple of months ago. Dean lived about four hours away in Michigan, but he was originally from McHenry County. Dean and Graham were buddies since the first grade. They were best men in each other's weddings. He was a high school mechanics teacher and on family emergency leave until the end of the school year. He came back to Illinois for the weekend to see his parents.

"He needs a shoulder to cry on, Alex. Like I did so many times after the tragedy."

Shit. Did I feel like an ass or what?

"He's hurting. And that kiss last night meant nothing. It was a mourning response. He needed to feel something...anything." She let that sink in and started speaking quickly, as if she needed to get it all out before I interrupted. "You know how I feel about you. Well, I hope you do. But you and I just met. Well, I know we met last year, but we just began speaking to each other regularly a few months ago. Dean has been a friend of mine since high school. If he needs me, I'm going to be here for him. People forgot about me after my family died. They didn't know how to treat me, so they never came around. I can't let that happen to him." She paused for a moment to gather her thoughts. "But he and I are only friends. Please don't worry about me anymore."

"Not possible," I stated without hesitation. She walked in the direction of my Jeep, which I guessed was my cue to go.

"Well, okay, fine. Then trust that I can look after myself in certain situations." We were at the door of my vehicle when she gently placed both her hands on the sides of my neck and kissed my cheek. A shiver ran down my spine and then straight into my groin. "I have to take care of a lot of stuff today, but I'm looking forward to our picnic tomorrow."

I took her hands in mine and kissed both of her palms. "I am as well." Time alone together in the middle of a field was just what I needed after the last twelve hours. I entered the Jeep while I kept my eyes on her. It felt more difficult than normal to leave her side. Maybe because I knew there was a tall, half-naked man full of tattoos waiting for her in the house—a man who needed a lot of comforting at the moment. I waved the thoughts out of my head before I did something reckless again.

I started the engine as she walked back to the house. Before she was too far away, she shouted at me in a playful tone. "Don't worry about me, Alex!"

"Not possible, Jane," I repeated my sentiment from earlier.

Her carefree laugh that followed became my favorite sound in the world.

11

Jane

"THAT DOUCHEBAG IS in love with you," Dean blurted out as soon as I entered the front door. He was casually resting against the kitchen counter with his ankles crossed. He had always been very comfortable at the Cora residence. It was his safe space as a kid and continued to be his home away from home.

"Oh my gosh, Dean. No, he is not." I rolled my eyes, downplaying the idea. "And don't call him that."

He raised an eyebrow. "I heard he declared his love for you. And he took you to Montana?" He turned his focus toward my in-laws, who were awkwardly looking anywhere but at him. Or me.

I gasped. "Traitors!"

"Janey, anyone who's paying attention can see Alex's love for you," Deb explained, as if it were a very obvious fact. She moved around the kitchen, pretending to be busy doing nothing. Robert grumbled something unintelligible under his breath.

"Do you love him?" Dean asked me abruptly.

It was the wrong time to take a sip from my mug. "*What*? No!" I croaked while trying to prevent coffee from going up my nose. Robert either suppressed a growl or coughed, I couldn't tell. Deb clasped her hands by her face in elation. I crossed my arms to show my dissatisfaction with the conversation and all their different, unspoken opinions. "He has a crush on me."

Dean huffed a laugh. "Who doesn't?"

I rolled my eyes. "Oh, stop. You're making me blush," I drawled sarcastically and went to find a towel to wipe my face. "Are we done with the inquisition yet?"

"Are we making you uncomfortable?" Dean grinned, showing his beautiful white teeth. For the record, I'd known him for more than half my life. He didn't *actually* care if he was making me uncomfortable. Teasing me had always been one of his favorite pastimes.

"No. But you *are* giving me a headache," I said to all of them. Deb raised her hands in surrender. Dean continued to wear a cocky grin. Robert turned around to get back to his TV viewing.

It seemed as if they were giving up. *Good*. I had more important business to tend to. "Wait, Robert, stay here for a second. I've been thinking about something for a while. Kind of the 'elephant in the room.'" They all looked confused, so I kept going. I directed my attention to the Coras. "I wouldn't have survived the last fourteen months without your support. You've let me stay here. You've taken care of my house. You've kept me fed." I hoped they saw the gratitude in my eyes. "I'm indebted to you both."

"We wouldn't have had it any other way," Robert said. For as grumpy as he could be, he truly loved me like a daughter.

"And I can't thank you enough. I'll never be able to repay you."

"Janey, what are you getting at? What 'elephant in the room'?" Deb looked concerned.

I took a deep breath through my nose and let it out. "I think it's time I go back to Maple Street."

All of their eyes became wide at once. Deb's mouth popped open in surprise.

"I'm not certain that's a good idea," Dean countered.

"Jane, are you sure—" Deb choked out.

"Not yet, dear," Robert stated matter-of-factly.

So that was how it was going to be? Three against one? I sighed, closed my eyes, and rubbed my aching temples. I wasn't strong enough to argue with them. I knew they had my best interests at heart. I diverted to Plan B. "Okay, how about I go for a visit then?"

"Jane." Deb had her mothering voice in place. "You were discharged from the hospital less than a week ago. Your new medications might not have kicked in yet. You haven't been to a grief group this week or to your therapist. You just started back at the salon yesterday." Her tone was concerned. "How much are you willing to put on yourself in such a short amount of time?"

I didn't know how to explain to them that I knew I was ready to visit my home. It was something I'd been thinking about for the last couple of weeks. There wasn't much more that could hurt me. My family wasn't coming back. Seeing our home and their possessions was not going to sink me into another downward spiral. I wouldn't let that happen. It was time for me to start thinking about the future. Or tiny parts of the future I could mentally take on.

"Don't you guys want your privacy back?" I looked at my in-laws. "I've been a burden long enough."

"You've been the opposite of a burden!" Deb exclaimed, sounding panicky. "Yes, we've helped you this past year. But, Janey, we need your help too! We wouldn't have made it without you either. Please don't feel like you're imposing. I assure you that you are not."

Robert shook his head in agreement. "You're welcome to stay as long as you need." He came over to me and wrapped me in his arms. Once again, I was so thankful my in-laws weren't afraid to embrace me.

We hugged in silence for a moment as I was contemplating my next words. "Thank you." I was not going to let Plan B go. "I've some errands to run first, but I'd still like to go to Maple Street today. I'd love for all of you to join me."

All three eyed me warily. After a silent and thoughtful deliberation, they agreed to come along.

DEAN CONVINCED ME to let him drive to all my errands. I informed him they were nothing significant and would probably bore him, but he insisted and said it would beat spending time at his parents' house. I refrained from reminding him that he came into town to actually *see* his mom and dad.

Dean had always had a strained relationship with his parents, hence why he gravitated toward the Coras' home. Any time I had ever gone to his childhood home, I could feel the tension in the air. Knowing that he was trying to heal from some heavy trauma at the moment and tension wouldn't help, I decided my errands were the lesser of two evils.

It turned out to be the nice day we were expecting. Dean had the windows down in his truck and I silently thanked the weather gods for the warm spring. Northern Illinois can and does get snow in April. We were a thankful group if there was no white stuff on the ground by springtime. For months we were stuck inside all day unless we wanted to brave negative degree weather. Every year on the first truly warm day, there would be a positive vibe in the air. Nobody wanted to stay in their homes. Everyone would be out walking, biking, and on motorcycles. Sitting in Dean's truck, I felt the good weather vibes radiating in. It felt amazing to breathe fresh air and feel my hair whip around in the warm wind.

We made it through all my tedious stops quicker than anticipated, which was a bonus. I was anxious to get to Maple Street before someone talked me out of it. I refused to let the worry in my heart surface. I kept reminding myself it was going to be okay. Easy? Maybe not. But definitely tolerable. Dean was right to insist on joining me on my errands. He distracted me enough so I couldn't dwell on what I was about to do later. Nineties alternative blared on the radio while I hummed along. At that moment, I paused to focus on something significant...

I felt *good*. Happy, even.

The Grinch immediately came to mind. My heart had shrunk a few sizes over the last year. However, it had grown by a fraction recently. Nothing too significant, but a step in the right direction. I said a little silent prayer to thank everyone above for giving me such a gift.

Dean seemed to sense my contentment. Every so often, he'd look over at me and grin. We'd always had an easy friendship. If oil and vinegar were opposites, we were oil and...oil. I shook my head at my silly analogy and thought about all the years we'd known each other. There were countless fun, carefree times in our teenage years. I chuckled when my brain sparked an old memory.

Dean heard my giggle and eyed me curiously. "What are you thinking about?"

"Remember that time you and Graham accidentally locked yourselves in that port-a-potty?" My giggling continued.

He groaned. "Don't remind me."

"It was so funny. The other guys and I thought it would be a good idea to bang it around to see if the lock would become unlatched..." I couldn't stop laughing hysterically. I was glad Dean drove. "And they pushed so hard it tipped over!" Happy tears pooled over my lids.

Dean glanced at me in between looking at the road. He had a grin on his face. "It's nice to see you so happy. How long does it take to be able to laugh regularly again?"

I took a deep, cleansing breath and grabbed his hand. "There are some days I can't find any reason to smile. Other days, like today, I feel all right. But I'm still broken, Dean. Very much so." My heart ached for my friend. It wasn't that long ago when I was certain I'd never have another reason to smile. I tried to think about what changed in the last few weeks or months. Aside from new medications, starting back to work, and one handsome, attentive gentleman coming out of left field to sweep me off my feet, I had nothing to pin it on.

Maybe that's how it happens, deep inner voice chimed in. *Maybe one day you're wholly broken, and the next day, you have a few less deep wounds.*

I squeezed Dean's hand and continued, "I'm okay with where I am in my recovery process, though. I have to accept that bad days will happen too, but I'm hoping for more good than bad going forward." I brought our entwined hands to my lips to give him a supportive kiss. I needed to help him as much as I could and give him some advice to think about. "Have you started seeing a counselor yet?" He shook his head. "I recommend you go. After the accident, I couldn't sleep or eat. I wanted to die. My parents came in from Sweden and stayed with me at the Coras' for a few weeks. My mom could see I wasn't getting any better, so by the third week she started researching grief counselors." Dean was quiet and stared ahead as I spoke. I hoped my words were registering as important information. I couldn't be more thankful for my mom's decision that day. "I've been going regularly ever since. The psychiatrist prescribed some medications: one to help me sleep and one for depression. I take the sleeping pill when needed. I took the depression med for months, but I had recently stopped to see how I felt without it." Surface voice showed up to chastise me for making such a stupid mistake. "*That* landed me in the hospital and right back on medications."

Dean continued to stare straight ahead while he drove. He had sunglasses on, but couldn't hide the tears falling down his face.

"Dean, please pull over," I said, a little panicky. Any interference with driving made all my anxieties show up. He did as he was told and turned into the nearest parking lot. He parked and stared forward without speaking. I still had his right hand in mine, so I pulled his left hand off the steering wheel so he would be forced to face me. He wouldn't look at me. His head was facing as far down as possible. He seemed ashamed of crying. In all my years of knowing him, I had never seen him overly emotional. At Hillary's funeral, he remained composed with a mask of stillness the entire night. I had a feeling he hadn't grieved properly yet.

After my tragedy, everyone kept telling me "It will get better" or "They're in a better place." My favorite was "You're stronger than I could ever be," as if I had a choice in the matter. So instead of saying anything, I let him take the moment to grieve.

I hadn't known Hillary very well. Dean had met her right before graduating from college. After they'd earned their degrees, they moved to Michigan and got married. Dean and Graham kept in contact, but the visits became fewer and fewer. Life became busy with careers and kids. Hillary and I had never had a chance to become close.

Regardless, I had so much empathy for my friend. Such huge, terrible tragedies should not have happened to either of us. We were too young. But something grief group had taught me was that life deals all sorts of cards. We don't get to pick our fates. I also learned in the past year that heartache would be a permanent part of my day-to-day existence. I needed to work around it from now on. Dean would learn too. But first, he had to mourn her and the life they'd once shared.

We sat in silence for probably ten minutes. Once his breathing calmed and his tears subsided, I asked if he wanted me to drive. He shook his head, put the truck in drive, and headed off. The mood was somber for the rest of the ride home. Before we departed his truck, I kissed him on the cheek and told him a phrase people often told me that *did* give me hope in moments of darkness: time heals all wounds...eventually. I reminded him that he wouldn't feel happy or normal for a while, and that was *okay*! He nodded and thanked me. I nodded back with a caring smile, hoping I'd helped in some way.

We headed into the house, hand in hand, to gather Robert and Deb for the next task of the day.

MAPLE STREET WAS about a half mile long in what was considered the downtown Crystal Lake Neighborhood. "Downtown" was a loose interpretation. Crystal Lake was a safe, quiet, mostly residential area. No high rises. No overly congested roads. No terrible crimes. Just suburbanites moving about their days, with or without kids in tow. It was a town full of families and retired people alike. Therefore, the town always scheduled activities for every age group throughout the year to keep us all connected. There were great schools, a couple of beaches, and plenty of places to eat and shop. We had everything we needed. And if something was appealing to see or do in Chicago, the Metra train would take us downtown in a little over an hour. I loved it there.

So when we'd decided to purchase a house, I was unyielding in my desire to raise our future family in Crystal Lake. Graham didn't need much convincing, so when the market lowered enough for us to be able to afford a mortgage, we started the hunt.

Our house was one of only a few we viewed with our Realtor. Before we even entered, I had fallen in love with the three-bedroom, 1,500-square-foot house within walking distance of the little downtown area. It had the most charming closed-in front porch that was the perfect space to enjoy a cup of coffee and a good book. At first sight, I could see Graham and me old with gray hair, in rocking chairs, watching our little grandkids play at our feet on that porch. Never mind we hadn't even had kids yet.

The picture in my head had been so vivid. I knew it was the right space for us. We toured the house, which confirmed my good feeling about it. That same day, we put an offer in and it was accepted. We moved in six weeks later.

Robert, Deb, Dean, and I walked up to the house together, forming a straight line. Deb held my hand tight in both of hers. Dean showed his support by gently resting his hand on the small of my back.

"You sure you want to do this?" Robert asked warily.

I looked at the house in front of me—my home—the place I brought and raised my babies. It didn't worry me to go in there. I was ready. "Yes, I'm sure."

They let me be the first to walk up to the door of the porch. I took a steadying breath and pushed it open. I looked around. For being vacant for over a year, the cute little space between the indoors and outside was spotless. There were no spider webs and no dust from the outdoors. I turned to Deb. I placed my head on her shoulder and rubbed her back to show my gratitude. "Thank you for taking care of this place," I said to her. I looked at Robert next. "You too." He nodded in acknowledgment.

"Our pleasure, Janey," Deb replied. "Now let's get this over with."

I opened the front door to what appeared to be a time capsule of my past life. Everything looked the same as it had. I didn't know what I had expected, but I *did* know I hadn't expected to feel that it was like any other day when I entered my home. Deb left every bit of it in place, aside from anything perishable.

"When you came back to visit for the first time, I wasn't sure what would be worse...all your possessions gone...or still here..." Deb spoke quietly. "I decided based on what *I* would want. So I kept everything in place."

My eyes couldn't focus on one space for too long. Everywhere I turned, memories came back to me. Memories I had forgotten already. I pried my eyes and thoughts away for a moment to comfort Deb. She seemed regretful. "You made the right choice. Thank you so much." I gave her a brief hug and continued slowly exploring the rooms. I sauntered over to the fireplace mantle to take in all the family pictures displayed.

Each photo sparked its own remembrance. My babies were so beautiful. How blessed I was that they had called me momma, even for a short time. I stopped at a photo of newborn Arlo being kissed by his older siblings. The emotions formed in the back of my throat. My fingertips involuntarily brushed over their darling faces. I closed my eyes to send a prayer up to my babies. *I'll see you again someday. Wait for me.*

"Jane," Dean approached me cautiously, "we can go whenever you'd like. Just say the word." He took my hand in his and kissed it.

I wiped the tears away with my free hand. "No, I'm okay. I promise. I'm not overwhelmed."

I continued to tour the house for another half hour or so, pausing in places that sparked a memory or emotion. The Coras and Dean had walked around with me for a few minutes but then made their way to the porch to give me privacy. They asked me many times if I needed them near me, but I refused their help. I had to view and reminisce on my own, at my own pace. Tears were going to be a necessary part of the process. I knew that going in.

The only rooms I was hesitant to enter were the kids' bedrooms. Arlo had slept with Graham and me, but the older two had their own rooms. When I made it to Clare's door, I took in a deep inhale before I entered. As expected, it looked exactly the same as it did the last day she was alive, aside from her bed being perfectly made. I chuckled softly to myself. My stubborn girl had always refused to make her bed.

I lay on her twin bed and closed my eyes for a moment. Immediately, a movie reel of Clare throughout the years filled the back of my eyelids. I took in every image and studied it—bringing her home from the hospital. Her first steps. Her first day of preschool. Meeting her baby brother. Her first day of kindergarten. Meeting her second baby brother. Getting her ready for the birthday party before I went to work that fateful day.

I let myself feel all the emotions tied to the beautiful snapshot of her life. It did not negatively overwhelm me the way it would have a few months ago. Tears and all, I was thankful for the recap of her milestones. As much as I didn't want to leave Clare's room, I was anxious to get to see reels of my other babies' lives.

I moved on to Marric's room and had the same experience. His snapshots were from a shorter amount of time, but significant nonetheless. I lay on his bed and took in a deep breath from his comforter, hoping there would be a remnant of fragrance from my sweet boy. After a few minutes of seeing his precious face behind my eyelids, I sighed and stood up. I couldn't smell any part of him as I had hoped, but I refused to let myself be disappointed. Scent or not, being in my kids' rooms was bringing back priceless aspects of their lives that I needed to commit to memory.

The last room to visit was the master bedroom. *Where the magic happens.* I snorted to myself. Not so much magic happened once three kids were involved. Besides Arlo sleeping with us, we expected at least one of the other two to join us each night. Much to Graham's disapproval, I was always happy to invite them in. I knew time was fleeting and they wouldn't want to cuddle us forever. Maybe somewhere deep inside I knew the stage of cuddling my kids would be cut short. I paused at our bed to recall all the different ways we would fit two grown adults and at least two kids on our queen mattress. I chuckled to myself. The things you were willing to do as a parent...

I made my way back downstairs to the others. They were still on the porch, doing their own reminiscing with each other.

"Janey, you are so strong. I'm so proud of you," Deb said, rocking in my favorite chair.

"Thank you. I feel a little strong tonight." I took a look around at my favorite part of the house. "I think I want to sell it," I announced abruptly.

"Sell it?" Deb sounded confused.

"There's no rush, dear. We don't mind tending to it," Robert assured me.

I nodded at them. "I appreciate that, but I feel this house deserves a family. It's not just four walls and a roof. Not to me anyway. It's a warm, cozy, welcoming space to make memories with loved ones. It's not meant to sit empty. The energy is too good here to waste."

"Jane, sweetie, you don't need to make any decisions tonight. Why don't you sleep on it?" Dean asked.

Knowing that they had my best interests at heart again, I couldn't argue with them. "Okay, if it will make you all feel better." I winked, but they probably couldn't see it with the sun setting. "I'll sleep on it. But I'm pretty firm in my choice." I made a mental note to call a real estate agent on Monday.

"Okay, we can talk about it again soon. You ready to go?" Robert asked.

I sighed. I didn't want the feelings of nostalgia to end yet, especially if I was going to sell it soon. "I think I'm going to stay a little longer. But you guys should go. It's dinnertime. I'll call you for a ride when I'm ready."

"I can stay with you," Dean suggested.

I couldn't refuse him when he had such a look of melancholy on his face, so I nodded.

We decided Dean would drop my in-laws off at home, pick up take-out, and come back. When he arrived back at the house, I was on the porch, rocking away in my favorite chair, humming one of the lullabies I always attempted to sing for Arlo before bed.

"You look very relaxed." Dean carried a bag of dinner and a bottle of red wine.

"I really am." I could sense the relief in his features that the afternoon did not tear me to shreds. Maybe it provided him hope for his own healing journey.

We ate mostly in silence. Dean gave me a lot of space to be in the moment with my memories. He would look up from his food occasionally but did not say whatever thoughts he had. After dinner, we moved to the couch to enjoy the rest of the bottle of wine. We made small talk for a while and also shared stories we could remember about the good ol' days.

Dean and I had known each other for a very long time. We had a lot of history together, including dating for nine months when we were in high school. In fact, Dean was the one who introduced me to his best bud, Graham. I'd had an instant connection to Graham, even while dating Dean. It was not a romantic connection at first, but more of an "I think I know you from a past life" kind of feeling. Graham told me later he felt the same way the first time he'd met me.

Dean woke me out of my daydreaming. "How are you doing? It's been a long afternoon."

I cleared my throat, trying to wipe away the emotions that had started to brew over thinking about my younger years. "Mixed emotions, I'd say. Of course there's sadness, but I also feel a sense of...peace." I closed my eyes to replay some of the images from the day. "I'm really glad we came here."

"So it wasn't a mistake?" Dean asked.

"Not at all," I replied firmly.

Dean was thoughtful for a moment. He took a sip of his wine and turned to face me a bit more. "What's the biggest mistake you've ever made?"

His question caught me off guard. I tried to think of the worst thing I've ever done and came up pretty short. "Hmm...maybe forgetting to feed my goldfish as a kid? I guess you could say I'm a murderer," I mused lightheartedly.

Dean chuckled quietly and looked down. He seemed...shy? Nervous? I couldn't place the emotion. "I guess I meant 'regret.'"

"Oh, well that's much harder." I ran my finger along the edge of my wine glass as I pondered his question. I always wondered if I'd made the right career choice. I wasn't an artist by any stretch. I had always felt I could have been a better hairstylist if I had even the slightest amount of artistic abilities. That being said, I didn't regret my path. After thinking for a moment more, he had me stumped. "I'm not sure. I can't think of anything significant. What about you?"

He didn't answer right away. There had to be a reason he asked me such a random question. His cheeks were a little flushed from the wine and he fidgeted. Yes, he was nervous.

"Dean." I leaned forward a smidge and willed his eyes to look at me from across the couch. It worked, and he gave me an awkward smile in return. He had the kind of face grandmothers loved to pinch. Not a baby face, necessarily. But one you would trust right away because of his looks. He had beautiful blue eyes and a bright white smile. His sandy blond hair was the perfect mix of short, messy, loose waves. He also kept a short beard. Not a five o'clock shadow, but more like an "11 p.m. the following day" shadow. He was very handsome.

However, at the moment all his appealing features were twisted in anxiety. "Has anyone told you lately how adorable you are?" I asked with a grin. He smiled and the flush in his cheeks became more intense. "I'm curious why you're asking me these questions. What is your biggest regret?"

"Well, I have two," he finally answered.

"Mmmm'kay. The first?" All the anticipation was making *me* anxious too.

He took a deep breath. "My first regret is being unfaithful to you when we were dating." My heart skipped a beat. He was speaking from such a long time ago. I was shocked that it still bothered him. We were kids when we dated. We weren't very serious. I had gotten over it as soon as I started seeing Graham. I'd forgiven him over a decade ago. I started to say just that when he continued, "The second is not fighting for you."

My mouth popped open in surprise. Those were not admissions I had expected. I couldn't help but giggle nervously. "Dean. I—" I didn't know what to say. He was a close friend of mine. I had no romantic feelings for him. He felt like...home to me, but not in a boyfriend or spouse kind of way.

"No, it's okay. I know you don't feel the same. I just needed to get it out, finally, that I've never stopped loving you." He looked at his wine glass and mumbled, "I've been holding that in for well over a decade." He sighed heavily, as if a huge weight had been released from his shoulders.

He had me stunned in silence. I understood why he kept that admission in for so long. He loved his best friend. There was no way he would have intruded on our marriage. Not to mention he had also been with his wife for a long time. "What about Hillary?" was my best follow-up question.

He knew what my question implied. "I guess you can fall in love with more than one person."

Overwhelmed with the new knowledge, I took in a big breath and closed my eyes. In the four heartbeats that my eyes were closed, Dean moved to my side of the couch and laid a gentle kiss on my unsuspecting lips. It took another heartbeat for me to figure out what was happening. I gasped in shock, which he mistakenly took for me inviting his tongue to the party. I pushed him away with all my strength.

"*Dean!*" My eyes went wide in surprise. "This is *not* what you want," I borderline shouted, "or need!" He sat back on the couch with the expression of a wounded puppy. "You're hurting. I totally understand. But you do not want me. You want the *feeling* of me. There is no way you are ready to have a healthy relationship with someone." I tried not to be preachy, but my words flowed fast. My filter couldn't keep up. "Not to mention I'm also healing from losing my spouse—and children. This would never work!" I was on a roll now. "*And* you're one of my closest friends. Do you want to mess it up? To risk almost two decades of friendship?" He went to speak. "Don't answer that," I ordered flatly.

I stood up from the couch and walked to the kitchen to put the wine glasses in the sink. I was agitated now. "*Way to ruin the night, Dean,*" was all I could think. And then I abruptly stopped myself from such negative thoughts. I was certain I had ruined plenty of nights, and days, for others over the last fourteen months. Even though I did *not* appreciate his attempts to kiss me, he needed me right now. It was my job to show him more empathy and establish some boundaries. So I walked over to where he was still sitting—more like sulking—grabbed his hands, and pulled him off the couch.

"Behave," I instructed sternly before I put my arms around his waist. He was too tall to hug in a conventional way so I did my best. I squeezed him tight to try to bring him the therapeutic aspect of a hug. *At least twenty seconds*, someone once had told me. I counted slowly in my head to get all the time in. He gently rested his chin on the top of my head and sniffled away some tears. Being so close to his body heat, I could almost feel his torment exuding off him in waves.

"I love you, Jane Cora," he choked out quietly as he kissed my hair.

My heart continued to break for him. I felt his pain, quite literally. "I love you too. Just not in the same way. And even if it was the right way, it wouldn't be the right time," I said into his T-shirt.

"I know," he replied and placed another kiss in my hair.

12

Alex

I WOKE EARLY on Sunday, full of too much adrenaline to sleep. The Coras always attended late morning Mass, so I had more than a few hours to kill before I went to pick up Jane. I wasn't sure what to do with all the unwanted free time; I could only focus on the upcoming afternoon. I played back a part of yesterday's conversation that nagged at me...

"I still hardly know you..."

Those words were a punch to the gut. I desperately needed some alone time with her to show her who I was. She was right. I'd been avoiding personal topics to prevent triggering her in any way. Unfortunately, it seemed to have backfired on me. So the current goal was to get to know each other on a much deeper level. I never wanted to hear "*I still hardly know you*" out of her mouth again.

I rose from bed and headed downstairs to start my morning routine. I went through the motions of making breakfast, drinking coffee, and reading the paper, but I was not fully present. My picnic fantasies, both grand and small, had taken over my brain. Many times I had to reprimand myself for wandering to licentious levels. Jane was strong in many ways. She was also a delicate flower in other ways. I could accidentally crush her if I wasn't careful. Going forward, I was hopeful my conscious mind would remind me of how fragile she was when my more primal desires started to take over. It had been a long time since I'd been with a woman. I could feel every part of my body getting impatient.

I had promised her I would behave in Montana. I'd kept to that promise and was happy to have done it. For some reason, once we returned, my subconscious felt like all bets were off. But that was just me. I didn't know where her headspace was.

After trying to stay busy at home for as long as possible, I headed to FLEX to work out and also take care of some neglected tasks in my gym office. I had a home office too, but it was always easier for me to focus on business outside of the house—especially on days when the distractions were endless.

Sunday mornings were always very quiet at the gym. One person I *could* count on being there was Reese, as Sunday was her day off from the salon. She never missed a chance to kick her own ass on the one day a week she could rest from everything.

That fact worked in my favor. She was just the person I needed to see.

As soon as I entered the main floor, I found her sprinting on a treadmill with a heavy incline. She had a weighted vest on for more resistance. She really was a fiery little beast.

I couldn't resist heading over to her right away. I was too impatient to wait for her to finish. "You know, running outside is a lot more fun," I said, attempting to break the ice. Her attempt to ignore me was obvious immediately. "Of course, there may not be enough hills for you to run up around here," I mused.

Reese eyed me quickly while continuing her sprint. She looked as if she was deciding to engage or keep ignoring me. She knew I wouldn't come over and interrupt just to make small talk. Therefore, after a minute or so—and not without a few obvious sighs of annoyance—she slowed to a walking pace and looked at me expectantly. I took it as my cue.

"You ever seen this Dean character who's in town right now, hanging all over Jane?" I asked, trying to hide my bitterness.

Reese's eyebrows rose in surprise and then narrowed. It was clear she didn't approve of my question. She didn't answer right away; she was breathing too hard from her run.

Finally, after what felt like forever, her breathing slowed enough to form sentences. She was still winded, so her response came out in fragments. "Of course I know Dean....He's a friend of mine...He was Graham's best friend... They did everything together...before Dean moved to Michigan to be closer to...his wife's family."

Nothing surprising there. Okay, not so bad. I nodded at her in thanks and walked away. I didn't want to poke the bear too much. I refused to let her do or say something to ruin my good mood.

"Did you know that Dean and Jane dated in high school?" she hollered at me when my back was already to her. I stopped in my tracks and turned on my heels to face her again. She had my attention and she knew it. She continued, "Only for a short time, maybe during sophomore year. Dean cheated on her and shortly after that, she started dating Graham." I couldn't hide the shock on my expression. Jane had made it sound as if Graham introduced her to Dean. She'd casually left out they dated in high school.

Reese's smug smile made my stomach turn. She loved letting me in on the information between Jane and Dean. She wanted to make me jealous.

"Sounds like a real winner if he cheated on her..." I stated, more to myself than to her.

"Like you can freaking talk!" Reese stopped the treadmill completely and stood there with her arms crossed. "You haven't been a saint in the dating department either."

I crossed my arms in defense too. "I've never cheated on a girlfriend."

"Maybe not, but when you lose interest in someone you've been toying with for a while, you leave her high and dry without a second glance—or reason. Try to argue *that*, Mr. Lombardi. Because I can provide you with a list of names if you'd like." She gave me those fierce eyes, showing me she wasn't going to lose. "I can *guarantee* you have hurt more women than Dean has. *Tenfold.*"

"I thought you said you weren't going to give me a hard time anymore." I tried to keep my tone nonchalant. I wouldn't let her win.

"You haven't met your end of the bargain." She crossed her arms a little tighter. She looked keyed up. Was she still truly worried about her friend? Or was it something simpler, like she hadn't gotten laid in a while? Reese enjoyed the male variety. A lot.

Didn't matter. She was not going to ruin my day. The good mood was still in place.

I backed away from her. "Working on it." I smirked with a patronizing wink. It wasn't like me, but I couldn't contain the rude gesture. She deserved a taste of her own medicine.

She made a noise that sounded something between a grunt and a growl and restarted the treadmill.

WHEN I KNEW I had given Jane more than enough time to get ready after church, I headed to the Cora household. I turned the corner onto their street and saw her sitting on the front stoop. I took in her outfit, as I always did. Analyzing Jane's wardrobe was one of my favorite pastimes. She was wearing a floral skirt that flowed to right above her ankles. Her upper half had a short-sleeved white top that showed about an inch of her midriff. Her hair was down and in waves. She looked like a perfect boho princess. More importantly, I noticed she was not looking nearly as thin or sickly as she had when we first met. She had a naturally petite frame, but her bones meant to be covered weren't sticking out anymore. Her curves were showing in perfect places. It made me smile to see her becoming healthier, inside and out. She was ravishing, more than ever.

I silently reminded myself to behave.

When she saw me arrive, she stood and flattened out her skirt fabric. Bending down to grab a large square basket in one arm and a blanket in the other, she headed my way. When she reached me, I took everything out of her arms and put it in the back of the Jeep. "What's all this?" I asked, with a wondering grin.

She grinned back at me. "We can't have a proper picnic without supplies."

I chastised myself silently. I hadn't thought about anything past just being together. "Thank you for thinking of such details," I said and placed a kiss on her cheek. "Shall we?"

JANE HAD A spot picked out already. We walked about a mile of trail at a nature conservancy and found an area with just enough shade and sun—and privacy. Jane spread the blanket as I opened the basket to see what she packed. I pulled out a bottle of cherry wine and gave her a raised eyebrow.

"I didn't know what you preferred," she admitted shyly.

"I'm more surprised you're a 'drink in the middle of the day' kind of girl," I replied with a low chuckle.

"Day drinking is the way to go. Start early and end early. No hangover." She had a smile that met her eyes.

"You should have told me that at the ranch. I would have loved to pop a few back with you at noon."

She giggled. "Hmm. Well, considering we had a hard time staying upright on a horse while sober, I'm thinking we did the right thing by not drinking much."

"True story," I said with a wink. "How are your bruises?"

"Just fine," she replied. "Yours?"

"Just fine," I repeated. I was still bruised, but the pain was lessening by the day.

Jane settled herself on the blanket as I rummaged through the basket to find the wine opener and glasses. I kept glancing in her direction as I went through the motions of opening the bottle and pouring it. A perfect breeze played with her blonde locks in the subtlest of ways. A couple of times, the light gust brushed a few strands of her hair over her exposed collarbones and into her cleavage area. Parts of me—who weren't invited to the picnic—were already trying to crash the party. I closed my eyes and shook my head quickly to settle my instincts. Behaving was not going to be easy.

Delicate flower. Nothing has changed since Montana, I reminded myself.

Jane woke me from my internal dispute. "Are you hungry? I brought cucumber sandwiches, almonds, and fruit."

"I'm hungry if you are," I said and placed a stemless wine glass into her hand. She rolled her eyes playfully and directed me to where the plates and napkins were hiding.

"So what did you do yesterday?" I asked as I sat down across from her with a plate. I couldn't help my curiosity. I knew sweetie Dean was probably part of her day.

She smiled and shook her head once. "Nope. We're going to talk about you today."

"Hmmm. Okay," I replied tentatively with a smile. "I'm an open book. What would you like to know?"

She swirled her wine glass. "I thought we'd start off simple. How many siblings *do* you have?"

"Pass," I uttered swiftly.

"Aww, come on. What about the open book? Is that not an easy question?" she teased.

I narrowed my eyes. "Not so easy." I couldn't help the worry that my sibling story would upset her. I didn't want to ruin the mood—well, ever—but at least not so soon.

"Okay, we'll come back to that one." She paused and took a sip of wine. "What's your birthday?"

"Pass," I said again, in an attempt to make her laugh. It worked. Her giggle was a beautiful sound. "January 9th. Would you like the year?" I teased.

"Only if you're willing to disclose," she replied playfully.

"Nineteen ninety. I barely made it into the next decade. My parents have always said I'm an '80s kid at heart."

She giggled again. "So, January 9th. Hmm..." She was thinking hard. "You're a Capricorn. Earth sign," she mused.

"Is that a good thing?" All of a sudden, I was a little self-conscious. I had never paid much attention to astrology. It always felt like everyone's personality could fit into every sign, if you wanted it to.

"Depends on whom you ask," she said in jest. I willed her with my eyes to explain more. "Capricorns are driven. They often are their own bosses or are high up in their companies. They are natural-born leaders and also self-reliant. They're motivated by money."

"Those traits don't sound so bad." All the qualities she listed were spot on to my personality. Maybe there was something to astrology after all. "What are the negatives?" I asked curiously.

She rattled some characteristics off quickly. "Moody, domineering, not able to show emotions..."

I chuckled and took a sip of the wine. "Well, you know the last one isn't true. For me at least." I stared at her with eyes I hoped reminded her of every intimate confession I had made since meeting her.

It worked. She blushed and looked at her skirt, keeping her hands busy by flattening it out around her bent legs.

"Any more questions for me before it's your turn?"

"Plenty," she stated. She wanted to know about my childhood and my parents. She asked where they lived and if they were still working. I filled her in that their main residence was currently in Manhattan. They were both born and raised in Chicago. When I was a toddler, my mother convinced my dad to move to the suburbs to have a quieter lifestyle for us kids. The idea of taking the train to work daily was not an exciting concept for my father, but he agreed to it because he knew it was the right thing to do. They'd settled on moving to the suburb of Cary, which was the little village next-door to Crystal Lake. I'd lived there until I went to college in Chicago.

When I'd graduated with my MBA, my father was ready to give me responsibility and part-ownership of his business, Lombardi Enterprises. Once a few years had passed and he saw I was holding my weight in the company, he relocated to New York City to be more involved with business dealings there. My mother was more than happy to move out east. They still had a condo in Chicago on the Gold Coast for when they come into town on business or to visit family.

"Something I'm really curious about is why you're a personal trainer. It doesn't sound like you need the income." She looked at me, puzzled.

I shook my head. "I don't need the money, no. But I like to help my clients find their path to fitness. Going to a gym is very intimidating, especially if you're out of shape or just unhealthy in general. I always try to get my clients to trust me and be comfortable the first time we meet. I want them to be excited for their next session and want them to take care of themselves."

She looked away from me and chuckled under her breath.

"What? Did I say something amusing?" I smiled.

"Not at all, keep going," she smirked.

"Anyway, I also just enjoy being at the health club. I've always been a gym rat. It's where I'm most at ease. Training clients keeps me there for more hours of the day." She nodded in understanding. "Why is it that you teach fitness classes? I'm assuming for the same reasons?"

"Nah. I just wanted a free membership," she giggled. I laughed out loud at her response. "I'm just joking. Yes, I like helping my customers get healthier. I also like being forced to work out a few times per week. It keeps me accountable, you know?"

"I totally understand." And I did. As much as I loved the gym, there was always an occasional day that I would rather have skipped. Having clients relying on me never allowed me to slack off. "So, when do you go back to teaching spin?"

"Soon. Hopefully in the next few weeks. It has been hard tracking Luis down. He's the manager at the rec center. I'm cutting his hair on Friday, so I'll ask him then." She looked excited and ready to get back to it. My heart skipped a beat at her elation. Maybe I would win the bargain with Reese.

Although I'm not so sure I was the one who was bringing out the happy side of Jane. Time would tell, I pondered to myself.

"Enough about me," Jane said firmly. "Back to you. What are your roles in your business? I know you're involved with the gym. But what else?" She looked interested in what I considered a boring aspect of my life. I hadn't had any choice in the matter of my career. My father was a strong, stubborn, and convincing man. As soon as I was old enough to start thinking about what I wanted to do, he guided me toward the path of working alongside him.

I sighed. Not in frustration. It was hard to describe all my positions within our company. "My father is the CEO. He makes all the final decisions and oversees everything. I'm the president. Second in command." I paused to try to break it down in a brief way, so I didn't bore her. "Admittedly, I currently don't handle many time-consuming tasks on the corporate level. I oversee a couple of employees for the Midwest region—the Director of Ethics and the Director of Employee Affairs." She looked at me questioningly, so I explained further. "I like to make sure everything is ethical, legal, and morally sound. Often with big corporations, dealings are happening illegally or unethically. It's my job to make sure nothing like that happens at Lombardi Enterprises."

"That sounds like a tough job."

"Only if you have untrustworthy employees." I smiled and raised my eyebrows. "We don't. Well, not that we know of at least. They only call me if there is a problem, either with a current employee, client, or any other business dealing. Fortunately, I don't get called often."

"Very interesting. Are those all of your roles?" she asked curiously.

"No. Locally, my father and I own the gym, as you know. But I also own a share of Marley's Pub." I looked at her nervously. I hadn't wanted to bring up Marley's, for obvious reasons, but needed to be fully transparent in the businesses I was involved in. "We own a bowling alley..." She looked surprised by that one, "and an antique shop. All in Crystal Lake."

"Antique shop? Are you interested in vintage items?" She chuckled with a playful tone to her voice. I nodded silently while keeping my eyes on hers. I had thought, while being out of state last week, her mood had been so light because nothing had upset her there. She had been living in the moment every day without much thought of her past. But it seemed as if Montana had indeed had lasting effects so far.

Her joyful demeanor overwhelmed me to the point I needed to reach out and touch her to make sure our time together wasn't a dream. I tentatively moved toward her on the blanket, so I could grab her feet from under her long skirt. She looked curious and confused, but let me slowly pick them up and put them on my lap. Unhurriedly, I started unbuckling her sandals to expose her bare feet. I grabbed one of them and started massaging the bottom of it with my thumbs. Her eyes closed and she took a deep breath.

"Back to your question about antiques," I said as I rubbed from the ball of her foot to her heel. "I appreciate heirlooms, old treasures, or anything that was built of greater quality than today's standards. The current motto seems to be 'cheaper quality at a higher price.' I much prefer how things were made a half-century ago or longer even." I worked on her other foot. She appeared to not be listening as intently anymore. Her eyes were closed. She was enjoying my foot massage. "Am I boring you, Ms. Cora?" I teased.

"Hmm?" She opened her eyes and looked a little dazed. "No, not at all."

"Does this feel good?" I asked, knowing the answer already. She nodded lazily and closed her eyes again.

When I had thoroughly taken care of both feet, I was at a crossroads... Stop? Keep going? Keep going, but *higher*? I didn't want to ruin her relaxed mood, but couldn't imagine my hands leaving her skin.

Right as the angel and devil on my shoulders were arguing about appropriateness, Jane's phone rang. She instantly shook her feet out of my grasp and rose to find her phone. "I'm sorry. I have to answer this..."

"No worries at all."

She found her phone and answered with happiness in her voice. "Hallå? Morsa...Hur mår du?" She sat down on the blanket and crossed her legs.

My eyes popped open wide. She obviously wasn't speaking English. I guessed it was Swedish. Her features told me she was overjoyed to hear from whoever was on the other end. I assumed it was one of her parents, but I'd have to wait until she was finished. It had to be the middle of the night over there. Whomever she was speaking to was a night owl.

While she was preoccupied, I uncrossed her legs to pull them toward me and mindlessly rubbed her feet again. I was in my own thoughts—and fantasies—as I listened to the beautiful foreign words coming out of her. With a little courage from the devil on my shoulder, I traveled up to her calf muscles. She glanced my way but didn't make any motion to stop me. One leg at a time, I rubbed up and down, from the back of her knee to the bottom of her calf. I used my knuckles to allow for more pressure on her muscles. She was still very engaged in her conversation but sent looks and grins my way on occasion.

When both her lower legs were evenly rubbed, I got on my knees to continue higher up. Paying attention to her body language and cues, I slowly pushed her long, loose skirt up just past her knees to allow me access to the back of her thighs. With one leg flat on the blanket and the other with a slightly bent knee and foot down, I pressed my fingers at the junction of her hamstring and the back of her knee. She jumped and winced. "Sorry," I muttered softly.

The person on the other end of the line must have caught her being distracted because her cheeks flushed pink in an instant. Even in another language, it sounded as if she was explaining what had just happened. I was curious if she told the truth or made up a story.

She continued her conversation, more serious now, but made no motion for me to stop, so I tried again. I pressed gentler than before in the same area. Yes, it was very tight, but she didn't react with a wince. She seemed more involved with the conversation than my light touch. Her tone changed; she was ending the phone call soon.

"Jag älskar dig. Hej då." She finished the call and then took a deep breath.

"Welcome back to America." I grinned and kept massaging her tight hamstring.

She took in the view of my hands on her leg. "I'm sorry. It was my mom. She's been up all night with my grandpa. She wants me to visit him soon. He's starting to decline."

I frowned at the news. "I'm sorry to hear that," I murmured. She did not need any more death in her life.

"It's okay, thanks. I don't know him well. I was never close to any of my grandparents." That made sense. She had been born in the States and all of her family lived in Sweden. "Either way," she continued, "I'm due for a trip there. I really should go see him and my other grandparents, while they're still around."

I nodded in agreement. As much as I didn't want her to leave for any length of time, I saw the importance. "When did you tell her you'd go?"

"She said I didn't need to rush onto a plane this week. She knows I just started back at the salon, so within the next few weeks." She kept her eyes on where I worked.

"You're very tight," I informed her and then chuckled under my breath at the dirty double meaning that entered my mind.

She must have caught it because she grinned and blushed. "I haven't had a proper massage in years."

"I hope this helps then. May I continue?"

She nodded slowly and lowered her torso to the blanket.

I continued my work with my knuckles pressing a little firmer on the tight area just above the back of her knee. When I felt it release, I moved up her leg to the center of her hamstring. I rubbed up and down the long muscles, pressing higher with each stroke. I took my time and enjoyed the silkiness of an area I hadn't felt yet. When I made it to the top of her leg, I anticipated feeling an undergarment. However, only her bare, soft skin met the back of my hand.

Immediately, those parts of me that had been awake and ready to crash the picnic—but forced to stay contained deep inside me—clawed to the surface at rapid speed. Without thinking it through, my fingers pushed her skirt higher. I lowered down and placed my lips above the inside of her bent knee. She gasped quietly but made no attempt to stop me.

Delicate flower.

I needed reassurance.

"If this is not okay, please tell me." She didn't reply which I took as permission. Feeling brave, I pushed her skirt even higher while I placed a hand on her opposite hip. Every movement she allowed me to make felt like a gift. These were uncharted waters for me. I wasn't used to taking it so slowly. Nevertheless, I had to admit I enjoyed it. The baby steps I've been taking were way more pleasurable than anything I'd ever done in the past.

With her skirt as high as it could go, and bunched in the middle to prevent the revealing of her intimate areas, I continued my path where I'd left off. With slow and measured movements, I placed my lips on her soft skin. I paused each time to take in her scent—and taste. Kiss by kiss, up the inside of her leg, I felt the atmosphere changing. My heart rate increased by the second. Her body temperature rose each time my lips explored the new, higher area. Every move I made, even the simple act of holding onto her hip, felt like a dream. There had been times I'd doubted she'd ever give me permission to touch her—or taste her. But she was allowing me to kiss her delicate skin.

Unreal.

When I was more than halfway up her thigh, daydreaming about all the areas I wanted to taste, she ever-so-slightly pressed her leg out to the side, as if she'd read my mind and was allowing me easier access. That small gesture lit a fire in me I couldn't describe. I had never been hungrier in my entire life. I raised my head to look at her; I needed confirmation her movement was to intentionally send a message. She had one arm behind her head for support, and the other one rested over her eyes. If I had to guess what she was feeling, I would have said she had a few conflicting emotions—calm, embarrassed, and...horny. Yes, there was no doubt in my mind she was also hungry in the same way I was.

Satisfied with what I saw in her expression, I found where I had left off and proceeded upward. I reached a more sensitive area, so I brushed my lips very gently up and down the highest part of her inner thigh. I inched my way closer and closer to the site of her pheromones. *Fuck*, she smelled so good. The stubble of my five o'clock shadow tickled her skin as I continued to kiss her. Her hips and waist moved around ever so slightly, getting impatient for what they anticipated to be next.

When I was at the junction of where her leg met her unmentionable area, a very irritating, unwanted thought popped up to the forefront of my brain before I could swat it away:

I could not, in good conscience, go any further without first kissing her properly on the lips.

I had kissed many areas of her body, but our lips had never met. I'd been dreaming of our first kiss for months. The experience couldn't be rushed or done out of order. Not with Jane. In all my years, I had never cared, nor even thought about, the steps in courting a woman. Most women threw themselves at me on the first night.

Jane was different. *A delicate flower.* She was worth the effort to run the bases in order, and we hadn't even made it to first yet. While my primal instincts snarled and reminded me of the long, sexless week I'd endured with my girl in the beautiful state of Montana, my more reasonable side was proud I'd paused to recognize such an important step. It was the gentlemanly thing to do.

With a sigh that surely tickled her skin, I kissed back down her leg and met her knee again. I released my hand from her hip to bear my weight as I pressed myself forward. Her arm was still draped across her face, so I gently pried it over her head and intertwined our hands together on the grass. She opened her eyes and stared back at me with nothing but deep, desiring anticipation. I leaned down slowly for what would finally, after waiting so long, be our first official kiss.

"Umm, *hey* guys."

We both jumped when we heard a voice holler from about forty feet away.

Fuck. Me. Can't a guy catch a break? The sexual tension that had been building popped like a balloon as Jane hurriedly pushed me out of the way to sit up and lower her skirt. In her haste, she knocked over one of the wine glasses, which frazzled her even more. She quickly rose to her feet to find something to clean the mess as our unwelcome visitor neared closer. She blotted the blanket with napkins and stood up again with her hands on her hips, brushing her loose tendrils away from her face, sighing loudly and looking guiltier than a thirty-something-year-old should. I chuckled to myself and stood with her.

"Hello, sir," I said, realizing it was a park ranger.

He smirked. "It's approaching dusk. The park is closing in thirty minutes." He narrowed his eyes at us, one at a time, as if we were students who had been caught cheating or something. "It's time to take your picnic elsewhere."

Had we sat there for six hours?

"Yes, sir," I responded respectfully. The ranger turned and left as quickly as he'd come. Jane packed up immediately. She shook out the wet blanket and folded it away from her body to not stain her clothes. I helped where I could, but she was on a mission to get out of there. She had a wide grin on her face while she worked.

"What's so funny?" I grinned back at her. Her expression was contagious.

"Oh, nothing," she remarked and went back to removing the evidence that we'd spent a half a day together in the field.

I glanced at Jane a few times on the walk back. She had that same smirk the entire time. It was times like these when I wished I could read her mind. What could be so amusing? I felt anything but amused. While I was happy to be anywhere as long as she was by my side, I was more than a little aggravated that a park ranger had interrupted us. I had been patiently waiting for well over a year to touch those lips. I finally had the moment. We were alone. She seemed willing and ready. And it was ripped away from me.

About halfway to the parking lot, I couldn't contain my annoyance anymore. "Are you as frustrated as I am?" I asked her. She looked surprised and hurt by my comment.

"With what?" Her brow furrowed in confusion.

I had no words. I would have to show her. I stopped her right on the trail, turned her toward me, grabbed the sides of her face, and went for it. It wasn't exactly how I wanted our first kiss to be, with so much force coming from me, but I needed the yearlong desire to be fulfilled. I needed the deep ache from the last week to disintegrate. I grabbed her neck gently and pressed her soft lips to mine over and over. The connection was electric. My heart jumped into my throat, then down into my stomach, at the sensation of her mouth on mine. It was the most amazing feeling I'd ever had. I wrapped my hands in her hair and let my needs take over. I could tell she enjoyed it, but she seemed a little shocked...or nervous. Her arms were down at her sides in a stiff position. Without breaking the kiss, I let go of her hair, found her hands, and put them on the sides of my neck. I then placed my hands on the back of her shoulders and pulled her deeper into my grasp. Her smell intoxicated me. I didn't know if I could ever stop. Our embrace may have lasted thirty seconds or five minutes, I wasn't sure. Time stood still.

Unfortunately, as if he hadn't spoiled enough of the mood, the park ranger walked up behind us. "Okay, you two love birds, beat it," he teased. We let go of each other and turned toward the parking lot, without looking the ranger's way. Jane's cheeks were flushed with embarrassment.

"Oh, one more thing," the park ranger yelled, making us turn in his direction. "It's tick season. You may want to check yourselves out before you sleep."

"Thank you for the info, sir," Jane said. When she turned to continue the trail to the car, I kept my gaze on him. He winked at me, as if he just scored me an opportunity, before he turned to walk in the other direction.

I shook my head, chuckled under my breath, and caught up to Jane.

13

Jane

HOW SHOULD A girl thank a guy for almost—but not quite—kissing her most sensitive of areas? For getting her aroused and excited in ways she hadn't been in at least a decade? Was it an unspoken assumption that he knew of the gift he gave her, even if it wasn't completed in the way he—or she—wanted? Did she need to tell him his actions took her very close to a place she didn't think she could go again? Was a thank you even necessary?

Did a widow need to apologize to her late husband for what had happened in the field? Did she have to say sorry for allowing herself to feel all the incredible sensations another man gave her? Should she feel guilty about any of it? Did her family members in heaven think it was all too soon?

My mind was on overdrive on the way back to my in-laws'. There were so many thoughts and questions spinning inside my head that I couldn't grab onto one single portion long enough to find a solution. A loud part, my surface voice, shouted at me for not keeping my legs closed. She questioned how I had just spent many nights under the same roof as Alex without any funny business, but one afternoon on a picnic blanket somehow weakened my resolve.

On the contrary, deep inner voice was proud of my bravery. She hastily climbed on her counterpart's back, attempting to cover surface's mouth from berating me any further.

Even louder than my internal dialogues fighting with each other was the *feeling* I still experienced between my legs. I had a hard time sitting still in Alex's Wrangler. Every way I put my legs had my lower central area throbbing. Each time I felt the throbbing in a new position, my cheeks burned hot with fresh blush. Therefore, I kept my face turned out the window and stayed quiet. I hoped he wouldn't misunderstand my silence as being upset. As much as my inner turmoil was overwhelming, I was far from upset with *him*. He had been incredibly patient with me. He knew I needed to take everything at a snail's pace, but I didn't blame him for allowing his hormones to take over.

Regardless, hormones or not, I didn't know if I was ready for what he wanted. In that acute moment on the picnic blanket, I had been ready. Now heading back home with my head a little clearer, I didn't know what I wanted.

No. That wasn't correct. I knew what I wanted. I didn't know if what I wanted was okay and appropriate.

I was a mess of conflicting emotions.

I shook my head and took a deep breath. All the answers didn't need to be figured out right away, I reminded myself. Deep inner voice patted me on the back for being so level-headed. I looked at Alex, who glanced over at me with a deeply concerned look. My heart sank in an instant. *I was a terrible person.* The beautiful man next to me had probably been watching all my different anguished faces for however many minutes we'd been in the Jeep, and having a much different inner turmoil in his own head.

It was at that moment, looking at the pain in his eyes, when a significant shift happened in my mindset. It felt like a lightning bolt shot right down my spine to awaken me to some important realizations: Alex was here, present with me. He was trying to do right by me. He would never pressure me. He'd proved that to be true at the ranch.

That being said, there was no denying how much he adored me. Plus, he was very much alive. And he had needs. I needed to do right by him too. I could at least try, with no promises. I was sure I was not ready to jump into any sort of relationship. Also, I *wasn't* certain I was willing to give him *all* of me. Only one person knew every part of my body. I didn't know if I was ready to take that privilege away from Graham. I had to keep something sacred in honor of him, at least for a little while longer.

Not too long, deep inner voice whispered.

Hussy, Surface voice scolded. The loud internal insult shocked me like a slap to the face. Deep inner voice tackled her and covered her mouth again. I suppressed a giggle. My internal dialogues were amusing when they weren't making me feel like I needed a padded cell.

While they were distracted, I tried to figure out the dilemma on my own...

So maybe I wasn't ready to give Alex *all* of me, but he could have *some* of me. It did not have to be all or nothing. Did it? I could commit to some. I wanted to actually. And that would have to be enough for now.

If I knew what the heck to do. My inexperience made me blush again.

I reached over to his side of the Jeep to grab his hand. I wasn't sure how my face appeared, but I tried to make it look reassuring. I hoped he saw in my eyes that I wasn't going to run out of his vehicle screaming for the security of my in-laws as soon as he parked.

It was about then when I realized we should have made it back to the house already. I looked out the window as we were turning into an unfamiliar driveway. I eyed him questioningly.

Alex slowed down to a stop. He still had the concerned look on his face. "Yesterday you mentioned you hardly knew me." He put on a shy smile, but the worry was still there. "I thought maybe you'd want to see where I live." He paused and kissed the hand he held. "I can take you home if you'd rather—"

"No." I squeezed his hand. "I'd love to see your place." I peered out the window to get a good view, but it was mostly dark outside. I did notice the house was of considerable size. Not surprising. I couldn't see much detail aside from that. I'd have to wait until daylight to examine it further.

He pulled the Wrangler into his multicar detached garage, which stood behind the house. I knew of him having only two vehicles: his Jeep and the one we took on our first real date. Turned out, he also had a vintage car. If I were into that sort of thing, I'd know the year, make, and model. But since I knew nothing about cars, all I could tell about it was it was green, large, a convertible, impressive-looking, and old. It was the kind of car you took out for long joy rides on Sunday mornings. The thought of doing just that, with Alex next to me at the wheel, made my heart skip a beat. I could picture the wind whipping through my hair while listening to Breakfast with the Beatles on the radio. We would stop for coffee in some remote town and all the locals would walk around the big green machine and whistle at how fine she was. The fantasy felt so real I could taste it.

Tucked to the side of the garage was a yellow and black motorcycle that looked as if it could only go one speed—very fast. I shuddered at the thought of him, or anyone else, speeding down the road with no sort of protection around them. I wasn't against motorcycles, but they had always seemed very reckless.

Alex noticed my shudder. "Would you like to take it for a quick spin around the block?" he asked, obviously teasing me.

"Sure. Take me for a ride," I replied sarcastically.

"I'd love to." His eyes were intense in an instant. There was definitely a double meaning behind his words, which made blood rush to my cheeks once again. He blinked away the intensity and continued, "One day I'll take you out on it. Not at night. And not with wine in me." He grabbed the picnic basket from the Jeep in one hand and took my hand in his other. "Speaking of wine, let's go finish our picnic."

Alex brought me in the back entrance of his home, which opened into a huge, spotless mudroom, if you could call it that. There was no mud to be seen—or anything else dirty for that matter. He led me into the kitchen which opened up to the rest of the first level. Next to the kitchen was a large dining table. Adjacent to the kitchen and eating area was the living room. I immediately took in his style and decor. It wasn't riddled with the common fads I'd seen in most homes. Everything was not white or gray. There were no farm signs to be seen.

Instead, his house exuded bachelor pad class with hints of vintage. The kitchen cabinets and island were black with brassy gold hardware. White granite counters lay on top of the cabinets. The appliances were flat black and screamed expensive. They belonged in the fanciest of cooking show kitchens, especially the range. There was minimal on top of the counters, but everything on display—a kitchen aid mixer, a fruit bowl, a scale, a clock, and a basket to hold keys—was from another time period. There was a stark difference between modern and antique, but somehow it all fit so well together. He must've had help from a designer...or an ex-girlfriend.

Alex went to work finding wine flutes to pour us each a fresh glass. "Make yourself at home," he told me as he moved about his kitchen. I moseyed into the living area which featured two beautiful tan leather couches, a recliner, and a coffee table. Everything was impressive-looking and high-end. My hand grazed across the back of a couch. It felt like butter. The furniture was set up to focus on his grand fireplace and giant TV above the mantle.

I walked a slow loop around the open floor plan, taking in every bit of his home—the expensive-looking rugs, the large art pieces on the walls from a different time, the giant windows covered with sheer curtains. There was something about the space that reminded me of the last book series I'd read many years ago—pre-kids—when I'd had time to read books. I couldn't place exactly *why* his home made me think of the books, aside from the masculinity emitting from every square inch. Either way, remembering that book series sparked my curiosity about the rest of the house.

I made my way back to the kitchen where Alex was standing at the island, ready with our wine. He handed me a glass. "So what do you think?"

I strolled away from him, toward the dining table. Those books were still on my mind as I headed to the opposite side of the table from him. If I was going to be brave, I needed a buffer between us. "Mmm," I stated pensively as I took a sip of wine. "It's very nice. You have good taste." I kept my distance so he wouldn't see the flush of my cheeks. "This is a big house for one person." His eyes narrowed as he nodded his head slowly. He definitely didn't know where the conversation was headed, but I had him intrigued. I kept with the vague comments. "Lots of rooms." I took another sip of my wine and walked farther away from him, toward the row of windows on the opposite wall of the kitchen.

"Lots of rooms. Yes," he replied, still confused.

"Rooms that get used for different purposes..." I stated, feeling braver than I have in....well, maybe ever.

He stared at me and nodded again. The curiosity was blazing in his eyes.

For over a year, Reese had continually reminded me of Alex's history with women. Just about every time Alex's name had been mentioned, she'd let me know I was flirting with fire. So it wouldn't be *too* far off to wonder if he had ever dabbled in the dark world of BDSM. I couldn't tease him any longer. I needed to know. "There's no red room of pain here, right?"

Alex's mouth dropped open in complete amazement. He quickly recovered and narrowed his eyes again but included the sexiest smile I had seen to date. "Ms. Cora, are you a fan of Mr. Grey?"

I took a sip of wine for more courage, keeping my distance from him. "You didn't answer my question." Alex chuckled quietly and looked to the floor. It appeared he had some sort of private or inside joke running through his head.

A moment later his eyes were on me as if I was his prey. He took his time heading in my direction. Now it was his turn to tease me with evasiveness. "I've never read the *Fifty Shades of Grey* series." His tone was light, non-threatening. "But naturally, I've heard all about them." Every step toward me was calculated. "Are you interested in that sort of thing?"

I pressed my lips together firmly. I refused to answer or react until he told me what I needed to know.

"Is that a fantasy of yours?" he asked, rewording his original question. I kept my face as neutral as possible while he taunted me with his words. A layer of light sweat started to build on my skin. My heart was beating out of my chest in anticipation.

When he finally made it to where I stood, he took my glass and set it on the table. My heart continued to race. It was so loud in my ears that I wondered if he could hear it. He placed his hands on the sides of my neck and kissed me for the second time ever. His tender touch took my breath away.

It felt so good to be kissed.

I hadn't realized how lonely my lips had been. I kissed him back the best I knew how. I was definitely out of practice. He trailed kisses onto my cheek and then found my neck. Pulling me closer to him, he took my hands and placed them on his hips. There was an urgency building with his touch. He was desperate for the connection.

You need it too, deep inner voice whispered.

My head became cloudy with his mouth and aroma all over me, but I wasn't going to let him totally distract me. I needed to know what I was getting myself into. I needed to know what *he* was into and if there was a playroom somewhere in his house. It took a lot of strength to be able to talk in the moment, with his soft, greedy lips all over my mouth and neck, but I managed a few words. "You still haven't answered," I said breathlessly.

He kept up the exploration of my skin with his mouth. His lips pulled up into a smile as he placed kisses under my chin. "I forgot the question." I let out a nervous giggle and attempted to pull away from him. He held me close so I couldn't escape and brought his lips to my ear. "Only if you want there to be," he whispered.

A shiver ran down my spine. I attempted to pull away again, just enough so he could see my wide eyes and shocked mouth. "What kind of sideways answer is that?" I asked, stunned.

He pulled me back into him. "Feel free to tour the upstairs." He brought the kisses up to just behind my ear. "See if you can find it." He made his way back to my mouth and kissed me gently once. "I can meet you up there if you like what you see." His stare was intense again. My entire body was singing with desire. Did I want that? So soon?

Yes. Yes, you do, deep inner voice answered.

I shook her opinion away. *Want* and *should* were two separate categories in life.

I honestly couldn't tell if Alex was serious or bluffing, so I played it safe. "Hard pass," I said playfully as I pulled all the way away from him to grab my wine glass and take a breath. He chuckled, grabbed my hand, and guided me to the living area.

ALEX AND I chatted on the opposite ends of his couch for a while about nothing important. We finally finished the bottle of wine I'd brought to the field, so he opened another one to share. After sitting there for maybe a half hour, he stared at me with a grin on his face.

"Are you going to tell me what you did yesterday?" he asked.

I assumed his curiosity had to do with Dean. I didn't want to lie to Alex, but I needed some information in return. "That depends. Are you going to tell me why you're being secretive about your siblings?" I retorted, with an eyebrow raised.

"Not secretive. Just trying to protect you." My face must have shown my confusion, so he continued, "We've had a really good day. I don't want to ruin it." He focused down at his glass. Whatever he was hiding was hard to talk about.

"Nothing you say to me about your siblings will ruin the high I've been on all day."

Alex looked at me with pleasant surprise in his eyes. He took a deep breath and let it out through his nose. "Before I share, I want you to know I'm totally healed. I am at peace with the past. There's no need to feel sorry for me, okay?"

I nodded.

"We moved here when my identical twin brother and I were three years old. My sister, Molly, was five."

Identical twin brother. My heart sank. Maybe I didn't want to know about his siblings after all.

He must not have caught the hesitation on my face, because he continued, "My mother joined a mom's group right away to meet girlfriends and also socialize us. On a hot day in the summer, we were invited to one of the other mom's houses in town that had a pool. There were a ton of kids running around the backyard, hopping in and out of the pool. My mom lost track of my brother, Tony. He either fell into the pool or jumped in without floaties. Nobody saw it happen."

My eyes teared up. I knew the obvious end of the story.

Alex looked down and traced the rim of his wine glass with his finger. "He was found lifeless. There was nothing anyone could do."

I immediately left my side of the couch and landed on top of him so I could give him a proper hug. I couldn't help the urge to embrace him. He'd lost his twin brother at such an early age. That had to have impacted his entire life. I nestled into him the best I could. "Alex, I am so sorry," I said with all the sincerity in the world. "I wish you would have told me sooner."

"It's okay. Truly. Over the years, I've willed myself to believe I will see him again one day. I went to therapy as a kid and as an adult. I even went to a grief summer camp for a few years." He put down his wine, draped his arms around me, and laid a kiss on my forehead. "I didn't tell you because I didn't want you to think I understood what you're going through. I can relate to an extent, but I cannot compare the two tragedies. It didn't feel right to mention it when your pain is so much deeper than mine."

He'd hidden his story to protect me from his pain. As much as I appreciated it, it made me a little uneasy. "You're too good to me," I mumbled into his chest.

"You're worth it," he stated with another kiss on my forehead.

I lay there for a while in Alex's arms, my head resting just under his collarbone. I tried to picture two of him in the world. Alex seemed so one of a kind. It was a difficult vision to have. I shook away the thought and said a prayer for little Tony. I silently asked him to play with Marric and Arlo up in heaven.

We cuddled in comfortable silence for a long while. Every couple of minutes, Alex kissed my hairline and squeezed me a little tighter. At some point, I closed my eyes and concentrated only on the soothing beat of his heart beneath me. I must have fallen asleep to the rhythm of his pulse until he stirred a bit underneath me and cleared his throat.

"You seem very comfortable in my arms," he said, sounding satisfied.

My mini nap had me groggy. "Mmm. Guess I am."

"Have we turned a corner this week?" he asked with a little excitement in his voice.

"Mmm," I repeated, turning my face in to nuzzle his chest. "I don't want to get your hopes up."

He chuckled quietly. "Can I ask you a question?"

"Depends on what it is," I stated cautiously.

He kissed the top of my head again and rubbed my back gently. "Did it feel good this afternoon? To be...touched?"

My cheeks flamed crimson. I nestled my face deeper into his shirt to hide. "Yes," I mumbled.

He burrowed his hands under the fabric of my top to tickle my bare skin. He was so warm. "Do you wish I could have finished what I started?"

If cheeks could start on fire, mine would be ablaze. My inner turmoil came back to me in an instant, but my physical desires and needs were louder than any worries I'd felt earlier. "Yes," I said directly into his chest, part of me hoped he didn't hear me.

I was so inexperienced in every single part of dating and beyond. Only having one sexual partner will do that to a person. Alex had given me no reason to feel so self-conscious. Unfortunately, that didn't stop my worries and hesitations. All of a sudden, I had an irresistible urge to lay it all on the line for him. Right at that moment. No holds barred.

"Alex?" I was going to do it. I needed to do it.

"Jane?" he mimicked, sounding amused.

"How many partners have you had?" I felt my heartbeat in my ears again.

"How many girlfriends?" His tone was laced with hesitation.

"No. How many partners." I nuzzled my face into his neck. I had a reason for asking him such a personal question. He needed to provide me with his answer to see why.

He was quiet for a minute or so. I could feel his pulse quickening in his neck. "Can I say it doesn't matter what the number is? That you're the last person I plan to share myself with, if you'll have me?" He sounded very sincere. And very worried.

"I need to know," I said quietly. I'd get to the point eventually.

He let out a breath. "Honestly, I'm not totally sure. If I were to guess, I'd say...in the forties?"

My mouth popped open in shock. That was a lot of women.

"Do you think less of me?" His tone still sounded concerned.

I shook my head as my lips grazed his neck. And I truly didn't. It wasn't about how experienced he was. It was about how grossly inexperienced *I* was.

"May I ask yours?" he asked.

I held up one finger, another wave of red hitting my cheeks.

He tried to move to see my face, but I resisted. "Jane, are you embarrassed by that?"

Emotion bubbled up from my throat. I couldn't answer him. How could I ever compare to all those women?

"Jane, please look at me."

I could not get myself to move. He leaned away from me and raised my chin so he could see my tear-filled eyes. I kept my gaze away from his; I was too mortified for eye contact.

"I may have a high number, but you're the only one who matters."

I closed my eyes and let the tears fall.

"What are you thinking? What has you so upset?"

Such a loaded question. "I don't know. This is humiliating. I have no idea what I'm doing in *that* department, Alex." I wiped the tears from my face. "Sure, we had three kids, so I know *some* things. We were always satisfied with each other. But I assure you I don't compare to any of those other girls. How can I even compete?" Fresh tears pooled over my lids.

He kissed my forehead again and pressed his lips where my tears were falling. "Silly, gorgeous girl, there's no competition. I don't care about what you know. I want you, all of you, the way you are right now."

I shook my head. "You say that, but I don't think you've been with someone like me."

"I'm a good teacher." He kissed me so tenderly that it almost made a new wave of tears erupt. He grabbed my hips to smoothly press me to the inside of the couch. "Let me lead you." He kissed me over and over as he was positioning his body to get out from under mine. "Let me show you how good it can be."

"It wasn't bad with my husband," I mumbled, feeling the need to defend Graham.

He released himself from my body weight and somehow in an instant had my body pinned under his. He looked down at me with honest, caring eyes, but I couldn't get myself to keep eye contact with him. "I understand every relationship is different. It's good that you both were happy. But if you're saying you two weren't adventurous, I'd like to show you...other things. Maybe things you've never done. Things that you may love." He bent down and kissed my forehead. "Not tonight necessarily. But eventually." He straddled me with his lower half, leaving my legs close together. His arms bore his weight next to my shoulders. "Please trust me." I still couldn't look at him. He noticed and gripped my chin so our eyes had to meet. "There's nothing to be embarrassed about." His face was so sincere; it was hard not to believe him.

I still did my best to avert my eyes, but at least the tears were drying up. Alex kissed my lips again before he moved to the side of my face. "Do you know what makes you feel good?" His whisper tickled my ear.

I shook my head.

He moved down my neck, trailing his lips slowly from below my ear to my collarbone. He lifted his head so he could see my face. "Do you have a vibrator?" he asked, as if it was a perfectly normal question to ask someone.

I put my hands over my face and shook my head. My cheeks were on fire once again.

"Have you ever owned one?"

I shook my head again, thankful my face was still hidden.

He pried my hands from my face. "Jane, please look at me." His tone was so sympathetic that I complied. "Have you never pleasured yourself?" He sounded surprised—but not judgmentally. More in a "you've been seriously depriving yourself" way.

I shook my head once again, looking away from his burning stare. "I never felt like I needed a...vibrator." Whatever the next level past "humiliated" was, I'd hit it. I wished I could crawl into a dark hole and never come out.

"So you don't know what makes you tick," he mused. He restarted the trailing of his lips, but headed lower, to the area between my breasts. Even through the fabric of my top, the sensation was amazing. He was waking up that throbbing I'd had earlier in his Jeep. I involuntarily squirmed my lower half underneath him to calm the building ache. "Hmm, we'll have to change that very soon," he stated, still exploring my cleavage, or what would be my cleavage, if I had any. "You need to know what pleases you. And you need to be able to tell me. Communication is very important to me." He trailed his fingers on my abdomen and then grabbed the hem of my shirt. "May I?" he asked. His eyes still had sincerity shining back at me.

Before I could change my mind, I nodded. He lifted my shirt over my head, leaving me in my white lacy, sheer bra. He looked down at me with hunger bright in his eyes. He let his fingertips explore the skin he'd just exposed which sent yet another shiver through my entire body. "This will be lesson number one. I hope you're a good student," he teased, probably trying to lighten my mood.

"I'm a dropout," I replied, attempting to hide the quiver in my voice. I could not remember the last time I felt so nervous...or turned on. "Might as well fail me now."

He explored my newly exposed garment with his mouth and nose, as if he was trying to breathe in as much of my scent as possible. His hands were on the sides of my lower ribs, holding me where I was. That simple placement had my hips writhing again. He was too damn sexy for his own good.

"There's a 'no fail' policy with me, Ms. Cora." He kept exploring until he found one of my nipples through the lacy fabric. My breathing halted while he enjoyed the area with his tongue before he sucked the tender spot into his mouth.

You're way out of your league, surface voice informed me. I tried to keep my heart from beating completely out of my chest.

"You're dangerously beautiful, Jane. Everything about you," Alex whispered, as if he heard my internal self-doubt. He tenderly rubbed his thumb over the wet fabric that had just been in his mouth while he moved on to my other breast with his lips. The stroking of his thumb made my nipple stand at attention and my back lift off the couch. "Do you like that?" he asked, already knowing the answer. I didn't say anything. The anxiety of totally sucking at making out with Alex was overwhelming. I closed my eyes to prevent the insecurities from showing on my features.

Apparently, my attempt didn't work. He met my face to give me a brief kiss on the lips and to rub our noses together. "Baby girl, there's nothing to be embarrassed about," he repeated the same words from earlier. "It's just you and me here. You've had my heart in your pocket since the moment I laid eyes on you. There is nothing you could do that would push me away. Not even your lack of experience. In fact, your innocence will make this even better." My eyes were still closed, but his pep talk helped. The nerves calmed down. "Please open your eyes." It was more of a request than a demand. My eyes were greeted with Alex's beautiful, caring face staring back at me. "You're perfect the way you are, minimal experience and all." He kissed the tip of my nose, which made me smile hesitantly. "Back to my question. Did you like that feeling?"

I closed my eyes again and nodded, cheeks on fire once again. It was going to take time for the insecurities and self-consciousness to subside. I hoped he was a patient teacher.

Alex went back to touring my upper half with his mouth while the back of his hand traveled down my waist, my hip, all the way to the back of my knee. He lifted my knee so my bent leg could rest on the side of the couch. With slow, calculated movements he found the bottom of my skirt and tucked his hand under the fabric. He used his knuckles to tickle my skin, from my calf all the way up to the back of my thigh. His light touch sent more electrical impulses all over my body. After he traveled up and down a few times, he gingerly ran his fingers over my most sensitive of areas. My body reacted to his touch, which gave his fingers some moisture to play with.

It felt so good to be touched.

He swept his fingers side to side in the wettest area and then backed his hand out from under my skirt. "Jane, open your eyes," he ordered softly. I complied and when he saw he had my attention, he placed those same wet fingers in his mouth and sucked. My eyes shot open wider in surprise.

His eyes brightened back at me. "You are delectable." My mouth went wide, matching my eyes. I couldn't contain my shocked expression. He was too good at this. Way too good. *Next level* good. "Would you like to taste?"

"I think I'm good." I was trying—and failing—to sound in control of myself.

He laughed under his breath. "More for me," he said as he pulled my skirt down past my hips and tore it away from me. My one knee was still resting on the side of the couch, so he gently pulled my opposite leg away from my body. My heart beat faster than it had in at least a year. I could hardly hear anything aside from the whooshing of blood running through the vessels in my ears.

"Is this okay?" Alex asked suddenly, with the faintest of worry in his eyes.

I nodded, very sure it was okay. My body was more than ready.

He brought his mouth to mine as he searched for something on the floor with his hand. He found what he was looking for, a flat throw pillow, and lifted my body to place the pillow under my hips. Yes, he knew what he was doing. Instead of worrying about it, my hips became more excited. I could hardly lie still.

Alex smiled at the reactions my body made to his touch. He slowly dove his hands under my bra line to unhook and remove the only part of clothing left on my body. He sat upright to take me in. His intense chocolate eyes worshipped every inch of my exposed body. I resisted the urge to close my eyes and cover my face. Instead, I looked back at him, trusting that he liked what he saw.

Speaking of liking what *I* saw, he was way too clothed, especially compared to my nakedness. I went to grip the edge of his shirt to remove it, but he grabbed my hands in protest. He shook his head at me while maintaining eye contact. "Oh no, baby. Not yet. You first." He kissed my hands and swept them over my head to rest on the arm of the couch. "Always you first." He held them firmly in place for a moment, willing me to keep them there when he let go. I complied while he moved down my body, painfully slow. He started with his lips to mine. Then he kissed straight down to my chin, to the center of my neck, and down in between my breasts. He chose a side to taunt with tender kisses while he used his thumb to stroke the opposite nipple. My entire body was on fire. I swore I could climax right then and be totally satisfied. However, the deprived side of me really wanted to finish the way I knew he intended, so I kept myself together.

Barely.

When he was done stroking my nipple, he moved his lips to that side while he trailed his hand down to the area between my legs. It was wet and ready for him. He played there for a moment, teasing me. An involuntary and very unexpected moan escaped my lips. I could feel his satisfied silent chuckle from his lips on my hot skin. He moved his mouth down to my stomach, trailing kisses in a straight line. As he traveled south, he subtly spread my legs apart a little more. Once he made it to the goal line, he took the thick part of his palm and pressed it onto my pubic area. Pushing upward, toward my navel, he exposed more of what he was after. He licked my clit and I almost came right then. My belly contracted and my legs tensed.

"Not yet, baby," he repeated his statement from before, only for a different reason. He knew I was already on the edge. "I'm just getting started." There was excitement hanging in his words. My hips thrust slightly in his direction. He grabbed onto them and went in to savor some more. He let out a soft, deep moan. His tongue was an expert. He mixed it up between slow strokes and then quick. Each change was a different and better sensation. "Do you like that?" he stopped briefly to ask. I couldn't answer. No words came out when I tried. At some point, my hands landed in his hair. I lost all track of time and space. I felt the pressure building in my veins. I heard Alex moan my name in contentment on occasion.

After another minute or so, the pressure was at near peak. "Don't stop," I told him in between deep breaths. Conscious that I was close, Alex revved up his motions. And that was it; I exploded into a sea of ecstasy. Nothing else existed except Alex, me, and my first orgasm in....I don't even know how long.

He kept going with his tongue until I told him he could stop. He took one last long lick and came right up to my lips to share the flavor. I was too busy enjoying the high to concern myself with my own taste.

Alex let me recover for a moment, with an intense and triumphant look on his face. "Hi," he said shyly before he kissed the sensitive spot below my ear.

"Hi," I replied. My voice hoarse.

"How was that?" he mumbled into my skin.

Like he even had to ask...

"Okay. Mediocre," I teased. He stopped and looked up at me. My joke made him smile for a second, but then his features became contemplative. Did he have some insecurities too? I couldn't tell what he was thinking, but after what he'd just done for me, I owed it to him to be truthful. "It was..." I had a hard time describing what I was feeling, "phenomenal. Thank you."

He bent down to kiss me again. "No. Thank *you.*"

"I haven't even done anything yet." He was still fully clothed. I brought my hands to his shirt and he let me lift it over his head. I was working on his belt while he stared at me with the most appreciative eyes.

"Oh, I disagree. You've done so much for me." He watched me struggle with his belt, but he didn't assist. "You just gave me everything I've been wanting. Everything I have fantasized about." He leaned down to kiss the nape of my neck again and then stared right into my eyes. "You have no idea, Jane." His voice was quiet with a hint of pain. "I've waited a year to taste you. It was better than I imagined," he whispered. His dirty words made my insides tighten once again.

I finally had his belt undone and was working on his jeans. He put a hand over where I was fumbling with the button, to hold my fingers in place. "You don't have to give me any more of you tonight," he assured me. "I know you need to take this slowly." I continued to mess with his button as he spoke. "I can still taste you. That's all I need."

Oh, his voice was so sexy. And I believed him. But there was no way I was going to prevent him from having a release too. I continued to try to unbutton the top of his jeans as he stared down at me.

"Jane." He slowly closed his eyes. "I'm more than satisfied. Please..."

My hands were too sweaty and shaky to release the button. I needed help. "Well, I'm not satisfied yet. So if you could help me remove your chastity belt, that would be great."

He laughed out loud and reluctantly unfastened the button. His eyes went back to worried in an instant. "Are you sure?"

"Yes," I said firmly. I finished the job by unzipping his pants and pulling them down. My eyes went wide at the sight of him in boxer briefs. I grabbed him through his briefs and watched his eyes roll back at my touch. I carefully pulled his briefs down too. He pushed both articles of clothing down his legs and off the couch. I took a moment to admire his marvelous, chiseled body. He was breathtaking. Complete perfection. His eyes stayed fixed on mine, as if he didn't want to miss any reaction I had to him. I stroked him up and down a few times and then directed him inside of me.

"Wait." He stilled himself. "I'm clean," he said firmly. "I assume you are too?"

I nodded.

"Are you on the pill?"

"I have an IUD," I stated, thankful he was asking important questions when I didn't.

"Even better," he replied with a grin. He stared down at my naked body. "You are the most incredible sight I have ever seen." He lowered himself to kiss and nuzzle my breasts before he came back up to my face. He cupped my cheek with one of his hands. "Are you sure you want this?" He repeated his concern. "There's no rush."

I grabbed onto the most intimate part of him again and stroked up and down. "I'm sure," I said with conviction.

He bent down to press the sweetest of kisses to my lips. I picked up where I had left off and guided him into me. I was still wet, so he slid in with ease. Our breathing hitched at the same time. He stared down at my face and body with overwhelming adoration. I blushed and closed my eyes to concentrate on the fullness of him in me. It felt incredible to have him in my darkest, most private of areas. I didn't know why I'd had so much inner turmoil. Our bodies connected felt nothing but right.

Alex pulsed slowly and rhythmically for a few minutes but then pulled out abruptly. I was in my own world of pleasure when it happened, so he caught me off guard.

"Wha—" was all I got out before he gently lifted me and placed me on my knees with the front of my body facing—and touching—the vertical side of the couch. He was behind me and tilted my hips up and back so he could insert from behind. He felt so *deep.* He took his hands and placed them on my breasts as he started pumping into me. *Oh my God*, it was a totally different sensation. I gripped the top edge of the couch as if it was a lifeline. He was far too good at this! And if that weren't enough, Alex took his fingers and started stroking my clit with one hand while holding onto my hip with the other. Another involuntary moan escaped my lips as he continued to both thrust his hips and play with me simultaneously.

And then a thought hit me to wake me up from my euphoria. A thought so strong that it was worth interrupting what we had going on. "Alex, I want to see you," I announced through my pleasure. Talking was not easy when it felt so good.

He didn't stop the motions of his body. "I'm right here, baby," he said breathlessly and kissed the side of my neck.

I shuddered at the culmination of his touches but needed to get my point across. "No, I want to *see* you. I want to watch the first time I make you—"

I couldn't finish the sentence.

He understood my request and in an instant we were in a totally different position. He sat on the couch and lowered my body onto his. That meant I had to do most of the work, which I was willing and ready to do. I moved up and down as his hips did their best to meet mine.

"Better?" he asked.

I looked into what I needed to see—his eyes. His wonderful, caring eyes that gazed up at me like I was the center of his world. "Yes."

The new position wasn't in the same pleasure category as how we'd just been, but being able to watch his reactions to my movement was more important. I did my best to please him with the pace of my lifting and lowering. His eyes closed and he rested his head on the back of the couch. The pattern of his thrusts went at a rhythmic, faster pace, so I knew he was almost there.

"Alex, open your eyes." He listened and locked his warm eyes right on mine. I didn't know why it was so imperative for me to see him, all of him, in the moment. Maybe to remind myself that he was there with me. That our intimacy was real and it was so coveted. I'd deprived him for a long time while he patiently waited for me to be ready to have any sort of connection. I needed to see his ecstasy up close. He pulsed hard a few more times as his breathing increased more and more. He let out a moan as he met his end and I smiled as I watched his whole body tremble in the aftermath.

We stayed in each other's embrace while he recovered. It didn't seem like either of us wanted to move—to end what had happened between us. I leaned forward to nestle my face into the side of his neck. "Lesson one complete." I smiled on his skin. "Did I do okay?" The self-conscious feelings surfaced again.

His breathing was still increased and he chuckled a low, throaty sound. "Mmm. I don't know. May need to try again," he teased. I lifted my head to face him in surprise. He grabbed the sides of my neck to bring me in for a kiss. "You are divine. Absolute perfection." He looked at my naked body and ran the back of his hands along my skin. "Have I ever told you how beautiful you are?"

I shivered at his gentle touch. "Hmm, I don't think you have," I replied with a grin.

He gently grabbed onto my breasts and started thrusting his hips slowly. "The most beautiful woman I've ever seen." I blushed. My heart skipped a beat at his words and touch.

He lifted me so he could kiss and lick each of my nipples. He played with them while he brought one of his hands down in between my legs. My eyes closed involuntarily. The pressure that had just been released not too long ago came back strong. How could I be ready again? I didn't think I was capable of it.

"How would you like me to please you this time?" he asked. My pulse raced and I felt beads of sweat form all over my body. I looked at him with a clueless look on my face.

How many ways were there?

"Hmm. Dealer's choice then." We were still on the couch, but he lifted me to my feet, so my sex was right in front of his face. He laid his hands on my backside and pulled my body to his lips. He kissed and nuzzled my tender area over and over. My hands dove into his hair for support. I couldn't believe I was going to experience him taste me again so soon. It felt unreal. Too good to be true. Like make-believe—

Until his doorbell rang and woke us both out of our real-life fantasy.

14

Jane

FOR THE BRIEFEST of moments, we tried to ignore the interruption. That was until whoever was on the other side of the door became so impatient that they rang the bell at two-second intervals until neither of us could tolerate it anymore.

Alex growled and mumbled something under his breath. It sounded like he said the name Tanner, but I wasn't sure. He pulled me back to my knees to kiss both my breasts one last time before reluctantly lifting me off him. He hopped up and quickly put his jeans on as he headed toward the door. I made quick work of finding all my scattered garments. Of course, they were mostly inside out. I fixed them and shimmied into my skirt as he turned around to make sure I was decent before he opened the door. I threw only my top on my upper half; the bra would have to wait.

Alex opened the door and I knew who it was in a quarter of a second. He didn't even have the chance to say hello before she barged right past him.

Reese.

She stomped about eight feet into his foyer and stopped abruptly. She raised her nose and looked around the house. "It smells like sex in here," she remarked and then narrowed her eyes, evaluating my appearance from across the room. She then turned to Alex with his gloriously bare chest and messy hair. He had a shit-eating grin on his face and couldn't look at her.

She turned to me again and all I could do was smile sheepishly and shrug my shoulders.

"Jane..." My name came out in a sigh. It was the sound of a mother's disappointment. She shook her head and rubbed her temples. Whatever Reese was thinking, she snapped out of it quickly. There was an obvious reason why she was paying us a visit. "Yo, do *either* of you check your phones?" We both looked at her, confused. "Well, I guess I now know *why* neither of you has answered any of the texts or calls from the last hour."

"What's going on, Reese?" I asked.

She glanced at Alex quickly, then back at me. It was obvious she didn't want to say too much in front of him. "Robert and Deb need you back at home." There was urgency in her tone.

"Are they okay?" I asked, concerned.

"Yes. They're fine."

"Then why do they need me home?"

"Umm..." Reese hesitated. "It's getting late?" It came out more of a question than a statement. She was eyeing me in an intense way, like I was supposed to understand the hidden meaning behind her words.

My eyebrows furrowed. "Seriously? They couldn't wait?" I looked at the clock on Alex's wall. "It's not even ten o'clock!" I crossed my arms defensively.

"Let's talk in the car," she ordered. "Get your things."

"No, Reese. I want to know why you rudely interrupted us before I decide if I want to leave with you." I could count on one hand how many times Reese had ever upset me. It didn't feel good to speak to her in such a way, but being forced to go home, without even knowing why, was beyond ridiculous. "I'm above curfew age, you know."

She looked flustered. She was trying to have patience. Reese didn't do patient.

She must have realized I wasn't going anywhere without more information. She sighed and explained, "No, it's not that, Jane. It's—Dean. Apparently he's been at the Coras' all day, waiting for you to get back." Reese looked uncomfortable.

My eyes went to Alex, who had a mask of calm plastered on his face. "Dean? He was supposed to go home this afternoon," I stated, confused.

"Yeah, well, I guess he wanted to say goodbye to you again. He drank all of Robert's Old Style and won't leave until you get home. He's drunk, Jane. Really drunk. The Coras want to go to bed but can't let him drive home, and they don't want to leave him unchaperoned in their house. You need to go talk some sense into him."

I nodded, finally understanding the urgency. She was right to come find me; I had to go. "Give me a second to get my stuff." I went to collect my things from the back of the house while Reese remained by the front door to wait.

Alex followed me into the mudroom and pulled me in for an embrace. "Please don't go." His whispered plea tickled my ear.

"I have to. I'm so sorry." I pressed away from him and sat on a bench to put on my sandals.

Alex bent down to be at my level and placed his hands on my legs. "Please," he repeated. "This isn't your problem."

His eyes were intense. They were making my body heat up again. I shook my head to clear the desire that was brewing from within. I had to go home. "Dean *is* my problem if he's making my in-laws uncomfortable while he waits for me."

Alex sighed and dropped his head. He knew I was right. "Let me come with you at least."

That would not be a good idea. Drunk Dean plus Protective Alex equaled *nope*. "Alex, I'll be fine. I'll text you when he passes out." I gave him a quick kiss on the lips. "Today was..." I didn't know how to properly describe it. "There are no perfect words. Unbelievable. The best day I have had in a very long time. Thank you. For everything."

Alex took my face in his hands and gave me a long, passionate kiss goodbye. "My pleasure, Jane." He kissed my lips one last time as my cheeks flushed a bright pink. "Today was the best day of my life."

"Hmm, I think I've heard you say that before," I teased.

He let out the quietest of chuckles and nodded. "The days keep getting better and better with you."

"Jane! Let's go!" Reese's continued lack of patience shone through.

"Please text me tonight when he's either gone or sleeping," Alex requested. He was trying to hide his concern, but I could see through his mask.

"I will. I promise." I raised myself off the bench to leave, even though I'd rather do anything else but walk out that door. Tonight had been magical. I'm not sure it could ever get better.

Reese was quiet in the car at first. I knew her chastising was on its way, so I waited in silence until she was ready to let me have it. It didn't take long.

"Did you at least use a condom?" she growled. What a way to start the lecture...

"Reese!" I exclaimed.

"What? You've been out of the game for a long time. Safe sex is important, especially with someone like Alex."

"Okay, Mom," I mumbled with an eye roll.

"No, seriously. There are some nasty diseases out there."

"Mmhmm." I was already done with the sex talk.

Reese wasn't. "Besides, we don't need a mini-Alex running around," she grumbled.

She was making my blood pressure increase. "Oh my gosh, Reese. Be nice, please. He's really good to me."

"For now—"

"*Reese,* please! This is hard enough on my brain without you criticizing me over who I chose to sleep with after my husband died. Besides, I have an IUD." I looked out the window, now equally as riled up as she was. "Do *not* tell my in-laws." My statements caught her off guard. Even in the darkness of the car, I could see her features soften and remember what I'd been through.

She reached over to grab my hand. "I'm sorry."

"I forgive you. Please remember that Alex has yet to do anything even remotely hurtful to make you lose trust in him. We spent four days together in Montana, and he didn't try to get in my pants once, okay? He's trying to do right by me. I allowed this to happen tonight. He asked me many times if I was okay. He didn't rush me. I wanted it." My heart skipped a beat with my admission.

I wanted it.

I turned toward her. "I'm going to say it again because it is worth repeating. He didn't force me. So please try to have less judgment and more of an open mind."

She sighed. "You're right. I'll try. No promises, though, okay? He triggers me."

"He does?" I asked sarcastically. She gave me a sideways glance and grin.

"So how was it?" Reese asked with the grin still on her face.

My heart skipped a beat once again. "Good. So good," I admitted, trying not to be shy about it. I was in dire need of some girl talk and Reese was the perfect candidate to discuss sex with.

"How many times did he make you come?" she asked. I envied the way she could talk about sex with no inhibitions. I wasn't sure I could ever be that way.

My cheeks became hot in an instant. "Once. I was on my way to number two when you interrupted us." I kept my face forward, too embarrassed to look at her.

"Well, shit, Jane. Now I feel bad."

"Yeah. You should," I teased.

"Sorry. But I had to find you. Dean really needs you." She glanced at me with concern in her eyes.

"Yeah..." As much as Dean might need me, she'd interrupted something that felt so...special. I needed time to process what Alex and I had done together. Did I regret it? Was it the right choice? It was too early in my over-thinking process to know the answers.

Reese interrupted my inner thoughts. "So Alex really didn't try to put the moves on you in Montana?"

"He found every opportunity to kiss my cheek or neck, but other than that, he was a perfect gentleman."

"Wow..." Genuine surprise rang through her tone.

"This is what I've been trying to tell you, Reese. He promised me before we left that he would behave and he did. He wants my trust. And he has it."

Reese didn't reply. She was deep in thought.

A few minutes later we pulled up to the Coras' house. "Would you like me to come in?"

I gave her a hug. "No. I'll take care of it. Thank you for bringing me home."

"Any time, my love. Good luck. Call me if you need reinforcements." She chuckled.

"Thanks, I will. Love you." I really hoped I didn't need help getting his drunk ass to bed.

"Love you too."

"*JANE!*" DEAN WAS waiting for me in the closest seat to the front door.

"Oh, thank God." Deb sounded more than relieved when I walked through the door. She came over and gave me a hug. "I'd love to ask how your date went, but we have more pressing matters on our hands." She turned to face Dean, who rocked and swung around on a recliner.

"When was his last drink?" I whispered.

"Over an hour ago. He ran out of beer, and we hid all the other alcohol." Deb looked mostly disturbed but also amused. She was always down for some interesting action, even on a Sunday night.

"Jane, sweetie, come over here and hop on my lap," Dean slurred.

Robert let out a big sigh. "Jane, you need to check your phone messages more often," he muttered. Robert was never down for any sort of action on a Sunday night.

"I know. I'm so sorry. I had my phone on silent after my mom called and wanted to have a thirty-minute conversation." I put my phone and picnic basket down on the coffee table and headed toward the issue at hand. I bent down next to where he sat and forced him to sit still. "What's going on, Dean?"

"Where have you *been*? I've been waiting here for houuuuurrrss. How many hours now, Robert?" He pointed to my father-in-law, who had obviously been keeping track.

"Eight—"

"*Eight hours*, Jane. That's a whole workday. What have you been doing for a *whole* workday?"

"I was out with a friend." I tried to sound casual.

"Who?" He grabbed my hands a little too tightly. I squeezed him back to see if he would release his grip. It didn't work, so I got to my feet and pulled him up with me.

"How about we go upstairs and tuck you in?" I asked in my sweetest tone.

Letting go of my hands hastily, he swayed, so I put my hands on his hips to steady him. "I'm not a child. I don't need to be 'tucked in.' Besides, the party is just getting started, am I right, Robert?" He turned to Robert, who had quickly made an exit with Deb when Dean had been distracted.

"Robert and Deb are tired, Dean. They're going to bed. Let's head up that way too."

"I'll only go if you sleep with me."

My eyes went wide in surprise. "Dean, I—" I didn't know what to say or do to get my intoxicated friend into bed, but I did know what I was *not* going to do.

"Not '*sleep with me*' sleep with me. Get your mind outta the gutter, Jane," he mumbled. He swayed toward the stairs which was a good sign; the bedrooms were upstairs. I walked next to him and made sure he was steady with each step. He placed his arm around me and pulled me in tightly as we walked. His arm was wrapped around my waist and his hand landed up under my cropped top to rest on my bare midriff.

He chuckled quietly when he felt the warmth of my skin. His hand was rough from working on cars for years. "Mmm, Janey. You're so soft," he mused. "When are you going to let me kiss that soft skin?"

I knew better than to rile a drunk person up by saying, "Um, never," so I didn't say anything at all. He'd forget about it by morning.

I thought about Dean's drinking history. He had always liked his beverages, but I hadn't seen him very intoxicated since our dumb drinking stage the summer after high school. Throughout college, he drank as much as any other student. But after college, he calmed down. He focused on his teaching career and his six-pack—and not the beer kind. He still had defined abs, so I knew drinking a case of beer in a day was not a regular activity.

Over the last few days, however, he had drunk a lot. At dinner on Friday, he'd had three glasses of wine to my one. When we'd returned to the Coras' after dinner, he'd started and finished a bottle of wine before we went to bed. Yesterday, his breakfast was coffee and a few cans of beer. On Maple Street, I'd had one glass of wine and he'd finished that bottle too. I hadn't paid attention, but it seemed as if he was using alcohol as his coping mechanism. That was a dangerous road to travel. We would have to talk about it when he sobered up.

I led Dean to the bathroom so he could try to pee before he got into one of the Coras' beds. He might be too old to be tucked in, but I'd known plenty of drunk people who wet themselves, awake or asleep. It didn't take too much convincing, thank goodness. While he was preoccupied, I ran to my room to get into pajamas. I had a feeling I wouldn't be able to leave him alone, and there was no way I would allow him to watch me get undressed while he was hammered and handsy. I'd barely pulled up my pajama bottoms when he called me into the bathroom where he sat on the closed toilet seat.

"Jane, I need a favor." He looked up at me with his big blue puppy eyes.

"Yeah, bud. What do you need?" Drunk people asking favors made me uneasy.

"I need you to brush my teeth."

I snorted and then tried to cover up my reaction with a cough. "You need me to brush your teeth," I repeated. "Can't it wait until tomorrow?"

He shook his head with drunken force. "*No!* I need you to brush my teeth tonight. I can't sleep with dirty teeth."

Ready to give him just about anything at that point so he would get to bed, I went on a hunt in the cabinets for a clean toothbrush. I found one quickly, along with toothpaste. I bent over to start and he pulled me on top of him with my legs straddling his. "Isn't that better?" he asked. "Now you can see." He kept his hands on my hips, then closed his eyes and opened his mouth. His teeth were a moving target as he swayed, so I did the best I could. I chuckled to myself. The experience would have to be filed in the category of "Never would I ever have thought I'd do this." I shook my head and smiled. The lengths you'd go to get drunk friends to comply. When I was done, I attempted to stand, but Dean's muscles locked in and held me where I was.

"Dean, you need to spit," I demanded. He raised his eyebrows up and down and gave me a sly smile. I had no idea how that comment was dirty, but I could see in his eyes that he was thinking something inappropriate. When he smiled, part of his toothpaste-laden saliva dripped out of his mouth. He used the back of his hand to wipe the mess off his face, which allowed me to escape his grasp.

Once we were done in the bathroom, I walked him to the guest room and pulled back the covers of the twin bed. He plopped down and pulled himself to one side of the mattress. He looked up at me with raised arms, as if to invite me in.

"I'm going to head to my room now. But thanks for the invite." I turned to walk away and he caught my wrist.

His big blue eyes gazed up at me. "It wasn't an invite. It's a compromise. I don't want to sleep. You want me to. I said I would sleep if you stayed with me." He sounded more sober than he had a few minutes ago.

I sighed, feeling very fatigued all of a sudden. Dean was harmless. He wouldn't make a pass at me. Well, sober Dean wouldn't. I was pretty sure drunk Dean wouldn't either. Lying down next to him was my best bet for getting any rest—for both him and me. I turned off the light and crawled into the small bed. It was too tight for us both to be on our backs, so I turned away from him to lie on my side. Dean did the same and swung his arm over me to pull me into him.

"Behave," I ordered.

He chuckled quietly. "Where's the fun in that?"

I rolled my eyes. Staying quiet was the best option. Drunk people loved to hear themselves talk. They also loved having the last word. I'd let him have it since he was in bed, somewhat quiet, and most importantly—not irritating Robert and Deb.

After a few minutes of silence, his breathing became heavier. I thought about making a break for my room but didn't want to risk him waking up and having to start the process all over again. At that point, I prayed he stayed asleep and didn't hurl on me. And if I was being honest with myself, it was nice to sleep next to someone again. It felt like a lifetime ago when I shared a bed with a warm body. It might not be the warm body I would choose first—or second—but Dean was special to me too. He was family.

I had probably been lying there for an hour, unable to sleep. As tired as I was, I couldn't calm down. My mind was solely focused on what happened with Alex. Somehow I went pretty quickly from "*I want to honor my late husband and not go all the way*," to "*Yes, I'm totally ready*." I didn't know how I felt about it. Had I *actually* been ready, or was I just caught up in the moment with a beautiful man? I didn't know that answer.

One thing I *was* sure of was my body needed what Alex gave it, both on the picnic blanket and the couch. The release that had exploded out of me must have been building for quite some time. My whole self felt lighter, less on edge. It was obvious to me that after our time together lately, my body and mind were on the mend. Not even close to perfect, but headed in the right direction.

My battered and broken heart was a different story. I didn't know if it was prepared for the aftereffects of what Alex and I did together. Time had repaired some of the cracks since the accident, but it was still broken. It wasn't on the same healing path as the rest of me. It trailed behind and got lost a lot.

All that being said, I had to admit that the feeling of Alex's lips on my skin was beyond therapeutic. The way he cared for my well-being made all parts of me feel less broken—even my heart.

I sighed. My mixed emotions overwhelmed me. And those mixed emotions didn't even consider Graham. What did he think about my actions? Was he angry? Or jealous? Did he watch?

I squeezed my eyes tighter and shook my head to get that image to disappear. No. Heaven didn't work that way. There was no sadness with God. If I was going to get through life without my husband and kids, I had to force myself to believe they were rooting for my happiness. Instead of imagining them judging me and giving me sad eyes for trying to build a life back, I promised myself right then that I would only imagine them being my cheerleaders from above. I only hoped they were distracted with something else during moments in my life that were not G-rated. Because I was ready to admit that I yearned for more wild nights on Alex's couch or bed—or naughty room.

I WOKE EARLY, overheated by Dean's body wrapped around mine. He was still in deep sleep. I softly shimmied out of bed to allow him to get a few more hours before the inevitable hangover set in. Robert and Deb talked quietly downstairs in the kitchen. It was obvious they didn't want to wake Dean either.

"Good morning, dear. How was your night?" Robert asked.

"It went fine. Once he saw you two go to bed, he didn't fight it," I said as I searched for a coffee cup. "I'm sorry, you guys. I should have kept my phone near me." Deb went to say something in response. Before she could, I stopped what I was doing and stared off into space, remembering a promise I'd made last night.

Shit. I'd forgotten to text Alex! I immediately went in search of my phone and found it dead. *Of course.* I felt terrible. I hoped he wasn't too upset with me. I needed to talk to him right away. I had two options: I could wait until my phone charged enough to call him...or I could go to the gym and apologize directly. Seeing him in person seemed like a better option, so I hustled to my room, dressed, and headed out with a brief goodbye to my in-laws.

I hastily opened the front door, trying to decide what I would say to Alex, and ran right into the man I was headed to see.

"Alex! Hi!" I exclaimed as I pulled him in for a hug. I shut the front door for some privacy and stepped back after our embrace to notice his appearance. He was in a tailored business suit, a look I hadn't seen yet. He was more handsome than ever, but there were subtle hints that something was off. His hair was disheveled, and he had bags under his sleepy, red-rimmed eyes. His face looked somber and anxious. "I'm so sorry I forgot to text you. I was just on my way to the gym to explain and well, here you are! What a coincidence!" My voice was too high-pitched.

Not at all because I'd slept next to another man in a very small bed. A man who had kept his arm around me, spooning the back half of my body the entire night. And not because I had enjoyed sleeping next to him. Or that it had filled a void I didn't know I had. Definitely not because of any of that.

Alex woke me out of my guilt fest. "Not a coincidence at all, actually." He ran his fingers through his messy hair. "Jane, do you have any idea of what I went through when you didn't contact me last night as you promised? I texted you with no reply. I called you, over and over, hoping you'd answer. I even drove over here at three o'clock because I couldn't handle the silence anymore. The only reason I didn't ring the bell was I didn't want to wake or upset your in-laws after Dean had already outstayed his welcome. So I sat here, in my Jeep, watching the house like a crazy person. The scenarios that played on repeat in my head got worse by the hour. You had me very worried in more ways than one."

My heart dropped. I understood in an instant. I could conjure up all the different scenarios in my head too—Dean being belligerent—Dean's drunk ass harming me, by accident or intentionally—Dean hitting on me—sleeping with Dean.

I instantly had empathy for Alex. He didn't know Dean as I did. He didn't know that Dean would never force himself upon me, drunk or not. Okay, well, Dean *had* forced a few kisses on me the past few days. But that was as far as he'd go. I was certain of that. Alex, on the other hand, was obviously not certain at all.

I took Alex's hands and rested them on the small of my back. I wrapped my arms around him and pressed my body to his chest so he could see, feel, and smell all of me—to know I was safe and everything was okay. He pulled me in equally as tight and rested his lips in my hair. After a minute or so, he led me backward a couple of feet until my back rested up against a wall of the house. He let go of me and placed his hands on the brick, next to my head. "You own every part of me, Jane." He leaned in slowly to kiss me. My heart started racing in an instant. His lips felt so good. Too good. I realized right then that I thoroughly enjoyed being pinned by Alex. Deep inner voice woke up at my realization and gave me an air high five. She had been awfully quiet, considering what had transpired recently.

"Every part of me," Alex repeated. He gingerly ran the tip of his nose and his lips over the nape of my neck, stopping every few seconds to lay a kiss on the sensitive skin. My breathing became heavy. For the briefest of moments, my brain reminded me we were outside, on the front porch, for anyone to witness our intimate moment. It felt so good that I couldn't get myself to make him stop. Instead, I tucked my hands under his suit coat and placed them on the fabric over his tight abs. It took a lot of willpower to not untuck his shirt to reach his warm skin. He pushed into me deeper when he felt my touch through his clothing. "Can I make a request?" he mumbled into my neck.

"Mmhmm..." Words were so hard when Alex's mouth was on me.

He lifted my chin so we made eye contact. "Please remember that when we're apart."

"Remember what?" I whispered, a little dazed.

A deep, low chuckle escaped his lips. "Remember that you own me. I am yours."

"Alex." I placed my hand near his heart. "That's a lot of pressure." I backed out from under his suit coat to grab his hands and place them by *my* heart. "Yesterday with you was…I still have no proper words." I pulled our hands up to my lips. "I was awake most of the night too, unable to escape the feeling of you. Last night, on your couch…I've never felt that way before." His eyes brightened. He leaned in for a kiss, but I put my hand up to stop him. "That being said, I am still not ready for a relationship." I looked down. I didn't want to see his disappointment. "I'm not saying never—"

"Jane," he interrupted me with an understanding tone. "I'll wait as long you need. Take ten years if you have to." He pulled my chin up and grinned at me.

A nervous giggle bubbled up. "I sure hope it doesn't take ten years to figure out the mess in my brain."

"Me too." He chuckled quietly.

"I was worried you'd expect more from me after…"

His eyes met mine with only sincerity shining through. "I don't."

"But your request—"

"Is for you to keep in mind that I already belong to you. Even if you aren't ready to belong to me."

I shook my head in confusion. "That seems so one-sided."

"You're worth it," he repeated his sentiment from yesterday.

"If you say so." I smiled. "So what has you in a business suit?"

"I came to check on you, but also to let you know I've been called to New York for a few days. I thought maybe you'd like to know I won't be back in town until Friday." He looked unsure of himself as he spoke, which made my heart drop again.

"I *would* like to know that. Thank you for telling me."

He grinned. "I have to go. I have to be at O'Hare soon."

"Text me when you land?" I requested.

"I will…or maybe I'll forget," he teased and winked. My mouth popped open, offended. He laughed under his breath, kissed me, and reluctantly retreated to his car. I turned in that direction too and noticed he had the fancy SUV parked in front of the house with Stan at the wheel—Stan, who'd just witnessed a very private moment between Alex and me. I waved at him casually. I couldn't help the blush that formed, but hopefully he couldn't see it. I wondered what the conversation to the airport would entail. Oh, to be a fly on the wall...

With a sigh, I headed back inside. I still had another man to tend to today.

Dean was awake when I reentered the house. He sat at the breakfast bar next to Deb, who looked at me with a very confused face, considering I'd rushed out of the house about five minutes beforehand.

"Hey, bud. How are you feeling?" I asked Dean as I went to get some coffee.

"Like I drank a case of beer yesterday." There was a hint of rudeness in his tone. He wouldn't meet my eyes.

Hmm, he looks a little embarrassed. Good.

"Yeah, about that. Would you like me to lecture you now or later about how alcohol will not become your coping mechanism?" I tried to keep my voice light. The sternness would come after the hangover wore off.

"Later sounds good," he stated flatly while attempting to rub the sleepiness off his face.

Yes, he was avoiding eye contact. I poured my coffee while shaking my head at him. Dean was a very stubborn man. I was concerned that anything I said to him would not prevent the potential path of destruction he was on.

"Okay. Later then. When are you headed home?"

"After this cup of coffee." He hopped off the stool and headed upstairs. "So your lecture will have to wait."

I followed him up the stairs to the guest room and closed the door behind me. "What's going on? Why won't you look at me?"

He searched the room for his things, still avoiding my eyes. "I have to go, Jane. I was supposed to be back home yesterday." His tone was accusatory.

"And that's my fault because...?" I asked, crossing my arms.

He finally met my eyes as he sat down on the bed to don his socks and shoes. "Because *you* decided to fuck the first man who came into your life after your husband died."

I recoiled from his harsh words. "*Excuse* me?" He could have slapped me across the face and it would have hurt less. "How in the *hell* do you know that? And how is that *any* of your business?" My cheeks were on fire for a new reason.

He sat on the edge of the bed for a moment without saying a word. His head dropped below his shoulders. "I'm sorry," he whispered. "I'm so sorry." He wiped away the emotion from his face. All the anger flushed out of me at once. I bent down in front of him. I had been where he was. I had felt hollow, angry, and resentful all at once. I'd had outbursts. I understood him completely.

Well, almost completely.

I took his hands in mine and rested them on his lap. I knew the first thing I said should be something to comfort the hurting man in front of me, but all I could think about was his knowledge of my night with Alex. Only one other person knew. If Reese was somehow involved, I didn't think I could forgive her. It wasn't her business to tell, and I would surely let her know it.

"Dean, how do you know—" I couldn't finish the sentence. I hoped he would catch on to what I was asking.

He took a deep breath and shook his head. "Does it matter? You're right, it's none of my business."

"It matters," I stated firmly.

He nodded at me. He still had tears in his eyes. "I wasn't snooping on purpose, okay? I promise you. Your phone was plugged into the charger at the breakfast bar. When I sat down to have coffee, all of your messages and voicemails were making your phone blow up with alerts. I glanced at it and saw a few texts from Alex. They didn't leave much to the imagination."

"And why would *that* make you so furious with me? We didn't have plans yesterday. I didn't tell you to wait all day. *You* decided to stay and drink all of Robert's beer."

He stood and slid past where I knelt on the floor. "I can't talk about this right now. I really have to go."

"Then when?" It made me anxious to leave on a sour note. We both knew how precious life could be.

"I don't know," he replied as he headed for the bedroom door.

"Dean, wait." I hurriedly stood. He stopped before turning the handle, refusing to look at me once again. I wrapped my arms around him and squeezed tight. "I'm sorry if I've upset you." I knew how much pain he was in. I didn't need to add to it. "I won't blame you if you don't want to see me next time you're in town."

Dean chuckled a deep, low sound. "Don't be so dramatic," he muttered before he kissed my forehead. "I'll be back soon. I'll text when I know when."

Hearing his mood change calmed my anxieties. I squeezed him a little tighter. "Okay, sounds good. I still owe you a lecture," I teased before I released my hold on him.

"Can't wait." He chuckled again.

I took his hand in mine and kissed the back of it. "Seriously though. Please take care of yourself."

He nodded and pulled me in to kiss my forehead again. "I'm sorry for what I said."

I wrapped my arms around his waist once more. "That really hurt." My throat tightened with emotion. "Don't ever talk to me that way again."

"I won't," he said with conviction as he rested his cheek on my hairline. We stood there for a moment, enjoying the comfort only a lifelong friend could bring. "You know I love you."

"I love you too, Dean."

He took a deep breath and let me go. "Not in the same way," he repeated my sentiment from the other night.

One of the cracks in my heart, which had recently healed, broke open at his words. One step forward, two steps back. I resigned myself to the knowledge my heart would never be completely whole again.

15

Jane

WHEN DEAN LEFT, I went straight to my phone to see what kind of messages he—and no doubt Deb—had read. Deb had moseyed off somewhere, so I was alone to inspect the damage. Some texts were from Reese earlier in the night. Aside from some vibrant language, they were harmless. Most of the texts and phone calls were from Alex:

> 10:45 p.m.- missed call
>
> 11:57 p.m.- Hey, I'm headed to bed, but just want to make sure you're okay? Please text me when you can.
>
> 12:34 a.m.- I hope your silence isn't due to what happened on my couch tonight. Because I can't imagine it ever getting any better than that.
>
> 12:36 a.m.- I can still taste you. I hope you still feel my mouth all over your beautiful body.
>
> 12:37 a.m.- Can you still feel me inside of you?

My body reacted to the words in his messages. He was even good at sexting. I shook my head to snap out of it so I could keep reading.

12:40 a.m.- But seriously, text me soon because I can't sleep when I'm worried about you.

1:28 a.m.- missed call

1:56 a.m.- missed call

My phone must have died around 2:00 a.m. Seeing all the evidence of his concern made me feel terrible again for forgetting. I'd have to make it up to him somehow.

His naughty texts had me thinking, though. Prior to what I'd just read, Alex had never gone past G-rated in any text. Was he playing a dirty game? Or did he not realize anyone else could walk by and see his smutty messages? I wasn't sure, but if I were a betting gal, I'd say the former option.

Boys. I rolled my eyes. They're always trying to mark their territory.

You're not Alex's territory, surface voice reminded me.

I sighed. I was done having that conversation with Alex. He knew where I currently stood. Hopefully he would respect it.

My mind then trailed to Dean and the last ten minutes before he left. His words were so hurtful and took me completely by surprise. He had never spoken to me that way. I'd never heard him speak to anyone so harshly. He had to have been in a lot of pain to allow his anger to show through his usual easy-going demeanor. Hurting or not, there was no excuse for being so nasty.

I closed my eyes, took a deep cleansing breath, and headed up the stairs to my room. The last twenty hours of my life had exhausted me in more ways than one. My body and mind deserved a morning in bed.

I KEPT MYSELF very busy the following few days, which made them fly by. I had been neglecting some responsibilities, so I diligently worked down my list of to-dos to keep myself from fantasizing about Alex. On the top of my task list was to call a real estate agent about my house. I met her Tuesday afternoon on Maple Street to go over the asking price, comparables in the neighborhood, and any work that needed to be done before putting it on the market.

The Realtor, Sarah, was excited about listing my home. "This house is in great shape, especially for being vacant for over a year. It's clean, not cluttered, and decorated well," she informed. "The market is hot right now. I don't think you're going to have any trouble getting offers within a few days. I think you should keep your furniture in the house until it has a pending sale. That way you don't have to stage it." I agreed with her plan and asked to have it listed immediately. My only request was to not post a "for sale" sign out front. I hadn't told Deb or Robert yet. I didn't want them to stop by and see it before I could share the news.

My little Maple Street home went on the market Wednesday afternoon and by Thursday I had three full-price offers. That evening I brought my laptop to bed, so I could go through all the bids in private; I still hadn't told my in-laws. I was about to go over the second family's negotiation when Sarah called me to let me know I had another one to add to the list. "Jane, they're very serious about buying your home. They are offering fifteen percent over list price, cash, no inspection."

"Wow," I replied, a little stunned. "That sounds like whom I should go with, right?"

"There's a catch," Sarah warned. "They want you moved out by May 16th."

There was a light knock at my door before Deb walked in. "May 16th?" I looked at the date on my phone screen. "That's only a little over two weeks away."

"I know," she sighed the words. "It's tight."

Packing up, selling, and donating everything in my home in the next two weeks felt a little daunting, but I knew I could get it done. I'd require help, though.

Deb sat on the edge of the bed and waited for me to finish my phone call. "Sold," I told Sarah, who then had a few logistics to share with me before she ended the call.

"Did your home sell?" Deb asked with a sad look in her eyes.

"It did. How did you know I was talking about my house?"

"Robert went over there after dinner last night to check on it and there was a real estate agent inside with some clients."

"Oh." I looked away from her, feeling a bit ashamed I kept it a secret. "I'm sorry I didn't have a chance to tell you guys. I put it on the market yesterday. I didn't think it would sell *this* fast."

She patted my arm. "No, it's okay. This was your decision to make when you were ready."

I put my hand over hers. "You two have been carrying the burden of maintaining that house for over a year. It feels like the right time to let it go and let you both have your free time back."

"Thank you, Janey." She had tears in her eyes. "Does this mean you're moving out?" Her tone was so sad.

I grabbed her hands and squeezed. "I love staying here. I don't have any plans to move out right now, but once the sale of the house is final, I may start looking for a condo."

Her tears pooled over her eyelids.

"Hey, what's wrong?" I scooted closer to her so I could give her a hug. As soon as she put her arms around me, it hit me in an instant. Deb had been able to hold it together the last fifteen months because she'd distracted herself with taking care of me and my house. She'd had to mother me, which healed some of the brokenness in her heart. "Deb, you'll still see me all the time. I won't go too far. I'll still attend church with you. I'll come over for dinner and watch movies."

Her tears started to flow harder and faster. Yes, she worried I'd forget about them—or not need them anymore.

I squeezed her a little tighter. "We can go on walks together. I'll drop into Jewel when you're working. You're still my adoptive mom and always will be. You're family. I love you so much."

She calmed down and let go of the embrace. "I love you too." Her voice quivered with emotion. "Do you promise you'll still come around often?"

"I promise!"

"Okay, good. I'm going to hold you to it." She wiped her tears, stood, and reached for my hand. "Now we have to break the news to Robert."

THE FOLLOWING MORNING my head spun at all I needed to get done during the following two weeks. Robert and Deb had volunteered to help, naturally. I asked them to set up a garage sale for next weekend, as well as to take everything to the donation center that didn't sell. That gave me a few days to go through and find what I wanted to keep, either for a place of my own or as a keepsake.

I planned on getting rid of most of the large furniture, but there were some pieces I'd want to have in my next home. Therefore, I needed some heavy lifters to help me. I evaluated my options—Dean, Reese...and Alex.

Dean needed some healthy distractions. It was a good excuse to check in on him and see how he was doing in the alcohol department. Also, it would be good for him to do some manual labor. I immediately texted him, explaining everything I needed and when. Dean replied quickly. He said he was on board and could get back to town next Friday evening.

Next up was Reese. I felt a little guilty asking her because she worked so much. However, she loved that house almost as much as I did. She'd want to be part of the move. I texted her next but asked her to only help on Sunday for a few hours. I didn't want to take up her Friday and Saturday evenings after she worked all day. She agreed in an instant.

Last was Alex. I didn't know if I should invite him. I wanted him around, but Alex and Dean together in close quarters didn't feel right. I settled on seeing how it went with the help I'd gathered and if we needed more brute strength, I'd call him.

I looked at the clock. It was time to get ready for work, so I had no more time to over-analyze the choices I made. They would have to do for now.

"JANE! IT'S BEEN way too long!" exclaimed my last client of the night, Luis, as he entered R & J's Salon. He walked toward me smoother than a model on a runway in Paris. If you were to mix chocolate with caramel, you would get Luis's skin tone. His hazel eyes and full lips complemented his perfect complexion. His hips moved better than most straight women's. Until I met Alex, I would have said he was the most beautiful man I knew. He demanded the attention of both men and women. And he won. Every time.

He met me with a swift kiss on both cheeks, then grabbed my hands to pull me in for a hug. "Hi, Luis. Way too long indeed." I refrained from reminding him that *he'd* forgotten about *me* during the worst year of my life. Instead, I decided to forgive and try to forget. "How have you been?" I asked with a genuine smile as I directed him to my chair. He ignored my question, and my cue to sit. Instead, he headed right to Reese, who had just finished her last haircut of the night and was cleaning up. He picked her up and swirled her around. "And where have *you* been, my girl?" he questioned as he put her down. "I haven't seen you at any bars or clubs in—at least a year."

"I know, right?" Reese agreed. "I'm in desperate need of an evening out. Let's plan one soon!" Reese and Luis had always been big fans of the night scene. They had stopped asking me long ago if I wanted to join them, for obvious reasons. For years, I had been in a whirlwind of pregnancies, co-sleeping, late-night feedings, diaper changes, and sleepless nights. Young motherhood wasn't very conducive to clubbing, which had always been fine by me.

"*Yes*! Let's!" Luis shrieked, already ecstatic about the idea. He then turned to point at me. "And *you* are coming with this time."

"Yes! That would be awesome. And so needed! Have you ever been to a club?" Reese asked me.

"Oh yeah, all the time. I'd always head out right between breastfeeding sessions," I answered sarcastically with a smile. It hit me immediately that I could joke about such a thing without my chest feeling like it was caving in on itself.

For the first time, my internal dialogue ladies agreed with each other and in unison whispered, *You're healing*. I closed my eyes for a brief second and sent some love above to my crew.

Reese and Luis must have noticed my lightheartedness too, because they both were very still, staring at me with matching concerned looks on their faces. "You guys, I'm okay." I grinned reassuringly at them. "Luis, get over here and sit down, so I have a chance of *actually* making it to a club tonight," I teased. My playful banter made him at ease again. He sat and let me place the smock over him.

"So what's new in your world?" I asked him as I set up to start on his hair. Luis was always good at creating entertaining conversations.

"Girlll, I've been great. I'm seeing a new man. His name is Timothy. We met at the rec center a few months ago. He's an *at-tor-ney*," he emphasized each syllable and raised his eyebrows up and down. "He took my step class and fell off the step *three times* during the warm-up." He giggled. "I finally had to bring him to the front and teach the rest of class holding his hand to keep him balanced." Reese and I chuckled at his story. "At that point, I wasn't sure if he was gay or straight—because you know, gay men usually have *some* coordination—but all I knew was he was going to break his damn neck if I didn't hang on to him." He stopped for a moment to explain how he wanted his hair cut and then continued, "Anyway, he asked me out to dinner as a thank-you for saving him from rolling an ankle, and the rest is history." Luis had a little twinkle in his eye.

"Aww, that's so great, Luis," I said. "I'm happy for you. I can't wait to meet him."

"You'd love him! He'll be at my spin class tomorrow. Maybe you could come say hi and take class?"

"Funny you mention that. I was going to ask if I could get back on the spin schedule soon."

"*Yes*! I thought you'd never ask! Your regulars have missed you, girl. They need you. I'm so tired of having conversations with them about how much better you are than all the other instructors. I've had no answers about if you were going to return. And it didn't feel right to ask you. I figured you would reach out to me if and when you were ready." He had the concerned look on his face again.

"Thank you for your patience, Luis—"

He interrupted me before I could finish my sentence. "So I've been teaching most of the spin classes since there were so many complaints after you left. They're satisfied enough, but most of them don't want to stare at this beautiful face for forty minutes. I don't know *why*." He pretended to be offended. I chuckled quietly at his silliness. "But in all seriousness, they want their Jane back. I can't wait to tell them you'll be there soon."

I felt a little speechless as I was tending to his hair. I didn't realize anyone had missed me. After the large bouquet of flowers had shown up at the funeral from my normal spin class crew, I hadn't heard a thing from any of them. It once again reminded me how terrible most humans were at coping with death. I'd had a lot of lessons in not taking things personally over the last year.

Luis woke me out of my internal thoughts. "Want to teach tomorrow?" he asked abruptly with a huge smile on his face.

A nervous giggle bubbled out of me. "You're cute, but no. I need to actually *take* class a few times before I teach again."

"Fine, not this Saturday. What about next Saturday? We can do a dual ride to ease you back in." Luis held his hands in prayer, pleading with me to say yes.

I had so much on my plate the next two weeks, but the pull to teach a class was strong. It would give me a break from packing and help me focus on something else. Without thinking about it too much, I agreed.

"*Yay*!" Luis squealed. "Come take class tomorrow and meet Timothy!"

"I will. Can't wait." I smiled at him through the mirror. It was the truth. "Thank you for letting me back on the sched—"

Luis's attention turned away from me to the front door. "Ooooooh, who is this *fine* specimen comin' in here?" Reese and I rotated our heads at the same time to follow his gaze. "Dibs," Luis stated firmly. He clearly forgot he'd *just* told us all about his new beau, the *at-tor-ney*.

Reese growled something under her breath as Alex opened the door to the salon. He wore a business suit again and had a small white gift bag dangling from his hand. My heart skipped a beat. I hadn't seen him since our porch rendezvous. He must have been preoccupied with business in New York, because we'd hardly had any texting correspondence, aside from "good mornings" and "goodnights." I hadn't realized how much I missed him until that moment.

"We're closed," Reese hollered at him, obviously knowing he was not there for a haircut.

"Reese! Is that any way to speak to a potential client?" Luis lectured. Reese rolled her eyes. "Hi." Luis welcomed Alex with a sultry voice. "I'm Luis." He pulled his arm out of the smock to delicately shake Alex's hand. "What brings you in here tonight?" Dang, Luis could turn on the sexy sass when he wanted to.

Alex shook Luis's hand but his attention was on me. "Nice to meet you. I came to bring Jane a gift."

Luis looked confused. "You two know each other?" His attention went back and forth between Alex and me.

"You could say that," I answered with a smile. "Luis, this is my friend, Alex." I refused to look at Alex after I'd just given him such a trivial title, so instead I stared intently at Luis's hair, trying to suppress a grin. I assumed that word—friend—would vex Alex, but after he'd sent me those naughty texts for the world to see, I felt the need to play his game. The intense brown eyes that currently bored into me proved my assumption to be correct.

Reese, who had only been observing until that point, let an involuntary satisfied giggle bubble up from her throat. Her reaction was contagious and it took everything in me to not burst out laughing. She seemed to see right through me. I wasn't as good at playing games as Alex was.

Luis seemed too enamored by the handsome man in front of him to recognize anything else going on. "Why do you look so familiar?" he mused.

Alex shrugged his shoulders and was about to answer when Reese beat him to it. "Maybe he's slept with one of your friends and then ghosted her the next day."

My mouth dropped open. She was so blunt. And so rude! Alex didn't seem fazed at all. He looked like he'd heard it before.

Luis turned his attention to Reese. "*You* know him too?" he asked in a high-pitched tone.

"Unfortunately," Reese mumbled and mindlessly picked at her split ends.

Luis was quiet for a brief moment before his eyes lit up. "Wait. I know you. You're Alexander Lombardi."

Alex chuckled quietly. "In the flesh."

Luis sat up in my chair a little taller while he checked out Alex from head to toe. "Wow, you're even finer in person."

"Um, thank you?" Alex's words came out as a question. I wondered how often gay men hit on him. My guess was all the time.

"Well, what did you bring her?" Luis took the bag out of Alex's hand and handed it to me. "Open it!" Luis demanded with a lot of animation, seemingly trying to break up all the intensity in the air.

Alex still was taken aback at my introduction. His eyes narrowed at me as he forced a grin on his face. He turned a quarter turn to head to the door. "Open it now or when you get home. I recommend when you're alone. Your choice." His attention went to Luis. "It was nice to meet you," he said before he turned all the way around and walked out the door.

Luis had a stunned look on his face as he focused his gaze on me. "Oh my word, you have been holding out on me, Janey girl. Alexander Lombardi? Chicago's Most Eligible Bachelor? Did you see how he looked at you? *Clearly,* he is not just a friend."

Reese grumbled something unintelligible from behind me.

Luis pointed toward Reese. "We'll get to why you're growling in a moment." He faced me again. "Please explain how you two met." He looked like an interrogator on one of those crime TV shows.

I waved my hand in the air. "Oh, it's a long, boring story."

"Well, at a minimum you need to tell me how good he is in bed. If I can't have him, I can at least daydream about it."

I had finished his haircut and was brushing off his shoulders and neck. "I'm not the kiss-and-tell type," I told him with a wink.

"Kiss? Oh honey, please tell me you've done more than just kiss that beautiful man." Luis crossed his arms and lifted an eyebrow. He would be disappointed in me if I didn't share my sexcapades stories soon.

Well, *story*. Singular. Only one so far.

I shrugged at him with a big smile plastered on my face. It didn't feel right to share such an intimate moment with him. I hadn't spoken to him in a year. I loved Luis, but he wasn't going to get anything out of me.

He must have sensed my decision to stay quiet. "Let's at least see what he brought you!" he exclaimed as he handed me the bag.

Something about the look on Alex's face before he left made me think twice about opening his gift in the company of others. But since I wouldn't share any details about my sex life, I'd give Luis something to satisfy him. How bad could the little gift be? I pulled out the tissue paper and grabbed the unwrapped box. Before it was even out of the bag, I knew what it was.

Bad. The little gift could be really bad. My cheeks flushed in an instant as I dropped the box back into the bag and shoved the paper on top.

"Wha—?" Luis eyed me, confused.

"What is it, Janey?" Reese asked. She walked over to me casually, then ripped the bag out of my hand and ran. I tried to chase her, but it was a lost cause. She reached inside, grabbed the box, and then dropped the bag. A sealed envelope flopped out of the bag onto the floor with my name on it. I grabbed the envelope and the bag and headed toward her to reclaim my gift. She inspected the box with the most shocked expression I had ever seen on her face and then raised it in the air at an angle to show Luis.

He squinted from across the salon and then his eyes tripled in size. "Excuse me right now, is that a *vibrator*?"

Being taller than Reese had its advantages because I ripped the box out of her hands pretty easily. I immediately put it back in the bag and covered it up again. The two of them had the same looks on their faces: shock, curiosity... and pity. Added onto Reese's face was—of course—disgust. The only look on my face was complete and utter humiliation. Tears formed as I thought of what to say to my friends: *Don't worry about it, I'm just* that *inexperienced...*

Alex was going to pay.

They were still quiet as I went over to my station and cleaned up for the night. I couldn't meet their eyes. For the first time in as long as I knew either of them, they were rendered speechless at the same time. Maybe it was the look on my face that kept them quiet; I wasn't sure. Luis lifted from the chair and gave me a swift hug and kiss before he paid Reese and left. Reese locked the door after him and sat at the station next to me.

"Do you want to talk about why Alex gifted you a vibrator?" Her tone was calm and comforting.

I kept up my busy work with a broom while avoiding her eyes. "No," I barked, but I really meant yes.

"Janey, there's nothing to be embarrassed about," she repeated Alex's sentiment from the night on his couch. "You were so young when you got married. It's to be expected that you may have less..." She paused, as if she was trying to find the right word, "experience." She grabbed onto the broom handle to force me to stop and focus on her. "You know I don't approve of Alex courting you. But it seems he truly adores you. So he must have really thought about the pros and cons of bringing you this gift. He's an ass, but with you—

he's different. I don't think he was attempting to embarrass you. Try to think of it as him caring about your well-being."

"Are you *actually* defending him?" I scoffed. The one time I wished she wouldn't...

She chuckled quietly. "I guess I am. Jane, we all need *that* sort of release. It's good for our mind and body. Look it up if you don't believe me."

"I believe you," I mumbled, still mortified.

"If he's giving you a vibrator, I'm assuming he's discovered it's been over a year since you've had regular orgasms."

My eyes pinched closed at the "O" word. I needed to take a course in being a grown-up and saying embarrassing words out loud comfortably.

"Or maybe much longer than a year?" she inquired.

My cheeks went red in an instant, which gave away my answer. She took the broom away from me and grabbed my hands. "Take that gift home and use it. Don't overthink it. It is a totally normal, natural, and needed thing to do." I nodded, keeping my gaze away from hers. "Just remember to lock your door when you use it. Speaking from experience, it's no fun to be caught in the act."

"Good to know." I pulled her in for a hug; her pep talk helped. I wasn't sure I was going to use it, but she made it seem less intimidating. Once again, I thanked my lucky stars that Reese Delvani entered my life all those years ago. "Thank you, Reese."

"Any time, sister," she said with a wink.

SATURDAY MORNING WAS the most fun I had—outside of a certain couch escapade—for as long as I could remember. Luis was such a talented instructor. But more so, he was completely entertaining. You didn't even feel like you were getting your ass kicked because he kept you distracted in the best way. I was so glad he'd convinced me to go. I sure missed taking his classes and looked forward to our dual ride the following weekend. After class, I met Timothy, who was a lovely gentleman. They seemed nothing alike. But as the old saying goes: opposites attract.

The rest of Saturday and Sunday was dedicated to the house. I started with the least sentimental areas: the kitchen, basement, and shed. By Sunday night, everything in those spaces was boxed up to keep or in the garage sale pile. After two full days of nonstop moving, I was thoroughly exhausted but satisfied with my efforts. I would be ready to completely move out in time. I slept well Sunday night and was ready to tackle the next busy week.

I woke up Monday morning and stared directly at Alex's little gift. That damn white gift bag had mocked me all weekend. When I had gotten home Friday evening, I'd set it on my dresser in my line of sight from the bed. I'd decided it would be better *not* to tuck it away somewhere to try to forget about it. Reese was right. Alex must feel really bad for me in that department. He was only trying to help. Regardless, he could have easily given me the box in private and saved me the indignity of opening it in front of others. I still needed to have words with him about his choice of delivery but had decided the silent treatment would be best for the weekend. I didn't want to be angry when we spoke and I'd needed to let some time lapse so I could cool off about it.

He had texted me a few times over the weekend, to which I kept my replies short. When he'd asked if we would meet Sunday, I'd told him I had plans after church, and I couldn't make it. As much as I wanted to spend time with him and get the sourness out of my body for the humiliation he caused me, I was way too overwhelmed with my house. It had already been emotional work, and I hadn't hit the hard stuff yet. I had nothing left in me for Alex.

I stayed in bed for a moment, continuing to stare at the seemingly harmless white gift bag. My curiosity started to take over. I went to retrieve a cup of coffee and to see what my in-laws were doing. Deb was at work, and Robert was out running errands. I wouldn't have any help at the house until the afternoon, so nothing stopped me from testing out my new toy.

Nothing besides my hesitations, of course.

It was rare to have the house to myself. Hesitations aside, being alone gave me the courage to at least open the packaging and look at it. I brought it back to bed with me and stared at it. With a deep breath, I pulled the tissue paper out of the bag and the little envelope fell in my lap. I had forgotten there was more to the gift than just the box. I ripped open the envelope and pulled out a small card.

There was a handwritten note:

> *When you use this, think of my tongue and mouth all over you. Next time we're together I want to hear what you've learned about yourself.*
>
> *Yours always,*
> *Alex*

His words made a deep part of me ache for his touch. I was certain a little plastic vibrating object could never make me react the way he had. However, feeling braver by the moment, I removed the outer plastic from the cardboard box and opened it. I grabbed the silver bullet-looking device and rolled it around in my palm. It was no longer than the span of my hand. I closed my eyes and took a deep breath. Why did this feel so terrifying?

Because new things are scary, deep inner voice reminded me.

I figured out how to turn it on and giggled when it tickled the skin of my palm. I closed my eyes and pulled strength and confidence from Reese's pep talk on Friday night. She'd made it sound so easy, so normal.

I took off my pajama bottoms and slipped under the covers. I already felt embarrassed and I hadn't even done anything yet.

You can do this! Deep inner voice was a great cheerleader.

I took it slow by letting the vibrating bullet graze my inner thighs. I tried to think about what Alex would do, but A) I wasn't a dude, and B) we hadn't had enough experiences together yet to mimic his moves.

When I had more courage built up, I gently rested it where it was supposed to go. It definitely didn't feel like Alex's mouth, but it was enjoyable. *So now what?* Doing it alone didn't seem so fun. I had nobody telling me how good I tasted. Nobody spoke dirty to me. Nobody kissed me in all my sensitive spots. It kind of felt anticlimactic...pun intended.

Concentrate, deep inner voice scolded.

Concentrate on what? I wanted someone on top of me, doing it for me.

No. Not just someone. I wanted Alex.

Pretend he's here, she said.

I took a deep breath and tried to do what my internal dialogue told me to do. It *was* what his note had instructed, after all. I imagined his couch and the way he looked at me with passionate eyes. I thought about how his tongue grazed and explored my most sensitive of areas. I concentrated hard on the memory of being with Alex so intimately...

The next thing I knew, I was writing my mental list of what I needed to buy at Home Depot later so I could keep packing up my house.

"Ugh! I can't do this!" I shouted to nobody but myself. Sometimes you can't teach an old dog new tricks. Disgruntled and irritated, I threw the covers back and angrily hopped out of bed. I rummaged through my drawers quickly to find a pair of jeans. There were none to be found. Hrmph! Working and sweating at the house created more laundry than I was used to. I found a mustard-colored knee-length bohemian skirt hanging out on the top of my drawer. I looked down at the black tank top I was wearing. It would match well enough.

I took one look at my hair and face and realized I was in great need of a shower. I didn't have patience for that, so I put on a black baseball cap and headed out with the offensive silver bullet in the pocket of my skirt. As I headed to my car, I asked myself why I had just cared so much about what I looked like. I had rarely given it a thought around Alex.

It's because you're already feeling so self-conscious that you wanted to at least make your outer appearance more presentable, surface voice informed.

So nice of her to show up.

I started my car and backed out of the driveway, grumbling to myself about how it was probably very unhealthy to hear pretend voices all the time.

I needed to get the offensive thing out of my possession as soon as possible, and I knew exactly who the giftee should be. I found his Wrangler when I pulled up to the gym. Relief washed over me at the sight of his vehicle. Returning it would only take a moment. Then I would be free of the disappointment that I was a failure.

I entered the gym and scanned the whole first level. He was often with clients at the weight machines. If that were the case, I'd have to find a way to stealthily return the gift. Or I could wave it in front of him and his client for a good show—and a little payback. I'd have to see what option appealed to me in the moment.

After making a full loop of the club and unsuccessfully finding him, I walked toward the check-in desk to see if the employee could help me. Patti was there, chewing her gum obnoxiously and looking at her phone. She wasn't my favorite employee, but hopefully she knew Alex's preferred hiding spots.

I approached the desk. "Hi, Patti. I don't know if we've ever met officially. I'm Jane, one of Alex's friends." The words came out more nervous than they should have.

She forced a smile. "I know who you are."

"Oh! Well, hi. Nice to meet you." A nervous chuckle escaped my lips. "Anyway, do you know where he is?"

"He's in his office," she replied. Her focus went back to her phone, sending the hint that she was done assisting me, and it was time for me to carry on somewhere else.

"Right. Okay." I paused. "Um...could you tell me where that is?"

Without breaking eye contact with her phone, she pointed to the corner of the second-level walking track. There was indeed a door and row of windows up there I had never noticed before. She ignored my thank you as I headed toward the staircase in the same corner. I leaped up the stairs, two at a time, more anxious by the second to get rid of the toy in my pocket.

When I made it all the way up, I could hear Alex speaking on the phone through the crack in the door. For a second, I thought about waiting to knock until he was done but quickly determined Alex being distracted was the better option. So instead of being polite, I barged right in. Alex was in workout clothes, sitting in an office chair with his legs crossed on top of the desk. As soon as I entered, he swiftly uncrossed his legs and brought them to the floor.

His face lit up in surprise and delight at seeing me, but he was still in conversation, so he couldn't ask questions. I rummaged into my pocket to find the silver bullet, my shaky hands struggling to find it in all the fabric. I finally grabbed hold of it, lifted it to show him what it was, placed it on the desk where his feet just were, and turned to march out. I hadn't even crossed the threshold and already felt better. I was free of the pressure that terrible gift brought me.

I made it only to the edge of the staircase, a few feet past the door jamb, before a strong hand grabbed hold of my arm and prevented me from going any farther.

16

Alex

"GOING SO SOON?" I held Jane's arm and guided her back into my office. She didn't fight my grasp, thankfully.

"Who are you talking to?" my father asked on the other end of the line.

"Dad, I have to call you back." I hit end before he could say he wasn't finished discussing the upcoming charity gala he'd organized. The gala wasn't for almost two weeks. My dad could wait.

The beauty in front of me obviously could not.

I closed my office door to prevent nosy members from overhearing our conversation. Jane paced back and forth, clearly agitated. "What a pleasant surprise to see you this morning," I said sincerely, leaning carefully on the floor-length mirror that was attached to the back of the door. She didn't say anything or look at me, but instead kept with her pacing. She reminded me of a wild animal at a zoo—the ones who have so much unused energy that they pace their enclosures all day. "Do you want to tell me what's wrong?" I tried to keep my voice smooth enough to avoid irritating her even more.

She stopped abruptly and looked right at me. "Not really!" she exclaimed and crossed her arms. Her cheeks were flushed, and tears were about to escape her eyelids at any moment.

I had known giving her that gift would make her uncomfortable at first. I expected a little pushback and maybe minor annoyance. I did not expect her to be so upset. Anger was the exact opposite emotion that I'd been looking for.

I needed to fix my mistake. *Now.*

The blinds were open on the windows, so I slowly closed each one while I kept my eyes on Jane. She didn't look like she wanted to make a run for it, so my nerves relaxed a bit. Instead, she leaned against my desk, looking down at her skirt, with her arms still crossed defensively. Once I knew we were truly alone, I met her at the desk and slowly picked up the vibrator. When I had her attention, I put the tip of it to my nose and inhaled. A blast of her scent hit me at once. *Damn, she smelled so good.* Just inhaling her aroma had my body reacting. Her eyes opened wide, but only for a second before the mask of anger returned. I turned the vibrator on and let it trail around and tickle my fingers. "Has my gift offended you?"

"Yes," she snapped.

I picked up her hand and made it tickle her fingers. "Are you ready to tell me why?"

She didn't respond to the touch; she was too irritated. "You could have given me a more obvious warning that I should have opened the bag in private. You *humiliated* me in front of my friends. What if I would have had a client that *wasn't* a friend, Alex? How inappropriate would that have been?" She nearly shouted, pain and embarrassment plastered all over her face.

I had no good excuse. The "friend" comment had completely thrown me off at the salon to the point of rudeness. "You're right. I'm really sorry," I apologized as I kissed just below her ear. "It was wrong of me," I whispered onto her skin. "Very wrong. Do you forgive me?"

"Maybe. Probably not," she mumbled sarcastically, which made me chuckle quietly.

I kept my lips at her ear. "Can I make it up to you?"

She took a deep breath before she answered, "Don't embarrass me like that again."

"I promise I won't. I'm sorry," I repeated the apology. "Is there anything else upsetting you?" I had a feeling deeper issues were going on.

She took another deep breath. "I can't do it. I tried. I can't concentrate. I don't know what I'm doing. I have too much in my life to worry about. I don't need to be worrying how to do *that*. And how terrible I'll be at it."

I still toyed with her fingers as I chose my words carefully. "I respectfully disagree. I feel you have so much going on in your life that you cannot afford to deprive yourself of a much needed release."

Jane shook her head in firm disagreement. "I can't do it," she repeated. "Besides, didn't we do fine—on your couch together?"

I raised an eyebrow at her. "More than fine, I'd say."

Her cheeks turned crimson. "Okay, much better than fine. But that's my point. What good does it do to force this new—skill on me, if I can have a professional do it for me?"

"Valid point." I let the vibrator trail to her wrist, then up her forearm. I rested it at the sensitive crook of her elbow before I kept moving upward. She looked confused, but let me continue. "It's not so offensive right now, is it?" She shook her head slowly. I curved it around her shoulder and headed back down toward her breasts. "I still disagree with you." She went to say something, but I put a finger to her lips. "Don't say anything yet. Just feel," I instructed as I brought the vibrator to the thin fabric covering one of her breasts. I trailed it around in circles a few times before I let the tip graze her nipple. Her breathing increased. "How about now? Is this offending you?" She didn't reply. Instead, she wrapped her hands around my arms to pull me in for a kiss. It wasn't often that she initiated physical touch. I vowed to myself I would never deny her when she did. Seeing and feeling her reaction to my teasing with the vibrator made me want to skip the lesson completely and ride her right there on top of my desk. I refrained, though, since the task at hand was far too important.

The waistband of her skirt was perfectly loose for easy access. Once I teased both of her nipples, I trailed the vibrator down to her navel and then under her waistband. Then an idea hit me. Without pulling back out of her skirt, I rearranged our positions so I was leaning on the edge of my desk and she was in front of me. Both of us were facing the mirror hanging on the door. I pulled her in to me tightly and guided her legs apart. She caught herself in the mirror for a brief second and then closed her eyes.

"I want you to watch," I whispered in her ear. I placed the vibrator on her clit so she could get a feel for what was to come—only with *her* hand in charge instead of mine. Her mouth parted and she arched back in satisfaction. "Open your eyes, Jane," I demanded gently. She complied but looked anywhere but the mirror. I continued to play with her delicate area but wanted her to understand my reasoning behind the lesson. I didn't know how long she'd last and we still had to get to her turn holding the toy. "Back to your argument—yes, I would love nothing more than to pleasure you all day, every day, for the rest of our lives."

Her breathing became heavier so I lifted the vibrator away from her body. I couldn't let her come yet. Her disappointed eyes went to the mirror in an instant. I chuckled under my breath and kissed the side of her face. I rubbed her spot lightly with my fingers so it wouldn't be too lonely while I pleaded my case. "There are a couple of reasons why I'm teaching you this skill. The first one is I'm not with you all the time. You need to be able to take care of yourself when I'm not around." She looked as if she wanted to argue, but didn't have the words or energy to fight. I replaced my fingers with the vibrator, which made her backside instinctually push into me. She swayed her hips slightly right and left, as if to invite other parts of my body to the party. "Not yet, baby, remember? Always you first," I whispered in her ear. That was a policy I'd created for Jane during the long year of fantasizing about intimate moments. I had never given it much thought prior to her, but my delicate flower needed to know she would always be the priority. It was a rule I vowed to stick to if she ever let me get close enough. So far, I was thoroughly pleased with the decision.

I found one of her hands and brought it under the skirt fabric to meet me and the vibrator. At first, I had both my hands and one of hers holding on to the little toy. Then, casually, I set her hand directly on it and put my hand on top of hers, letting her take the lead. I gently guided her to explore herself as I finished my argument. "The second reason is what I've told you already. I need to know you're confident enough to tell me your desires—what you like, what you don't like, and what you need at the moment. All of that stems from practicing on yourself."

I let go of the vibrator and rested my hands on her hips. She didn't stop in protest, which is what I'd expected her to do. Instead, she leaned into me a little deeper and kept exploring. Her eyes were closed again, and her head rested on me. As much as I wanted her to see what she was doing to herself, I had to concede. I watched intently through the mirror as her breathing increased and her hips moved around again. I thought about giving her more pep talking but stayed quiet and still. She needed to experience it on her own.

After a couple of minutes, I could feel the heat radiating off her body. She was close, which had my lower half standing at full attention through my shorts. Jane's mouth opened and her breathing increased even more. I held on tighter to her hips to steady her. A moment later a soft moan escaped her lips as she, for the very first time, brought herself to orgasm. I let her recover for a couple of minutes without saying anything, but my hands and lips immediately found her body. I reached under her tank top to find her breasts and trailed my lips over every part of her face and jawline.

"See, baby, not so bad, right?"

Jane didn't reply. She was still recovering. She opened her eyes and looked right into the mirror at me. Even after what she'd just accomplished, she looked hungry. She turned around to face me and ran her hand down to the hardness under my shorts. She started rubbing and stroking it the best she could through clothing. "Would you like me to use my mouth?" she asked, still hot and breathy from her climax.

My heart raced at once. I hadn't expected her to offer so soon—or ever. She was trying to please me with communication, which meant she had taken everything I'd said to heart. She leaned in to kiss my neck and collarbone. I closed my eyes and enjoyed her volunteer touch. I didn't deserve such a perfect woman. I would never stop proving to her how much I loved her, even if her history would never allow her to reciprocate.

I used my finger to pull her chin up for a long, deep, appreciative kiss. "Only if you want to," I whispered, finally answering her question. Her eyes lit up as she pushed the waistband of my shorts to the floor. She held on to me, stroking up and down. Her hands were made of silk. I couldn't even imagine how good her mouth would feel. The pressure started building inside of me, so I willed myself to slow down the moment.

Jane pulled the chair around to sit in front of me and then guided me to rest back on the edge of the desk. She pressed my legs apart to give herself room, ripped the baseball hat off her head, and bent over to kiss my most sensitive part. My breathing hitched as the sensation ran up my spine. She trailed kisses up and down, taunting and teasing me with her lips, tongue, and hands. I wanted to tell her to use her mouth before it was too late, but we would do it her way, no matter how quickly my climax came. She must have sensed I was close already because she put her mouth around me and sucked deep. I nearly fell back in pleasure. For a girl who'd been so worried about being inexperienced, she knew what she was doing.

As expected, it didn't take long for me to feel the pressure build. I involuntarily put a hand in her hair and delicately pulsed up into her mouth until I met my orgasm. My entire body lit on fire. *How was this even happening? What had I done to deserve it?* One by one, my dreams were coming true. Even while living it, I couldn't believe it.

Jane dutifully sucked and swallowed as my whole body quivered in satisfaction. When my hips stopped pressing into her, she pulled her mouth back with one last suck and raised herself to my lips to kiss me. The act made another shiver run up my spine.

"You're better at this than you give yourself credit for." My voice sounded low and throaty. "No lessons needed there." I chuckled quietly. "You are exemplary. Thank you." She smiled slyly, placed another kiss on my lips, and pulled away from me to allow me to stand up and redress.

We were silent for a minute as she went to find her hat and I moved the chair back where it belonged. I looked at the clock. I didn't want our time together to end, but I had a client soon and needed to calm my body down in the thin basketball shorts I wore. It wouldn't be professional to walk around my gym with a boner. I found the vibrator and put it in her skirt pocket. She didn't fight it, but instead gave me a shy grin.

I pulled her in for another deep kiss. I needed to ask her something before we parted. "When you came in, I was on the phone with my father. He has arranged a black-tie charitable gala in Chicago for the Vietnam Veterans of America Foundation. It's in two weeks and he needs me to attend." She listened intently, probably wondering what my point was. "It would be my honor if you joined me."

"Black-tie?" she questioned, with a little anxiety in her voice.

I nodded.

"What's the date?"

"May 13th."

She thought about it for a brief moment. "Alex, thank you for the invite, but I don't think I can." My face fell in disappointment. "I'm so sorry. I have a crazy two weeks ahead of me. I'm not sure I'd even have time to go dress shopping." She stared into space, pensive for a moment. "No, I'm certain I don't have time to go dress shopping." I wondered what was on her plate for the next two weeks, but really had to get out on the floor and find my client. For the time being, I just needed her to accept my invitation.

"Don't worry about the attire. I'll have everything ready for you before that day." I gently kissed the tip of her nose. "Please." The word came out more of a plea than a request. I brought my lips up to her forehead while she pondered her decision. "Please," I repeated.

"Okay," she said quietly.

My heart skipped a beat at her acceptance. The idea of walking into a gala with Jane, her arm resting on mine for the world to see, had me beyond elated. "I look forward to it, Ms. Cora." I leaned in for one last kiss and guided us to the door, making a mental note to delete the security camera footage from my office at some point in the day.

EXACTLY ONE WEEK before the gala, my father, Anthony, surprised me at my home with dinner and a bottle of our favorite bourbon. He had flown in a few days beforehand to oversee the final arrangements. My dad and I had a unique relationship. We were family, friends, but also business partners. And yet somehow it worked. We didn't see each other in person all that often anymore. But when we were together, it was like no time had passed. He was my hero, role model, and one of my best friends. He was also interested in my dating life and always worried about why I hadn't settled down. It was a topic of conversation every time we were together. So it didn't take long until he brought it up.

"So who's the latest flavor?" Anthony asked after we finished dinner and moved to the three-season room to chat. I took a sip of my Blanton's to buy myself a moment to decide how much I wanted to share. Jane had encompassed all parts of me for over a year, and I hadn't spoken much about her to anyone. I still had the strong desire to keep our relationship private, but my dad was the most trustworthy man I knew. He also was happily married to the same woman for over thirty years. He knew how to keep a woman satisfied long-term. Maybe he'd have some advice for me.

All of a sudden I had a strong urge to share with him how much Jane meant to me. "Well, I wouldn't call her a flavor." I chuckled, feeling a little nervous. "She's much more significant than that."

Anthony's eyes opened wide in surprise. "Alexander, are you seeing someone, and you didn't tell us?"

I shook my head. "Unfortunately, we're not official. But I'm working on it. It's a slow and steady race with her."

I had not seen my dad light up like that in years. He must've been truly concerned about my long-term happiness. For the next hour, Anthony made me divulge everything about Jane and our budding relationship.

Well, almost everything. I left out the obvious parts that should stay confidential.

I had to admit it felt really good to talk to someone about her—someone who listened intently and gave advice when asked. When my dad left for the evening, he and I both were more at ease than when he'd arrived. I was thankful for the much needed conversation. He seemed grateful that I wasn't going to be married to my work forever. We shook hands, hugged, and left on a note that he couldn't wait to meet the young lady I spoke of so fondly. I felt heat in my cheeks at his parting words. There was nobody I'd rather bring home to my parents than Jane.

When I lay down for bed that night, I couldn't help but think about the week I'd just had. Monday had been a very good day. It didn't happen often that my week peaked on a Monday. Just *thinking* about her mouth on me got my lower half excited. And the vibrator lesson I had been trying to teach her could not have gone any better.

Well, with one exception—we hadn't been able to decompress or even talk about our experiences afterward. I'd had to leave abruptly, which bummed me out. It mimicked the first time, on my couch, when Reese interrupted us before we could communicate. Those details probably hadn't fazed Jane at all. I, on the other hand, was irritated. I hoped our next intimate moment could be a bit slower. I wanted to make love to her all night and wake up next to her beautiful naked body to do it all again in the morning. That was my next goal and I hoped to accomplish it the night of the gala.

In regard to the gala, another fantastic part of Monday had been getting Reese on board to help me dress Jane for the event. I knew it would be a long shot to convince her to do me a favor, but she was my best option. I chuckled quietly to myself while recalling the conversation we'd had, and my remark that made her comply:

"If you don't want to help me, fine. But you're hurting Jane more. She could show up in a garbage bag, and I'd think she looked perfect. She's going to this gala whether you help or not, and I'm pretty sure she doesn't want to wear a big piece of thin plastic."

That had sold Reese. She might despise me, but she'd never let Jane down. I thanked her, told her I owed her, and gave her a few specific requests regarding Jane's attire. My input riled Reese up once again, and so I—once again—told her the favor was for Jane. She growled and hung up on me. Angry or not, I knew she'd get the job done.

As if Monday could have gotten any better, I'd received an anonymous text that afternoon. It was a screenshot of the recreation center schedule for Saturday. Jane's name was listed on the schedule for an 8:00 a.m. dual ride with Luis. I assumed the anonymous number was Luis's, but since he didn't offer his name, I only replied with "Thank you." I was thankful for a couple of reasons—for the information to be included in her first class back. And also for the support. Whoever had texted me had to be supportive of my courting Jane. I smiled to myself and was grateful my reputation hadn't ruined the impression of me for *everyone* close to her.

With the help of the bourbon and therapeutic conversation with my dad, I drifted off to sleep quickly, very content with how far Jane and I had come. It might not be at the pace I'd prefer, but it was heading more forward every day. Before sleep took over completely, I wondered if she would ever allow my ring on her hand. I imagined sliding a large, clear diamond on her finger when the time was right.

"Yes" was the only answer I'd allow myself to dream about.

"ALL RIGHT, PARTY people! Are we ready?" Jane asked her spin class as she set up her mic at 8:00 a.m. exactly. I looked around to estimate how many bikes were filled with riders. The room was mostly dark. The only lights spotlighted on her and Luis, so it was hard to count. My guess was around fifty, all filled. Jane was met with a room full of loud "Woos," and hollering at her question. "I love the energy! Let's do this!" she exclaimed as she clipped into her pedals. She hadn't seen me walk in, which was fine by me. I wanted to see her in her element without the potential nerves my presence could bring.

She started cycling, which prompted all of us to follow suit. "If you don't know or remember me, my name is Jane." The class erupted in cheers again. "I'm so happy to be back with you all today." More cheers from the crowd. It was obvious she was a favorite instructor—or maybe *the* favorite. "And you all know the man riding next to me." The crowd cheered again, but definitely not as loud.

"Yeah, yeah, we all know they're here for you," Luis said with a wink in Jane's direction.

Jane laughed and looked at her bike, seemingly embarrassed. Her hair was in her signature style down her back. She wore a simple black sports bra and black leggings. She had makeup on, which was rare for her. The most beautiful part of all was the smile she had plastered on her face. Genuine, carefree happiness exuded from her.

She was so fucking hot.

Jane continued the warmup as "Good as Hell" by Lizzo blared in the background.

"You all are aware of our leaderboard, right?" Jane asked the crowd. They cheered back. "If this is your first ride, listen up. There is a leaderboard behind us. It will light up in a little bit with the results of the top twenty riders. If being competitive is not your jam, no worries. Just ignore it." She told us to increase our bike resistance before she continued her explanation, "But if you *are* competitive..." She smiled a flirtatious smile. "Good luck."

The next twenty minutes or so were beyond any expectations I had. She came alive on that bike. She was funny, witty, and very knowledgeable. She and Luis bantered back and forth at just the right times. The workout was tough, but it felt so much like a show that I forgot I was working hard.

After one of the more challenging intervals, the leaderboard popped up behind them. They both had screens attached to their bikes, so they could call out the top riders. "All right, let's see what's happening out there," Jane said as she was reading her screen. "We've got Peter M in lead. Followed by Dean C and Alex L." Both Jane's and my faces were surprised in unison. *Dean*? I looked out at all the riders to search for him at the same time I heard Jane call my name. "Alex Lombardi? Where are you?" I hesitantly raised my hand. She saw me and smiled. "You guys, I have a couple of special friends here today. Please give Alex," she directed her hand my way, "and Dean," she directed our attention to the other side of the room, "a warm welcome." Everyone clapped and cheered for us. Dean and I were in the same row, on opposite ends. The rows were set up in a shallow U, so Dean and I could see each other from where we rode. I nodded at him in acknowledgment, out of obligation. He did not reciprocate the gesture.

So that's how it was going to be. All right. Bring it on.

She removed the leaderboard so the class would focus on her and Luis for the next instructions. Jane was all smiles as sweat dripped from every inch of her skin. A large part of me was irritated that at least half the riders were male and they were all—no doubt—watching her body in the same ways I was, Dean included.

"Nice work on that last climb. After this short break on a flat road, we'll start the next climb. It's a bit steep so adjust that resistance! It should be in your medium to high range." Jane looked around to make sure we were all ready. "Now let's rise out of the saddle. Pedal strokes on the beat!" Jane instructed firmly while lifting herself off her bike.

Her instructions put my head back in the game. One thing I knew for sure—I was not going to let Dean beat me on that leaderboard. I kept the resistance higher and pushed harder. I was soaked with sweat. My legs were on fire. At some point I looked down the row to see Dean looking the same way. It appeared he had the same goal.

While Luis instructed, I caught Jane glancing both Dean's and my way. She giggled into her mic. "Just so all you newbies know, there's no prize for the winner. Only bragging rights."

That was prize enough for me.

The rest of class went quickly. We cooled down and used some small weights for arm work. I was anxious to see that leaderboard pop up again. As soon as I thought it, Jane spoke. "Okay, everyone. I hope you had a great class." The crowd cheered again. She pushed a button on her screen—the moment of truth.

The leaderboard displayed my name first. *Fuck yes.* As much as I wanted to look down the row at Dean, I refrained. "Looks like Alex came out on top. Followed by Dean and then Peter. Amazing job, guys! And awesome job to all of you! Thank you for the warm welcome back. Have a good rest of your weekend!" Jane exclaimed.

I stayed on the bike for a minute, peddling slowly. My body needed to recover from the ass-kicking. Once I caught my breath, I unclipped my shoes and headed to the common area to find my girl. She had a crowd of people around her, so I waited my turn. Jane saw me waiting and excused herself from the group.

She came over and raised her arm for a high-five. I met her hand with a clap and then grabbed it to pull her in to me. "That was unbelievable," I whispered in her ear. She giggled, appearing to still be riding the high from class.

"Thank you." She smiled at me with pride. It was obvious how much she loved what she'd just done in there. "I didn't know you were coming."

"I didn't either until a random phone number sent me a screenshot of the schedule." I couldn't hide the hurt in my voice that she hadn't invited me herself.

She looked down as she spoke. "I wasn't sure it would be appropriate, since you own a gym close by. I don't know what the rules are," she replied with chagrin.

I was about to respond when Dean came up behind Jane and put his arm around her waist. "Jane, we've got to go. We have a long day ahead." Dean must have been referencing why she'd felt so overwhelmed recently. I glared at the hand that touched her bare midriff. My heart raced immediately. I wanted to rip his arm off.

Jane casually stepped out of Dean's grasp. "Okay. I'll meet you outside in a sec," she said to him.

"What are you up to today?" I asked her, no longer willing to be on the outside of important information.

She watched Dean walk away. "Uh…I sold my house. I have to be out soon. Dean is helping me pack and move the items I'm planning on keeping."

The hits kept coming. "And you didn't ask me to help because…?" I tried to keep my voice calm. She had some big moments happening in her life, and she purposely was not including me in any of them. It wasn't the time to talk deep, so I would have to accept however she responded. For now.

She looked a little guilty. Her words came out faster than usual. "Because I wasn't sure if I'd need more help. Dean's on leave from work. He needs to stay occupied at the moment. And I didn't think having you two in a house together all weekend would be a good idea."

All. Weekend.

I took a breath to relax the jealousy that simmered to the surface. What could I say that wouldn't cause conflict between us?

Luckily, I didn't have to respond. Dean came back into the common area. He grabbed Jane's hand and tried to pull her toward the door. "Jane, let's go!" He said it so forcefully that my primal instincts to defend my girl took over.

I batted his hand away from her, which landed me right in his face. "Do *not* talk to her that way." It came out almost as a growl. Dean was about to say something back, but Jane was right there in an instant, trying to diffuse the situation.

"Hey, Alex. It's okay." She put a comforting hand on my chest. "He didn't mean anything by it." Raising on her toes to first place a slow, gentle kiss on my cheek, she spoke quietly in my ear, as if she wanted the moment to be just between us. "I'm glad you were here. I'll see you later. Thank you for coming."

I turned my head to bring our lips together. She wasn't ready for the kiss but didn't pull away immediately, which I counted as a win. I explored her lips for a brief moment before she let go.

"My pleasure," I said, hoping she remembered me saying the same sentiment after our couch endeavor. She blushed and looked away just before Dean pulled her toward the door.

She remembered.

17

Jane

DEAN AND I headed to Maple Street right away after spin class. He was right; we had a lot to accomplish today, so in a way I was thankful for him rushing me out of the rec center. I had taken care of as much as I could at the house in the past week, and of course my in-laws helped a lot too. But, some tasks I couldn't—and didn't want to—do alone. We changed out of our sweaty clothes into outfits we packed for the day and got right to work.

"What do we have to accomplish in the next two days?" Dean asked.

I sighed. Just thinking about everything that had to be done gave me anxiety. I waved around the first floor, which was looking bare. "I've packed up and organized everything on this level. Aside from the kitchen table and chairs, couch, and end tables, all of this furniture is for sale. Deb and Robert should be here any minute to run the garage sale and they'll let any customers know what furniture inside is up for grabs. Anything not sold in the next two days will be donated." I took a steadying breath before I went on. "I need to go through the bedrooms and decide what I want to keep." I fought the emotion that had already started to build. "I didn't want to do this part alone and didn't want to obligate my in-laws to help. They've done so much for me already." I lowered my eyes to the floor. I had been doing so well with my emotions lately. However, the process of packing up my kids' rooms was going to try to break me. I could feel it.

Dean closed the distance between us and took my hand. "This is why I'm here, Janey. You're going to get through this." He pulled me through the hall and up the stairs. "Which room first?"

I wanted to work through the rooms from oldest to youngest, so we started with my bedroom. I pulled out a couple of articles of clothing that were Graham's favorites and asked Dean to box up the rest to take downstairs to the garage sale. I sorted out my clothes I hadn't worn in over a year, wondering why I'd kept so many articles that I didn't even like. We worked in silence for a while. Every so often, Dean would hold up an old nostalgic shirt of Graham's to make sure I wanted to donate it. Some of the shirts I chose to hold on to while others jogged memories that made the shirt far too painful to keep. I had to teeter a fine line between keeping materials that reminded me of my loves, without throwing me into a depression every time I looked at them. Grief was a sneaky bitch at the current stage of my healing process. Most of the time I felt okay. Then out of the blue, I'd hear or see something that reminded me of my past happy life. It would trigger so much pain that it would feel as though my heart and lungs were collapsing into themselves.

I could already sense the black pit forming in my chest and we had just started. Plates, coffee cups, coasters, leftover liquor, couches, and throw blankets did not hold a fraction of the sentimentality that the second floor held. I'd been kidding myself all week when I thought I'd get through the process unscathed.

After I was done with my clothes, I went to the little dresser that held Arlo's small wardrobe. I took a deep breath and opened the top drawer. Most of Arlo's clothes had been Marric's, so they held even more memories. I saved some of the cuter pieces that didn't have spit-up stains and threw most of the rest in a trash bag. After being through two babies, most pieces were not worth donating.

I paused for a moment to analyze the black pit in my heart. Pulling out Arlo's clothes felt exceptionally painful. The little dude hadn't even started walking, and his short life was already over. A pang of guilt shot through me that we'd created a little being that didn't live the life he deserved. As much as I believed in God's will, I struggled with why He would take all my little babies away from me so abruptly. I know, without a doubt, they would have had happy, prosperous lives. The pain of losing my family felt insurmountable, but losing little Arlo felt even worse than that. He was too young to even understand he was alive. He had very little awareness of life, aside from the few people he loved. His opportunity to live was taken from him in a flash. I was not sure if reincarnation was a real thing. Catholics didn't believe in it. But for Arlo's sake, I secretly hoped he came back again as a little boy in a loving family. He deserved to try again.

When Dean took a load downstairs, I sat on Graham's side of the bed and closed my eyes, trying to remember our last night together. Did we watch a movie in bed? Did we talk before we drifted off to sleep? How had his day been? Did the kids do anything funny that had made us giggle softly in the dark as Arlo nursed himself to sleep?

As much as I attempted to extract any memory, nothing showed up in the forefront of my brain. It was frustrating but also made me sad. I had already lost everything; the least I could get was some of the last memories. I let myself feel the grief and wiped away the tears when I heard Dean approaching.

We finished my room in a little more than an hour and headed to Clare's room. Clare, my baby girl—the only girl besides me in a house full of rambunctious boys. Clare and I had a bond that was special to girls. We would always make faces at each other when the boys made fart jokes. We ran away quickly when a playful tackle session broke out. We'd bake together while the rest of the family was more interested in the final product than the steps in production. We understood each other.

I walked around her room, trying to decide where to start. I couldn't help but mourn the loss of being able to watch her sprout into a gorgeous young lady. She would have been a wonderful wife and mother one day if she had desired. I opened her drawers and took out her clothes. I set a few items aside for my memento bin. Drawer by drawer, I emptied the contents and put everything in a laundry basket to bring down to my in-laws. I pulled many of the clothes to my nose, hoping to smell even a fragment of my daughter. Just like the last time I was on Maple Street, trying to do the same to Marric's bedding, I smelled nothing but detergent. After about the tenth piece of clothing, I crumpled to the floor and held a piece of her clothes to my heart.

If I couldn't smell anything, maybe being near her belongings would make me feel closer to her. I was desperate for any connection.

Dean had left the room to bring a load downstairs, so I was alone. I didn't know how long I sat there, rocking back and forth with one of Clare's pajama shirts pressed into my chest. The next thing I knew, Dean pulled me up from the floor and wiped away the tears from my eyes.

"Janey," he breathed out. "If this is too much to do in one day, we can stop after this room and work on something else." His eyes were wide with concern.

"No," I said, wiping my eyes and nose with the back of my hand. "I need to do this today." Spreading out the painful task would only hurt more. "I don't need to keep any of her toys, so all we need to do is pack them up for the garage sale and then we can move on." Dean nodded in understanding and headed to Clare's closet. I added the pajama shirt I snuggled to the "keep" pile, along with her favorite teddy bear, and went to grab more laundry baskets to tote everything downstairs.

We entered Marric's room next—my sweet middle child, who had never stopped smiling. I swore the baby came out of the womb happy. He was my easiest labor, easiest breastfeeder, and best sleeper. He followed Clare around anywhere she went, much to her dissatisfaction. He loved all things fire trucks, garbage trucks, and construction trucks. He was a special little boy. I remember looking at him in the hospital the day I'd had him, thinking he was the most beautiful baby boy I had ever seen. He had me wrapped around his finger on day one. He was my charmer and my comedian. At his young age, he would already do anything for a laugh.

After going through all his belongings, I lay on his bed to let myself feel the pain of never coming back into his room to tuck him in for the fourth time in one night. He'd always needed "just one more kiss goodnight." Never would I read him another Dr. Seuss book. I'd never see his bright smile the first thing in the morning. I'd never kiss him goodbye and send him off to preschool. Never again would I watch him run out of his classroom with a poster board of art he was so excited to show me. I'd never help him get ready for sports events, or his first date, or for prom. I'd never get to watch him graduate from high school or college. All of those milestones and memories were stolen from me. And from him. And from all my other loves.

I hadn't realized I was vocally sobbing until Dean came in from wherever he had been and immediately laid on Marric's bed with me. He tucked my back into his chest and held me tightly. He kissed my hair and my shoulder over and over until my sobs subsided and my breathing slowed. I said a few silent prayers to God and my family, asking for support to get me through the rest of the journey of selling our home.

The prayers calmed me down to the point that I was ready to get up and keep going. I grabbed Dean's hand, which had been draped over me, and kissed it a few times in thanks. He kissed my shoulder once more before I moved out of his grasp. I forced myself out of Marric's bed for the very last time. I tried not to think about that fact too deeply.

We worked in silence, which I was thankful for. Nothing he, or anyone else, could say would help. I needed to let myself feel all the feelings. Unfortunately, I had learned over and over that feeling grief was part of the healing. I would call my grief group to ask if I could attend more than one session next week. The black pit took up most of my chest, but I refused to surrender to it. I had worked so hard on getting my grief to a manageable level. I would not let the sorrow set me back too far. Yes, I needed to grieve. No, I didn't need to dwell indefinitely or fall into a deep depression.

Once the last of Marric's belongings had been packed up, we headed downstairs to see how the garage sale was going. Deb and Robert were finishing up for the afternoon and assured me they'd be back in the morning after church for day two. I thanked them over and over for their continued help. They both gave me a big hug and kiss and headed home.

We felt accomplished at the end of the day. Dean and I were completely done upstairs. The donation center would be at the house on Monday to take anything that hadn't sold. We didn't need to come back Sunday because my in-laws insisted on doing the garage sale on their own. Reese wouldn't have to give up her day off, which made me feel better about it all too.

Dean and I ordered take-out before we left my little home for the night.

My tears had fully subsided, and I wanted to spend more time there while I could. I knew my time on Maple Street was coming to a close. As much as I felt like it was the right decision, it was still going to hurt to say goodbye.

We settled into the couch once our takeout had been delivered. "What's going on with you two?" Dean asked randomly after a moment of silent eating.

He didn't need to elaborate. I knew whom he was talking about. I ate my salad in silence, ignoring his question. I didn't feel like having that conversation at the moment.

"Why are you avoiding my question?" It was as if he could read my mind.

I looked up at him questioningly, hoping he would catch on that I didn't want to talk about it. "Hmm?" I asked, playing dumb.

He stared at me with speculative eyes. "You and Alex. Are you in a relationship?"

I looked down and pushed my food around with my fork. "We have a relationship, yes."

"Jane," he chided.

I looked up at him. "I don't know what we are exactly, Dean. I know I care for him. But there's a lot I don't know right now."

"Do you see yourself ever being in a relationship again? With what happened, I mean?" His face was pained. I understood the underlying question. He wondered if I thought I could ever love again.

"Something my therapist has taught me is to stay in the present if the future gives me anxiety, which it does. Worrying about the future won't help me right now. So I'm not sure if I'll ever marry, or even be in a serious relationship again. One day at a time."

He nodded in understanding. "Without planning your future, do you care for Alex enough to consider having a relationship?" He basically reworded his two questions into one. He obviously wasn't going to let it go.

I stared off into the corner of the room, recapping all the memories I'd made with Alex already. I did my best not to blush at *some* of the recent images popping up. "Yeah, I think so. He's really good to me."

He huffed out a quiet breath. "I'm really good to you too," he stated shyly.

"Yes. You are." I met his eyes so he understood my gratitude.

He set his lips into a thin line before he spoke again. "Would you ever consider having a relationship with *me*?"

I closed my eyes briefly, not knowing how I was supposed to keep him in the *friend zone* without hurting his feelings. "I do have a relationship with you. You're family."

His beautiful blue eyes became more serious. "You know that's not what I mean."

I took a deep breath through my nose and let it out. "Dean, we went over this recently. You're hurting—"

He interrupted me. "I know what I want."

I shook my head in exasperation. "I don't doubt it. But do you honestly feel like it's a good idea to jump into a relationship right now?" My voice sounded a little higher pitched.

"I think it would do us both good to be together," he stated matter-of-factly.

I looked at my salad, all of a sudden too nauseated to eat. I didn't know what to say. I didn't want to hurt him. I didn't want to lead him on. I changed the subject and prayed he wouldn't double back to ask more relationship questions. "Have you looked up any therapists or support groups yet?"

Dean shook his head. Stubborn man.

"How about church? Have you tried going?"

He chuckled under his breath. "I'm not really the church kind of guy."

"I disagree. I think you could get a lot out of it if you found the right one for you." An idea hit me. "Come with us tomorrow. To church."

"Hmm. I don't know," he mused with a grin. "Do they let guys with tats in there?"

I snorted. "Of course. God doesn't judge you for having tattoos." I leaned over and laid my hand on his arm. "Please come."

"Only if you agree to make out with me in a confessional." He raised his eyebrows up and down.

"Dean!" My mouth opened wide in shock as I dug a tomato out of my salad to throw at him. Maybe I couldn't get him to church, but I'd still nag him about therapy. And I needed to make sure his alcohol consumption was not excessive. He hadn't had any booze while helping with the move, so I prayed he'd given up the heavy drinking after the case of Old Style a couple of weeks prior. "Thank you for helping me today." I was feeling very grateful to him.

"Anytime, sweetie," he replied with a smile.

THE FOLLOWING DAY I really looked forward to attending Mass. It had been a long week. As hard as some of the moments became during the packing up of my home, I was proud of myself for getting through it. It was too soon to tell, but I hoped it didn't damage me any further than I already was. The black hole didn't feel quite as large or dark as it had the day before. That being said, I was exhausted—mentally, emotionally, and physically. I knew that the service would bring me peace, help calm my mind, and hopefully push the darkness away from my heart.

We arrived at Mass early so we could mingle with our friends in the large gathering space adjacent to the front door. I casually listened to Mrs. Potter explain to me the difference between her homemade apple cider and juice, when I caught the image of my darling friend, in a button-down shirt and jeans, walking into the building. I excused myself from Mrs. Potter and greeted him at the door.

"You came. I'm so happy you're here." I wrapped my arms around his waist.

He chuckled quietly and then bent down to my ear. "I'll meet you in the confessional after Communion."

I released my grasp and smacked him playfully. "Yeah, I don't think so."

Dean greeted my in-laws before we headed into the sanctuary. We sat in our usual row and waited for the service to start. Dean grabbed my hand during the first reading and didn't let go. I knew I should have pulled away at some point. I didn't want to give him the wrong impression, but I kept my hand in his. He had come to church at my request, which I was sure was hard for him. The least I could do was give him some comfort. Besides, it felt nice to have a warm hand in mine. Every so often, he would pull our hands up to his lips before resting them back on his leg. I smiled at him and squeezed his hand. I said a little prayer in my head a few times, asking God to help heal Dean's heart.

During one of the hymns, my mind wandered to a life in which I could hold a partner's hand again at church. Understandably, I'd dismissed the idea for a while. But holding onto Dean reminded me how good it felt to be physically connected to someone I loved. I sighed quietly and asked God to continue to heal me too. Dean and I were the same that way. We'd always understand how much it hurt to lose our spouses. He didn't quite understand my pain from the loss of my children, but he had experienced losing the most important person to him. We related and were empathetic to each other's situations. We could pick one another up when the other was down. We could check in with each other in ways others couldn't. Or wouldn't. We had bonded because of something so terrible. It was the tiniest bit of good out of the worst possible circumstance. Dean was a priceless part of my life.

Not priceless enough to agree to make out in a holy space, but priceless all the same.

Right about the time my mind was creating mental pictures of being caught shirtless by the priest, Deb elbowed me back into reality and pushed me through the pew for Communion.

As Mass ended, I felt my phone vibrate in my bag. I usually wouldn't check my phone at church, but since nobody ever texted or called me before noon on Sundays, I figured I'd better check it to make sure it wasn't an emergency. It was a text from Alex:

> I want to see you today. Let me know if you can make that happen. I'll happily come help you pack if that's where you'll be.

I sat and thought about what could have sparked Alex's request. It didn't take long to put the puzzle together. One, it was Sunday, and church was ending. We'd spent most Sundays together for the past few months. Two, I hadn't invited him to my spin class or to help me move. He felt left out and probably hurt. Three, he knew Dean was in town.

I felt a little guilty for not including him in my recent significant moments. Even though I didn't exclude him maliciously, it bothered me I had upset him. I knew how much he cared about me. I shouldn't have been so careless in return.

I waited until we left the sanctuary to text Alex back:

> We are done at the house, but thank you for offering. Would you like to meet somewhere for lunch? Or I could come to your house?

He replied in seconds:

> My house works. Are you on your way then?

Soon, I replied. I looked up from my phone and realized I had gotten lost in the sea of parishioners entering the gathering space. I needed to find my people and say goodbye.

Dean's height helped me locate him quickly. I thanked him for coming and also for helping me move. I told him the busy week had exhausted me, and I needed to go rest. It was only a half lie. I *was* exhausted. He nodded in understanding and picked me up for a hug.

"We'll have to hit that confessional next time," he whispered in my ear.

I wiggled out of his grasp with a giggle. "Um...not happening!" I countered before I walked away to find my in-laws.

As I headed to my car, I realized I had no idea where Alex lived. I had only been there once, and I wasn't paying attention to the route. Right when I was about to text to ask for his address, he beat me to it and sent it to me. I shook my head and chuckled. Alex never seemed to miss any detail.

I put his address in my GPS. It was only ten minutes away. My heart skipped a beat in anticipation. Aside from a couple of quick moments, we hadn't spent much time together lately. I'd been so wrapped up in cleaning out Maple Street that I'd been neglecting him.

I pulled into his wraparound driveway and was able to get a good view of where he lived in the light of day. I was familiar with the two-story home in front of me. Just about everyone in Crystal Lake knew it too. It was a beautiful property, tucked into a more modest neighborhood. In fact, I was pretty sure it was considered the same neighborhood as Maple Street. I'd driven by it a thousand times, admiring the ornate stone exterior and perfect landscape. The house was probably 5,000 square feet and sat on just under an acre of land. It had a subtle way of hiding those features. That didn't diminish its beauty though. It belonged on a hillside in France, not in Crystal Lake, Illinois. The property screamed class and wealth. It was a home sought after by many locals. I shook my head while I took it all in. I couldn't believe I hadn't put it together the first time I'd been there. Even in the dark, I should have recognized it.

Alex saw me from the backyard as I pulled in front of his garage. He grinned and headed my way. My heart skipped a beat at his smile. Why did I feel so nervous? Was it simply because I enjoyed being in his company—or was it that my deep inner voice really wanted to see if he *actually* had a naughty room?

Both. Probably both.

Yeah! Deep inner voice pumped her fist.

I blushed at my dirty thoughts and tried to cool off my cheeks before he was at my car.

"Good morning, Jane." Alex opened my door and offered his hand.

"Hi," I replied, a little more breathless than the situation called for.

He chuckled quietly and guided me toward the backyard. "I thought we could have brunch on the patio."

"Sounds good to me. Thank you for the invite."

"Thank you for accepting it," he said with a sexy grin. "Did I interrupt your plans?"

"Not at all. I was supposed to be at my house packing and moving, but we finished yesterday. I close a week from Monday." I heard the pride in my voice. It had been a hefty task to move five people's entire lives out of a house in just over a week, but somehow we'd done it. He directed me to sit on the patio couch while he poured something bubbly out of a big bottle. He handed me one of the champagne flutes and sat next to me at an angle so we could see each other. I stared at the flute. "I love Prosecco. Thank you." I took a sip. "Are we celebrating something?"

"Not necessarily. I suppose we could celebrate your hard work at your house." He brought his flute to mine and we clinked them together.

The guilt of not including him weighed on me. "I'm really sorry I didn't ask you to help. I had a lot of conflicting opinions about it."

"Conflicting opinions?" He looked confused.

"Wrong word, I guess. Conflicting emotions. There was a battle going on in my head, in all different directions. It's too much for me to be able to explain."

Alex took a deep breath and looked down at his flute. He seemed different. More somber. "Could you try?"

I shook my head, more in confusion than a refusal, while tears formed in my eyes.

"I told you I wouldn't push you and that still holds true." Alex's voice was understanding. "But it seems I'm not the only one pining for you. If I'm not who you want, and if there's no way to change your mind, please tell me. I'll let you go. Not because I don't *want* to fight for you. But because you need to be happy. If I can't do that for you..." He ran his hand through his hair and shook his head. His eyes were closed tight as if he was in pain. "Walking away would be the most agonizing thing I've ever done, but I'd do it, for you."

"Alex—" I didn't know what to say.

He continued, "If you *do* want me, even a little bit, even in the smallest of ways, I need to know. I'll fight for you. I'll fight for you every day for the rest of my life. But..." he paused and took a sip of his Prosecco. "I can't promise I'm going to fight fair."

Tears escaped my eyes and I wiped them away. "I *do* want you." That was something I was sure of. I always felt better in his presence. He made me come alive and have desires I'd never had. His kindness and attentiveness helped heal those little fissures in my heart. He was so good to me in every way possible.

Alex's eyes closed in relief. "Do you want *all* parts of me?" he whispered.

I furrowed my brow. "I'm not sure I know what you mean."

He sighed and looked away. "Forgive me for being blunt. But lately, it seems Dean gets to be a part of your day-to-day life. And you keep me around for the sex." My mouth popped open and made an involuntary foreign noise at his words. "Maybe I'm even the sloppy seconds. I don't know..." he murmured and looked away from me.

What in the hell was he talking about? "Alex!" I hopped up from the couch. "That is *not* how it is!" I exclaimed. I couldn't help but shout. He was so far off.

"Isn't it?" he replied, still calm. "I see how he looks at you. How he touches you."

"Dean may not be able to keep his hands to himself, superficially, but that is as far as it goes!" Anger bubbled up to the surface; I didn't need such false accusations in my life. "Honestly, Alex. Is that the kind of girl you think I am?" I grabbed my bag, keys, and phone and turned away from him.

"Jane, please don't run away." His words halted me in my tracks. How did he remain so relaxed when my blood was boiling? Could I be *any* more defensive? My mind went to an article I'd read once about infidelity. It stated that those who get extremely defensive are most likely the ones who were cheating.

Leaving will make you look like you're lying, both my internal voices informed.

"I'm *not* running. But you are *so* wrong. I can't tell you how wrong you are. You are the best thing that has happened to me since—well, you know. The absolute best!" My tears flowed hard and fast.

I tended to not overthink my relationship with Alex. When I tried to overanalyze, it put me into a spiraling hole of anxiety, doubt, insecurities, and depression. For months I had been "living in the present," as my therapist recommended. That being said, the walls have crumbled down. He'd torn them right off the foundation that kept me grounded. "I don't know if I want a committed relationship. I'm sorry I can't give you that. But it has nothing to do with Dean! I cherish you, Alex. You're a gift who came right from heaven onto the gym roof that cold day in March last year. You might not realize how much you've helped mend my wounds, but you have. I'm healing and getting better every day, and you're one of the few people I can thank. You've been nothing short of amazing. And you're ruining it with jealousy!"

Alex raised himself off the couch to stand in front of me, inches from my face. He was still masked with calmness; there was no anger in his eyes. He placed his hands on my hips. "Then why are you sharing all of your important moments with someone else?"

Valid question. "I don't know! Maybe because I feel Dean needs me more than you do right now. Maybe because I'm a heartless bitch. Maybe because I'm subconsciously trying to keep you an arm's distance away because I'm scared. Or maybe it's all those things." My chest shook with tension, but my anger at Alex subsided. If roles were reversed, I'd feel the same way. Every bit of the conflict was about me and my commitment issues. I didn't know how to fix it, but I had to try harder if I wanted to keep such a caring, wonderful, attentive man in my life.

A light bulb moment flashed brightly across the span of my brain. How would I feel if Alex walked away from me and didn't look back? If he gave up on me? Or worse, if he gave up on me and married another woman? How would I cope?

I knew the answer in an instant: not well at all. My heart dropped in anxiety at the thought. I wasn't sure if I could be any more heartbroken than I already was, but it would be another layer of absolute, unbearable pain.

If you would be devastated if he left you, then you need to let yourself love him. Just try. See what happens, both my internal voices whispered.

They were right. Again. I couldn't resist anymore. I had to stop holding myself back from long-term happiness. I had to believe in a plan bigger than my own.

Alex watched me with guarded eyes. He could tell I was in heavy contemplation because he didn't interrupt my internal haze. I blinked back to reality and pulled him in for a kiss. I let our mouths explore one another's briefly before I pulled away.

"Alex, I'm sorry for how I've been treating you. It's not fair to you. Please know it's not because I don't care about you. I care about you so much..." I grabbed his hands and kissed them. "I've only fallen in love with one man. The start of that love happened a long time ago. I don't know if this feels the same as it did then. I can't remember. I was really young when my heart chose Graham." I paused for a second to gain some courage. "But I think that I'm headed that way again. With you. The feelings are more pronounced every day—"

He interrupted my confession by crushing his lips on mine. His mouth trailed everywhere on my face and neck. The sensations were so powerful I had a hard time staying upright. My knees wanted me to fall over. "Alex, listen. Please." I panted. I needed to get the rest out.

"I'm listening," he mumbled while grazing my neck.

I tried to concentrate. "I don't know if it will ever be enough," I admitted.

His exploring stopped at my collarbone as he ingested my words. "I cannot promise I'll ever be enough for you."

"You will," he argued.

I placed my palms on his chest. "You say that now, but think about how you felt today. How I hurt you."

He pulled away to look at me. "As long as you want me, all parts of me, you're enough."

I stared right back into his warm, brown eyes. "I do."

He put his forehead to mine. "And nobody else?" he whispered.

"Nobody else," I confirmed.

"That's all I need." He picked me up in a hug and wrapped my legs around his waist. He walked to the couch and lowered us down slowly, so I could meet the cushions with my knees while I stayed in his lap. My burnt-red church dress had buttons that ran a straight line down the front of my body. I unbuttoned the bottom button and shimmied my dress up my thighs to have space to straddle his legs.

"I told myself we wouldn't do this today," Alex mused as he unbuttoned the top buttons of my dress to lay gentle, unhurried kisses against the newly exposed skin. My nerves immediately lit on fire. Kneeling over him became one of my favorite places to be. My heart pounded heavily inside my ribs.

"Why would you do that?" I attempted to unhook his belt, but he caught my hands in his and guided them away.

"Because I want to talk with you too. I want to know what's going on in your life." His eyes were so sincere.

"We just talked a lot." He wouldn't let me wiggle my greedy hands away from his.

His eyes stayed focused on mine. "Jane, I need our relationship to be more than sex."

I huffed a sigh of defeat and sat back on his legs.

He smirked. "Trust me. I *want* you all the time. Every moment of every day and every night. But I want this too." He pointed at my temple, indicating my brain. "And I want this more than I can express." He put his hand over my heart.

"You have those already," I explained, feeling a little shy.

"Not every bit of them. It's a work in progress. I'll be fighting until I have all of you. And once I have you completely, I'll fight forever to keep you." My heart leaped at his words. I truly didn't deserve Alex Lombardi. I leaned in to place a thank you kiss on his lips.

"These strong feelings go away, you know. They fade with time," I informed.

"What feelings exactly?" he asked while kissing the skin above my breasts. It seemed he couldn't help himself, even when he tried to refrain.

Fine by me.

I closed my eyes at his touch. He was so distracting, but I needed to make my point. I wasn't sure he understood what an aged comfortable relationship actually was. With a lot of effort, I continued, "The young love feelings and desires. The lust. Haven't you noticed that couples in the 'new love' stage touch each other all the time? They steal glances at each other while blush flushes their cheeks. It's intense. It's what we've got right now."

"So you think my desire to do this," he kissed along my collarbones, "will fade?"

"Somewhat. Yes," I whispered.

He kept his lips on me. "Never."

"You'll see. Before you know it, we'll be fighting about who stole the blankets last night and who took up more of the bed."

Alex quit his kisses to look me in the eyes. "You can have all the blankets and the bed."

I rolled my eyes playfully. "We'll argue about who has to go out and shovel the driveway for the fourth time in a night."

He picked up my hand and trailed slow kisses up the inside of my arm. "I always hire a snowplow company," he mumbled onto my skin.

Those tiny sensations of touch up my arm made my insides clench tight. "Our sex life will become monotonous and dull."

He stopped abruptly and snorted in disagreement. "Now you're just getting crazy. *That* will absolutely not happen."

I giggled. "Easy to say in the young love stage."

"Jane." His tone was serious. "The intensity of my feelings for you will never fade. I'll never stop craving you. You can count on that." He continued his kisses where he left off on my arm and landed on the soft upper part of my breasts. With a deep inhale and exhale he began buttoning my two top buttons.

"So just talking today?" Disappointment laced my tone.

He kissed my cheek. "If you don't mind."

"What if I do mind?" I asked with my best version of a seductive grin.

"Then we'll do what you want." He grinned back at me.

I sighed and raised myself off of him to grab and raise my flute of Prosecco. I understood where his head was at and wanted to respect his needs. "To give myself the allowance to move ahead in life without guilt. And to give *you* enough patience to deal with me."

He chuckled quietly and clinked my glass.

"You really are so patient with me," I said as I took a sip.

"You really are so worth it," he countered.

18

Jane

REESE POINTED TO a large garment bag hanging in the closet. "Would you like to see it before or after I do your hair?" she asked on the afternoon of the gala.

"After will work. Reese, I can't believe you took the afternoon off for this. You really shouldn't have. I can do my own hair and makeup." I'd spent the last ten minutes thanking her and apologizing. She had insisted on helping me get ready.

"Stop it right now!" she blurted. "I *want* to be here with you. I only had one client and she always ditches me last-minute. She can wait until tomorrow."

"Well, thank you. I owe you."

"Oh, you don't owe me a thing. It's Alex who owes me big." She winked at me and pulled me toward the makeup vanity so we could start on my hair. "So are you excited? You haven't been this dressed up since prom."

She was right. The only event even close to as fancy had been my wedding, which was a casual gathering of friends and family without all the pomp and circumstance of a regular wedding day.

"I'm looking forward to tonight, yes. Not only because I get to feel pretty for an evening, but because I'm going to view Alex in a new light. I've never seen him at work, aside from the gym, which is a totally different atmosphere. I also get to meet his parents."

"Mmm," Reese hummed. "Big step."

"True story. I don't know much about them. I'm a little nervous." Alex seemed very fond of his parents. I was sure they were kind and welcoming. But meeting his parents definitely felt like we were taking it to the next level. That idea both warmed my broken heart and scared the crap out of me. What if they didn't approve of me?

"Just turn on your Janey charm and they'll fall in love with you right away," Reese answered my silent question. She had a natural way of making everything sound so easy.

I nodded and watched her hands work in the mirror. I told her to do whatever she thought would complement the dress, so I had no clue of her plan.

"What time is he picking you up?" Reese asked after a few minutes of concentrated silence.

"He isn't. He had to be in the city all day with his dad. Stan's picking me up in a couple of hours." Hopefully that would be enough time for her to create her masterpiece with my hair.

"Perfect," Reese said while she continued with her work.

She had me turned away from the mirror for most of the time and I found myself daydreaming of *after* the gala. Alex had a suite reserved at the same hotel. My heart fluttered in anticipation at what the night could bring. We hadn't touched each other *that way* since that day in his office. My body ached for more endeavors with him.

Jeez, get through the night as a lady before you turn into a sex kitten, surface voice scolded. As much as she bugged me most of the time, she was right. Meet and mingle first. Get down and dirty in the bed sheets later.

Reese started my makeup after my hair was done. When she was satisfied with her work, she turned me toward the mirror. I stared at myself in disbelief. I didn't even look like the same person. The makeup erased any proof that I'd had a tough year. I looked ten years younger. My hair was curled and set into a loose, low bun. There were perfectly placed tendrils flowing out of the bun and around my face.

"Reese—" She looked at me through the mirror with pride in her eyes. "Thank you so much." I resisted the emotion building in my throat. I didn't want to smudge the perfect makeup.

"Of course! Happy to help!" She loved playing dress-up more than anyone I knew. "Gown time!" She went to where the bag was hanging in the closet and unzipped it carefully. I was really looking forward to seeing what she'd chosen for me. As if she heard my thoughts out loud, she replied to my unspoken words again. "I had some say in this dress, but Alex insisted on a couple of details." She unzipped the bag completely and pulled a forest green gown from the bag. "He was firm on this color, which I can't deny was the perfect choice. Your skin tone will look stunning in it."

I hardly listened to her because I was in awe of the sleeveless dress in front of me. The entire A-line gown was the same color, but the V-shaped top portion was embedded with tiny green rhinestones from the one-inch shoulder straps down to the upper midriff section. Where the rhinestones ended, layers of green tulle began.

"This gown is gorgeous." I reached over to put my hand on the fabric and get a closer look. "Maybe too gorgeous for me."

"Nonsense!" Reese looked at her phone. "We have only a few minutes before Stan will be here. Time to try it on."

I stood there in a daze, wondering how I would pull off such an exquisite gown all night. There was no way I could do such a perfect dress any justice.

Reese shook me out of my panic. "Jane! You're the most beautiful person, inside and out. You always have been at the top of my list of stunning women. You're not going to let this dress wear you. *You* are going to wear it! Now let's go!" Her speech woke me up enough to start undressing.

"*Oh*! I almost forgot. There was another part Alex insisted on," she grumbled, rolled her eyes, and pointed to a corner of my room. "The bag over there has what you're supposed to put on *under* the dress." My eyes went wide. I could only imagine what was in that bag. She caught my shocked response. "Yep," she said with a sigh. "I told you he owes me." She headed to the door. "I'll be right outside. Let me know if you need help zipping up the back. And hurry!"

I went over to the bag and peeked in. My breathing stopped when I pulled out the contents. It was meant to be a black lingerie teddy, I believed, but it couldn't even count as that. The only part of it with actual fabric—sheer fabric at that—was the lowest area of it. Aside from that, it was a plethora of straps. The highest straps went over my shoulders and then met my bodice area. My breasts would be exposed, aside from the thin outline of straps around them. They then crisscrossed all over my stomach area until they met the sheer fabric in between my legs.

I put my hands on both sides of the sheer fabric and pulled it apart. As expected, the fabric had easy access for indecent activities. My deep insides pulsed in excitement, but I had no time to fantasize. It would take me twenty minutes to figure out how to put it on.

"Jane! Hurry up!" Reese repeated.

"Almost done!" I shouted. Shockingly, I had managed to get the teddy on without breaking any of the straps and glanced in the mirror quickly before I went for the dress. As much as I instinctively wanted to avoid my reflection, I allowed myself to admire what I saw. I wasn't nearly as thin as I had been. My subtle curves had come back at some point without my notice. Between the hair, makeup, and teddy, I looked hot and didn't feel bad admitting it.

Atta girl, deep inner voice professed.

I pulled the dress off the hanger and stepped into it with ease. It fit perfectly. I hadn't noticed before, but there was a slit in the tulle that ran up my left leg to my mid-thigh. Exposing so much skin wouldn't necessarily be my usual choice, but the swaying tulle prevented my whole leg from showing at any given moment. It was the perfect touch. I called Reese in to zip me up. When she was done, I turned in the mirror to make sure no teddy straps popped out anywhere. None were showing, surprisingly. It probably hadn't been easy to find two articles that would fit together so perfectly. Reese had done well.

She helped me with my heels and grabbed my hand as we headed downstairs to say bye to the in-laws. They were both in the kitchen, waiting in anticipation. Deb had a wistful look on her face. She was a sucker for fairy-tale nights out.

Much to my surprise, Robert had a grin peeking through his usual grumpy face. He walked over to me, laid his hands gently on the sides of my face, and kissed me very delicately on the cheek. "You look so beautiful, Jane." He emphasized every word, which brought the lump back to my throat.

"So you approve?" I was barely able to speak without my voice breaking.

"I approve," he replied with another grin.

"Do you approve of Alex?" I asked, feeling brave.

"He hasn't given me any reason not to. Until that time comes, you can be sure you have my blessing." He kissed the back of my hand and gave me a gentle hug.

"Thank you, Robert. You have no idea how much that means to me." I couldn't escape the tears that formed.

"Ohhhkay, no ruining my hard work!" Reese informed me with a giggle. She brought me a tissue to catch the tears before they fell.

As I was cleaning up my eyes, the doorbell rang. "Time to go, Cinderella!" Reese exclaimed. I quickly hugged her and Deb and headed to meet my chauffeur.

At five o'clock exactly, Stan waited for me at my door in a tuxedo. "You look lovely, Ms. Cora. Are you ready?" I nodded at him as he reached for my overnight bag. I gave Reese one last thank-you hug and headed to the vehicle with my arm in Stan's for balance.

"Alex wanted to be here to ride with you into the city. He sends his apologies and asked me to give you this." He lifted his hand to reveal a small white envelope. He opened the back door and helped me get all the layers of fabric into the car. As soon as we were on the road I opened the envelope to find a handwritten note:

> My girl,
>
> I'm sorry we couldn't start the evening together. I assure you Stan will get you to Chicago quickly and safely. I'll anxiously await your arrival at the gala.
>
> Reese would not show me anything she chose, so the anticipation is nearly breaking me. I assume and hope she fulfilled all my requests. It will be a long night of wondering before I find out if she totally complied.
>
> While you're headed my way, remember the last

time we were in the Alpha Romeo together—our first real date. You felt electric that night. I cannot wait to see how you feel tonight.

My love,
Alex

Damn, he had a way with words.

Stan turned the radio on, seemingly to prevent awkward silence. I knew driving to Chicago on a Friday afternoon could take well over an hour, and I didn't want to sit in my own thoughts the entire time, so I sparked conversation. "How long have you known Alex?" I projected my voice to the front.

Stan turned the music down. "A little over a decade."

It was an interesting work friendship they had. I didn't know Stan well, but he'd always been pleasant and friendly. More than that, he appeared to always be at Alex's beck and call, whether it was at the gym or driving Alex around somewhere. I hoped Alex paid him well.

"You seem very dedicated to him."

"I am," Stan replied. "He's a good guy. Kind of like a son I never had." I could see him smiling from the rearview mirror.

My mouth curved up into a smile at his words. "I can tell he has a special place in your heart."

"He does," he confirmed, "and you have a special place in his."

"So I've been told." I blushed and hoped he didn't notice.

"Alex gets a bad rap with some ladies. I can understand why. But he's changed drastically since he met you. He's a completely different person. A better version."

I sighed quietly. "Yeah. Sometimes history is hard to let go of." I spoke of my own history, as well as of Alex's hate club.

"Mmhmm," he hummed.

We were silent for a while before a question popped up that I couldn't let go of. I didn't know why the answer even mattered. But some part of my subconscious wanted to know. "Hey, Stan, do you think Alex will ever want to get married?"

He raised his eyebrows in surprise, which made me wonder what kind of conversations they'd had. Alex didn't seem to have a lot of buddies. I had a feeling Stan was a sounding board, which was fine by me. He seemed trustworthy and committed to his boss and friend.

"If you'd have asked me a year ago, I would've said there was no way he'd ever get married." He paused to look at me in the mirror. "Now I would bet he'll have a ring on your finger within a few months."

I huffed a breath at his prediction. "I don't know about that."

"You may not. But he does." My eyes opened wide in surprise. He looked straight forward, avoiding eye contact. Immediately he looked as if he'd said too much, so I dropped the conversation and stared out the window.

So Alex had marriage on his brain. My initial reaction was concern, but there was a deep part of me, run by my deep inner voice of course, that was flattered and honored that he would want to commit to me forever. I wouldn't let myself overthink Stan's admission. Alex would not force a ring on my finger at the gala. Or a hotel suite. Or ever. If it was meant to be, it would be. I needed to keep letting the chips fall where they may and accept with open arms the gifts sent from above.

Alex's letter was correct in stating Stan would get us to Chicago quickly. In a little over an hour, he pulled up to The Drake Hotel, where a bellhop opened my door and assisted me out.

"You look lovely, madame," the bellhop said formally as he walked me into the lobby.

"Thank you." He was the second person to say that already. It made me proud that I would not look unworthy next to Alex during such a special night.

I realized once we were in the lobby I didn't know where I was supposed to meet Alex. "You're Ms. Cora, correct?" the bellhop inquired, to which I nodded. "Come with me. Mr. Lombardi is waiting for you in the Gold Coast Room." He allowed me to wrap my arm around his and escorted me through the hotel. He opened the grand doors of the ballroom and led me inside. I thought he was going to let my arm go and have me fend for myself, but he scanned the giant room, searching for the man waiting for me. The bellhop must have had strict instructions to not let me go until I'd been delivered safely to Alex. It probably should have made me feel like a piece of property, but instead, it made me feel protected and adored. Alex was aware I wouldn't know a soul in the room aside from him. He was taking care of me the way he always did—thoroughly and thoughtfully.

There weren't many people in the room yet, so I helped in the search. The bellhop found him before I did and guided me toward one corner of the room. It took me a few paces forward before I recognized Alex. He chatted among a group with his back facing us. Once we approached him, the bellhop gently tapped his shoulder. "Sir," was all he said.

Alex turned around and took me in for the first time. I wish I could have taken a picture of his reaction. He looked as if the wind had been knocked right out of him. His hand went up to his mouth in utter surprise and then he scooped me in for a hug and kiss. I didn't let our lips meet for long, knowing we were not alone. Alex nodded at the bellhop in thanks and dismissal. I thanked him too as he backed away.

I turned my attention to Alex, who hadn't let me go yet. I pulled out of his grasp, merely because I wanted to see his attire. He was in a fitted black suit, white shirt, and black bow tie. It was the classic version of black-tie, but he looked better than most ever could. He had a forest green handkerchief peeking out of his coat pocket. I grazed my fingers across it. "Nice touch," I remarked with a smirk.

He pulled me in and whispered in my ear, "You look incredible. Absolutely incredible."

I blushed at once. "As do you."

"Ahem! Alex, don't be so rude. Introduce us!" A woman, who didn't look much older than Alex, put her arm on his shoulder and pulled him away from me. She was about my height, with the same brown hair and eyes that matched Alex's.

"Hi, I'm Molly, Alex's sister. It's so nice to finally meet you!" she exclaimed before she pulled me in for a hug.

"It's nice to meet you, too," I replied sincerely. I didn't know much about Molly, but her friendly demeanor toward me felt reassuring that she approved of me already.

Molly directed my attention to a handsome man next to her. "This is my husband, Jett." Jett shook my hand with a smile. Molly then looked at the last two in the group. They were older, maybe in their early seventies. The man was shorter than Alex but had the same color eyes and skin tone. He had a full head of salt-and-pepper hair. He was one of those people who looked powerful and wealthy just standing still.

Alex's dad, I presumed. And next to him had to be Alex's mom. She was taller than her counterpart by a couple of inches. She had blonde hair and blue eyes, a stark difference from the rest of the family. She was very beautiful.

Molly woke me from my analysis. "And these are our parents, Anthony and Loretta."

"Mr. and Mrs. Lombardi, it's nice to meet you both," I said with a quiver of nerves in my voice. I shook hands with Alex's dad and attempted to do the same with his mom, but she pulled me in for a hug and kiss on the cheek.

"Please." Loretta waved her hand in dismissal. "Call us by our first names. None of that formal crap," she spoke while hiccuping.

"Did you start early today, Mom?" Alex questioned with a chuckle under his breath. He looked at her empty martini glass.

"Oh, honey," Loretta slurred. "You know these events make me nervous. I'm taking the edge off." Another hiccup.

Molly directed my attention back to her. "I wish I could say Alex has told us so much about you." She looked at Alex with disapproving eyes. "But he's refused to share much of *anything* about you...or your relationship."

"Do I know more about Jane than you, Miss Molly?" Spencer came out of nowhere and raised his eyebrow mockingly at Molly.

"Jane! Hi! I'm so glad you're here tonight!" Betsy exclaimed as she ran over for a hug.

I returned her embrace and pulled back to see her beautiful black gown. "Oh my gosh, I didn't expect to see my favorite Montana ranchers. You two clean up nicely!"

"Thanks!" Betsy exclaimed. "We wouldn't miss such an important event to Anthony!"

Molly pushed herself into the center of attention. "Wait. Spencer and Betsy are besties with Jane, and I haven't even met her until right now? Alex! Not fair!" She crossed her arms and pouted.

Alex didn't look like he wanted to formulate a response. Instead, he pulled me into his side protectively, then shrugged and grinned at Molly.

She looked back and forth between Alex and me, and then at Spencer and Betsy. "I think we need to get to know each other, Jane."

"I'd like that," I said with a smile. I wasn't sure of her intention, but I had nothing to hide. Plus I found myself *wanting* to get to know his family.

Alex looked uncomfortable. "Okay, we're going to head to the bar for a drink. We'll see you guys in a bit." He practically pulled me away.

"It was nice to meet you all," I announced to his family as Alex tugged me in the opposite direction. They waved and had the same excited smile plastered on their faces. My guess was they were all equally happy and relieved that Alex showed interest in someone being more than just a booty call.

There were bar stations set up in every corner of the room. Pulling me behind him, Alex was on a mission to get me to the farthest bar from where we had just stood. I pulled back from his grasp to get his attention. "Why are we running away from your family?" I questioned with a grin and inquisitive eyes.

He slowed his gait to match mine and put his arm around my waist. "They can be a lot to take in at first." He glanced at me and matched my grin.

"They weren't a lot at all! They're all so friendly!" I exclaimed. "I'm looking forward to chatting with your sister more. She seems great."

We made it to the bar, where Alex ordered two Tito's and sodas. "They're friendly and yes, she's great," he mused. "But they're also piranhas." He chuckled. I looked at him questioningly. He leaned in and stole a quick kiss to the nape of my neck when the bartender wasn't looking. His touch shot a shiver up my spine. He kept his face close to mine and whispered in my ear, "They want me to have a wife. Preferably sooner than later."

"Oh," I gasped.

Alex had a little color to his cheeks. Unlike me, blushing was rare for him. "They mean well," he ensured.

"Alex, there's no need to defend them. They want what is best for you." I took a sip of my drink. "Now let's go back over there."

Alex caught me before I had moved even an inch. "Not so fast," he demanded. "I want you to myself for a moment. The doors will open soon. It's going to become crowded very quickly."

"How many people are you expecting?"

"Roughly five hundred."

I scanned the room, imagining five hundred people in there. It was an intimidating image. "You're going to stay by me, right?" I gulped back a little fear.

Alex pulled me in and kissed my forehead. "Of course—"

"Wow, Alex. Now I know why you've been keeping her secret," an unfamiliar voice spoke from right behind me. I turned around to find an unfamiliar face attached to the voice. He was a natural blond with blue eyes. He was maybe an inch taller than Alex but had the same build. As I was evaluating his appearance, Alex and the stranger shook hands and shared a brief hug.

"Tanner, thanks for coming," Alex stated.

"I wouldn't miss it," the man replied while keeping his eyes on me. It didn't feel like a sexual stare, but more like he was analyzing everything he could about me. It made me a little uncomfortable, so I kept my eyes anywhere but on him.

Alex remembered his manners after a moment of lapse. "Jane, this is my very good friend, Tanner."

I shook his hand. "It's nice to meet you, Tanner."

"Likewise, Jane. I wish it hadn't taken so long to meet you." Tanner eyed his friend.

"Yes, well. Add your name to the list of those disappointed in me for keeping her all to myself," Alex instructed with a soft chuckle. His eyes were not on us. He was watching all the guests arriving through the doors. I wasn't sure if he averted his eyes because Tanner made him uncomfortable, or if he was anticipating the busy night ahead.

"Not to worry," Tanner announced, demanding Alex's full attention. "We can make up for it tonight. Jane, I am officially reserving a dance with you later." I looked at Alex, who had placed a mask of calm over his face while he stared at his friend. It must have been some sort of silent bro language because Tanner laughed under his breath and retreated. "I have to find my date. I'll catch you guys later. Jane, the dance. Don't forget!" Tanner hollered as he backed away from us.

I nodded in his direction before I turned to Alex. "He seems...nice." I giggled and took a sip of my drink.

"Mmmhmm, nice," Alex repeated. He watched Tanner become hidden in the sea of people gathering in the large room. "You're not dancing with him."

I giggled at his intensity. "You can't keep me a secret forever," I teased.

He pulled me in and kissed my temple before he made his way to my ear. "Is that a challenge, Ms. Cora?"

The blush formed on my cheeks in an instant. He was so incredibly good at making my heart skip a beat. I smiled and hesitantly pulled away from him, strictly because of the volume of guests around us. Nobody wanted to see our public display of affection. "Let's go back to your parents."

We found our way to the table where Alex's family sat and enjoyed each other's company. I didn't know how galas worked, but I assumed it rolled similarly to a wedding—dinner courses, speeches, dancing, mingling, more dancing...

As it turned out, I was right. A few minutes after we arrived at the Lombardi table, an announcer let everyone know that the silent auction would be open for the next two hours. The announcer asked everyone to head to their seats after they had a chance to peruse the auction items.

About ten minutes later, Alex's dad walked over to a podium and tapped on the mic. "Good evening, everyone. If you don't know me, my name is Anthony Lombardi. I'm the CEO of Lombardi Enterprises, and on behalf of everyone at our company, I want to thank you all for coming to support the Vietnam Veterans of America. This is a foundation near and dear to my heart...and my ass." The crowd erupted in laughter, including Anthony himself. "Most of you know that I was wounded in Vietnam. I was shot in ...you guessed it..." He raised his hands for air quotes, "'my buttocks,' just like Forrest Gump." There were a few chuckles in the crowd. "I am a lucky man that my war wound did not affect me long-term. However, most wounded soldiers do not have that luxury. This foundation was started in 1978 to aid soldiers in recovering and recuperating after their time in the military. They provide avenues for treatments and services to improve both the physical and mental health of our men and women who sacrificed their minds and bodies to protect their country. Every dollar we raise tonight will be sent to this foundation. So please make sure you head over to the silent auction in the next couple of hours before it closes. Thank you again for being here. It truly means a lot to me, my son and business partner, Alexander," Anthony pointed our direction and Alex raised his hand in a wave, "as well as all of our employees. Veterans often are forgotten once they leave their military branch. It's my mission to prevent that from happening for as many of them as I can reach. Enjoy the night!" The crowd clapped as he left the podium.

As if it were on cue, multiple doors opened simultaneously on one wall of the room, and carts came with our first course. Alex and I enjoyed our meal at the same table as his parents, sister and brother-in-law, and four others I'd just been introduced to. Two of them were employees whom Alex oversaw at the company. One was Amanda Grier, the Midwest Director of Employee Affairs, and her husband, Todd. The other employee was Kendrick Booker, the Midwest Director of Ethics, and his wife, Amaya. They were all friendly people and we hit it off quickly. You never know how a table would vibe at certain events, but besides me, the rest of the group knew each other well. The employees felt like an extension of the Lombardi family.

When dinner was complete, the music became louder, and the guests left their chairs to head to the auction table and dance floor. Alex and I walked around the room, saying hi to faces he knew. He introduced me to so many people I couldn't keep them all straight—family, friends, employees, and people connected to him through his businesses. Every one of them greeted me with friendly handshakes or hugs.

"You have a lot of really wonderful people who surround you," I mentioned to Alex after being introduced to his mom's best friend, Mary, who had been beyond happy to meet me. She let me know that she'd been in Alex's life since he was a toddler and she never thought he'd settle down.

Alex had informed her many times in a respectful way that we were not an item. His explanation to her made me feel super guilty that I'd been stringing him along with the notion that I wasn't ready to commit. While he and Mary chatted, it hit me like a ton of bricks, again, that what I was doing to

Alex wasn't fair to him. And since I didn't want to walk away from him or what we had together, I needed to figure out how to be comfortable being in a committed relationship with someone who wasn't Graham. I'd had a similar pep talk with myself on Alex's back porch, but I couldn't break through the anxieties of having an official relationship title. Mid-conversation with Mary, I realized I needed to speak to my therapist about my relationship issues and why a title gave me so much anxiety.

Mary knocked me out of my silent turmoil when she waved her hand at Alex and told him that titles meant nothing in the long run. She went on to say she could feel our love and chemistry for each other, and that's what mattered. Her words gave me a pause. *She could feel my love for him?* I didn't even know if I could feel my love for him. She was presumably a pretty magical, intuitive, and empathic woman. Even though her comments were raising my heart rate, I liked her already.

Alex must've sensed my discomfort with the topic, so he excused us politely from the conversation. We walked around a bit more and then he asked if I would be okay alone for a moment while he used the restroom. I nodded, hoping he'd be back soon. Once he left my side, I headed right to the auction table. I was curious about what types of goods and services were being bid on at an event so grand. I stopped and read every auction sheet.

My eyes went wide. The level of fundraising was not what I had been used to with my kids' activities. We would sell pizzas, wrapping paper, Christmas wreaths, and flowers. Not one of the sheets in front of me had a bid of less than $1,000. They were all high-ticket auction items—expensive clothing, handbags, and shoes. There were week-long stays at swanky resorts, season tickets to sporting events, box seats and backstage passes to concerts and shows. The impressive list was endless.

I stopped at one of the sheets where I saw "Alexander Lombardi" written on the paper a few times. I didn't know how he'd kept track of his bid because I'd been with him the entire evening. He must've had a helper.

Stan, who I presumed was in the room somewhere, had to be watching over the sheet to make sure Alex stayed the highest bidder. It worked, because Alex was indeed at the bottom of the list with a bid of $13,000. My eyes opened wider as I looked to the top of the sheet to see what he would pay such a high amount on. It was a seven-day vacation at the luxurious St. Regis Bora Bora Resort. I ran my fingers over a photo of the villas, which were built over the water. Aside from visiting family in Sweden a few times in my life, I had never left the country.

Alex came behind me and wrapped an arm around my waist. "Busted," he confessed with a soft chuckle into my ear.

I turned to face him. "Thirteen thousand dollars?" I squeaked. That was so much money.

"It's for a good cause." Alex shrugged his shoulders. "I'd pay much, much more than that if it meant a week of guaranteed time alone with you." His eyes were so intense; I had to look away. Instead, I looked down at the photo of the villas and shook my head. I couldn't imagine myself being there. Those were places in fairy tales. He lifted my chin to meet his lips to mine. "I cannot wait to see what is under that dress." He intentionally changed the subject, probably because I made it obvious how uncomfortable such a fancy trip made me.

His distraction worked. "Hmm. I thought you wanted us to be more than sex," I teased.

"I do." His intense eyes bored into mine again. Just his look alone made parts of me throb under my dress. However, I remembered the promise to my more pragmatic internal voice—I had agreed to meet and mingle first. I didn't want the night to end anyway. It felt amazing to be at the gala, surrounded by great people who were there for a good cause. Plus I felt more confident in my dress than I had been in a long time. I didn't want to take it off—yet.

Eric Clapton's "Wonderful Tonight" came on over the speakers. "Care to dance?" Alex asked with a shy smile.

"Sure," I replied with a matching grin. He pulled me out to the dance floor and grabbed my hand while his other arm wrapped around my low back.

He led me effortlessly along to the tempo of the music. I placed my head on his shoulder and closed my eyes. He smelled so good. I took a deep breath and allowed myself to enjoy the moment. Being with Alex felt so easy. I didn't know if it was because his efforts made it that way, or if it was because of our natural, loving chemistry that Magical Mary spoke of. All I knew was every time I was physically close to him, all my deep, underlying anguish became quieter.

"Are you having a good time?" he asked after a couple of minutes of comfortable silence.

I reluctantly lifted my head off his shoulder so he could see my eyes. "I really am. Thank you for inviting me."

"My pleasure," he said, which made me blush. The saying brought me back to his couch every time.

The song ended as an announcement blared from the speakers. "Ladies and gentlemen, the silent auction will close in five minutes. Please head to the tables to check your bids."

"Do you need to go check?" I asked him curiously.

"I do not," he said with a wink.

At that moment, I was one hundred percent sure Alex would win the Bora Bora vacation, no matter the cost. The realization had me excited—and nervous—in more ways than one.

We were on our way back to our table when a couple of things happened simultaneously. First, Kendrick Booker, Alex's employee, advanced toward us with a stern look of concern on his face. "Alex, we need to speak privately for a moment," he stated firmly. Alex looked as if he wanted to argue, when Tanner approached us to remind me of the dance he'd insisted upon.

Tanner grabbed my hand and pulled me away before Alex could stop him. I kept my eyes on Alex as Kendrick pulled him in the opposite direction. Before I knew it, I couldn't see them anymore.

Tanner brought me to the center of the dance floor as "You Are the Best Thing" by Ray LaMontagne played in the background. He, like Alex, led me effortlessly. I tried to keep a little more distance between our bodies than I had with Alex. If he noticed, he didn't mention anything.

The silence with Tanner was not so comfortable, so I started up a conversation right away. "So how did you and Alex meet?"

"High school," Tanner informed me.

"That's nice," I replied sincerely. "Do you live locally?"

"You don't really want to know everything about me, do you?" he asked with a chuckle. He didn't say it rudely. More like, I didn't need to make small talk on his behalf.

"I don't mind getting to know Alex's friends."

Tanner nodded. "I appreciate that, but what I really want is to know what's going on between you two. I've been able to pry some information out of Alex, but it hasn't been much. I'm hoping you'll be more forthcoming."

"What would you like to know?" My voice was laced with nerves.

Tanner must have noticed my uncomfortable tone because he looked away and chuckled. "Don't worry, Jane. Like all of Alex's family, whom you met tonight, I want what's best for him."

I eyed him speculatively, wondering how he would know that I had just met the Lombardis for the first time.

Tanner answered my unspoken question. "Yes, Alex has been a hot topic this evening among his family. I'm not sure you understand what a difference you've made in him—and his behaviors." Tanner looked away again and grinned. "Alex wouldn't change that way...that drastically, for anyone. He's madly in love with you. It sounds ridiculous, but I would even say he's desperately in love with you. The sense of desperation in him is foreign to all of us. We are happy for him, but we're also waiting with bated breath for the floor to drop out from under him. I hope you can try to understand that."

I nodded, feeling a little stunned at the bluntness of Tanner's words.

"So my question to you is why are you holding back?"

I looked down, trying to hold in the tears about to escape.

He continued when I didn't say anything, "I know you lost everything. I'm not asking you to replace your late husband. All I'm asking is for you to—"

Alex came out of nowhere and gently but firmly pressed Tanner away from me. "I've got her from here. Thanks, bro."

Something about Alex's expression made Tanner not fight it. He nodded at Alex warily and let me go. "Thank you for the dance, Jane," he said before he walked away.

Alex directed his attention to me, looking more than anxious. "Are you ready to go?"

I nodded, mainly because it appeared that *he* was ready to go. We collected our things at the table, said a quick, abrupt goodbye to his family, and headed to our hotel room. Alex practically dragged me behind him.

"What's the rush?" I asked once we were in the elevator. His demeanor had me anxious.

"No rush," he replied, which was obviously a lie. He wouldn't meet my eyes. Something was definitely not right.

19

Jane

NOTHING ELSE WAS mentioned in the elevator ride, which gave me a moment to try to figure out what in the world had made Alex's mood shift so drastically. My first and only guess was that he was jealous of my short dance with Tanner.

That theory didn't add up. Tanner was Alex's good friend and he obviously had just met me. One dance was harmless. It meant nothing. Surely he wasn't jealous of *that*. I tried to play back the moments before my conversation with Tanner. Alex had been whisked away by Kendrick. Maybe there was some business issue I didn't know about? It seemed unlikely for him to have dragged me out of there so quickly because of business.

We walked the long hall to our suite with silent tension surrounding us. I grabbed his hand, hoping for some sort of connection to come back. He squeezed my hand and brought it up to his lips. Once we entered the suite, Alex immediately found the bathroom and shut the door. I couldn't help but huff a quiet laugh. Was *that* the problem? Digestive issues? I shook my head in disapproval of my thoughts. I basically had him hating my guts over one dance and the issue was he had to poop?

I took a deep breath of relief, let it out, and found the bedroom so I could sit down and take off my high heels. I hadn't worn shoes with a tall heel in as long as I could remember. My feet were aching. As I sat there waiting for Alex,

I was in the awkward position of taking my dress off...or not. I had imagined entering our room with Alex's lips all over me—with him not being able to wait to rip my dress off to view what I wore underneath.

As it turned out, the night wasn't going according to plan. So I wasn't quite sure if I should undress and put on my pajamas—or wait for him. I checked my phone to delay having to make a decision. I had a few texts to read; one of them was from my mom. She informed me that my grandpa was doing worse every day, and I needed to get there as soon as I could. I texted her back immediately, telling her I had to stay in town until Monday morning to close on my house, but I would search for a Monday evening or Tuesday flight. I then texted Reese, letting her know I was going to have to cancel my Friday clients for the next week. I was midway through Reese's response, letting me know it was no problem, when Alex appeared at the threshold of the bedroom. He looked pale.

I put my phone down and examined him from top to bottom. "Are you okay? Are you sick?"

He walked toward me very slowly. "I'm not sick."

"Are you okay?" I repeated the question he hadn't answered. "What's going on with you? What happened in the last twenty minutes I don't know about?"

Alex pulled me up from the bed, hugged the sides of my neck with his warm hands, and kissed me so tenderly it almost brought tears to my eyes. If I hadn't felt the desperation that Tanner spoke of before, I felt it in that kiss. He kissed me over and over, each time pushing harder into my lips. He willed my mouth to open so our tongues could meet while he brought his hands to the zipper of my dress. He unzipped me with ease and slowly pulled the straps from my shoulders. The anxiety building in me was blocking my sensory receptors. I pulled back from his grasp to see his expression. He still looked distraught.

His demeanor made me self-conscious about nothing. "Alex, please tell me what's wrong. We were having the best night. Did I do something—"

"No, baby," he interrupted and bent to kiss the exposed lingerie straps on my shoulder. "You did nothing wrong." I believed him, but it didn't help the concern in my body. He pulled the dress sleeves farther down my arms until they were released. His eyes widened at the first sight of the strappy black teddy. "Oh my God, Jane." I felt his mood shift. He pushed the dress down to the floor, allowed me to step out of it, and then took in every part of me as if I was the best prize he could ever win. He ran his fingers along all the black straps that encased my body. His thumbs found the straps around my breasts and trailed the area as he continued to relish the view. My entire body heated up and then shivered at the intensity of his admiration. "You are magnificent," he declared with heavy desire in his eyes.

I went to unbutton his suit coat, but he grabbed my hands before I could get too far. "You know my rule." He grinned as he lifted me and lowered me to the middle of the bed. He hovered over me, holding most of his own body weight, but he positioned his knee in the right spot between my legs to tease my lower half. His mouth met my body, exploring every strap from top to bottom.

"The rule doesn't say you have to stay fully clothed, does it?" I asked breathlessly. I felt a little pouty that once again I was basically naked, and he was not. "I want to feel your *body* on mine, Alex, not your clothes."

My simple request worked. He raised onto his knees, unbuttoned his coat, and shook himself out of it. He had the sexiest grin on his face, as if he was proud of me for telling him what I needed. I lifted my body to a seated position under him and untucked his shirt. Alex removed his bow tie and started on the buttons of his shirt. I didn't know if I was imagining things, but he appeared to be trembling. He had a hard time releasing each button, so I started from the bottom to help. As soon as his shirt was off his body, I pressed my lips to his bare, hard, beautiful chest. He let out an audible breath at my touch.

I knew I didn't have long before he reminded me of the rule again, and I wanted to kiss parts of him I hadn't yet. He closed his eyes and let me explore his skin before he lowered me back down to the bed so his lips could return to my body. Even though his mood seemed better than it had a few minutes ago, I had a hard time letting go of what could have upset him.

"Alex, are you okay? I asked the question for a third time since we'd been in the bedroom.

"Yes," he whispered without taking his mouth off me. He found one of my nipples and twirled his tongue around it while he grabbed my opposite breast. He almost had me distracted enough to let it go.

Almost.

"Are you *sure*?" He must have heard the despair in my voice because he lifted off me just enough to look me straight in the eyes.

"I'm okay as long as you're with me." There was pain in his voice.

"I'm here." I put my hands on his chest. "I'm not going anywhere." I kept my eyes on his. "Alex, you can tell me anything. If there's something upsetting you, please tell me." He stared at me silently with his intense, liquid brown eyes. I raised myself up to my elbows to kiss his collarbone and pull him down to me. Our lips met again, and I willed myself to let the distraction go for now. I had tried enough times to get it out of him. When he was ready to tell me, he would. I knew we were both looking forward to a special night together. I refused to let it be ruined.

I ran my fingers between our bodies and onto the zipper of his pants. He pulled in another audible breath at my touch before he pushed my hand away so he could lay on top of me completely. He scooted himself down my body and placed gentle kisses on the crisscross straps at my stomach. While keeping his lips on me, he grabbed my thighs, pulled them apart, and then ran his fingers in between my legs to evaluate the mesh fabric. He chuckled hot breath onto my skin when he located the easy access opening.

"When we were in Montana, all I did, every night, was fantasize about doing this to you," Alex admitted. As if to tease me, he slowly ran his thumb around the fabric over and over without touching my skin. When my hips couldn't stay still anymore, he placed his thumb in the center and pushed upward. I let out an involuntary gasp when he hit his mark. I felt the moisture on his fingers; I was more than ready for him. He held onto my hips to keep them from moving and trailed his lips down the center of my stomach to where the mesh began. He stayed there for a moment, taunting me. "I fantasized about how you would taste. How your body would respond to my tongue and fingers."

Between his words and his touch, the pressure and ache in my belly had built to a point I knew I wouldn't last long. "Alex—" I moaned.

"I knew you would taste good, but—" He kissed every intimate inch between my legs. "You taste better than I could've ever imagined."

My body was screaming for his mouth to send me into a much-needed release. "Alex, please," I whimpered.

He listened to my plea and sank his tongue into the right spot a moment later. My hands grabbed onto his hair as he drew shapes right on my pink button. He brought his hands up to the sides of my ribcage and continued to keep me in place. Not being able to squirm around made the pressure in my body almost unbearable. His thumbs grazed my nipples in an expert fashion while his mouth had fun down below. I gasped again. I could live 1,000 years, and nothing would feel as good as Alex's mouth on me. My heart raced and my breath became heavier. The pressure built higher and higher. With Alex still holding onto my ribs, I thrust to meet his tongue. I felt my body heating up and knew my release was very near. Alex must have felt it too because he abruptly lifted his tongue from me. I opened my eyes to look at him, wondering why he'd stopped. He smiled at me for the briefest of moments, kissed my clit, and then played again. And that was it—the pause was all it took for me to detonate over the edge. It was as if all the worry and torment of the last hour—and last year—exploded out of me. My body shivered in the aftermath, relishing in the contentment that only an orgasm could bring. Alex slowly traveled up my body to connect our lips at the same time he used his fingers to gently rub and soothe in between my legs. He didn't stop with the kisses or caressing until my breathing calmed.

When he sensed my body had recovered, he lowered back down to kiss in between my legs again. My heart, barely back to a regular rhythm, started racing once again at his delicate touch. Keeping his mouth on me, he wrestled with his belt and pants and then threw them to the floor. A moment later, his hands traveled up to my shoulders and started removing my teddy. I didn't know it was possible to desire another orgasm only minutes after I'd had one. But Alex's tongue greedily enjoying my most sensitive of spots had my body yearning for a release once again. He made light work of pulling the teddy straps from my upper body and released his mouth from me so he could pull the garment down my legs.

"I want us to finish together this time," he whispered as he lowered his whole body on me to connect us in the most intimate of ways. He pushed up and into me with slow, deliberate movements. I wouldn't have taken Alex for a vanilla sex kind of guy. But in the moment, it felt right—and damn good. I held onto his hips and tried to meet his movements. He lifted his chest off me for a brief second, so he could look to see where we were connected. He then gazed up toward my face with a seductive grin before he bent down to kiss every inch of my neck. *Oh, he was so good at this!* He let more of his weight rest on me, which made him push deeper into my body. That feeling alone, of his hard body fully pressed against mine, made my insides quiver with desire even more.

While still keeping his lips on my neck, he took one of my hands off his hip to connect it to his. He brought our intertwined hands to the mattress and laid them right by my head. I didn't know why, but holding hands while Alex was on top of me, cherishing every part of me, felt—hot. We were connected in every way we could be.

His skin became damp, and I knew he was close to his climax. As much as I didn't want the moment to end, I couldn't help but feel the satisfaction of making such a beautiful man have so much pleasure. Undeniably, it was mostly him and his expertise that pleased us both. But that deep inner voice cheerleader of mine was reminding me that *I* was helping too.

Alex's thrusting became harder and more rhythmic. I did my best to keep up with his pace. "Baby girl, you need to finish with me," Alex ordered.

He lifted some of his body weight off me and placed his free set of fingers on my clit. He started playing as he thrust into me deeper and deeper. I closed my eyes and let the sensations overtake my body. It didn't take long before I felt the build in my deepest of areas. The primal pleasures took over and I began panting from the pressure.

"Don't stop," I whispered. I was close.

Alex continued his playing and thrusting. "Open your eyes, Jane."

I did as I was told and immediately crashed into my climax at the sight of his adoring expression looking back at me.

Less than two seconds later, he moaned while meeting his end and cried out my name over and over. I smiled to myself and tickled his back with my fingers as we both took a few minutes to recover. I kissed his shoulders, his collarbone, anything I could reach. He kept the pulses going but at a much slower, softer pace.

Once we'd recovered, he whispered the softest "I love you" into my ear. My breathing stopped suddenly. He hadn't said those words to me since the first day we'd spoken to each other. At that time, I thought he was a little delusional for confessing such intense feelings to a stranger. But we weren't strangers anymore. Far from it.

Even so, I wasn't ready to repeat those words. "Alex," I said his name with a worried sigh.

"You don't have to say it. Not if you don't want to. But you need to know how much I love you." He placed his lips to mine. "I love you, Jane Cora. I'll never stop loving you." His words made my heart sink. They sounded more like a goodbye than a confession. I closed my eyes to prevent him from seeing the tears form. I didn't know what to say in return.

Alex lifted his body up and out of me and went to turn off the light. While he was up, I scooted off the bed to find my pajamas. He must have heard me rummaging through my bag and knew what I was after. He came to my side of the room, grabbed my hands, and led me back to the bed. He pulled down the covers and guided me onto the sheets, spooning me once we were both lying down. "I hope you're okay with this."

I assumed he was referencing sleeping in the buff. "Mmhm," I replied, still riding the high of what we'd just done together.

He intertwined our hands and pulled them to my heart. "You are my world, baby girl. I love you so much."

I closed my eyes and replied in my head, *I think I might love you too, but I'm not totally sure yet.* Saying it out loud felt too terrifying and concrete.

"DID YOU HAVE a good time?" I asked Alex on the way home the following morning. We were almost to my in-laws' house, and he'd barely said a word to me in the car.

He grabbed my hand and kissed the back of it. "I did." He had a smile that didn't reach his eyes. "You?"

I replayed the entire day from start to finish. Aside from Alex's somber mood, it was one of the best days I'd ever had. I'd felt glamorous in my gown. I was able to meet many of Alex's loved ones. The gala itself was impressive. We'd made—*love*—so hard for me to say, even in my own head, many times throughout the night and into the morning. So much—*love*—I had trouble walking in the morning. My lady parts weren't prepped for an all-night affair. I had no regrets though. The entire day was a once-in-a-lifetime kind of experience.

I squeezed our entwined hands. "I had a great time. Thank you again for inviting me and taking care of all the details."

"My pleasure," he replied. His smile met his eyes, thankfully.

My phone rang, which made me jump. Alex's mood had me edgy. I fished my phone from my bag and looked at the screen; it was my mom. I apologized to Alex for having to take the call and then answered. I had a feeling I knew why she called instead of texted. Through her tears, she let me know I was correct in my assumption—my grandpa had passed away the previous night. I comforted her, let her know how sorry I was, and told her I would still be on the first plane available on Monday or Tuesday.

She told me the memorial would be Wednesday, so I had to make sure I was in Sweden by then. I assured her I would be, did my best to console her some more, and then ended the call. After I hung up, I filled Alex in on the conversation since as far as I knew, he wasn't fluent in Swedish. "So I'll be heading out once my house sale is complete," I informed him.

"I'm so sorry about your grandpa." His eyes were caring and worried. "How long will you stay?"

"I'm not sure. Depends on flights. Probably until next weekend."

We drove the rest of the way in silence. As much as I usually loved his company, I needed to separate myself from the anxiety that exuded from him. I didn't know how to help him if he wouldn't tell me what was wrong. I hoped by the time I arrived back after my trip, he'd either feel better or be ready to talk about it.

We pulled up at the house, and he walked me to the door. "Please extend my condolences to your family."

"I will. And thank you again for everything."

He leaned in to place a tender kiss on my lips. "I'll miss you."

"I'll miss you too. Don't be too bored without me," I teased, attempting to lighten his mood.

He gave me one last kiss and then brought his lips to my forehead. "I'll try."

I WOKE UP Monday morning feeling a lot of different emotions. I was sad to say goodbye to my home but was thankful a new family would be able to enjoy it as much as we had. I didn't have to be at the closing, but it felt like the proper thing to do. The closing meant *closure*. A chapter has ended for me. No, more like a novel. I was starting Book Two of my life.

I also felt down about my mom losing her dad. I was obviously not a stranger to grief and needed to be there to comfort my family. I felt a magnetic pull to get to my parents as soon as I could. Luckily, when I arrived back from the gala on Saturday morning, I was able to find a direct flight out of O'Hare Airport for five o'clock on Tuesday afternoon. If flights ran on time, it would get me to Sweden around nine in the morning Wednesday, their time. I gave my itinerary to my in-laws, and Robert offered to be my airport shuttle. I'd be with my parents before I knew it, but first I needed to finish the last paragraph of *Jane's Life—Book One*.

About an hour before I had to be at the closing, I headed to Maple Street to say goodbye. It was early and the street was quiet when I arrived. I took my time as I walked through every room one last time. In each area of my home, I stopped and chose a favorite memory to think about. Some made me laugh, like when Clare tried to make smoothies for us and forgot to put the lid on the blender. We'd had to scrape blended frozen fruit off every surface of our kitchen for weeks.

Some of the memories made me cry, like the image of Graham on the couch after dinner with his three little loves piled in his lap for bedtime stories. Clare and Marric would fight about which of their books was read first and Graham would always say if they fought about it then Arlo's books would go first. The two big kids would prop themselves on Graham's legs and the baby would sit in the middle. Clare would play with Graham's hair while he recited the lines of each book with perfect character voices. That was my time to get the kitchen cleaned up for the night, but I often paused my work to listen and watch the nightly tradition.

I closed my eyes and let the tears stream down my face. It was reliving moments like that when I honestly didn't know how I would survive the next several decades without them.

I kept moving about the house, feeling all the good and all the pain that went along with my final walk-through. I saved the porch for last. There was no rocking chair anymore, so I rested on the windowsill and closed my eyes. I thought back to the very first day I'd seen the porch—the day I fell in love at first sight. I rested my head on the window and let myself mourn the loss of being able to watch my grandkids play at our feet while we rocked away on our chairs. I would never greet any guests right there again. For some reason, saying goodbye to the porch felt as hard as saying goodbye to the entire house. At that moment, I didn't ever want to leave what used to be my comforting, happy place.

I sighed and checked my phone. My walk down memory lane took longer than expected. I had just enough time to get to the closing, so I headed to my car with one last glance at my beautiful, perfect home. I sent a silent thank you to the property for everything it had given us over the years and sank into the driver's seat. It was time for me to seal the deal on the end of an era.

The closing went quickly and I was back at the in-laws' in no time. Deb was at Jewel, but Robert was home. I didn't want to be alone in my thoughts after such an emotional morning, so I poured myself a cup of coffee and planned to go sit with Robert while he watched the local news. I was stirring the creamer into my coffee when something the newscaster was saying sparked my attention.

"Move over Pamela and Tommy Lee, Kim and Ray-J, there's a new hot sex tape breaking the Internet and it comes from Chicagoland's Most Eligible Bachelor." Choking on the sip of coffee I'd taken, I made my way closer to where Robert sat so I could clearly see and hear the TV. Surely they hadn't just said what I thought they'd said.

"That's right, you all know him as Alexander Lombardi, President of Lombardi Enterprises. His personal and professional emails, as well as his Internet cloud storage, were hacked last Friday, which unveiled a pretty raunchy sex video of Alexander with an unidentified woman. The recording is too vulgar to share, but we *can* show you a still from the video." They then displayed a black and white, pixelated photo of Alex's office with a very blonde, pale girl in a baseball hat. She was pressed up against Alex. The lower area of her body was blurred out, but anyone could assume his hand was down her skirt. Somehow my hands lost the ability to hold anything, and my coffee cup crashed to the floor. Neither Robert nor I reacted to the dropping of the mug. Our eyes were glued to the TV.

The newscaster carried on. "It appears the video was shot from a security camera in his office at FLEX, the health club he owns in Crystal Lake, a far northwest suburb of Chicago. It has been confirmed that the security system has not been compromised, which means Alexander had transferred this video into a personal cloud account." They paused for dramatic effect. "The irony of it all is Alexander oversees the Director of Ethics of his company. While nothing else found in his personal files has been reported as illegal or unethical, he'll be in the hot seat for his video editing for a while..."

"I wouldn't want to be him today," a male newscaster stated. "That's the first time I have ever said *that* sentence before." They both chuckled and went on to the next story.

I didn't know how long I stood there, with broken mug pieces and coffee all over my feet. The world spun around me. I could vaguely recognize that Robert stood next to me, saying something. I couldn't hear him over the whooshing in my ears. It sounded like ocean waves had taken over my hearing canals. At some point, Robert walked me away from the wet mess and sat me on the couch. He left me for a moment and my ears cleared enough to hear him talking to someone on the phone.

"Uh, yeah. Hi. What time are you off today? Hmm. Okay. Well, we have an emergency at home. If you can leave early, that would be helpful. I can't talk about it now. Just get home soon if you can. Okay. Love you too. Bye."

I may have been sitting on that couch for two hours. Maybe less, maybe more—I wasn't sure. My brain had shut down into survival mode. The next thing I knew, Deb knelt in front of me. At first I couldn't register her words, but she shook me, literally, out of my dark haze.

"Jane! Listen to me! Do you want to go to the hospital?" she shouted. The worry in her voice was palpable.

"What?" I whispered without looking at her. "Hospital? No. I just need to go to my room."

"Are you sure? They have counselors and psychiatrists on staff at hospitals. They can talk to you. And give you something to calm down what you feel on the inside."

Her offer woke me from my staring fest. There was no way I would go to the hospital. How could I explain what happened to a doctor without feeling more mortified than I already was? No way. Not going.

"Thank you, Deb. But no." I stood up to head toward the stairs. "I need to go pack. I leave tomorrow." I was aware of every step I took. It felt as if the air was thick and I had to work hard to push through it.

I finally made it to my room and shut the door. I could vaguely hear my phone in the kitchen blowing up with texts and phone calls. I didn't want to know who was trying to reach me, nor did I care. I could've stayed in my bedroom for the rest of eternity, and it wouldn't be enough time or protection from the humiliation. Not just humiliation, but betrayal and devastation.

Alex knew what I'd been through. He'd seen my pain firsthand. He'd literally picked me up when I was down—more than once. Unlike most people, he had actively tried to heal me since he met me. He knew how fragile my mental health was.

So how could he have *done* this to me? Alex, of all people. The one who was extremely protective of me. The one who took care of me. The one who made me feel like I was the most important person in the world. I sat on my bed and tried to calm my anger and soothe the pain that ripped my already broken heart apart. I honestly didn't know what to do. Call him and scream at him until I had no voice left? Should I never talk to him again? Maybe I should let him come over and grovel on his knees.

The image of him begging for forgiveness with a look of distress on his face slammed an acknowledgment to the forefront of my brain...

I gasped out loud and covered my mouth in shock.

Alex knew.

HE. FUCKING. KNEW! My heart beat out of my chest. That must've been what his employee, Kendrick, had told him on Friday evening. It all came together quickly. Alex's mood had shifted because he *knew*. He'd needed to get me away from the gala because he'd known some of his employees had already heard the news, and he didn't want me to pick up on any staring or gawking. He confessed his love for me in bed because he knew.

And he hadn't told me. Or better yet, *warned* me. I was beyond furious. I couldn't remember a time I felt so livid. My entire body trembled with rage.

Just then the doorbell rang. I would bet my life I knew who was on the other side of the door. I opened my bedroom door a crack as Robert opened the front door. As expected, Alex was there, asking to see me. He sounded distressed. Robert spoke so quietly I couldn't eavesdrop. I had a decision to make: let Robert send him away, or deal with him myself.

Since Alex was all about transparency, I had a sudden urge to let him have it. I pulled my door open and pounded down the stairs so quickly that I almost tripped. Robert saw me coming and held me back from marching out the door and into Alex's face.

"How *dare* you, Alex? How *could* you?" Robert pushed me in the opposite direction.

"Jane, I am so sorry! I—" Alex looked terrible. Absolutely wrecked.

Good.

"After everything I've been through...how could you do this to me?" I did my best to pry myself from Robert's hold. Heat emanated from my entire body. Adrenaline surged through every vessel and tears pricked the corner of my eyes.

"Jane, please listen—" Alex attempted to speak; his voice was weak.

I wouldn't let him get a sentence in. He needed to see and hear what he'd done to me. "And the worst part of all is you *knew*!" I glared at him. If only my eyes could've thrown fire. "You *knew* on Friday. And you didn't even have the decency to tell me!"

"Jane, I was going to tell you. Please believe me. I didn't expect it to be on the news. I was going to tell you—" Tears formed in Alex's eyes. They didn't affect me the way they normally would. He deserved to suffer.

"*When*, Alex? When were you going to tell me?"

"I—" he paused and looked at his feet. "I don't know," he whispered while he shook his head.

"So much for communication," I spat out. I pushed Robert's arms away from me so I could walk away. I couldn't look at Alex anymore.

Alex called to me, his voice heavy with emotion, "Jane, please don't go."

I ignored him and walked upstairs, without another look in his direction. Robert murmured quietly again and a minute later, the door closed. I sat on my bed and evaluated if confronting him had made me feel better. In a sense, yes, it had. But I still felt all the same embarrassment and mortification as I had before.

And now I had Alex's tormented expression flashing over and over in my head.

Great.

I raised myself from my bed and started packing. My trip to Sweden could not have come at a better time. I needed to get the hell out of Crystal Lake.

"PLEASE TEXT US when you land. You brought your phone, right?" Robert asked as he was pulling into Terminal 5 at O'Hare Airport.

"I did. It'll be the middle of the night when I land, though."

"That's fine. Please text us."

There hadn't been much communication at the Cora house in the last twenty-four hours. My in-laws gave me space to pack and collect my composure after Alex had left. They must have turned off my phone at some point. That, or it died from being overworked because I'd stopped hearing the incessant ringing and text tones by evening. Either way, I was fine with the silence. I couldn't even imagine what kind of—and how many—messages I would see and hear once I turned it back on. The idea made me want to keep it off the entire trip. Or maybe forever.

Robert probably knew that fact already, which was why he was persistent about letting them know I'd made it safely. "I'll text you. I promise." *I could text them and* not *look over my unread messages*, I reminded myself.

"Thank you for driving me."

"Any time, dear." Robert exited the car and wrapped around the back to unload my suitcase. "Tell your parents hi for us and give them our condolences."

I nodded and gave him a hug and kiss on the cheek. I was about to head inside when he grabbed my hand gently. "Jane, try not to think about anything at home. Take this time to rest your mind and be with your family." Robert appeared a little misty-eyed—a look I didn't see on him often. He must feel really bad for me, which made my heart sink into my chest.

I gave him another quick hug. "I'll certainly try."

As soon as I walked into the terminal, I felt a little paranoid that someone would recognize me from my recent few minutes of fame. I purposely wore a baseball cap and kept it low on my forehead to cover up my features. I made it through check-in and security in a little under an hour without anyone actively staring, which made me relax the tiniest bit as I went to find my gate.

I checked a nearby clock. I had an hour to wait. I had no appetite, so going to find food was out. I refused to turn on my phone for entertainment, so I headed to the nearest gift shop to find a book. I would need it on the plane anyway.

I was perusing the autobiography section when a familiar male voice whispered in my ear, "Find anything good yet?"

20

Jane

THE LOW VOICE startled me. For the briefest of moments, my brain had Alex following me to the airport to apologize again. However, I knew that voice. And it wasn't Alex's.

I whipped around to see my tall, adorable buddy smiling his most genuine smile, standing next to my very best girlfriend.

"Oh my gosh, you guys!" I pulled Dean in for a hug and then did the same to Reese. I squeezed her a little tighter and longer, almost to the point of falling over. A lump formed in my throat. Seeing them was like feeling warm sunshine after a brutal, freezing blizzard. "What are you doing here?"

"We're coming with you," Dean informed with a huge grin still on his face.

"What?" My hand covered my mouth in surprise. "But why?" I asked, delighted by the news but still confused.

"Deb called us yesterday. She said you could use your friends," Reese explained.

I couldn't hold the tears back any longer. They pooled over my eyelids as I went for another hug from each of them. "It has been a very rough thirty-six hours," I mumbled into Dean's chest.

"We know, sweetie. That's why we're here," Dean stated as he kissed the top of my head. I squeezed him a little tighter and let my falling tears soak his shirt.

Suddenly I thought of a few things all at once. "Wait. I don't have a return flight yet. Do you guys?"

"Dean will have to head home in a few days. I'm staying with you until you decide to leave," Reese explained.

"What about the salon?" I asked.

"It's handled," she stated flatly.

My face showed disapproval. "Reese, please tell me you didn't cancel a whole week."

"I didn't. I found coverage. And don't worry about it." She chuckled and grabbed my hand. "Let's go find our gate."

An hour later, we were boarded and ready to take off. Unfortunately, my friends and I were assigned seats nowhere near each other on the plane.

That's okay, deep inner voice mollified. *At least they're here.*

I needed to remember to thank Deb when we landed for reaching out to them. She could not have given me a greater gift to help soothe my anxious and angry heart.

I settled in to the middle seat of the very last row and glanced at the passengers next to me. The man to my right was probably in his mid-fifties. He already had a neck pillow in place and was leaning against the closed window shade while wearing sunglasses. He definitely planned to sleep the entire way and not hold any conversations with his row mate, aka me.

The girl to my left appeared to be in her early twenties. She was taking selfies from every angle and posting them on her social media accounts. She had an e-reader tucked into the seat pocket in front of her. I cursed myself for not buying a book. If I couldn't sleep, it was going to be a very long nine hours.

Just as I buckled my seat belt and waited for the flight attendants to go through the safety protocols, Dean walked down the aisle and stopped at my row.

"Excuse me, miss?" He directed his attention to the girl next to me. She reluctantly looked up from her phone to meet his eyes. As soon as she saw Dean towering over her with his best sexy grin, her demeanor changed. She sat up in her seat a little taller and dropped her phone in her lap.

"Hi. My wife is sitting next to you, and she gets motion sickness on planes.

I was wondering if you wouldn't mind switching seats with me so I can make sure she's okay. My seat is up in the front. It's in the aisle." Dean did his best attempt to convince her with his beautiful blue eyes.

The girl glanced at me, and I tried to appear sick. Either I'm an amazing actress or Dean's proposal was too good to pass up because the girl quickly unbuckled her seat belt and gathered her things.

"Thank you so much. 1D," Dean informed her as she squeezed past him. He sat down next to me and smiled again. "Hi, wife." I sighed and rolled my eyes.

Dean and I made small talk once we were in the air. He didn't bring up my last two days of misfortune, which I was grateful for. When the flight attendant came down the aisle asking for drink orders, Dean requested a Jack Daniels and Coke. He saw the disappointment on my face and huffed out a low laugh while he shook his head. "I'm okay, Jane. I'm not going to get plastered. Besides, what else is there to do on a plane?" As soon as he asked the question he raised and lowered his eyebrows at me with a sexy grin.

I knew in a second he was thinking about the mile-high club. I rolled my eyes and rested my head on the back of my seat. I already was involuntarily part of the sex tape club. I definitely wasn't interested in adding any other saucy clubs to my list.

My mental exhaustion from the past couple of days must have taken over, because the next thing I knew my head was resting on Dean's shoulder with the smallest amount of drool coming out of my mouth. I quickly lifted my head and wiped my lips and face. "How long have I been out?" I asked Dean, who had three empty mini Jack Daniels bottles along with empty cups stacked on his tray table.

"Good morning. It's 6:30 in Sweden, so maybe five hours."

I evaluated his movements and mannerisms, worried about all the empty bottles. He didn't seem drunk, which quieted my concern. "Did you sleep?" I asked, already knowing the answer.

"I can't sleep on planes."

"Is that because your teeth are dirty?" I giggled, wondering if he remembered his silly bedtime request from me a few weeks ago.

He chuckled under his breath. "Probably. Want to head to the bathroom and brush them for me?" He raised his eyebrows up and down again.

"What's with you and wanting to make out in enclosed public spaces?" His little fantasy had me genuinely smiling and laughing.

It felt good to laugh.

Dean shrugged his shoulders at my question, but based on his intense stare, he was looking for an answer. I shook my head and laughed under my breath. He was relentless.

A flight attendant came down the aisle, collecting trash and asking if anyone needed anything.

Dean pointed to his empty bottles. "I'll have another. And she'll have—" He turned to me to let me finish the order.

"No, I'm good," I remarked.

"She'll have a vodka and lemonade," Dean informed the attendant. I didn't want to argue in front of her, so I nodded in agreement instead.

When she walked away, I whispered in disapproval, "Dean, it's 6:30 in the morning. I don't need to drink vodka."

"Well, it's 11:30 at night in Chicago, which is a perfectly appropriate time to have a cocktail," he retorted. He had me there. I couldn't argue.

After she brought us our beverages, we clinked our plastic cups together before taking a sip. The alcohol burned my throat, but it felt good to drink something. I hadn't had much to drink or eat since Sunday night.

After a few sips, the vodka had already gone to my head. I didn't dislike how it made me feel. Everything felt a little less serious. I could see why Dean, or anyone else going through a tragedy, could resort to alcohol. It was a temporary, easy fix. I looked at Dean, hoping his beverage consumption was solely because plane rides were boring. It still worried me that he was not taking the right steps to heal himself, but that would have to be a conversation for another day. He was there with me when I needed him.

I grabbed his hand and kissed the back of it. "Thank you." My gratitude for him grew with each sip of vodka.

"For what?" Dean asked with a hesitant grin.

"For dropping whatever plans you had this week to fly across the world with me. For all your help on Maple Street." I kissed his knuckles before I continued, "For caring about me. And loving me. For making me laugh." I took a sip of my drink with my free hand. "For the vodka."

Dean chuckled at the last part. "Is that all it takes? Get you a little liquored up and you think I'm a saint?"

"Not a saint." I giggled. "But definitely someone I'm grateful to have in my life."

He turned his body toward me as much as he could in the tight quarters and brought his free hand to my chin to guide my face to meet his. He forced our eyes to connect. "The feeling is mutual."

I didn't know how long our eyes stayed locked, but I woke up from our intimate moment when surface voice started scolding me. *You're leading him on,* she warned.

She was right. Even with my body buzzed from a little liquor, I had to agree with my conscience. With a deep sigh, I let go of his hand and looked away from his intense eyes. I heard Dean sigh too as he straightened in his seat. He brushed his wavy hair back with his hand and hit the call button. I looked at him with a furrowed brow. He smiled at me and waited for the flight attendant.

She arrived a moment later, looking annoyed. "Can I help you?"

"Yes, uh, hi. I was wondering if we could get one more round?" Dean put on the charm again.

The attendant looked a little uncomfortable. "Um, sir. We have a four drink limit. You've hit your maximum."

"Hmm, okay. Well, then she will have a Jack and Coke and a vodka lemonade," he insisted, showing as many white teeth as possible in his smile.

It must've been Dean's lucky day, or she didn't feel like arguing with a passenger, because she nodded once and went to prepare the drinks.

"Dean, do you really need another drink?" I asked, feeling more than a little buzzed from my first one. I couldn't imagine having *five.*

"Janey, don't be such a square. I'm fine." He glanced my way with another sexy grin and finished his fourth beverage.

OUR PLANE LANDED right on time, which had me very thankful. Before my world had come crashing down for the second time in two years, my mom had texted me that the memorial service would start at noon the day I arrived. That meant we had a few hours to get through customs, head to my parents' house, get ready, and sober up.

We met Reese on the jetway and walked up the ramp into the airport.

"How was the flight?" I tried to not sound as intoxicated as I felt.

Reese stared at me speculatively. "It was fine. Are you drunk?"

"No! Why do you ask?" I mumbled, annoyed that my attempt failed. Nothing got past her. Reese looked at me again and then at Dean, who seemed as sober as a judge.

"You're drunk! You both are! Why didn't you invite me to the airplane party?" She looked offended.

"Shhh. I'm not drunk. Besides, there was no way we were getting the grumpy fifty-year-old out of his seat next to me. Sorry, bud."

"Well, you'll just have to give me a rain check for the flight home." She pouted.

"Deal," I agreed.

We headed to retrieve our checked bags, and I remembered I needed to text my in-laws. I thought about asking for Dean's or Reese's phone to send the message but realized I'd better contact my parents as well. With deep hesitation, I pushed the little button on my phone to power it up. I watched the conveyor belt go around a couple of times before the vibrating text alerts stopped. When they finally did, I looked down to see how many unread messages I had.

Three hundred eighty-seven.

Three hundred eighty-seven unread text messages and seventeen missed calls. It was worse than I had imagined. I went to Robert's name and texted him that I'd arrived safely. Then I scrolled to Deb's thread to thank her for knowing what I needed when I didn't. I called my mom, told her my status, informed her that I had a couple of guests with me, and we would be there soon. I hung up quickly and shoved my phone into my pocket. In no way was I ready to take in almost four hundred texts.

After being distracted by my phone for a few minutes, I looked around the baggage claim area. Reese had her luggage, but Dean didn't, and neither did I. The conveyor belt had the same three suitcases going 'round and 'round. It made me dizzy watching them take their journey around the curvy track. None of the passengers from our plane were anywhere to be seen anymore.

I turned to Dean. "Um, where's our luggage?"

He shrugged his shoulders and scratched his head.

"Shit! They're lost!" I screamed.

"Hey, you don't know that. Let's give it a few more minutes," the sober one advised. We did as we were told with no new luggage added to the conveyor. We waited there until the next plane's suitcases arrived.

The panic set in. "They actually lost our bags!"

Reese couldn't deny it that time. I immediately went to find someone who could help with our dilemma. After forty-five minutes, the lost luggage people agreed that they indeed had misplaced our bags. We'd have to wait for them to be delivered in the next few days. Panic vibrated through every part of me. "I cannot miss my grandfather's funeral!" I screamed to anyone listening.

Luckily we had a level-headed one in our group. "Jane, you're not going to miss it. Let's get through customs. Then we'll taxi to a store close to the church. We'll make it, I promise."

Reese ushered us to the customs line, where she finagled our way past many people with her charm. Before I knew it, we were in the taxi, headed to a clothing store.

My parents lived in Bromma, a borough of Stockholm. It was an area not far from the city center but had the atmosphere of a suburb. It was where they'd grown up and was one of the only areas in Sweden I was totally familiar with. I ordered the driver to take us to Bromma Blocks, a shopping center that would be our best bet to find funeral attire.

About thirty minutes later, the driver dropped us off and we ran into the nearest store that carried both men's and women's clothing. We went through the store at rapid speed. All three of us hunted for anything black that would be appropriate. Reese threw clothes at both Dean and me and pushed us toward the changing rooms. Dean and I hustled over the threshold of the dressing area, assuming there would be a men's room on one side and women's on the other. When we entered the space, we realized at the same time that it was just one large room.

Dean backed away from the threshold. "You go first."

Reese was right behind him, pushing him back into the room. "Dean, there's no time for courtesy. Get in there and try the crap on. We have to go!" She shut the door behind us before shouting that she'd look for more outfits in case our first round didn't work.

Dean locked the door and threw the clothes down in a corner. There were mirrors on the two opposite sides of the room, which would not allow for any sort of privacy. I felt the awkwardness set in, but pushed the thoughts aside. I had no time for modesty. Dean threw his shirt off and looked for his first outfit. I tried to keep my eyes off of his beautiful tattooed body as I searched for the first dress to try.

With a lot of hesitation, I removed my baseball hat, pants, and shirt to replace them with item number one: a solid black simple dress with no embellishments. I immediately knew it was too tight and too short for a funeral.

"Want me to zip you up?" Dean asked as he was tucking a gray and black button-down shirt into a pair of black pants.

"No thanks," I said as I wiggled out of the rejected dress. "You look good." He nodded in agreement. He was done already after one outfit. Ugh, sometimes it wasn't fair to be a girl. I reached for option number two: a belted black, knee-length dress with layered, subtle ruffles at the arms and skirt hem. I threw it over my head and attempted to zip myself with no success. Dean, who had been undressing when he saw me struggling, walked over and zipped me up while he stared at our reflections in the mirror.

"Thanks," I muttered. My cheeks flushed at his gaze. He stayed right behind me, keeping his eyes on mine while I evaluated if the dress would work. I took a swift glance at myself while trying to ignore his magnificent shirtless physique and decided it would be good enough. I swung my arm around to my back, futilely trying to unzip myself. Dean kept his gaze on me through the mirror and unhurriedly pulled the zipper down my back. If it was his attempt to slow down time, it worked. With each inch he unzipped, more goosebumps surfaced on my skin. It was hard to look anywhere but directly into his stunning blue eyes; they screamed exactly what he was thinking.

My heart raced for more than one reason. I glanced at the ceiling and corners of the room. Dean knew where my mind was in an instant. "There are no cameras in here," he ensured in a soothing voice. "Nobody is watching." He finished with the zipper and slid his large hands under the fabric and onto my ribs. My breath caught at the feeling of his warm, rough skin gently rubbing my midriff. I looked in the mirror again; our bodies were so close together. I instantly shook my head and closed my eyes. The image was much too close to the one I saw of myself on the news. Once again he understood my unspoken anxieties because he turned me around so I could only focus on him. There was no denying how beautiful his body was. I ran the back of my hand up and down his abs and chest, enjoying the feeling and the view. He leaned down and kissed my cheek before traveling slow kisses toward my ear. "Jane," he said breathlessly. "Do you want this?" His tone was pleading.

I didn't know if feeling so hurt and broken from the past two days had me yearning for the healing properties of physical touch. Or if the remnants of booze in my system affected my judgment. Maybe I felt the need to get back at Alex. Or maybe I was attracted to Dean more than I had let myself admit. Maybe I needed a stress release. I truly didn't know.

All I knew was in that moment, I did indeed want him. I leaned into him and placed a kiss on his collarbone. "Yes," I replied simply. Dean pulled in an audible breath at the feeling of my lips on his skin. He bent down to grab the bottom of the dress and pulled it over my head at the same time there was a knock on the door.

"Yo, we've got like ten minutes! Are any of those outfits working?" Reese sounded irritated. Clearly, time hadn't slowed down on the other side of the dressing room.

Dean put his finger to his lips in the classic "shh" sign. "We're almost done," Dean answered her calmly. "Give us a few more minutes." Reese sighed but didn't say anything else. We had very limited time and Dean knew it. He lifted me up quickly and walked to one of the walls where he put me down to stand on a very low bench. He rubbed the backs of his hands up and down my ribs and then traveled to find the back of my bra. He unhooked it easily, let it drop to the floor, and then ran his hands down to my panties to pull them down. I unbuttoned his pants and pushed his garments to the ground. I looked down at his majestic body. He was truly impressive from top to bottom. Dean pulled my chin up to meet his face and placed a firm kiss on my lips. He then turned me around so my back was against him and my front was pushing into the wall.

"We don't have much time. I wish we could take this slower," he admitted quietly as he trailed his hand down my body to explore in between my legs. "I want you to finish too...kill two birds with one stone." He used his fingers to caress and awaken my most sensitive of areas. It didn't take long for his fingers to be moist. "Feel how you're reacting to my touch." I closed my eyes, rested my forearms on the wall next to my head, and enjoyed the high his fingers gave me. "You've been holding back, but I knew it was there inside you. I knew you wanted this." He kept his fingers moving in a quick, rhythmic motion. When I was practically dripping with desire, he took some of the moisture and pressed them into my pink pocket. I gasped at his fingers pushing deep into me. "Do you like that?" I couldn't answer him. Not quietly, at least. So I nodded. He then pulled my hips up and back and inserted his hard self into me. I gasped louder.

"Shhh, Janey. You've gotta stay quiet," Dean instructed as he pulsed into me while keeping his fingers moving quickly. He took his opposite hand and trailed it up to my breast where he found the nipple and pinched it. The sensation made my breathing stop and my lower half contract. The pressure was building in me at the same pace it was for him. His breathing became a pant and his motions became harder and faster. I turned my head to the side and rested it on my hands in front of me. I couldn't help but steal a glance in the mirror. Dean's body looked so big. And so hard. Every part of him was sculpted. I'd never been a fan of porn, but watching him press into me with his glorious body was hot to watch.

Dean's eyes met mine in the mirror. "Do you like what you see?" he whispered. "Look at how good we are together." I couldn't respond. I closed my eyes and let the sensations of what he was doing to my body take over my consciousness.

For a couple of minutes, he kept up with his hands in the two different areas as he thrust deep inside me. His lips met the nape of my neck for a kiss, which was the final connection to put me over the edge. I closed my mouth to quiet the intense climax ripping out of me. Not even ten seconds later, Dean stifled a moan onto my skin as he met his end too.

"What the hell are you doing? Let's go!" Reese exclaimed.

Dean still pushed into me slowly, trying to recover, so I felt the need to respond. "We'll be out in a minute," I said, sounding more throaty than I wanted. "I got a zipper stuck."

Dean laughed into my neck at my attempt to stall my impatient best friend. He kissed the top of my shoulder before he pulled away and found his clothes. I hopped off the bench and quickly did the same. We were dressed with our funeral attire in our hands less than a minute later.

We opened the door and breezed past Reese. Neither of us looked in her direction. Dean paid for the outfits while I headed outside to order a cab.

Reese followed and stood next to me while I fidgeted with my phone. We stood there in silence for a few minutes before she spoke. "Want to tell me now or later what happened in there?"

Dean pushed open the door to exit the store as our ride pulled up. I glanced in his direction. "Later."

"Yep," was all Reese said before we piled in the cab. I was sure to grab the front seat before one of them could claim it. The idea of sitting next to either of them made me feel uneasy—Dean with his post-sex glow, and Reese with her wondering eyes. Yes, sitting next to the stranger in the front was the right choice. I rested my head on the back of the seat and closed my eyes.

The dressing room shenanigans had sobered me completely. The highs from the booze and Dean's touches had faded. I sank low in the seat, feeling pretty damn pissed at myself for what I'd just done. Every second that went by was a new lecture from my more judgmental internal dialogue:

Hussy! Do you open your legs for anyone now?

Dean was your husband's best friend. What were you thinking?

What about Alex? Does this seal the deal that you two are over? Is that what you want? How will he ever forgive you?

What is Dean going to expect from you now? You know how he feels about you. You're toying with his emotions.

You have created a lot of complications. More than you already had. All for a quick lay. Nice work.

The taxi stopped and I shook my head to push the negativity and self-hate away. I'd worry about it later. I needed to be present for my mom.

We ran into the church and went straight to the bathroom to change. Once we were in the right attire, I searched for my parents.

"Mom!" I found her surrounded by a group of her cousins and my grandma. Mom rushed over and hugged me tight. "How are you doing?"

"My darling daughter," she whispered as we hugged. "I'm better now that you're here. You?"

"Better now that I'm here," I mimicked her statement and squeezed her again.

The funeral went as all funerals did. There was a service and then speeches. Afterward, family and friends mingled quietly and shared stories about my grandfather for a couple of hours. A lot of my family came to me, extending their condolences for my losses. I hugged them all and thanked them. I introduced them to my friends and had to let them tell Dean and Reese their names. Most of these people were somewhat strangers to me. I had met them all only a handful of times. Nevertheless, they were family and I appreciated their sympathies. When it all got to be too much, I excused myself and walked outside for a breather. I found a bench and tried to think about anything but the mess going on inside my head.

It didn't take long for my friends to come out and find me.

"You okay?" Reese asked.

"Yeah. Just a long day," I lied.

"Yeah," Reese repeated. "So hey, um, Dean and I are going to get checked in to our hotel. We'll be back in a bit."

"Okay. But you don't need to come back if you don't want. You guys have done enough for me today." I kept my eyes solely on Reese because as soon as I spoke the words, I caught the unintentional double meaning that Dean may have heard.

If he'd caught it, he didn't let on. "We're here to be with *you*, Janey. So we're going to check in, and we'll meet up with you soon." There was a no-nonsense tone in his voice.

I met his eyes for the first time since the dressing room and blushed. "Okay. If you go to any stores, can you get me an outfit or two? And maybe a toothbrush?" All three of us chuckled at my request. I sighed to myself after they walked away. My stupid lost luggage had gotten me in a heap of trouble.

THE NEXT FEW days flew by. It was a whirlwind of spending time with family, sightseeing, and a whole lot of rest and relaxation. My parents told stories about when they lived in Bromma as kids. We all played a lot of Vändåtta, which was the Swedish version of Crazy Eights. My mom pulled out my baby books, much to my disapproval. We laughed a lot. And we cried a little too.

It had been a great few days. It was easy to be around my parents. My mother didn't probe or ask too many hard questions. I assumed she thought better of it, considering the year I'd had. And since I had a perfect mask in place, disguising all the anguish inside of me, there was no need for either of my parents to pry about anything. They seemed oblivious to my recent cameo on the news, which made me so thankful they lived in Bromma and not Crystal Lake.

Being surrounded by my favorite people the past few days was the best kind of therapy. It had soothed the anxieties. I could honestly say I hardly thought about my viral video. Or the hundreds of text messages that waited for me.

Unfortunately, the great time we were having could not have kept me from obsessing about a certain dressing room scene. Dean and I hadn't had a chance to speak in private about it. While I was mostly grateful that we'd been unable to be alone, there was a small part of me that wished we could've discussed the elephant in the room. The lack of communication was perpetuating the awkwardness. At some point, we'd have to talk about it. With my family and Reese around was not the time. It would have to wait until we got home.

Before I knew it, it was time for Dean to head back to the States. I had mixed feelings about his departure. I was sad to see him go. I would forever be thankful to him and Reese for coming in my time of need. But I also felt relieved. I needed time alone to think about what happened, why it happened, and how I would move forward.

I drove with my dad to take Dean to the airport. It was the least I could do since he'd traveled across the world for me. Dad stayed in the car once we arrived at the terminal, but I got out to say goodbye. Awkwardness or not, it was only right to thank him properly.

I pulled him in for a hug once he had his backpack on his back. "I appreciate you so much. Thank you for being here." I talked into his shirt. It felt too intimate to look at his face.

"Anytime," he said as he held on to my embrace with one hand and lifted my chin up with the other. We stared at each other for the briefest of moments before he leaned down and placed the gentlest kiss on my lips. "I'm sorry if I ruined our friendship."

His apology caught me off guard. I didn't expect to have the hard conversation in the drop-off lane of Stockholm Arlanda Airport.

"*You* didn't ruin anything, Dean," I replied honestly. "But we can't talk about this now. My dad has to move his car."

Dean nodded, kissed my forehead, and let go of all parts of me except my hands. "Text me if my luggage ever shows up."

I laughed at his request. "You'll be the first to know."

He backed away from me while our hands were still connected. "I love you, Jane."

"Love you, too." We let go of each other and he headed into the airport. I said a silent prayer for him to have safe travels before I opened the passenger door.

"Is that boy in love with you?" Dad asked in Swedish as soon as I sat down and buckled my seat belt. So much for my parents not prying.

"Why do you ask?" I spoke in English to annoy him.

"Jane Elizabeth," he scolded.

"What?" I played dumb on both accounts. I really didn't want to have the conversation with my father—in Swedish or English.

"Wasn't Dean best friends with Graham?"

"He was," I stated flatly.

He kept his face neutral and looked straight ahead. "Be careful, my girl. That boy is captivated by you."

"Thanks for the advice," I said, looking out the window.

We rode in silence the rest of the way.

Once Dean was gone, I booked Reese's and my flight home for the following evening. As great as it had been to be with my family and show my friends around Stockholm, I had the itch to get back home, even if "back home" meant a lot of hard conversations.

My parents drove us to the airport the next day with a promise to come to the States soon. I hugged and kissed them goodbye before Reese and I headed into the terminal. As soon as we found seats at our gate, Reese looked me dead in the eyes. "All right. We're alone. Spill it."

"You don't waste a second, do you?" I asked, mostly teasing.

"Jane, I've been watching you struggle for over a year. That was the worst type of struggle there ever could be. There wasn't much I could do for you but support you in the ways I knew how. This stuff, on the other hand—boy stuff—I can help with. I know you have a lot going on in your head. I've watched you all week, and I've been worried about you. Now it's time to talk about it. You're not getting out of it."

I took a deep breath to decide where to start. I figured the most recent dilemma would be the best opener. "So, you want to talk about me being a whore?"

"A *whore*?" Reese exclaimed, a little too loud for a public setting. I shushed her. "Why are you calling yourself a whore?" she whispered.

I raised one eyebrow at her with a look that said, *You know why I'm calling myself a whore.*

"Jane, you are allowed to play the field. You have no commitments to anyone. Don't forget...you did everything right the first time. Everything! You fell in love. You got married. *Then* you made love and had babies. All of that was ripped away from you. You didn't ask for this season of your life. It was decided for you. Now it's time to play by your own rules. You deserve this second chance. Do not call yourself a whore ever again." Reese had her serious face on.

"That all still counts when I slept with my dead husband's best friend?"

"Yes! Of course it does. Jane, Graham doesn't get a say in your life anymore. I'm sorry if that's harsh. I don't mean it to be. He's in a much better place than here. He's happy up there. You cannot think that way. Do you understand? It's too detrimental to your health. Don't do it."

I nodded in acceptance with tears in my eyes.

"So what else?"

"Well, Dean's confessed a couple of times that he loves me. He told me he never stopped loving me since we dated. I'd been downplaying it because I know he's hurting and looking for an emotional connection." I paused, trying to gather my thoughts. "But I think he actually is in love with me." I stopped again to find something to wipe the moisture away from my eyes. "I've been mulling this over all week. And I can honestly say I don't feel that way about him. I love him a lot. He's one of the most important people in my life. But I'm not *in* love with him. And now I ruined our relationship with what happened in the dressing room." I looked down at the floor, too ashamed to look her in the eyes.

"You did not ruin your relationship, Jane. You may have complicated it, so you'll have to explain how you feel. But he'll understand."

"Will he? What if I know I'm not in love with him because I think I'm in love with someone else?" Saying it out loud made my chest tight. I knew Dean's pain. To hurt him more, on top of the pain he already carried, should be illegal.

"You're in love with Alex." Reese made it more of a statement than a question, as if she was trying to figure it all out in her mind too.

I shrugged my shoulders gently. "I think so. I've been fighting it. It's like my body and mind already know, but my heart is resistant. I never thought I could love again after Graham. The idea has been so foreign that I'm having a hard time believing it could be true. But everything that happened this week has given me a new perspective. Being with Dean—intimately—was amazing. But I didn't feel half as incredible as I do with Alex."

"Well, there's more to a relationship than sex," Reese mused.

"Trust me, I know that." I chuckled under my breath. "But when I'm with Alex, I feel so loved and protected. His care for me seeps out of every pore of his body. I know Dean loves me, but it's a different kind of love. He just doesn't see it that way. He's hunting for something he's lost. Since he's always had a connection with me, he's grabbed onto me tightly during this tough time in his life."

Reese giggled. "What are you? Some sort of psychologist?"

I smiled at her. "No, I've just had a lot of therapy recently. And a lot of time to think."

"So, you love Dean, but you're in love with Alex." Another matter-of-fact statement. I nodded slowly, wondering how I'd gotten into such a mess. "That's a tough one."

"Yeah. It is," I agreed. "And then add in a sex tape to worry about."

Reese nodded, understanding. "At least the saving grace is you put a hat on that day."

"Yeah…" I looked down. Even with Reese, it was an embarrassing topic.

We were quiet for a moment before she spoke again. "That video was hot. I didn't know you had it in you."

I groaned and put my hands over my face. "You watched it?" I couldn't be more mortified if I was currently sitting butt-ass naked in the airport.

"Of course I did! Didn't you?" She looked stunned.

"No," I stated flatly. "I lived it, remember?"

"Well, I had to see for myself. You're my best friend. I need to be able to defend you any way I can if someone was to bring it up." Reese pried my hands from my face and took one in hers. She gave it a gentle squeeze. "There are some silver linings you need to recognize." I gave her a skeptical glare. "Hear me out. The first one—the hat hid your face and expressions. Once you were sitting in the chair for the…um…other part…your face was away from the camera. Sometimes expressions are the most intimate part."

I rolled my eyes. "That's a stretch, but I'll take it."

"Two—all the reports are saying there was nothing else of interest found in Alex's cloud or emails. Nothing, Jane. No other sex tapes, personal sexy pictures, pornography, or illegal business dealings. Nothing. Just that one thing you happened to be involved in, which brings me to number three—Alex has had a lot of women. You know that. If sex tapes were his thing, he could have easily recorded a hundred girls by now." I raised my eyebrow at her. "Okay, maybe that's a slight exaggeration. Anyway, they said the data went back over ten years. Ten years, Jane! In ten years he has never done anything like this. Not even when he was a stupid, young twenty-something-year-old. There's a reason he decided to keep that security footage. If I were to guess, I would say he kept it because he feels you could fall out of his grasp at any moment."

I shook my head. "Why does it feel like you defend him when I need you to hate him?"

She smirked at me and squeezed my hand. "I'm not done. Listen, Jane. You told me he declared love for you the first time you spoke. Back then, I thought it was bullshit. Now I fully believe it was love at first sight." She gave me a stern look to prevent me from interrupting. "I'm assuming you have not returned the sentiment?"

"Not exactly. I told him I thought I may be falling in love, but I wasn't sure." Tears formed again. Why couldn't I just say the words without the "maybes" attached?

Reese answered my unspoken question. "And that's okay, Janey. Nobody would expect you to know that yet. However, can you see the situation through Alex's eyes? I'm not saying what he did was right. All I'm saying is I can understand why he would want to keep such an intimate memento of you—of you two together. He's infatuated with you. And he has no commitment in return."

I couldn't deny her logic. When she twisted it into that angle, she made the whole issue seem much less serious. Regardless, I was still mad. Nothing had changed there. "Well, I'm still furious. He could've at least warned me."

"You can be furious. Just don't hate him forever. He came to talk to me at the salon before I left for Sweden. He didn't look good." My eyes lit up in surprise. "Yeah. He was hoping he could get to you through me. I didn't say much to him. Don't worry. I'm in your corner on this, I swear."

I nodded in understanding. Alex, of course, would reach out to Reese, even if it meant getting verbally abused by her in the process.

"And since then," she continued, "he has texted me at least a hundred times asking about you."

"He has texted me a lot too, but I haven't read any of them," I admitted.

"That's okay. Read them when you're ready. Just don't hate him forever," she repeated her demand. "He needs you."

"Wow, Reese. Never would I have thought those words would come out of your mouth. You've come a long way."

"Oh, don't get me wrong. I still think he can be a rotten guy. But not with you. Of all the terrible ways he could have hurt you, this is mild."

"*Mild*?" My mouth popped open in shock.

"Well, actually, it's pretty fucking spicy." She raised her eyebrows up and down and laughed at her corny joke.

I shook my head in disapproval. It wasn't funny to me, so I didn't share in her laughter. "So what do you suppose I do?"

"About which one?"

I took a deep breath and let it out. "Both."

"I think next time Dean is in town, you need to set it straight right away. Be completely honest. He may take it hard, but he's loved you for a long time. I have full faith he'll understand and come to terms eventually. Just have patience with him."

"And Alex?"

"I think you need to text him—before or after you read all his texts doesn't really matter. But give the guy something. Any sort of communication would probably be good." I nodded in agreement. It'd been a week since the news broke about the security footage. I'm sure it felt like much longer than a week for him.

"I'll text him now. Thank you, Reese." I grabbed her hand and squeezed. "For everything."

She nodded back and smiled. "Happy to help."

Reese went to find something to eat before we boarded, so I had a few minutes to myself. I still wasn't ready to read all my messages, but I had the urge to connect with Alex. I opened up his text thread and paused to figure out what to say...

Hey, was all I sent. Not very creative, but it was a good start.

He replied within seconds. Jane. How are you?

I could feel the relief in his words. I'm hanging in there. You?

Surviving.

Yeah, Reese was right. He was suffering.

Serves him right! Surface voice shouted at me out of nowhere. I mentally pushed her away. I needed to concentrate.

Alex, we need to talk. My heart dropped at the thought of having to tell him what I did with Dean. Somehow that seemed like the worst part of our impending conversation.

I'm ready whenever you are.

I'm about to board the plane to come home. I'll reach out soon.

I look forward to it.

I sent him a thumbs-up emoji and was about to turn my phone off when I felt it vibrate again.

Jane, I love you deeply. I am so sorry.

His words made my heart drop. I know. We'll talk soon. I turned it off before I could read any more.

21

Alex

"ALL RIGHT, UP and at 'em," a voice ordered from the edge of my bed.

"No, leave me alone," I demanded. I covered my head with a pillow to drown out any other requests. "How'd you get in here?" I mumbled to Stan from under the pillow.

"I have a spare key—you know that. Listen, Alex, you need to get out of bed. It's time. It's been two weeks. The gym needs you. Your clients need you. And you need to push through this."

I spoke from under my pillow. "I appreciate your concern, Stan, but I think I'll just stay here."

Before I could say any more, Stan ripped the pillow from my grasp. He then went over to my windows and opened all the curtains. The incoming light burned my eyes. I hadn't seen the sun in a while. He walked back to my bed and grabbed onto my comforter to yank it away next.

"I'll do it. I don't care if you're naked," Stan declared.

I lifted up to my elbows and stared at my annoying friend. "I am naked and I don't care that you don't care." I didn't even know what I meant by that, but it sounded like a good comeback. I pushed the blankets aside and stood up. Luckily for him, I lied and was actually wearing boxer briefs. "I'm up. Now will you go away?" I waddled to the bathroom. My legs hadn't had to work very much lately.

"No. I'm not leaving until you do," he shouted to me while I was at the toilet.

"Ugh, Stan. Why?" He gave me a headache. Or maybe I'd already had the headache.

"Because you're a wreck, and I'm here to help."

I flushed the toilet and met him back in my bedroom. I caught a glimpse of myself in the mirror. I looked terrible. There were bags under my eyes and my hair was beyond greasy. I hadn't showered or eaten a decent meal in days. I hadn't worked out at all. My reflection looked thinner and much less defined. I hadn't left the house since I'd spoken to Reese at the salon.

Stan was right. I was a mess.

"Maybe I wanna be a wreck," I muttered as I attempted to lie back down.

"Oh, no you don't!" Stan pushed me aside and hopped into my bed. "If you go back to bed, I'll snuggle with you until you can't take it anymore."

"You're annoying," I growled.

"I know," he agreed with a smile as he stood again. "Alex, listen. I know what happened sucks. You messed up. You feel terrible. I get it. But it's not the worst thing that could have happened."

I looked at him skeptically. "Copying secure footage to a personal file of one of the most intimate moments of my life without permission from the love of my life. Then, finding out it was leaked to millions of people and not having the balls to tell her, but instead letting her find out *from the news*." I ran my hands through my greasy hair. I assumed it was standing on edge at that point. "What could be worse than that? Honestly, I want to know." He didn't say anything, but instead just stared at me. I crossed my arms. "That's what I thought."

"Okay, it's really bad. I didn't say it wasn't. But at least she's alive, Alex. Think of how terrible you feel right now. Think about how Jane must have felt—how she feels—losing her entire family. How does this setback compare to her tragedy?"

"The two aren't even in the same category," I spit out. I was irritated with his argument.

"Right. You're catching on quickly. Alex, Jane is alive and she'll forgive you. I have no doubts. We gave you two weeks to stay in bed. Two weeks to grieve and feel sorry for yourself. But this isn't you. You need to pick yourself up by your bootstraps and get back to the gym. A gym that has never been busier—with mostly twenty and thirty-year-old women, I might add."

I raised my eyebrows at him in disgusted surprise. "Stan, please do not tell me my sex video has increased membership." I shook my head. *As if it could get any worse.*

He nodded at me in return.

I groaned. "If this is your way to get me back—to entice me...you're out of your mind."

"I'm not trying to entice you. I'm informing you that business is good. You have so many potential clients on your training request list we had to cap it. It's a mile long, Alex. And don't worry, not all of them are cute girls. Only seventy-five percent or so." He grinned at me.

I took a deep breath and let it out. "I have no interest in training attractive girls. And I honestly don't think I can go back until I talk to Jane. I won't be any good to any of them. Or any of you."

"Have you spoken to her at all?"

"Not much. She texted me last week from the airport, saying she wanted to talk. But she hasn't texted since."

"Maybe you should text her."

I raised my eyebrows. "Do you know how many times I have texted her? She hasn't replied to any of them."

"When was the last time you texted her?" He scanned my room for something.

"We only had that one text conversation when she was at the airport. That was it." I repeated what I'd told him a moment ago.

"So a week ago?" He continued searching.

I nodded, watching where his eyes were going.

"Give me your phone," he ordered. He walked around my bed, looking for it.

"Why?" I asked, feeling panicked at whatever he had planned.

"Just give it to me."

"No. Why?" My heart pounded with anxiety.

He pushed the sheets aside and found it. "Because if you aren't going to help yourself, I'm going to do it for you."

"Stan—" I warned.

He was already typing a message.

I slowly crept around to the side of the bed where he was, hoping I could grab the phone before he hit send.

He was too quick for me and backed away before I could reach him.

"Stan, please—" I stood still for a moment, in only my boxer briefs, to plead with him. "I'm walking on very thin ice with her. No, it's more like drowning under the ice with no escape."

He hit "send" and threw my phone back down on the bed. He walked past me and patted me on the shoulder. "Hope that helps. I'll be in the kitchen making you coffee."

"I'm not sure anything you do could help." I sat on the edge of my bed and ran my hands through my greasy hair again.

Before Stan walked over the threshold of my door, he turned around and stared at me for a moment. "When I drove her to Chicago, she asked me a very interesting question." I turned my attention to him. "I didn't tell you because I didn't want you to read into it too much. But now I need to let you know she asked me if I thought you'd ever get married—if you'd ever *want* to get married." My heart skipped a beat. "That may not seem like a significant question if it were asked by anyone else. But it was Jane Cora—your girl. Your girl who lost everything. Nobody would blame her if she chose to never love again. Could you imagine being in her shoes, Alex? Imagine the fear she'll inevitably have when and if she falls in love again. She'll always worry about losing the one she loves for a second time. If it happened once, it could happen again, right? And *she* asked if you wanted to get married."

Stan took a breath as I tried to process everything he'd just said. "She'll forgive you." He nodded in approval at his speech and turned to head downstairs. "Take a shower! You stink!" he shouted. I ignored his insults and found my phone to read the text:

> Hey, are you still open to talking? I need to see you soon.

Okay, not bad. He could have written much worse. Now I would have to wait and see if she'd respond.

I took Stan's advice and headed to the shower. I mulled over Jane's question and Stan's speech as I let hot water run over my body. I had thought Jane was holding back because she felt guilty about finding someone after Graham. I'd also thought her heart had to heal more before she could start a new relationship. Those roadblocks might've been true, but Stan was right. Maybe there was a part of her that was worried to love me and then lose me. Maybe it was a wall she'd put up around her heart and mind to survive. I wanted to soothe and heal all of Jane's worries and fears. I'd fix as much as I could. But aside from assuring her that I would do my best to stay alive, I couldn't help with that worry. I didn't know how to break down the wall so she could love without fear. Unfortunately, I'd probably added a big, thick layer to the wall with what I had just done to her. I hadn't died, but I had hurt her to her core, which was the next worse thing I could've done.

I washed my body and hair and tried to think of a way to make everything right with her again. For the past two weeks, I'd come up with nothing, hence the wallowing in self-pity in a dark room for days on end. But Stan was right once again. It wasn't like me to wallow. I didn't just accept defeat. I fought for what I wanted.

And I'd fight for what I *needed.* Because after the last couple of weeks of misery, I knew I couldn't live without her. I was not as strong as Jane. If something were to ever happen to her, I wouldn't survive.

And I'd been wasting precious time sulking alone in my bed.

I finished in the shower and dressed quickly. I found my phone and checked for a response. To my surprise, there was one:

> Hey, I'm sorry I haven't reached out. I've been helping Reese at the salon every day for the past week. I'm not used to working so much anymore. It's exhausting me by the end of the night and I crash into bed.

Things were looking up already. Jane being too tired to talk was much better than her hating me so much that she couldn't even look at my face. I replied right away:

No, it's okay. I just miss you. And I'm worried about you. I need to see you and apologize until you forgive me.

How about Sunday? Want to meet for coffee?

Sounds good, I replied, not even knowing how many days away Sunday was. I looked at my phone to check. It was Monday. I was never going to make it another week without seeing her.

An idea hit me.

I'm in need of a haircut. Do you have any openings today?

I waited there in my bedroom for a few minutes for a reply that did not come. She probably had a client, so I went downstairs to join Stan for some coffee. I kept checking my phone between sips. Stan didn't say much. I think he'd used all his words in his speech earlier. I was about to head to the coffee pot for a second cup when Jane replied:

I have an opening in fifteen minutes.

I texted her without hesitation. I'll be there.

"I'm going to see her," I said to nobody. Every nerve in my body came alive in a millisecond. I dropped my coffee cup in the sink and ran to get my keys, wallet, and shoes. Stan watched with confusion as I ran around my kitchen.

I ran over to Stan, grabbed the sides of his arms, and shook him. "I'm going to see her!" I went to walk away, but then swiftly turned back around to give him a big hug. "Thank you so much. I owe you."

He chuckled under his breath. "Happy it helped. Good luck."

"Thanks!" I shouted as I shut the door behind me.

The salon was in downtown Crystal Lake, so it was only three minutes from my house. I really didn't need to rush to get there, but even sitting in the waiting area and being in her presence would be better than waiting at home.

I entered the salon and saw Jane with a client. Nobody else was there. I sat in a chair and did my best to look away from Jane from time to time. I didn't want to make her any more uncomfortable than she probably already was, but it was hard to keep my gaze off her. While I waited my turn, I thought about what I could say to make her understand how regretful I was. Repetitive "I'm sorrys" and "I love yous" weren't enough.

Jane finished her client and walked her to the door. As soon as the client left the salon, the energy in the space shifted.

"I'm going to clean up and then I'll be ready," Jane said as she walked past me.

"Take your time." I watched her work and took in her appearance. Her hair was in a low bun and she had no makeup on. She wore loose black overalls with a white T-shirt. Her usual black smock covered her outfit. Even with her baggy clothes, I could tell she'd lost some weight, which made me worry even more about her. She had just started to gain some much-needed pounds. She couldn't afford to lose them again.

Just another reason to right the wrongs, I thought to myself.

"Okay, come on over," Jane called to me. Her tone was joyless.

I stood and walked toward her. My hands sweated and my heart raced. When I made it to her station, I leaned in to kiss her softly on the cheek before I sat down. "Thank you for getting me in."

"Not a problem," Jane replied as she draped the cape over me. Her eyes were blank. "Same as last time?"

I nodded.

Jane collected what she needed and started on my hair. It appeared I would be the one starting the conversation. "Where is everyone?" Usually there were two to four stylists and a nail tech.

"Most of the girls are off on Mondays. Reese will be here in a little bit," Jane replied without meeting my eyes.

"Why are you working so much all of a sudden?"

"Reese came with me to Sweden and had to move a lot of clients. This is how I'm paying her back."

"I see." I stared at her in the mirror, trying to get some sort of connection out of her. "How was Sweden?"

She raised her eyebrows. "It was okay. Sad for my mom who buried her father, but the rest was good…fine, you know…I mean good. It was good, I guess." My eyes narrowed in confusion at her words. There was something she wasn't telling me. Something that bothered her. Considering I was in hot water with her already, I didn't pry.

"I'm glad it went okay." I didn't know how much time we had until Reese showed up. I needed to at least start the hard conversation. I waited until she was near the front of my face to gently grab her forearm. I held it until she met my eyes. "What can I do to fix this?"

She closed her eyes and inhaled a deep breath. "I don't know," she whispered.

"I am so sorry," I whispered back. My throat felt tight.

"I know," she said softly. Her tears dripped down onto where my hand was placed on her arm.

I stood and ripped the cape off so I could have use of my arms. I lightly grabbed the back of her neck and rested my forehead on hers. I could no longer prevent the emotion from leaving my eyes. "What do I need to do for you to forgive me and trust me again?" I kept my hands on her neck and kissed her forehead. She was so still, as if she didn't know how she should react. I trailed kisses down to her temple and landed on her cheek. My lips became salty from the mixture of her tears and mine. "I'll do anything." Her scent was as intoxicating as the first time my lips touched her skin. "Anything," I repeated. Her eyes were closed and there was a continual trail of tears falling down her cheeks and off her jawline.

She inhaled deeply before she spoke. "In your office, when I came to return the gift, you told me you'd never embarrass me again. You promised." Her eyes were still closed, but that didn't mask the hurt. Her pain ate me alive.

"I know. I remember. I'm so sorry. If I'd known it would harm you, I would never have kept it. Please tell me what I can do."

"Tell me why you did it," Jane answered through her weeping. "Why did you save that footage without telling me? Or asking my permission?" She took a deep breath, wiped her face, and opened her eyes. "And why didn't you tell me in the hotel that night? I asked you over and over what was upsetting you. You lied to me." Her gray-blue eyes were swarming with emotion.

All of her questions were warranted. "I went to remove the footage after I finished with my last client. Instead of deleting it right away, I hit play first. Watching it back was...incredible. Being with you in my office was one of the best times of my life. I knew I wanted it cleared off the security footage, but I couldn't delete what you did to yourself that day. Or what you did to me. It felt wrong to erase a moment so significant." I brought my thumbs up to her cheeks where her tears fell and wiped them away before I continued, "To be honest, I'm unsure if I would have ever shown it to you. I have no answer as to why I didn't ask your permission. It was a spur-of-the-moment decision. I'm so sorry." I took her hands and kissed her knuckles. "I also wasn't sure if it would ever happen again, so it felt like a keepsake of sorts, in case you ever... walk away from me." I kissed the ring finger of her left hand. "Please believe me when I say I've never done anything like that before. I've never recorded myself with a woman. I've never sent inappropriate pictures, nor asked anyone to send them to me. This was poor judgment in an isolated incidence..." I trailed off.

I knew none of my reasons were good excuses. But it was the truth at least. "I didn't tell you the evening of the gala for a few reasons. I didn't know how to start the conversation after an amazing night. I was worried you'd run away and never speak to me again." I took a breath before I continued. My admissions were hard to say out loud. "I wanted to make love to you all night, especially if it was going to be the last time..."

Jane's tears had slowed. I waited for her to say something in response. She stayed silent instead, silently pondering my reasoning.

"What else can I do? I can't live like this. I can't keep you in pain. You've had enough pain for a lifetime. Tell me how else I can fix it."

She looked to where our hands were still connected. "I forgive you," she whispered.

I let out an involuntary exhale and closed my eyes in relief. One hundred pounds of weight left my shoulders. There were no words I'd wanted to hear more. I went to kiss her, but she stopped me.

"Alex, there's something I need to tell you." Her tone had me concerned in an instant. Jane's attention went to the front door. "But I guess not now because Reese is on her way in." Jane quickly found some tissue to wipe her face free from any residual evidence of crying. She then grabbed the cape from the floor to put it back around me before Reese walked in the door. She had almost been done with my hair before we took the break, so she finished up and tried to act as if we hadn't just had a deep conversation.

As soon as Reese saw me sitting in the chair, she stopped abruptly.

Here it comes, I thought to myself. I braced myself for the impact of her harsh words that were on their way. There was no denying I fully deserved them.

Reese retained her composure and headed to her workspace. "Hi, guys. How's it going?" she asked, trying to sound casual.

"It's going," Jane answered. She took the blow dryer and blew away any residual hair on my neck and cape before she unbuttoned it to allow me to stand.

"Good to see you, Alex," Reese called over to me after I paid and was about to leave.

I furrowed my brow and looked at Jane, as if to say, *"Is she okay?"* Jane raised her eyebrows and shrugged her shoulders. "Uh, good to see you too, Reese. Thanks," I said hesitantly. I directed my attention back at Jane. "Are we still on for Sunday?"

"Sure. I'll meet you after church."

"Okay, sounds good." I grabbed Jane's hand and kissed the back of it. "Thank you."

She nodded and looked down. She seemed uncomfortable around me. It would take time. That was okay. All I had was time.

I entered my Jeep, feeling as if my lungs had expanded to double the size compared to before I'd walked into the salon. I could finally breathe in deeply. I sat for a moment, staring at my steering wheel, not knowing what to do next. I didn't want to go back home.

My thoughts went back to Stan and the conversation about marriage. He didn't tell me how he'd responded to her. I assumed that was because he knew the answer. We'd had a few short conversations over the past couple of months about my dating history versus my current priorities. If Jane offered her hand today, I'd put a ring on her finger without hesitation. A fact came to mind—even if Jane was to be ready for a ring, I wouldn't be.

That could not stand.

Before I could talk myself out of the ludicrous idea, I put the Jeep in drive and headed to Northbrook, where the store I needed was located. The entire drive there, I imagined all the different ways Jane could say "Yes" to the most important question I'd ever ask her. Should I make a spectacle of it? Take her to a sports event and blast our special moment over the jumbotron? *No. No screens.* Maybe I should take her to Montana. I could propose on the top of a mountain. Or I could take her skydiving and ask her midair. There were about one hundred different scenarios in my head by the time I reached the parking lot of my destination.

I knew in my mind that none of them would be the way. When the time came, it would be intimate and beautiful, just like my girl. I walked into the building, more than ready to make the most significant purchase of my life.

An employee greeted me at the door. "Good morning. Welcome to Tiffany's. How can I help you today?"

22

Alex

I KEPT GLANCING at the bag on the passenger chair of the Wrangler the entire way home. I resisted the urge to untie the white satin ribbon and steal a glance. They had let me inspect and admire the ring as long as I needed, but it still hadn't seemed like enough time. I knew nothing about diamonds—cut, clarity, or carat. Luckily, they had a knowledgeable gemologist on staff to help me choose the perfect ring.

He had asked about Jane, about her personality, and what she did for a living. *"She sounds like a wonderful woman. I can tell how much you love her,"* he'd said. *"I have the right diamond for you..."*

I chose the diamond he'd recommended: a 2.5-carat solitaire square-mixed cut diamond unique to Tiffany & Company. The setting wasn't too high, since Jane worked with her hands in hair all day. They assured me it was the highest clarity they sold and also guaranteed she'd love it. As clueless as I was about jewelry, even I could agree it was the perfect ring.

I glanced at the bag again, realizing it could be months or years before I slid it on Jane's finger. We were on her time more than ever. I said a silent prayer it wouldn't take *too* long for her to want me in all the ways I wanted her. I was more than ready to officially start my life with her.

I was about fifteen minutes from home when I realized there was another step I needed to take before I was fully prepared for whenever the day would come. I'd never met Jane's father. I wasn't sure when or if that would happen. So before I could chicken out, I pulled into the Coras' driveway and grabbed the box from the passenger seat. I slowly walked to the house, building as much courage as I could, and knocked on the door of her current father figure—the man who'd taken care of her for over a year. Robert had seen Jane at her worst. He'd watched me court her for months. He knew firsthand about what happened a couple of weeks ago and how it had affected her. He had a good sense of what she wanted...what she needed. I needed Robert's blessing more than her biological father's.

Deb answered the door and seemed more than surprised to see me on her front stoop. "Alex. Hi. Jane's not here."

"Hi, Mrs. Cora. I'm here to see Mr. Cora. And you, of course." I tried to keep my tone light and respectful. I needed her to let me in.

"Okay..." Deb replied hesitantly. "Come in." She moved out of the way and guided me into the kitchen where Robert was eating a sandwich. He looked up from his meal and glared at me.

"Good afternoon, Mr. Cora. May I sit down?" He nodded once and took another bite out of his sandwich. I sat across from him and adjusted in my chair. Deb sat in a seat adjacent to us. I cleared my throat and tried to figure out where to begin.

My heart raced and I felt beads of sweat forming on my forehead. "First of all, I want to apologize to both of you for what I did—and what I didn't do—regarding our...viral video." I looked at them both before continuing, "It was the worst mistake and judgment call of my life. And to be honest, it was unlike me to do such a thing. I'm sorry for any pain or mental discomfort it caused you. And I'm sorry you've had to watch Jane suffer because of it." I paused to see if they wanted to reply to anything yet. When they didn't, I continued, "I know how much your daughter-in-law means to you both—"

"Daughter," Robert corrected. He spoke slowly. "She's my daughter. There's no difference between Jane and my biological daughter. Or Graham. They say 'blood is thicker than water,' but that's bullshit. Family is whomever you care about most. Jane is on that list. She's my *daughter.* Not daughter-in-law." Robert took a sip of his milk and continued eating his sandwich.

"And that, sir, is why I'm here." My hand and the box had been hiding under the table. I lifted it and placed it in front of Robert. He looked at it blankly. I turned to Deb briefly, whose eyes became twice the size they just had been. "I've never cared for anyone as I do your daughter. I love her with every ounce that I am. My thoughts are on her every waking hour. I'll worship and love her as long as I live. Even longer. And I'll spend my entire life doing whatever I can to make up for the mistakes I've already made. I can assure you without a doubt that I will never hurt her again. She's a treasure. I adore her." I took a breath and untied the bow from the box. "She told me a few weeks ago that she felt I was a gift from heaven sent down to her. I wouldn't disagree to her face because it would be rude to do so. However, she has it backward. Jane has ignited my soul. She has taught me how to love. She's made me want to fight for that love." I opened the box and pushed it toward Robert. "And when she's ready, I'd like to place this on her finger. With your blessing, of course."

Deb took in a deep, audible breath. "Alex. You bought Jane a Tiffany diamond?" Her eyes were still as wide as ever. "A very *large* Tiffany diamond? You don't even know if she'll say yes."

I chuckled softly and grinned. I looked Robert dead in the eyes. "You're right. I don't know. But my first priority is making sure *he* says yes."

Robert took a few more bites out of his sandwich without saying a word. Deb and I sat in silence, watching every move he made. Finally, he swallowed a bite, wiped the crumbs off his mustache, cleared his throat, and spoke. "'Resentment is like drinking poison and then hoping it will kill your enemies.'"

"Nelson Mandela," I stated.

"Mmhm," Robert hummed. He put his sandwich down and pushed the plate out of the way. "I wish you could've seen Jane's face after the newscaster displayed that photo of you two. I could see a million happy smiles on her face for the next fifty years and I'd *still* not be able to get that image out of my head." I closed my eyes and cringed at his words. He continued, "There's a difference between losing your entire family in an accident and having someone close to you purposely harm you—"

My eyes popped open in surprise at his words. I interrupted, "With all due respect, sir, I did *not* purposely harm her." Adrenaline pumped through my veins.

"Let me finish," Robert ordered. "Jane will never feel pain stronger than losing Graham and those kids. I honestly don't know how she has the strength and motivation to keep going. But somehow she does. She has worked hard to heal herself. All of us who are affected by tremendous loss know there will be setbacks...a song on the radio...a smell...seeing kids play at the park... You never know what's going to trigger you. So you brace yourself every single day, waiting for that one trigger that might put you over the edge. When it happens, you lean on the people ready to help you. Your only hope is those people, the ones who love and care about you the most, will never add to your pain. You trust they will protect you." Robert clasped his hands together and pointed his index fingers at me. "You're supposed to *protect* the one you love, Alex. You're supposed to be selfless enough to make choices to help and benefit your partner. You put your wants below theirs, if what they want or need is more important. That's what love is."

"I know, sir—"

"So you might not have purposely hurt her. But you purposely kept something from her that ended up harming her. Do you see what I mean now?"

I nodded. I couldn't argue. He was right.

"All that being said, if you don't count the last two weeks, I know you make her happy. I can see that you're good for her. Ever since she went to coffee with you that first time, she's been slowly coming back to life. She has color in her cheeks. She smiles and laughs again. Her eyes aren't vacant anymore. Without even knowing it, you motivated her to step back into her home. You motivated her to sell it. She's back to work and teaching fitness classes. Sure, she might have gotten to this point soon anyway. Time heals all wounds after all. But you spoke of her igniting your soul..." He paused, waiting for a response from me. I nodded slowly. "Well, *you've* ignited something in her too. I don't know if she's ready to admit it, but it seems she is slowly and subconsciously trying to restart her life. A happy life. And I'm pretty sure she wants to start a life with you.

"This last week or so... I can tell she misses you. Don't tell her I told you that." He huffed a laugh. "But she'll make small mentions of you. She checks her phone often and I assume she's looking for messages from you. She stares out the window very pensively, as if she's trying to figure out everything in her head at that moment. She's got a lot on her mind. I wouldn't consider myself intuitive. I obviously can't read minds. But if I had to guess as to what she was thinking about all day...it would be you.

"So, you two need to talk. Soon. You need to figure out how to fix what you messed up. You need to show her that you're worthy of her love. You need to *prove* that you'll protect her."

I interrupted as politely as I could. "We started the conversation this morning actually. She said she forgives me, but I know it will take time to earn her trust back completely."

Robert nodded. "You're on probation, Alex...with her. And with me. But if Jane can forgive you, then I can too. It will do her no good for me to hold a grudge. And since I love her and want what's best for her, I'll put my feelings aside. For her." He took the last sip of his milk before he continued, "If Jane wants to marry you, then you have my blessing." His lips lifted in a half smile, and he extended his hand across the table.

I shook his hand, but then stood and walked around the table to give him a proper hug. He awkwardly returned the embrace and then let me go to push me an arm's length away. "Probation," he repeated.

I dropped my head to prevent him from seeing the emotion dripping from my eyes. "I understand. Thank you," I whispered. I turned to Deb and hugged her next. "Thank you so much," I repeated. "I can't tell you how appreciative I am of you two. Thank you for taking such good care of her. You both have helped her heal too."

"We may have helped in our own little ways," Robert remarked. "Jane has done most of the work on her own. But you get credit for her coming back to life the last few months. You've expedited her healing." He paused and nodded to himself. "So, thank *you,* Alex. Now get out of here before she comes home and sees that ring."

I nodded and collected my things to head to the door.

"Oh. Alex," Robert called to me before I was over the threshold. "Jane's birthday is Saturday. She doesn't love celebrating her birthday, so make sure she feels special."

I nodded at him in thanks. "I will definitely do that."

I ENTERED THE gym the following day with a renewed amount of energy and ambition. And for good reason: my girl had forgiven me. The ring was in my possession, which she would wear as a symbol of my love and commitment...well, that she'd *hopefully* wear. I banked on her saying yes when I asked. Robert had given me his blessing. Things were turning around, and I couldn't be more appreciative. I'd spent the majority of the afternoon and evening trying to figure out how I'd make Jane's birthday special.

I'd texted Reese, making sure Jane had plans for Saturday. I wouldn't let her celebrate alone. Reese had assured me Jane would be taken care of on her birthday. She didn't give me any details, and I didn't ask further questions. I was somehow on Reese's good side. I didn't want to ruin it.

I walked to the main desk where Patti and Stan were greeting and checking people in.

"Welcome back," Patti said sarcastically.

I furrowed my brow and wondered where that attitude had come from. "Thanks, I think," I replied as I grabbed the newspaper.

Stan pulled the paper from my hands and replaced it with a clipboard. "Nope. You don't have time for that. You have sixteen clients today."

I huffed out a breath. "Sixteen?" Considering personal training was my part-time job, I averaged about four clients per day. "What the hell, Stan?"

"Don't look at me." Stan crossed his arms and brought his gaze to Patti.

Patti looked up from the computer. "What? You've been gone two weeks, Alex. You have regular clients who have been waiting for you. And now you have new clients. Get used to it for a while."

I looked around the gym, remembering what Stan had said about new customers. Indeed, the majority of the clientele were young women. Granted, the time of day would affect who was there; we tended to get more men in the early morning and afternoons. But Stan hadn't exaggerated; the women were out in full force. I looked over the clipboard of whom I'd be training today. There were a handful of familiar names, people I had trained for a while. Most, however, were women's names I didn't recognize.

I rubbed my face and sighed. Two years ago, I would have been amped up for such a schedule. Now it seemed daunting—and uncomfortable since most of the listed women probably signed themselves up because they'd seen me getting a blowjob in my office upstairs.

It is what it is, I thought to myself.

"Is my first one here?" I asked Patti.

"She sure is." Patti pointed to a bench along the wall.

After my first client warmed up, I had her start on a machine doing some lat pull-down reps. The view of her holding onto the bar overhead sparked an idea for Jane's birthday. I excused myself for a brief moment to call in a favor from a buddy. Hopefully he could deliver by Sunday when I'd see Jane. It was a risk to give her such a present, but I was willing to take the chance in order for her to reap the reward.

The next couple of days went by in a flash. Patti had my entire week stacked with clients. By Thursday, I was exhausted and over it. All the new women clients, and most of the men, eyed me as if I were some sort of candy. Most were respectful. Some were not. Many attempted to slip me their phone number after our first session. Every time, I politely declined and told them I did not date my clients. That was never a hard rule before, but it was getting me out of a lot of awkward situations.

After three full days of training clients, I told Patti she needed to cap it at eight a day. She begrudgingly agreed and started calling people to remove them from next week's schedule.

I was walking out to my Jeep on Thursday afternoon when I received a text from an unfamiliar number. Well, somewhat unfamiliar. It was the same number that had sent me the information about Jane teaching spin class. There was no screenshot like the last anonymous message. Instead, it was a written text:

> We're headed to the city tomorrow night to celebrate Jane's birthday. Here are the deets—

*Limo picking us up in CL at 5:45 p.m.

*Arrive at Fondue You for dinner at 7:30 p.m.

*NightBar 923 at 9:30 p.m. until ??

*Palmer House Hotel to sleep.

*Breakfast in the morning.

*Limo back home.

Feel free to join for all or some of it.

I read over the text a few times before I responded. I didn't know what to say to my secret messenger who had kept me in the loop. My curiosity was getting to me, so the first response was easy:

Is this Luis?

Wouldn't you like to know...

I rolled my eyes. He basically just confirmed it for me.

Thank you for the invite, but if Jane wanted me there, she would have invited me.

Okay. Suit yourself. The invite from me still stands.

I had one of those moments driving home when you get to your destination and you don't remember the ride. My thoughts were on the next night, and if I should or should not make an appearance. It was hard to resist the idea of seeing my girl out having fun. So before I could think better of it, I texted Tanner:

What are you doing tomorrow night? I need you to be available.

WE ARRIVED AT NightBar 923 at 9:00 p.m. I wanted to make sure I was there before Jane's party, so none of them would spot us. I wasn't sure if I was going to show my face or not. It would depend on how the night went. Tanner and I had a table and bottle service waiting for us, so we settled in to one of the darkly lit corners and waited. The large room was set up with tables that had been reserved all the way around the perimeter on a raised platform. The open dance floor sunk down a step in the middle of the room. A metal bar separated the two spaces, aside from accessways to and from the dance floor.

"Dude, you're so whipped by this girl," Tanner reproached.

I ignored him and took a sip of my bourbon.

"What *is* it about her?"

I shook my head in confusion. "I don't have an answer for that. It's everything about her."

Tanner shook his head in response and took a sip of his cocktail. "So we're just going to wait here for her to show up? And then watch her from the dark? You don't at all find this weird?"

"I don't have an answer for that either, Tanner. Let's just see what happens," I stated firmly. "I invited you here, but I don't actually have a plan."

"Got it. No plan," Tanner pronounced.

Jane, Reese, Luis, and two other dudes showed up a few minutes after their scheduled time. Jane looked stunning. Her hair was down in loose waves. She had on tight black leggings and sandals. Her upper body was in a long-sleeved mostly backless black crop top. The back had one 'X' of string that crossed over her spine and then crisscrossed around her waist a few times. The string came together and tied at the small of her back. I couldn't help but think about the black crisscrossed teddy I'd taken off her body the last night we'd spent together. I'd be hard-pressed to think that top didn't remind her of the same night.

Jane chatted with Luis and the two other guys while Reese went off somewhere. I stared at the men I didn't know. One of them I didn't recognize at all, but it was obvious he was Luis's date. The other one I knew I'd seen before, but couldn't place who he was. Reese returned and directed them to the opposite corner from where we were. They had a table and couches reserved on the far opposite side of us. They ordered their drinks and settled in to their area.

There weren't many people dancing yet so it appeared nobody from her group was ready to get out there. I watched as the one dude whom I couldn't place pushed himself down on the couch where Jane and Reese were sitting. He shifted himself right and left until he sat between them. Jane and Reese both laughed and smacked him. He put his arms around both of them. Without missing a beat, Jane grabbed his hand, pulled it away from her shoulders, and placed it on his lap. They all still laughed and smiled. It seemed as if she knew him well.

The waiter went over with a tray full of drinks and shots. I watched as Jane shook her head fiercely when Reese tried to push a shot glass into her hand. Jane was all smiles but continued to refuse it. Reese leaned over the guy sitting in the middle so she could reach Jane's ear. Whatever Reese said worked, because Jane grabbed a shot glass from Reese's hand, clinked it together with the guy's and Reese's glasses, and popped the one-ounce drink back down her throat.

She winced at the burning before she set the glass on the tray and grabbed her full drink. The guy in the middle clapped dramatically and kissed Jane on the cheek. She pushed him and shook her head in mild disapproval.

"Yo, Tanner, who is that guy next to Jane? Do you recognize him?"

Tanner narrowed in on the three of them on the couch. "I think that's Brooks."

"Brooks? Reese's scrawny brother? No way," I disagreed.

"Yeah, bro, I'm pretty sure it is."

I looked harder. I was too far away to really analyze him, but Tanner was right. Brooks's high school features were there. They were just hidden behind the maturity of a grown man's body.

For a while, I watched him continually flirt with the woman I loved. She'd laugh and smile at him, but she pushed away anything more than conversation. He'd put a hand on her leg, and she'd swat it away. When she stood to mingle, he tried to put a hand on her bare back. She stepped away quickly in order to avoid his touch. She made it obvious she wasn't into him and yet he wasn't taking any hints.

Another man after Jane's attention. *Fucking Fantastic.*

As much as I wanted to go over there and set him straight, her demeanor seemed light. She didn't look threatened. So it was better if I let her take care of herself.

After about an hour, the DJ's music became louder and more intense. You could feel the beat through your entire body. The lights in the room dimmed low while strobe lights flashed in every direction. The room was so crowded I had a hard time viewing the table on the opposite side. I saw as Reese pushed another shot into Jane's hand and then guided her out on the dance floor. They danced together for a while, laughing and chatting with each other while their bodies moved in sync. They were pushed together by the crowd, but they didn't seem to mind.

At one point, Reese's attention went to the corner of the room, where people entered from outside. She screamed in excitement and ran over to hug a tall, blond-haired man.

"*Fuck*!" I shouted and then slouched down in my chair, rubbing my eyes in frustration. "Fuck!"

23

Alex

TANNER STARED AT me and tried to figure out what had happened. He shifted his glance back and forth from me to Jane with concern all over his face. Jane was still on the dance floor but dancing alone, totally oblivious that Reese had left her. I narrowed my eyes at her, trying to get a better view. I had lost track of how many drinks and shots she'd had.

"Dean is here," I informed Tanner, but my concern shifted to Jane's alcohol consumption. She wasn't a heavy drinker. With her recent weight loss, I imagined she could get plastered pretty quickly—especially with Reese forcing shots on her.

Tanner had a clueless look on his face. I realized that he'd never met Dean, nor had I mentioned Dean to him. It was too much to explain with the electronic dance music on full blast. He'd have to get the short version.

I leaned in to his ear. "That guy with Reese. He wants Jane." I wasn't sure he'd heard me at first since the bass was bumping hard, but he stared at Dean and nodded.

"He's a problem?" Tanner asked.

"A big one," I growled as I watched Dean head onto the dance floor and lift Jane up in a bear hug.

"Well, you have a choice. Either show your face and let him know Jane is yours. Or...you don't." Tanner smiled and took a big sip of his drink. "I vote for option number one."

I sat in the chair and thought about what would keep me on Jane's good side. She might have forgiven me, but as Robert had said, I was on probation. "Option two."

"Boooo. You're getting lame, Alex. Have another drink. Maybe you'll loosen up." Tanner laughed and leaned far back in his chair. I ignored him and kept my eyes on the issue at hand. "So we sit some more." He looked around the club, and then at me. "I'm really glad you invited me tonight, Alex. This is really exciting shit." I could taste the sarcasm that emitted from him. I had to remember he had no stake in the game.

"Go take a lap. See if you can find some action," I told him.

Tanner appeared to want to take my suggestion, but was hesitant to leave me alone. "You sure?"

"Yeah. I'm fine. Go."

He grabbed his glass and lifted off the chair. "Text me if you need something."

I poured myself another drink and sat back in the chair again. The urge to feel sorry for myself was strong. They were celebrating Jane's birthday and I wasn't invited. It was the same scenario as it had always been with Jane and me—Dean was invited to events while I sat on the sidelines.

Jane's entire group was on the dance floor. I watched each of them but kept my focus on Jane most of the time. While sitting there, a voice of reason spoke from my inner conscience. As much as I wanted to, I couldn't deny the logic of why Jane or Reese didn't invite me. Jane and I had spoken only once in almost three weeks. It would've been awkward for me to be with them.

Still, I was pissed that Dean *had been* invited. The dude lived in Michigan. How was it that he could drop everything and come to Illinois all the time?

Because his wife died, and he's on leave from work, I reminded myself.

Either way, Dean continually got in the way. He complicated an already complicated situation. He needed to leave the picture if I had a standing chance at a long-term relationship with Jane. Maybe Tanner was right. Maybe I had to show Dean that Jane was mine.

I watched the whole party out on the floor while I pondered what to do.

As if the strobe lights, heavy bass from the music, and Dean's presence weren't enough to give me a headache, fog machines pushed cloudy air onto the floor from every direction. Before I knew it, my view was almost completely obstructed. I saw silhouettes dancing, but that was about it. Not being able to see where Dean's—or Brooks's—hands were placed, especially while Jane felt the effects of booze, put me over the edge. I grabbed my phone and texted the anonymous, otherwise known as Luis's, number:

> Hey, make sure you're taking care of Jane. She looks like she's been overserved.

I knew it wasn't guaranteed he'd check his phone, but I had to try. More than likely, he'd want to take a picture of a moment and then he'd read it. I put my phone in my lap and waited.

I was right. It only took a few minutes before he replied. I saw him leave the dance floor and stand on the couch to search the room: You're HERE?

> Yes.

Where? He still scanned. When his attention was closer to my area, I lifted my drink up over my head so he could pinpoint me.

> What the hell are you waiting for? Get over here!

> I'm not sure I'm welcome.

> Who the F cares if you're welcome? Do you see what's happening? Come fight for your girl!

"*What's. Happening?*" The fog and lights still limited my view, so I didn't know what he was talking about. I stood to take a lap to find out. I walked around part of the perimeter, trying to get a good view of Jane. I found a pocket of space where the fog was less dense. Dean had Jane in his grasp. He tried to pull her up against him while he held onto the strings around her waist with his thumbs. Jane had her hand on Dean's stomach, but it looked more like a barrier attempt than an act of affection. Dean kept trying to get their bodies to connect, but Jane's refusal was strong.

Dean then grabbed all her hair in one hand and pulled down. Her head tilted up in response, which was obviously his plan. With a huge smile on his face, he bent down to kiss her lips. Before he could reach her, she put her hand over his mouth and pushed his head gently. He shook out of her grasp and bent over to kiss below her ear. She immediately shrugged her shoulder to shove his lips away. Dean still had her hair in his hands and he pulled harder to have her look up again. He bent over to once again attempt to kiss her.

That was when my body started traveling toward the dance floor; my brain had no time to tell my feet to stop. I knew it was a terrible idea before I made it to them, but I pressed through the crowd anyway. With every step, the anger and jealousy were getting louder. Luis and Tanner were right. I needed to show myself.

When I almost made it to where they were standing, I angled myself so I would hopefully not harm Jane. Two steps later, I rammed into Dean with as much force as I could gather. His unsuspecting large frame fell backward into strangers, a few of them falling to the floor and screaming. He was taken aback for a moment and then locked eyes with me. I pushed Jane behind me and hoped someone from her party would grab her. Before Dean could even reach me, both he and I were dragged off the floor by security. I didn't fight it. I knew better.

Dean, on the other hand, did everything he could to get out of the grasp of the large bouncer. "I didn't do anything!" he shouted at them. "*He* attacked me!"

We were led to what appeared to be the back exit. They threw us both outside into the alley and told us there was zero tolerance for fighting. Before the doors even shut, Jane's entire group came out of the same exit. I locked eyes with Jane, who looked an equal amount of surprised to see me...and drunk. I knew I wouldn't get any alone time with her to explain anything, so I turned to walk away before I made bad choices.

"What the fuck, man? What's your problem?" Dean shouted at me.

I turned on my heels and looked him dead in the eyes. "My problem?" I scowled. "My problem is you still haven't taken a lesson in chivalry. You still don't understand cues from body language." I paused to get a good look at Jane. "And by the way, she is *my* girl. Stay the fuck away from her."

Dean scoffed and took a few steps toward me. "*Your* girl?" He laughed sarcastically. "Oh, your girl, right. Is that why you were invited tonight?" I planted my feet; my body geared up. He continued, "Oh, wait. That's right. You weren't. But I was..." He took a deep breath in and let out an audible sigh. "Hey, remember at Marley's when you told me you should only kiss a girl when she agrees to it?" I didn't reply. Instead, I stood and allowed the adrenaline to push through all my vessels. "Yeah, well, she agreed to it. In Sweden."

No. My attention went right to Jane, who seemed stunned to the point of paralysis. Without moving any part of her body, she directed her eyes straight at me with a tormented expression. "Dean...please..." she pleaded.

Dean turned toward her. "No, it's okay, sweetie. He needs to know." He turned back to me with the cockiest grin on his face. "In a dressing room." He took a couple more steps toward me. "She agreed to *all* of it, Alex. All of it."

My eyes went back to Jane in disbelief. I couldn't process what I'd heard.

"Dean! Please!" Jane shouted. Even in the dim light, I could see that all the blood had rushed from her cheeks.

I shook my head and rubbed my face with my hand. That couldn't be true. He had to be lying.

"Does it seem unbelievable, Alex?" He tipped his head to the side and took another menacing step toward me. Every ounce of my body trembled in anger. "What...is it hard to believe if it's not documented? You won't believe it unless you see it?" We were only a couple of feet apart now. "What do the younger kids say nowadays? 'Pics or it didn't happen'? Yeah, that's the saying. Or in your case, 'video'?"

I reacted without thinking. One second I stood there in complete disbelief, and in the next, I plowed my fist into his chin. There was screaming in the background, as well as an audible crunch as Dean fell backward to the ground. I went to walk away before I did any worse, but an arm wrenched me back. I turned and was met with Dean's fist cracking into my face. I saw stars for a brief second before my vision cleared. The ringing in my ears and the beating of my heart were excruciating. I quickly brought my hand up to my face to assess the damage. I was pretty sure he'd broken my fucking jaw.

I pulled my fist back to make my second move, but arms suddenly came around from behind me and pulled me backward. "Alex, walk away, dude," Tanner ordered in my ear. "It's not worth being arrested. Or on the news. Walk away."

Dean wiped blood from his mouth and spit on the ground. "Again...you mean. It's not worth being on the news again." He had a devil's grin plastered on his face.

I attempted to unhook the arms that were restraining me so I could knock that fucking smile off his face. Tanner locked down, so there was no chance to escape. "Alex, he's trying to piss you off. Don't let him win. Walk away," Tanner stressed in a calm voice.

Reese pulled Dean away with a sympathetic glance in my direction. I looked over at Jane, who had her eyes on the ground. Luis stared at me with the same sad eyes as Reese before she'd guided Dean away.

Tanner still had a hold on me as he continued to retreat. Once everyone had dissipated, he let go. "Do you need to go to the hospital?" he asked in a concerned tone.

I gathered the blood in my mouth and spit it out. "Nah. I just need to go home."

"Alex, you may have a broken hand or jaw. How about I take you back to my place in case you need to go see a doctor tonight?"

I agreed reluctantly. As soon as we were in Tanner's car, I sent Jane a text:

> I'm sorry I ruined your birthday.

She replied immediately:

> Luis told me he invited you. I wish you would have shown yourself sooner. But I'm not upset with you. Not at all, okay?

I leaned my head back on the seat and sighed in relief. I didn't know exactly how to process the news Dean had shared, but I was so thankful *she* wasn't angry with *me*.

A few minutes later, she texted again:

I am so sorry, Alex...

I read the text over and over. My mind went back to the salon last Monday when she looked distressed and said there was something she needed to tell me. The dressing room incident had to be what she was talking about. I couldn't imagine anything being worse than that.

At least she was going to tell me...

Once we arrived at Tanner's condo, he made up the guest bed, tossed a few ice packs and a bottle of ibuprofen my way, and told me to holler if I needed him. I lay in bed for hours, unable to calm down. The knuckles on my right hand killed me and every nerve on the left side of my face throbbed. My lower lip was split open, and I was pretty sure a few roots of teeth had been fractured. I had never been in so much physical pain in my life.

All that being said, none of the physical sufferings even touched the agony I felt about Dean's admission. After more than three full decades of life, I finally understood what heartbreak meant. The torment from under my rib cage screamed at me all night. No position I tried to lay in would ease the ache. When I closed my eyes, all I could see was Jane's and Dean's bodies connected. Every time the vision came into my head, I'd feel a heavier sharp stab directly into my heart.

At about four o'clock in the morning, I couldn't take it anymore. The Jane and Dean images became more graphic, plus the physical and emotional pains swelled to unbearable levels. I sent Tanner a text from my room that I was calling a cab to go to the hospital. He didn't reply, which was what I hoped. He'd figure it out when he woke up.

THE EMERGENCY DEPARTMENT staff dismissed me after a thorough evaluation and treatment of my face and hand. It turned out I didn't have a broken jaw. Dean had dislocated my TMJ with his blow to my face. They gave me medication and anesthetic before the doctor relocated my jaw back into place. I was given strict instructions to keep up with the pain medications and to not open my mouth wide for six weeks. The doctor stitched up my busted lip and told me that while it didn't appear that I had any broken teeth, the nerves of my teeth could have been traumatized to the point where they might die. I'd have to make an appointment with my dentist to have them evaluate further. As far as my hand, the doctor was pretty sure there were a few hairline fractures in my metacarpals. They placed a temporary cast and gave me the name of an orthopedist.

I walked out of the hospital feeling bandaged, bruised, and pretty fucking terrible. I'd never felt as low as I did in that moment. I made my way back to my Jeep, which had been parked near the nightclub, and headed home to Crystal Lake. The entire ride home I pondered what I was going to do about Jane.

After the long sleepless night, time in the hospital, and the drive back to the suburbs, I decided I wasn't angry with her. If I'd put myself in her shoes, with all the sadness, trauma, mental conflicts, and confusion, I could understand why it had happened. Not to mention the pressures she might have felt from me to start a relationship. Plus, the pressures of having a lifelong friend—whom she was very comfortable with—craving her attention. It made sense that she'd crack under pressure.

So no, there was no anger. Only pain. One of my father's favorite sayings was "Time heals all wounds." Robert mentioned the same quote when I asked for his blessing. Healing took time. Forgiving took time. And it would take a lot of talking. Plus, we'd barely fixed the sex tape issue. I stared out at the cars in front of me and wondered how our relationship had become so complicated in such a short time. We'd both made detrimental mistakes. We both felt awful about them. She'd already forgiven me for my mistake. I needed to do the same for her.

I hadn't replied to her final text the previous night. I didn't know what to say. When I arrived home, I texted her to make sure we'd still be meeting tomorrow after church. She replied only with a thumbs-up. I breathed a sigh of relief. I wasn't sure I could handle much more suffering without seeing her. With confirmation that we would be together the following day, I lay down in my bed and was finally able to rest.

I SLEPT ALL afternoon, through the evening, and woke mid-morning. My face throbbed from the lack of pain medicine. I found the pills, filled up a glass of water, and looked in the mirror for the first time since Friday night. My eyes expanded to twice their size. It was worse than I'd expected. Everything was swollen, and the bruises were turning a nice shade of purple. As much as I didn't want Jane to see me in such a terrible state, the urge to see her was stronger than my reservations. I drove over to her in-laws' when I knew I had given them enough time to get home from church.

Before I could ring the doorbell, Deb opened the door with a sorrowful look on her face. "Alex..." she put a hand up to her face. "Oh, my gosh. Look at you. Are you okay?"

"I've been better," I admitted. "Is she ready to go?"

Deb sighed with a look of pity. "She's not here." I stared at her, confused. She handed me a sealed envelope. "She asked me to give you this."

Still confused, I opened the envelope right there on the porch:

Alex,

I'm headed out of state for a couple of weeks—

I stopped reading. "What?" I said more to myself than to Deb. I looked at her. "Where did she go?"

"I've been instructed not to tell you," she replied regretfully. I nodded in acceptance and slowly turned away from her to leave. "She didn't say I couldn't tell you *how* she was getting there, though..." I turned back to Deb in surprise. "She and Robert left forty-five minutes ago. They're headed to O'Hare. Terminal 2, JetBlue. If you hurry, you may be able to make it."

I pulled her in for a hug and then looked her straight in the eyes. "Thank you, Mrs. Cora. Thank you so much."

She smiled at me. "You're welcome." I went to walk away, but she grabbed my arm to hold me there. "Alex, I know I don't get a say in any of this. But for what it's worth, she's extremely torn up about hurting you. I've seen just about every type of pain in her eyes. This is a different kind of anguish. It's from something *she* did. Something she could have prevented. She's so mad at herself. But she's a really good person. She messes up, just like anyone else. Please go easy on her."

"I understand what you're saying. I'm not angry. We have a lot to fix, but I have faith we can get through it."

"I have faith too. Now get out of here!"

I backed away to head to my Wrangler. With my hands in the prayer position, I pointed my fingers toward her, then brought my fingers to my lips and closed my eyes in appreciation. "Thank you again. So much. Wish me luck."

"Luck!" she exclaimed.

I ran to the Jeep and headed out. I didn't have a plan, aside from catching up to Jane. I didn't know where she was going or why. Whatever she was doing was obviously a last-minute plan, and I assumed it had to do with Friday night.

While waiting for the red light to change, I glanced down at my hand. I was still holding Jane's envelope. I almost forgot there was more to the letter:

> *I'm sorry I didn't say goodbye, but I didn't want you to talk me out of going. I was worried if I saw you this morning, I'd talk myself out of it.*
>
> *I'm headed to a grief retreat. This wasn't planned until yesterday. Deb told me about this place a while ago, but I dismissed the idea. Now with all the added confusion and pain in my heart and head, I feel it's the right step. I called them and they had an opening for the next session, which begins tomorrow.*

The light turned green, so I'd have to wait for another red light to finish.

A grief retreat.

I couldn't disagree with the idea. It was something she probably should've gone to sooner. Even though I wanted her with me, especially now so we could work out our problems, I knew the experience would heal and be helpful. For a brief moment, I thought about turning around and heading home, but the need to see her before she left was strong enough to keep me driving southeast.

I hit another red light and picked up where I left off:

> *I am so sorry for what I did. I can't put into words the deep regret I feel. It was wrong. I wish I could go back in time to undo it. I am praying you will somehow forgive me even though I'm not sure I deserve your forgiveness. I know we need to talk, so I apologize for leaving like this. I'm hoping once I return, I will have some of the conflicts in my head worked out, so I can focus on moving on to the next stage of my life. We can talk then.*
>
> *I hope to see you when I return.*
>
> *Jane*

I hit the gas pedal harder. I was more anxious than ever to get to O'Hare. I needed to tell her we *would* work everything out, and what we had together may have become messy, but it was all reparable. She needed to be reminded I loved her unconditionally. That still held true, even after what had happened with Dean.

I finally made it to the departures area of Terminal 2 and threw myself out of my Jeep. "Sir, you can't park here! It's drop-off only!" the traffic controller hollered my way.

"Tow it!" I yelled back at him. The airport was so crowded. I didn't know what she was wearing to help my eyes find her. I scanned the crowds, looking for anyone blonde. I searched all over the main ticketing area with no sign of her. My eyes scanned the security line, and by some miracle, I spotted her. She was on the other side of a very long line of people. She was putting her shoes on and collecting her things after walking through the metal detector. "*Jane*! JAAANNE!" I shouted.

She didn't react to my yelling. She was too far away. I pushed through the security line while disgruntled passengers around me yelled and sighed at my hastiness.

"Sir, I need to see your ticket and photo ID," the security guard ordered when I approached. I didn't listen and instead attempted to go past her. The guard pushed her hand on my chest and tried again. "Sir, do I need to call for backup? You're not allowed to enter this area without a valid ticket and a photo ID." *Shit!* I turned and ran to the ticketing area. Mercifully, there was no line.

"Where are you headed?" the JetBlue agent asked.

Uhhh. I had no idea where she was going. "Could you tell me where passenger Jane Cora is going?"

"No sir, I cannot. All traveling clients have full confidentiality."

"Okay, I'd like to go to the destination that is leaving out of this terminal in the next hour."

She looked at me speculatively. "Any destination?"

My annoyance started shining through at her questioning. "Yes. Any destination. Just pick one," I said curtly. She typed on her computer for what felt like an eternity before asking for my credit card. I ripped the boarding pass out of her hands and ran toward the security line without even a "thank you" her way. I pushed through the passengers again and handed my ticket and ID to the guard. She eyed me, then my ID, about five times. Considering I'd had a fist annihilate half my face recently, I could understand how my photo ID could look different than how I currently appeared. She must have been satisfied with the features she could connect to my photo, because she gave it all back to me and said, "Next."

I ran through the metal detector and stopped short when I saw the terminal was split into two concourses. I didn't know which way she went. *Shit!* I ran to the screens where all the upcoming departures were listed and honed in on all the JetBlue flights. It looked like they were isolated to one of the concourses. I picked that side and ran, my eyes weaving through all the different gates. There was no sign of her anywhere.

Over the intercom, an employee updated departure info for one of the flights. "Last call. This is last call for flight 3241 to Charleston International Airport. All ticketed passengers must board now." I looked down at my boarding pass for the first time. My arrival city was New Orleans. It wasn't supposed to board for thirty more minutes. I had no idea if I should look there or hover around other areas with boarding passengers. I could've thrown a dart in the dark and had a better chance of hitting my target.

My search lasted another forty minutes with no success. Up and down the concourse I went. I weaved through all the chairs at all the gates, a few times. I stalked the women's bathrooms and tried not to look too creepy while doing it, especially considering the condition of my face. She had to have been on a plane by now. It wasn't looking good, which meant I'd have to wait another two weeks to repair the damage to our relationship—and my tormented heart.

I was never going to make it.

24

Jane

ALMOST ALL THE anxiety left my body as soon as I sat in my seat on the plane. When Deb had told me about the retreat a few weeks ago, I informed her that being surrounded by so many grieving people for two weeks didn't sound like a good game plan for me. But the reality was I couldn't stop thinking about how two weeks away could possibly help. I had looked into it on their website and realized it might be just what I needed. I had sent a request for more information, and a pamphlet showed up in the mail a few days later.

I'd arrived home yesterday morning feeling wrecked, both emotionally and physically. I knew I had a choice to either fall back into a deep hole of depression or actively work on all my trauma so I could have a life worth living again. I'd grabbed the pamphlet off my dresser to read it once more. Spending fourteen days on the beach of South Carolina while meditating and practicing yoga became too enticing to refuse, especially after the last few weeks I'd had. I wasn't sure it was possible to heal all my fears, worries, trauma, and regrets in that short period of time, but at that point, I was willing to try anything.

I nestled into my seat, let out a few big exhales, closed my eyes, and wondered what Alex had thought of my letter. I felt guilty leaving so abruptly. I should have texted him when I'd made the plans to leave. Having the mental picture of him reading my words with a tortured face made me open my eyes, shake my head, and attempt to stop picturing him. I would fix my problems with him. But I needed to do the retreat first. I took the pamphlet out of my purse and read it again for the hundredth time:

Namaste Grief Retreat: A 1,000-acre sanctuary nestled up to the Atlantic Ocean off the coast of South Carolina. NGR is a place to process and overcome the tremendous grief that follows tragedy. We are open to those just starting their healing process, as well as those who have been processing their grief for years. All are welcome and encouraged to attend.

Each guest is assigned their own fully furnished bungalow, which offers a kitchenette and private bathroom. Enjoy light activities throughout the day—including yoga, horseback riding on the beach, relaxing in our saunas or hot tubs, hiking, and guided meditation. Massage therapists are on staff to provide deep tissue, hot stone, and/or Swedish massages by appointment. Other therapies are also available, including Reiki, ice bath therapy, chiropractic care, and red light therapy.

Peer and professional counseling are required daily activities. Both are group sessions, with peer counseling at 10:00 a.m. and professional counseling at 3:00 p.m. These sessions are mandatory and integral to our healing program. There are also counselors available for one-on-one sessions twenty-four hours a day.

*Every morning, as a group we show our appreciation for a new day with Sun Salutations on the beach. The dining area is open eighteen hours per day and stocked with only the most nutritious organic food. In the evenings, we offer a social gathering with staff and guests. Dinner is served in the dining hall, followed by our house band playing well-known tunes from every decade. *This is optional and only for those ready to mingle and test the waters of being in a large group setting. There is an alternate dining hall for guests not ready for social situations.**

If you're ready to take the steps to heal your body and mind, please visit our website for more information on how to register. We look forward to meeting you soon.

I closed my eyes and imagined myself there. Rereading the pamphlet had me antsy to start my session. I sat with my head on the back of my seat for a while until I realized there was no sign the plane would leave soon. Usually at that point, the flight attendants would be buzzing around, closing overhead bins, and asking people to get ready to stow their belongings under the seats. I opened my eyes and checked the time on my phone. We were supposed to have taken off almost an hour prior.

I looked to my right to find a middle-aged woman reading a book. "Excuse me. Do you know what the hold-up is?" I asked.

"I overheard someone say there was an engine issue," she answered.

Engine issue. *Super.*

I rested my head back on my seat again and tried not to be annoyed with the airplane for slowing down my journey to healing. We all sat there another ten minutes before we received an update from the captain.

"Good afternoon, everyone. This is Captain Brent speaking. It appears this airplane has a malfunctioning engine." The passengers erupted in disappointed groaning. "I know we're all anxious to get up in the sky, but I promise you we want the engines working properly before we take off. That being said, we will need to deboard this plane and board a different one just across the hall. The good news is the airplane we'll use has been fully inspected and is ready to go. I apologize for the inconvenience and will see you all across the hall at Gate E9."

Just as annoyed as everyone else, I gathered my belongings and shuffled out of the airplane. It was a slow shuffle, considering the number of people traveling down narrow passageways at the same time. While I walked at a snail's pace, waiting for the passengers ahead to move across the hall to Gate E9, I glanced around the terminal to people watch. My eyes immediately settled on a man sitting at an empty gate, slouched over with his head in his hands. He looked distraught. As I inched closer to him, I noticed he resembled Alex. I took a long look at his features and saw the evidence of a bar fight on the left side of his face.

Instant shock stung my body. I had a millisecond to decide what to do—either approach him quickly before I boarded the new plane or walk right past him. I stood there stunned, waiting for one of my opinionated internal voices to help me make the right decision.

Nothing. They were of no help.

I glanced at him again. He looked absolutely miserable. I thought about why he could be there, sitting alone. And more importantly, I thought about what I would want if roles were reversed. So I left the herd of passengers and walked the ten feet that separated us. I was directly in front of him, but his body didn't respond to my approach. "Alex," I said softly.

He immediately popped his head up at the sound of my voice. I tried to keep my features light as I studied his injuries. They were worse than I'd imagined. The entire left side of his face was twice the size of his right. The bruises ran from his chin all the way up to below his eye. His lip was crusty, with black stitches keeping the skin together.

His face had been damaged because of me.

The guilt encompassed my entire body. I blinked away my examination and bent to his level. "Hi," I whispered, because I didn't know what else to say.

"Jane," he replied.

"I don't have much time. But I saw you here and couldn't walk past you. I'm sorry I didn't text you my plans. And I'm sorry about..." The lump in my throat was forming. "We can't talk about this now. Not the way we should, at least." He looked at his feet and nodded. "I truly have to go." I kissed him very tenderly on his right cheek. "I hope you'll forgive me once I get back."

I turned around to leave, but he grabbed my hand. "I'm sorry too," he whispered with eyes so tormented that I had the urge to burst out crying—or vomit. I gently pulled my hand away from his and hustled to my gate.

I wasn't sure if I had made the right decision to stop and talk to him. His suffering seeped right into all my pores.

"HI, I'M JANE. My husband and three young children were killed in a car crash about a year and a half ago. One thing I've learned about myself so far is I am subconsciously preventing myself from being happy. Truly happy, that is. I have moments of happiness. But the thought of long-term happiness or contentment makes me feel guilty."

"Why does it make you feel guilty, Jane?" Dr. Francis, the therapist leading the group, asked.

"Because..." It was hard to put into words. "Because I'm here and they aren't. I'm getting a chance at life when it was ripped away from them."

The doctor nodded in understanding. "Survivor's guilt, in a sense?"

"Definitely," I admitted.

"And how could you push through that guilt?" Dr. Francis's voice was so calming.

"I don't know. Wanna tell me?" The group chuckled quietly, including the doctor.

"I think a good first step is to remind yourself that these are normal feelings. Give yourself grace. But also remember that you were given the gift of survival. You're meant to be here in this moment. Use the gift you've been given for good. It can be a long journey to heal from this type of guilt. But I promise you, Jane, it can be done."

I nodded in thanks before the next person gave their opening statement. I had been at the retreat for seven days, and it had been nothing short of amazing. The advertising in the brochure had not let me down. I was wrong when I thought being around other mourning people would be bad for me. Contrarily, it was the best idea. It wasn't so much "misery loves company," but more like "you understand my pain and maybe we can help each other heal."

I'd met so many lovely people in the last week. They were from all parts of the country and lived lots of different lifestyles. Their stories were all different, but the common denominator was grief and loss of loved ones. People—those who had not met grief as we had—could try to sympathize or empathize. They could imagine what they *might* feel if any of their loves passed away, but they didn't truly understand because they hadn't *actually* lived it. All sixty guests there with me had lived it. They understood it. And all of them wanted to heal. They wouldn't be there if they didn't.

I took full advantage of just about everything the retreat had to offer. I spoke with a one-on-one counselor daily. I scheduled different types of massages every few days. I had acupuncture sessions, as well as Reiki and red light therapy. The only therapy I didn't try was the ice bath. Everyone said how amazing it was, but I decided to take their word for it.

In group and private sessions, we talked a lot about what our lost loved ones would want for us. We were asked what we would want for our loved ones if roles were reversed. I knew in my heart that if Graham was alive and I was in heaven, I would want him to be happy, whatever it took. I wouldn't be upset if he found love again. I wouldn't feel as if I was being replaced. I'd be content if he was doing well.

Having that realization finally made me fully believe Graham was looking down at me every day, feeling the same way. He was content I was doing better. There was no other way to feel anymore.

In my private sessions, I asked if we could focus on my fear of losing any more loved ones. The fear was inhibiting me from being able to go forward with any new relationship. The therapist, Dr. Edwards, ensured me it was a common fear she helped work through with guests at the retreat. Dr. Edwards allowed me to talk through my anxieties the first few sessions but then gave me ways to train my brain to stop hyper-focusing on hypothetical situations. She called it Cognitive Behavioral Therapy. She warned me it would take time to rewire the strong "worries" embedded in my brain, but promised I would notice the fears subsiding if I worked on it daily.

In both private and group sessions, I was reminded that grief and fear would not disappear completely. But I had many new tools in my arsenal to cope and not let the pain prevent me from starting a new life. Because more than anything, I was *ready* to start a new life. For the last year and a half, I'd been living in a dead space of time. My past life was over, and I hadn't known how to start new. The retreat—the main missing tool in my healing arsenal—taught me, in many ways, how to move on. Moving on did not mean forgetting. Moving on meant creating a happy life that I deserved. I was anxious to get going.

The next week went too fast, and it was almost time to go home. I knew that once I left, I would be a different person than when I'd arrived. I felt it. I'd cried more tears in the past couple of weeks than I had in the past six months. And for me, that was saying a lot. The tears were nothing but cathartic. It never felt overwhelming, but instead felt like I was releasing deep trauma out of my body. I knew I wasn't going to be perfect. But I would be better. So much better.

During the last group session, we were encouraged to write a list of intentions or goals for the following weeks. I thought about my list as I was packing up my belongings the night before I flew home. The first item was to talk to Dean. I needed to set my feelings straight and apologize. I wasn't looking forward to the conversation, but I knew it was necessary. Number two was to find somewhere to live. As much as I loved my in-laws, the last two weeks of having my own personal space had me craving a townhouse or condo. Not only was it refreshing to have alone time, but I felt that staying with the Coras would impede my continual healing. For over a year, it did nothing but help. But it was time to move on. Starting my new life couldn't happen when I was still a houseguest in Graham's old bedroom. Number three was Alex. I couldn't think too much about Alex. I didn't want to lose the good vibes from the retreat. Because I knew what I wanted and worried my actions in Sweden might have changed his mind. I would focus on goals one and two first, and work up the courage for number three in a few days.

On the last evening before I returned home, I lay in bed feeling more at peace than I had in a very long time. I fell asleep quickly, which had been the norm for the entire two-week stay. It turned out, all the fresh air and different types of therapies were exhausting.

That night I dreamt of Graham for the second time since he had passed. The background was white and bright. Graham was wearing one of my favorite outfits: a fitted maroon button-down shirt with gray shorts and Birkenstocks. He looked like he'd just gotten back from a long stroll on a beach. He walked toward me with the happiest smile on his face. He was so handsome. He stopped when he was right in front of me, and then turned his head to the left so he could look behind him. He turned back toward me, his eyes guiding my gaze to what he'd seen in the background. I followed where he wanted me to look and found my three little loves, all in white, playing "Ring Around the Rosie" together. Clare and Marric had to lift Arlo up by his hands since even in heaven he hadn't mastered the skill of walking. They all fell down together on the last notes of the song. Then they stood up and sang it all over again. Each time they hit the last few words, they would belly laugh when their backsides hit the ground.

I couldn't say how many times I watched them go through the entire song and dance. Maybe a dozen? Finally, I looked at Graham, who had been watching along with me. I went to take a step forward to say hi to them, but he gently put his hand out to stop me. He shook his head very slowly with that same smile plastered on his face. I furrowed my brow, confused at what he was trying to tell me. He lifted his hand and placed it on my cheek. As soon as he touched my skin, a movie reel of still photos played in my head. The first few photos were of Graham and me as teenagers. They weren't photos I had ever seen before. It was as if he was showing me *his* memories. The next few pictures were of our little family of five. Again, they weren't images I had ever seen, so I tried to soak up every feature on my babies' faces before the pictures disappeared.

After those snapshots, there was a photo of myself with a dark-haired man, standing on a roof in the wintertime. I knew that setting. It was the first time I'd met Alex. In the next picture, Alex and I sat at a coffee place. My back was to the camera and blurry in the shot. The photo was centered on Alex and his beautiful face smiling at me. His eyes were bright with adoration. A few more images flew past my eyes...Alex and I on our first dinner date...us at our picnic...enjoying wine on his couch...sitting in the hot spring together in Montana...

Then the movie reel transitioned. The next pictures stayed around a few seconds longer. They were photos of memories I haven't lived yet...Alex and I on a beach together...hiking a beautiful mountain...a beautiful ring on my finger...a dark-haired, dark-eyed baby in my arms...

The movie lingered on the last photo until it became fuzzy and then dissipated. I blinked a few times and stared at Graham. The happy look on his face was set in stone. None of those images seemed to upset him. Quite the opposite, actually. I grabbed his hand that had rested on my cheek and kissed it a few times before I let go and backed away.

I woke up abruptly with sweat beading on my forehead.

Whoa.

I took a deep breath. *Did that really happen?* It would take me a little while to process the whole dream. It hadn't been bad by any means. Just intense. A dream that told a story—one that seemed to guide my new journey. I was disappointed to leave the retreat because I really wanted to decipher it all with Dr. Edwards. It would have to wait until I saw my usual therapist back home.

One thing I could reconfirm after the dream was that Graham wanted me to be happy, just as we spoke about many times in recent therapy sessions. As much as I had wanted to believe it for months, the guilt and doubt strangled the notion before I could affirm it in my heart. There were no doubts anymore. I had the retreat, and Graham coming to me in my dream, to thank.

ROBERT PICKED ME up from the airport and gave me the biggest hug before I entered his car. I could tell he'd missed me. My heart dropped a little at the sadness I'd cause them by moving out. I promised myself again that I would stay true to my word and visit them often. When I arrived back at the Cora home, I unpacked and settled into bed early. I needed to set up my meeting with Dean, which had me on edge. I pushed the negative worries aside and focused on calming my mind and body before bed. I was still on a relaxing sort of high from my retreat. I refused to let anything alter my mindset.

Relaxing high or not, I couldn't wait to get out of bed the next morning to text Dean. He was at the forefront of my mind. I needed to get the conversation over with so I could stop worrying about it:

Dean, we need to talk.

He replied immediately: No, we don't.

Yes, we absolutely do, I countered, feeling annoyed already.

Jane, no, we don't. I know what you're going to say, and I don't need to hear it.

I understood what he was doing—avoiding the inevitable hurt. Even so, we needed to work things out: Well, I need to say it. As soon as possible. Will you be out here soon? If not, I can come to you today or tomorrow?

I'm not in Michigan.

Where are you?

My phone rang a second later with Dean's name and picture popping up. "I'm actually about to check in to the Namaste Grief Retreat."

"What? You are?" I exclaimed.

"Yeah, I called Deb last week when you weren't answering my texts. She filled me in on this place. It sounded too good to pass up."

Pride beamed out of me that he was ready to work on healing. "Dean, you won't regret it. It was an incredible experience."

"That's what I'm hoping for."

"Hey, can you do me a favor? While you're there, would you talk to the counselors about your drinking?" My worry about his alcohol consumption had not gone away.

He chuckled quietly. "I plan to, sweetie pie. It's on my list of things to work out."

I sighed in relief. "So you really don't want to talk about...us?"

"I really don't," he stated firmly.

"Maybe later then? When you return?" I asked, feeling hopeful. I couldn't imagine sweeping such an important conversation under the rug.

"Maybe. We'll have to see."

"I'm so sorry, Dean," I choked out with heavy emotion.

He chuckled again. "I'm not."

"I do love you," I confessed. "A whole lot."

"I love you more."

I couldn't disagree. We hung up, and I sent a prayer above, hoping I hadn't ruined a lifelong friendship.

"WHAT ARE YOU up to today?" Deb asked a few days after my return. She'd been very interested in my daily itinerary since I got back. I hadn't wanted to be rude and ask her why she cared so much, so every day I'd rattle off my boring plans to her until she seemed satisfied. The past couple of days had been dedicated to finding a place to live. Thankfully, I had prepped my in-laws during the sale of my home because the news that I was actively working on moving out did not upset them too much. Maybe they also felt it was time? I hoped so. We were all in the same boat, and I wanted them to heal and move on too.

Either way, I met up with my Realtor, Sarah, who showed me a few local places each day. None of them had caught my eye, but Sarah assured me we'd find a home for me soon.

I turned to Deb to tell her my plans for the day. "Not much. If Sarah has any new places come on her radar, I'll go check them out. Other than that, I need to work on my spin class set for Saturday. And I have laundry that's been waiting for me. That's about it."

"Want to go on a walk?" she asked semi-abruptly.

"Sure, I'd love to," I replied sincerely. It sounded as if she'd planned to ask me to go. "Do you have somewhere in mind?"

"Well, it's a really nice day, and I've always wanted to do the Lake Geneva path—"

I interrupted her. "The Lake Geneva path? That's not a walk, Deb. That's a marathon. It's twenty-six miles." I giggled. Lake Geneva was on the south end of Wisconsin, not far from Crystal Lake. It was a beautiful town full of lots of history. The path ran between the gorgeous lake and the prestigious mansions that lined most of the shoreline. It would be a fun path to walk, but usually one would start early in the morning and walk most of the day because it's *twenty-six miles*. When Deb and I walked together, we never went farther than a few miles.

"Well, we don't have to walk the *whole* path. We can turn around any time we want." Her voice was higher pitched than usual.

"You don't want to go somewhere local?" I was so confused as to why she'd want to travel forty-five minutes to go on a walk.

"We could go shop around the town afterward, maybe get some lunch?" Her tone sounded more than high-pitched. It sounded...nervous, maybe? She must've felt worried about me moving out and spending time together was her way of coping.

If she wanted to drive almost an hour to walk, that's what we'd do. "Okay, that sounds great. Let me go get my shoes."

Deb insisted on driving, even though I offered many times. Just as before, her tone and demeanor were off. I tried to act casual and make small talk on the way up to Wisconsin. Maybe if I acted normal, whatever was brewing inside her would calm down. I filled her in about the retreat and how much it helped me. I told her about some of the other guests and what they'd been doing to heal that had been successful. I encouraged her to look into it if she felt it could help her.

"Have you talked to Alex yet?" she asked when there was a pause in my storytelling.

I looked down at my hands, feeling ashamed I hadn't reached out to him. "Not yet. It's on my list."

She glanced at me briefly as she drove. "Are you worried he won't forgive you?"

I nodded. "I am. Avoiding the issue has seemed like a better option than facing it head-on."

Deb nodded in agreement. "It's understandable that you're worried." She paused before she continued, "But, Janey, he made a mistake too. He needed your forgiveness, and you gave it to him. Don't you feel he'll do the same?"

"Two wrongs don't make a right. And my offense was far worse than his." I looked out the window. As much as I was still beyond humiliated that millions of people had watched a private video, Alex hadn't posted that video to the Internet. It had been stolen from him. That wasn't the same as actively deciding to cheat on someone.

You didn't cheat on him, both my internal voices reminded me. *You weren't in a relationship.* I shook their words away quickly. We were close enough to a relationship that there was no defending what I did.

We drove in silence the rest of the way. My Alex cabinet, which had been shut tightly for a couple of weeks, had been ripped wide open. Deb was right. I needed to contact him. It wasn't fair to avoid him. I vowed to text him when we returned.

When we arrived at the walking path, Deb found a place to park near one of the access points to the trail. We made some small talk but mostly walked in silence. I had a feeling Deb was letting me process my Alex cabinet.

After about a mile, Deb stopped abruptly. "I forgot my water in the car. I think I need to go back and get it."

I raised an eyebrow at her. "Want to go just a little farther and then we both can head back?"

She shook her head in disagreement. "I'm really thirsty. I think I need to go get it right now."

I furrowed my brow at her. She was definitely off today. "Okay, let's go."

"No!" she exclaimed and pushed her palm out at me. "I'll go. You wait here."

Before I could disagree, she turned around and ran away down the path. I stood there, completely stunned. I knew a lot about Deb Cora. And one of the things I knew to be an absolute fact was she did *not* run. Funny memes exist that say things like, *"If you see me running, you better run too because something is chasing me."* Not even if someone was chasing her, would Deb Cora run. She'd say, *"Jesus, save me, 'cuz I'm not runnin'!"*

So the fact that she hightailed it away from me during a hike in Wisconsin that *she* wanted to go on—for a water bottle—had me completely flabbergasted. There was a little bench a few feet in front of me, so I sat down and waited for her. After what felt like five minutes, I realized I would probably have to sit there for a while. Surely she wasn't going to run the entire time, right? I shook my head in disbelief. I didn't have my phone with me; I must have left it in the car. So I looked out to the lake and tried to figure out what the heck had just happened.

After a couple more minutes, I started daydreaming about how my conversation would go with Alex when I texted him later. My inner fears tried to convince me he wouldn't respond to my messages. I pushed the fears away before I talked myself out of reaching out to him at all. I was on the third or fourth scenario of how it would go when I saw someone in my peripheral approaching slowly. I turned my head toward the figure and stared right into the eyes of the man I had just been thinking about.

25

Jane

"HI JANE," ALEX said solemnly. His hands were in his pockets. He appeared nervous.

"Alex. Hi." I stood to give him a hug but then stopped myself. I didn't know if we were at hug status. My heartbeat doubled in time. "What are you doing here?"

He grinned and looked down at his shoes. "I asked Deb to bring you."

Well, *that* explained it! I immediately felt much better that my mother-in-law wasn't losing her marbles.

"Walk with me?" he asked with a shy, hopeful tone in his voice.

We traveled the path in silence for a few minutes before Alex started the conversation. "How was the retreat?"

"It was really good. I learned a lot about myself." I heard pride in my tone.

"I'm so glad to hear that." He kept his eyes on the path.

"How are you doing?" I looked at him briefly as we kept walking. The left side of his face almost looked back to normal. "Your injuries are healing."

He nodded in agreement and raised his right hand. "No cast needed."

"Good news," I replied as he walked off the path and into the grass of someone's private property. I slowed my gait while I tried to figure out what he was doing.

He chuckled nervously under his breath and looked at the grass. "This is my home." He pointed to the house behind him. "Would you like to come inside?"

My mouth opened in utter surprise. I had no idea he owned property on the esteemed Lake Geneva shore. "Um, sure."

He took me around to the front door and I caught a glance of the vintage green car I had admired in his Crystal Lake garage. I still had that image pop in my head at times of us driving down the road with the top down, blissfully happy, on a Sunday after church.

But first, you need to make sure he has forgiven you for what you've done, surface voice reminded me.

We settled in on one of the decks off the back of the home. He offered to brew some coffee for us and told me to stay and enjoy the view. My heart rate was still through the roof. I sat and waited for him to return, but couldn't sit still, relax or enjoy any sort of view.

When he returned to the deck with our coffees and sat down across from me, I started the discussion right away. No more small talk or beating around the bush. I hugged the mug of coffee tight in my hands for comfort. "Alex," I looked him right in the eyes. "I am so sorry." The emotion was already forming in the back of my throat. "I understand what you meant at the salon when you asked me how you could fix that situation. I've been through so many options in my head, but none of them suffice. I don't know how you're going to forgive me. But if there is something I can do, you need to tell me. Nothing I've come up with is good enough—"

Alex interrupted my tangent. "Jane, I forgive you."

"What? No. It can't be that easy." I closed my eyes and shook my head. "That's almost as bad as not forgiving me at all."

"It *is* that easy, actually. Not only have I made a mistake recently that you forgave, but I've had two weeks to process the whys of the dressing room. I understand, Jane. I really do. You were under a lot of pressure. So, *I* actually have to apologize to *you*."

"No." I shook my head fiercely. "No way. You are not putting the onus on yourself." My stomach felt sick.

"Please listen for a moment. You told me many times on many different occasions that you weren't ready for a commitment. You warned me over and over you weren't ready—"

"Not so I could go out and bang another guy!"

He scooted our chairs together and put his mug down so he could place his hands on my leg. "I know that. Trust me. I know it wasn't premeditated. Not on your end, at least. But you hit a breaking point that day. I'm not saying I'm okay with what happened. All I'm saying is I understand *why* it happened. And I forgive you for it. Your apologies are sincere. I can tell you regret it wholeheartedly. I still trust you. We're okay on my end. Are we okay on yours?"

I stood and rested my back on the deck railing. I still felt antsy and sitting wasn't helping. "We're okay as long as you think so. Thank you for forgiving me." I took a sip of coffee and tried to gain more courage to let out what I needed to say. "Alex, there's more I need to tell you." He stood warily. He had a look of concern all over his face. "Don't worry. Just listen. This retreat made me work through just about everything in my life. I can't begin to describe how beneficial and therapeutic it was. Not only did it help me process the traumas that I carry, but it enlightened me to the desire I have to start fresh. More than desire...the deep need, actually."

I thought about sharing my dream with him, but that could be a long story for another day. "Alex, I don't know why God took away my husband and babies. It still doesn't seem fair to them or to me. It will be a question I ask Him in heaven one day, hopefully far away from now. Because one thing I know for certain is I'm meant to be here on Earth. And something I'm even more sure about is I'm meant to do this next stage of life...with you." I'd been avoiding his eyes for most of my speech but glanced his way on the last line. He looked completely astonished. "I told you this before, but I had an experience at the retreat to affirm my belief that you saved me on the roof that day." I took a breath and let the tears fall from my eyes. "You were already mine; you've expressed and shown that many times already. But I am meant to be yours too, Alex. You are my savior—a miracle on Earth, sent to me by God." I walked toward his very still body and grabbed his hands. "Nobody has ever made me feel as loved or cared for as you do. Nobody has coveted me the way you have. Nobody heals me like you do." I kissed his knuckles slowly, one at a time, my tears falling on our entwined hands. "Nobody has made me feel as beautiful as you do. Nobody has made love to me like you have." I pulled our entwined hands to my heart. "I love you, Alex Lombardi." I kissed his knuckles again and then stared into his eyes. "I am in love with you."

His eyes filled with tears to match mine. I kissed away the tears dropping down his cheeks before I continued, "I have been for a while, but I didn't know how to let it surface. I was too afraid. I'm so sorry it has taken me this long to realize it, but there's no question now. I adore you. I love you. I want to be yours. And if you'll have me, I promise to never let you go."

Alex still seemed stunned by my admission. I let go of his hands and brought mine to the sides of his neck in an attempt to kiss him awake. At first, it was only me pressing our lips together, but after a moment, a fire lit inside him. I felt it as it happened. His touches became those of passion. Of love. His lips pressed on every part of me he could reach...my mouth, both cheeks, my neck, my wrists...everywhere.

"Jane," he whispered in between kisses, "I don't know what to say."

"Say you'll have me," I said, breathlessly. "Tell me you still love me."

"I love you. I'll always love you. You mean everything to me." Tears still rolled down his cheeks.

I pulled him in tight for a hug and smashed our lips together. Any amount of space between our bodies became too much. I pressed myself to him as if my life depended on it. Alex felt the same way; he embraced me just as tight.

In his arms was exactly where I was supposed to be. God had known it. My loves in heaven had known it. Even Deb had known it months ago. It just had taken my broken, beaten, and bruised heart a little while to catch up. But she was there now, alongside my brain and body. We were finally all on the same path again, ready to heal and love.

After a few minutes of worshipping each other's mouths and letting our tears dissipate, Alex picked me up and wrapped my legs around his waist. With the sexiest look I'd seen from him to date, he entered the house and carried me up the stairs to a bedroom.

Once there, he gently laid me on the bed while our lips still stayed connected. "I don't know what I expected today, but I can tell you it wasn't this," Alex confessed. He lifted my shirt off my body and unhooked my bra.

"You've made me the happiest man in the universe." My heart beat rapidly again. It felt like it was swelling to twice its size. He took off his shirt and then pulled my joggers and panties off. "And right now, I need to thank you for what you've done for me..." He bent to the floor, pulled my hips to the edge of the bed, and lifted my legs to rest on his shoulders. "You need to feel my love." I was speechless. Excitement for what was to come pulsed through my veins.

He went right in with his talented and eager tongue. There was no foreplay, which I was more than fine with. My lower half immediately contracted in pleasure at his touch. "Baby girl, I'll never stop demonstrating how much I love you." He played around for a while until he felt my body shift to almost climax. "You're mine." He kissed my inner thighs—teasing me—prolonging my release. "Tell me you're mine." His tongue explored some more before he looked up, waiting for me to fulfill his demand.

"Alex, please—" Every time he stopped, my insides screamed in dissatisfaction. Heat and deep desire radiated off me.

"Tell me," he repeated as hot breath hit in between my legs.

I squirmed around more, unable to concentrate on anything but my much-needed release. "Please—"

He used his nose to nuzzle and tease in between my legs. "I need to hear it, Jane."

"I am yours," I gasped, finally able to form a sentence.

Satisfied with my statement, Alex's tongue went back to work, circling me repeatedly until my back arched off the bed and I moaned with pleasure to the end. I wasn't even fully through my orgasm when he flipped me around and entered me from behind. He brought his fingers under me and played with my pink button as he pressed himself into my swollen area at a slow, unhurried rate. I could tell he wanted the moment to last, which made my insides squirm with pleasure. He kissed my neck and tickled my overly sensitive area as he continued to push into me. My breathing was at a pant due to my recent climax and the anticipation of another. The feeling and mood were different than our last times together. There was no desperation in the air. No sadness. No worry. No self-consciousness. No wondering if it would be the last time. It was love—pure, raw, intimate love. It was lust, worship, and love combined into something physical. Alex's love—our love—was unparalleled. It felt godlike. It felt unreal.

We made divine love for a few more minutes until Alex pressed a little faster with his fingers and pushed a little harder with his lower half. Since I was on my stomach, I couldn't see his eyes, but I knew what they'd look like. I didn't need to see them. There would be nothing but desire, reverence, and love looking back at me. The pressure built again in the depth of my body. I wanted to finish together, so I resisted the release that tried to break through until I could tell he was on the verge of climaxing. As soon as he let out his first moan, I let myself go and finished a few seconds behind him.

Alex lay on top of me for a quick moment to kiss my neck and shoulders while we both recovered and then he rolled to the side of the bed. I turned on my side to see his face after what we had just done together. He mirrored my movements. As expected, he had never looked more handsome. Or happy. I closed my eyes and kept the image of his peaceful, wondrous face behind my eyelids.

We lay there naked, face-to-face, for a long time without speaking. Alex closed his eyes at some point and his breathing became heavier. I let him sleep for a while, wondering if he'd had a good night's rest lately. He and I hadn't had the best few weeks as a couple. Well, 'sort of' couple at the time. I thought back to the night of the gala and how amazing it was before Alex had turned weird. I usually wasn't one to enjoy large social gatherings, but with Alex by my side, I was ready and willing to tackle anything.

Anything. That word in that context meant a lot. It was the honest truth. If we could overcome the last two major problems we had, and if we could get through my trauma and commitment issues, we could fix any challenge that came our way.

I took the back of my hand and lightly brushed up and down Alex's arm. He stirred a little before he opened his eyes. "How long was I out?" he asked.

"Not long." I leaned in so I could kiss him where my fingers had just touched. "Alex," I looked at him and hoped he saw into the heart of my soul. "Marry me."

He inhaled an audible breath and closed his eyes. He was not expecting those words to escape my lips. "Jane, there's no rush."

I let my fingers trail up and down his arm again and then over his chest and abs. "I'm not in a rush. I just want you."

He shivered at my touch. "You have me. Every part of me. We don't need to be engaged if you're not ready." His expression was so sincere.

I spoke slowly. "I am ready. There are no guarantees in life. Time is fleeting. We don't know how long we have, and I want to seal myself to you in every way I can while we're both here."

"Jane." His eyebrows furrowed in concern and ran his fingertips up and down my thigh. "You shouldn't want to get married because you're worried about one of us passing away."

"It's not so much a worry as I want to start my life with you. I know what I want. That won't change. I want all the traditional symbols that you're mine." I kissed the tip of his nose. "I don't want to wait."

Alex took a long look into my eyes as if he was trying to find doubt in there somewhere. He wouldn't find it. I was ready. He pulled in a deep breath and then moved to get out of bed. "Close your eyes," he instructed.

I did as I was told and wrapped a sheet around me while I sat upright. I heard him wrestling with his clothes and then heard some noise across the room from a drawer opening. I felt the weight of him returning to the bed as he told me to open my eyes. When I blinked open, a closed Tiffany blue box was on the mattress separating the space between us. My heart went into my throat. I stared at the little box for a moment before meeting Alex's eyes.

"I bought this a few weeks ago. I've been carrying it everywhere with me. I didn't know when or if I would ever be able to place it on your finger. I was hopeful, but as you said earlier, there are no guarantees in life."

He opened the box, and my hands flew to my face in surprise. I didn't care about the size or shape of the diamond. Or that it was from Tiffany's. It was the simple fact that he chose a diamond on his own to represent his love—our love. Alex, a man Stan said would never have wanted to marry before me. Alex, who brought a broken girl back to life. Alex, who had bought an engagement ring before he knew if that broken girl would say yes. He took a leap of faith. On me.

"I asked Robert for his blessing," he said softly.

I looked at him, surprised. He never ceased to amaze me.

"I know you asked me, but permission to be a little traditional?"

I nodded. The tears had already started to build once again.

Alex grabbed the box and slid off the bed to bend down on one knee. I moved closer to the edge so I could see every part of him. "Jane, you've had my heart since the moment I laid eyes on you. I've never needed anyone or anything as much as I need you. I love you unconditionally and fiercely. I will do everything I can to make you happy. You are my life. Will you do me the honor of marrying me?"

Alex looked up at me with giant tears welling in his eyes. Until recently, I'd never imagined I could be happy—truly happy—again. I thought back to my dream. The diamond was part of the plan. It was the right step. And my family above approved.

"Yes," I whispered, feeling more confident in my answer than anything in the recent past. Alex smiled a huge smile, took my left ring finger to slide the diamond in place, and stood up to kiss his fiancée.

We, of course, made love to consummate our engagement. I swear, every time became better and better. I had a feeling it had to do with me and my experience level. Alex had me on the fast-track program of lovemaking, and his teachings were stellar.

After we recovered, Alex grabbed my hand and pulled me off the bed. "I have a surprise for you," he announced, looking a little shy. "A belated birthday present." I went to grab my clothes, but he stopped me. "Don't bother." His eyes were bright. He was excited to show me whatever he had hidden.

I grabbed the sheet and wrapped it around me protectively as he yanked me away from the bed. There were a *lot* of large windows in his house. I really didn't need to be part of another sex video if he had any weirdo neighbors lurking around.

Alex pulled me down the hall to the last room. "Okay, are you ready?"

"Um, I think so?" I wasn't sure what I should be ready for.

He opened the door and let me walk in first. I studied the space inch by inch. The room was bright white with big windows and a large skylight. Everything I could see besides the walls and floors was black—the closet doors, the trim around the windows, and the trim around the many large mirrors. Black hooks were hanging from different heights and areas on the walls....and the ceiling. Black ropes were braided perfectly and hung on hooks. Black paddles in all different sizes were connected by leather straps to a horizontal rod. I opened one of the black dresser drawers. It had black lacy underwear and bras. The next drawer down had black leather whips. The third drawer had all black teddies.

I stopped and turned to face Alex with a grin. "Black and white room of pain?" I couldn't hold in my nervous giggle.

He chuckled and nodded slowly. "Happy birthday. What do you think?"

I couldn't answer yet. I took my time to walk over to one of the closets and hesitantly opened the door. It was organized full of all types of contraptions. I closed the door quickly when a sex swing came into focus. I didn't need the space to become too overwhelming before we were able to experiment.

I blushed a deep red. "I'm a bit speechless."

He smiled shyly. "There are different rules in here." My interest was piqued by his words. "Outside these walls, you own me." I went to disagree with that one-sided idea of a relationship, but he stopped me. "You own me out there," he repeated with a smile. "In here, we are equals. This isn't a sex novel, and I'm not a dominant. You're not my submissive. We can role-play if we want, but only if we both want to. There are no safe words because the word "stop" means stop every time. I don't get excitement out of seeing you in pain. So if we use a toy and you like it, great. If not, we burn it."

My entire body lit on fire at his words. Every ounce of my skin was hot and sweaty, and all I had draped around me was a bed sheet. Alex could sense the change in my body. He walked over to me and laid his palm on my cheek. His hand felt cold and nice on my overheated skin. "Do you like it?"

"I do," I managed to croak out. I had a hard time believing such a room was made for me. "Thank you."

"I decided to build it in this house rather than in Crystal Lake...in case it was a bad idea." He laughed quietly under his breath. "But maybe I should build one there too?"

I tilted my head to the side. "So that night when you told me to go upstairs and find the room...you were bluffing?"

Alex gave me the sexiest of smirks. "I was."

My mouth popped open in mock offense.

He beamed a beautiful smile at me and shrugged his shoulders.

"I think one sex room is enough." I giggled and shook my head. "Besides, it'll make me look forward to being here that much more." Blush flushed my cheeks again at my admission.

Alex took his cool fingertips and brushed them down my neck. "Do you want to play?"

I looked around again at my birthday gift. As much as I wanted to test it out, there was something else at the forefront of my mind. "Can I take a rain check for tonight?"

Alex smiled. "Of course. Do you have something else you'd like to do?"

"You know that old car you have outside?"

He nodded. His eyebrows furrowed.

"What kind of car is it?"

He seemed confused as to why I was asking such a random question while standing basically naked in a sex room. "Um...it's a 1960 Cadillac Eldorado. Why do you ask?"

I smiled at him and thought about what I wanted to say. "As I mentioned earlier, the retreat helped me heal so much. You've helped me heal so much." I gave him a light kiss on the lips. "However, I'm not naïve enough to think all my trauma and pain have been erased. I know I'll have emotional setbacks for the rest of my life." I took his hands in mine. "But I know I'll get through every setback easier with you by my side."

He listened intently, probably still trying to figure out what my speech had to do with his vintage car.

"The first time I saw that car was the night of our picnic. When we pulled into your garage, my mind involuntarily created a reel of us driving down the road with the top down on a beautiful Sunday afternoon. It was an image of complete contentment. You held onto me with your free hand and smiled my way every so often." Alex tilted his head and grinned. He looked so happy. He was enjoying my daydream. He placed his hand on the nape of my neck. I leaned into it, showing my love, and continued, "Our hair blew around in the warm Illinois breeze. Everything was right in the world." I placed my hands on his chest. "I've thought of that image many times since then. And every time I think about it, my mind tells me when that time comes, I know I've made it to the other side. I've overcome and I've won." I kissed his collarbones and neck to butter him up. "I know it's not Sunday, and we're not in Illinois. But it's warm out, and we have the time to do it." I looked into his chocolate-brown eyes. "I need that image to become a reality. Will you go on a joy ride with me?"

Alex smiled shyly, grabbed my left hand, and kissed my new ring. "Where do you want to go?"

"It doesn't matter. As long as I'm with you, we could go anywhere."

Alex smiled again. His face was full of so much elation that it was making my heart expand tight in my chest. "All right, let's go. Joy ride now. *Joy ride* in this room later." I couldn't help my nervous giggle at his corny joke. He ran his fingers gently along my cheek and stared down at me with pure adoration shining bright in his eyes. "I'll never tire of that sound."

I blushed at his words and stared down at the ring on my finger, my proof of dedication to a beautiful man with so much love to give me. Somehow, I was getting a second chance at happiness. For that, I needed to be grateful—To Alex. To God. To my lost loved ones rooting for me from above. And to myself.

I wouldn't let any of us down.

I placed a gentle kiss on his lips, trying my best to show my appreciation for his devotion. "Thank you, Alex. For everything. I love you so much."

"I'll love you forever, my girl."

J. Cova & A. Lombardi
602 Pine Circle
Crystal Lake, IL 60014

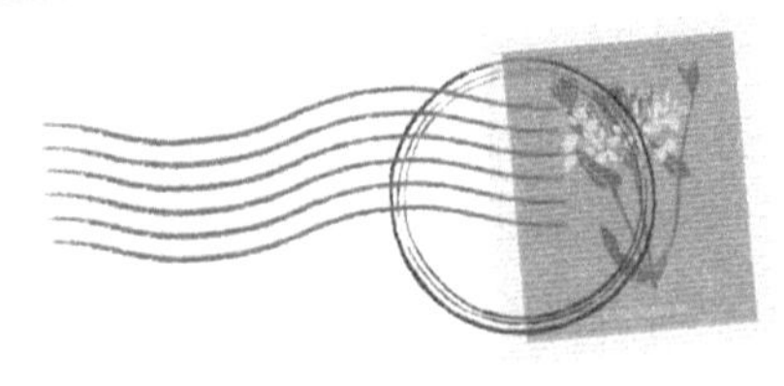

Mr. & Mrs. Martin Miller
1106 Sherwood Rd
Mountain Brook, AL 35223

Acknowledgments

I have learned throughout this process that it takes a village to write a novel. This book would not be complete without thanking those who helped me along the way.

Without further ado…

*First and foremost, to my husband, Andy, and our boys, Oliver and Everett—you all are my world. You're the reason I worked so hard on this novel. I'm so lucky to call you mine. Thank you for your encouragement and patience for the two full months it took me to get Jane's story on paper. And thank you for having even *more* patience during the many months of editing. Writing this book was a labor of love. I'm so grateful you three understood that and let me spend many, *many* hours at the computer. I love you guys more than I can ever express.

*To my early readers: Marci Sersen (my mom, best friend, and #1 fan), Tiffany Sersen (my sister and compound bow-wielding, fierce family protector. Think 'Katniss Everdeen'. She would volunteer as tribute all day, every day, to keep her family safe), Kathy Skalski (the best second mom I could ask for, aka my mother-in-law), Melissa Hinderlider (my friend, confidant, laughing buddy, and shoulder to cry on), and Liz Bickett (my friend and fellow book lover.

Special shout-out to Liz. She read my unpublished, messy, raw book...three? Maybe four times? The final time, she speed-read it to be my last eyes before I published it. It was a big job.).

Ladies above, I couldn't be more grateful for all your opinions, suggestions, encouragement, insights, and constructive criticism. It's an honor that you all helped me improve my rough draft. I truly believe you made the story better. Thank you.

*To my friend, Rachel Halihan, who got me all dolled up and took my author photos, you're always a riot and you'll always be the "sun on a cloudy day." We have twenty years of friendship under our belts. Most of that friendship has been spent laughing (more like cackling). I adore you, bud. Thank you.

*To my boss and friend, Dr. Randy Halihan, thank you in advance for *not* quoting my book every time you come in for a hygiene check. I assure you most of my patients don't want to hear your rendition of my novel. I look forward to your quiet, humble opinions with zero teasing. Oh, and thanks for employing me for the last seventeen years. You're pretty rad, Bossman.

*To my editor and proofreader, Jeannine Thibodeau, thank you for pouring so much expertise and love into Jane's story. Thanks for answering all my questions with patience. And thank you for being the first non-biased reader to read it and tell me you loved it. I'm so grateful I found you.

*To my cover artist, Robin Locke Monda, thank you for your beautiful design, your professionalism, and your patience with me as I learned how to publish a book.

*To my book interior designer, Alison Cnockaert, thank you for designing the elegant final touches for my novel. Prior to this experience, I'd never paid attention to how the inside of a book was designed. It takes time and dedication to make the words on a page come to life. Thank you for your help in making that happen.

*I was very inspired by one song in particular during my writing sessions. So to the musician, Emmy Meli, thank you for your song "I AM WOMAN." While writing, I listened to your song on repeat too many times to count. It also became Jane's theme song throughout certain parts of her journey. I especially imagined her thinking of the powerful words during a specific couch scene. IYKYK.

*Finally, thank you to the readers who took their precious free time to read this book. I hope you loved it. There are thousands of books to choose from, and you picked up mine. I will forever be grateful.

www.ingramcontent.com/pod-product-compliance
Lightning Source LLC
Chambersburg PA
CBHW020606310726
48979CB00008B/1363/J

* 9 7 9 8 9 8 7 7 7 0 1 2 2 *